PRAISE FOR MARVELLERS

"*The Marvellers* deserves the highest compliment I can give a book: I want to live in this world. You can stop looking at admissions brochures for all those other schools of magic. The Arcanum Training Institute for Marvelous and Uncanny Endeavors is definitely where you want to apply."

—**RICK RIORDAN**, #1 *New York Times*–bestselling author

"With fantastical twists at every turn, Clayton has created a world that readers won't want to leave. *The Marvellers* is magical!"

—**ANGIE THOMAS**, #1 *New York Times*–bestselling author of *The Hate U Give* and *Concrete Rose*

"A 'Marvellerous' middle grade debut! Delightful, charming, exceptionally clever, and filled with suspense and humor."

—**LISA McMANN**, *New York Times*–bestselling author of The Forgotten Five series

"Never in all my years of reading have I encountered a book that so seamlessly weaves together mind-bending marvels, cultural relevance, and powerful historical themes . . . all in a richly imagined world I would give anything to live in."

—**NIC STONE**, #1 *New York Times*–bestselling author of *Dear Martin*

"An expertly crafted amalgamation of rich, cultural representation wrapped up in a magic school adventure . . . sure to be a well-loved favorite."

—**J. ELLE**, *New York Times*–bestselling author of *Wings of Ebony*

"Dhonielle Clayton's beautiful prose showcases how honoring differences and sharing gifts can build the strongest friendships. *The Marvellers* illuminates stellar storytelling through the lens of a Black girl learning to embrace the full potential of her magic."

—**KAREN STRONG**, author of *Just South of Home* and *Eden's Everdark*

"A new classic. Clayton creates a luminous world where everyone can find themselves within the halls of the Arcanum Training Institute. I'm ready to be transported into the sequel!"

—**ZORAIDA CÓRDOVA**, award-winning author of *Labyrinth Lost* and *The Way to Rio Luna*

"The fantasy adventure the world needs. *The Marvellers* is a cultural reset, the kind of thorny, exciting, and magical story that I've needed my whole life. Where's book two? I already need it!"

—**MARK OSHIRO**, author of *The Insiders*

THE MARVELLERS

DHONIELLE CLAYTON

SQUARE
FISH

HENRY HOLT AND COMPANY
NEW YORK

SQUARE
FISH

An imprint of Macmillan Publishing Group, LLC
120 Broadway, New York, NY 10271 • mackids.com

Square Fish and the Square Fish logo are trademarks of Macmillan and are used by
Henry Holt and Company under license from Macmillan.

Our books may be purchased in bulk for promotional, educational, or business use.
Please contact your local bookseller or the Macmillan Corporate and Premium
Sales Department at (800) 221-7945 ext. 5442 or by email at
MacmillanSpecialMarkets@macmillan.com.

Library of Congress Control Number: 2021916756

Originally published in the United States by Henry Holt and Company
First Square Fish edition, 2023
Book designed by Liz Dresner
Square Fish logo designed by Filomena Tuosto
Printed in the United States of America by Lakeside Book Company,
Harrisonburg, Virginia

ISBN 978-1-250-87884-7 (paperback)
1 3 5 7 9 10 8 6 4 2

AR: 4.8 / LEXILE: 670L

THE PARAGONS

PARAGON OF TOUCH

"The hand has no fear!"

The brave

PARAGON OF VISION

"The eyes are wise!"

The sage

PARAGON OF SPIRIT

"The heart beats true!"

The intuitive

PARAGON OF SOUND

"The ears listen well!"

The patient

PARAGON OF TASTE

"The tongue tells truth!"

The honest

THE ARCANUM TRAINING INSTITUTE FOR MARVELOUS AND UNCANNY ENDEAVORS

———— LOWER SCHOOL ————

Salutations and Greetings of the Most Magnificent Kind,

We are thrilled to inform you that you've been accepted into the Arcanum Training Institute for Marvelous and Uncanny Endeavors. Only the marvelous can attend. It is an honor to be chosen by the Heads of the Arcanum, and this invitation means that you demonstrate what it takes to join us. But remember, only your work will guarantee that you can earn the proper degrees to stay with us.

Once your starpost arrives in the Stariary, you will receive a message noting the coordinates of the Level Ones' Stardust Pier and the Institute's location this year.

All the light to you and yours! Good marvelling!

Laura Ruby
Executive Assistant to Headmarveller MacDonald and
Headmarveller Rivera of the Lower School

P.S.: No Fewels allowed! If you share this letter with a non-Marveller, it shall disintegrate into dust. Don't test it. You will regret it.

PART I

A BRAND-NEW WORLD

CHAPTER ONE
THE LUCK ROOT

Marvelous.

The lucky kids got called that. Praise like honey drizzled on hot biscuits. But Ella's family didn't believe in gassing you up. Clothes ironed? Make your bed? Clean your plate? And most importantly, did you mind your business so nobody was minding *you*?

Even now, during the greatest . . . the awesome-est . . . the most spectacular thing that had ever happened in all eleven years of Ella Durand's life, her parents were squabbling and telling her what to do.

"Did you use the hangers? Gran pressed those mantles herself after the old iron did a poor job," her mama said. "I don't want to see them wrinkled."

Three juju-trunks floated in the middle of the Durands' living room with all of Ella's things neatly arranged and ready for inspection. Their silk linings glowed as a good-fortune spell infused itself into her belongings.

"Yes, Mama," Ella replied, annoyed.

"The conjure-cameo?" her papa asked.

"Yes, Papa." She patted her chest, the carved medallion of her parents' faces tucked just beneath her shirt.

"And the braid-hands?"

Ella pointed at the vanity case, where a wax copy of her mother's hands sat. "Of course."

Mama tugged one of Ella's long twists. "I *won't* have my baby so far away with her head looking a mess. I spelled them with your favorite styles. You remember how to work them? Their waking song?"

"Yes—"

"Aubrielle, my sweet, she has everything she needs." Papa looked above his newspaper, *The Conjure Picayune*. He tapped his black top hat, which made the ring of tiny human skulls on its brim smile at her. "We should get a move on."

Mama sighed. "Sebastien, I *still* don't know about this."

That sparked their eighty millionth argument about Ella attending the Arcanum Training Institute for Marvelous and Uncanny Endeavors.

Ella plugged her ears. They'd been fussing all summer. Mama and Gran wanted her to stay home and continue to attend Madame Collette's Conjure École. The whole community was conflicted about whether she should be going. But Papa thought it was time for a new adventure, and she was *more* than ready to leave home.

Everyone went silent as Gran's rooster companion, Paon, marched in from the gallery porch and crowed.

"Y'all quit all that hollering, you hear?" Gran shouted through the window. "You're ruining a perfectly good sunset.

This second line is loud enough. The parades are doing too much this year."

Ella hid her smile. "Can we put my trunks in the car now?"

"I'm coming! I'm coming! I'm coming!" Her little sister, Winnie, burst into the room. Her own little juju-trunk tailed her, the edges of it spilling over with toys.

Ella scowled at her. "We've been over this a thousand times. You're too little."

"Fine, but can I see your letter again?" Winnie gazed up at her.

"But you've got to read it to me—"

"I don't like to read," Winnie whined.

"Then you can't see it."

"I just want to *look* at it." Winnie pouted.

"A deal is a deal."

"Okay!" She stomped her tiny foot. "Okay!"

Ella's hand relaxed, and with a sigh she gave up the letter. Winnie fingered the night-black envelope like it was a slice of hummingbird cake, her mouth salivating, ready to gobble it up. She tilted it left and right to see it twinkle, squealing as the envelope's five symbols winked. An eye blinked, a mouth smiled and poked out a tongue, an ear wiggled, a tiny hand waved, and a little heart pulsed. That was Ella's favorite part too.

The five Paragons of Marvelling.

She couldn't wait to learn what was marvelous about her and to join a group based on her talents.

Winnie pinched the stardust seal and opened it, then began to read.

Ella would never get over how amazing it sounded. Her very own invitation. Her very own chance to be a Marveller.

"How do you get a marvel?" Winnie asked.

"You're born with one. They come from your family or community—"

Papa cleared his throat. "Many Marvellers I know have chosen their marvel as well."

Ella whipped around. "I didn't read that—"

"Much to learn, baby girl." Papa returned to his paper.

"What will mine be?" That had been the question Ella had toyed with all summer.

"A conjure marvel, of course," Mama replied like it wasn't even a question.

"There's coupons in here too. Did you see them? They move, and the numbers keep changing like they're fighting with one another. This one says it has the cheapest weather jars—WAIT! No, now it's that one." Winnie's eyes grew wide.

Ella was amazed by the wiggling coupons and their incessant battles. Sandhya's Splendiferous Sundry now boasted the most affordable astrolabes, and the prices from Woodfolk's Wonderous Wares flickered angrily.

"I want to go too," Winnie begged. "I want a marvel. Maybe I can talk to merpeople."

Ella swiped the invitation back. "Don't ruin everything, okay?"

Papa shot Ella a look and picked Winnie up like she was nothing more than a scoop of chocolate ice cream. "Cricket, in just five years, we'll be packing you up too. The second you turn eleven."

"If everything goes all right . . . ," Mama whispered under her breath, but Ella chose to ignore that.

Of course everything would be fine. Better than fine. Spectacular, in fact. Marvelous indeed.

Winnie sniffled and buried her face in Papa's shirt. His bullfrog companion, Greno, croaked as she climbed out of his pocket and got all tangled in his long locs while Mama's chubby alligator, Gumbo, tromped into the room, then nosed around Ella's open juju-trunk as if he were the missing piece.

"Is it really in the sky? How does it even float? Isn't an Institute too heavy to fly?" Winnie asked. "What are Marvellians *like*? Can we go to their cities?"

"You'll see, my beloved." Papa tried to calm her down. "You'll see."

Ella glanced at her satchel spilling over with all the research she'd done this summer at the Griotary, listening to all the books and pestering all the griots to tell her all the things they knew about Marvellers and their Training Institute. Mama and Papa interacted with very few Marvellers, so she didn't know as much as she wanted to.

"Conjuring ain't marvelling, that's for sure," Gran shouted from the porch with a laugh. "And living all the way up in the sky like that can't be natural."

Ella squeezed her eyes shut and let her imagination run wild. She had dreamed about what the Institute would be like all summer. But just like the Institute changed locations every year, she'd read, it also never looked the same way twice. While poring over old brochures, she noticed that sometimes it looked like an art museum, other times a grand hotel, occasionally a camp, and most often, a boarding school. Ella tried to guess how it would look now.

Her parents had told her as much as they could about the Arcanum Training Institute because they *too* had never visited. No Conjuror had ever been a Marveller before.

Until Ella.

Marvellers were born with marvels, light inside them that allowed them to perform magical feats. They lived in the skies above and away from non-magic-having Fewels . . . and Conjure folk.

They were decidedly *not* the same.

Conjurors were born with a deep twilight inside them, allowing the work of crossing spells and tending to the dead in the Underworld. Now Ella would be the first one to enroll, and when she passed all the tests, she'd be the first to join the Marvellian community. Officially. She'd make her family proud. Especially her papa.

Ella's heart beat as if a firefly had been trapped in her chest. She felt like she was ready for anything.

Mama took one last look into Ella's juju-trunks, then she nodded with approval, eyes softening. Ella waved her hand over the latches and the lids flipped shut. She hummed the sealing spell Mama had taught her to make sure everything stayed secure.

"Please get in the red car," Ella ordered.

They sparked and zipped through the back of the house.

Gran hobbled in from the gallery. "Give me some sugar before you leave me."

Ella dove headfirst into the soft, round middle of her grandmother, inhaling as much of her scent as she could: a little honey, a little lavender, and a little butter.

"Just remember you come from a mighty tree." Gran lifted her sleeves and flashed the conjure mark on her brown skin.

Intricate tangles of roots and writhing flowers grew in inky, raised lines along both Gran's and Mama's bodies. Over the years, they'd become more and more complex, traveling along their backs and arms and legs. Ella loved tracing her fingers over it when Gran let her oil her scalp, surprised at how it constantly changed—a new bud here, a new flower there as her grandmother used her skills. Both of them were covered with a road map of talents and abilities.

Conjure always left its mark.

Gran kissed a finger and touched the tiniest mole on the back of Ella's neck, a kidney bean–shaped spot that resembled a tiny birthmark to most, or an unfortunate puffy tattoo to others. It had sprouted like a new seedling ever since she started to work with Gran in their family pharmacy, learning that belladonna loves compliments, trips to the Underworld require pennies in your shoes, and conjure skillets are best seasoned with twilight stardust. The spot had been just the same for so long until it cracked open like a bean bud; a thin line similar to a pen stroke grew out of the mole. Her first mark as a Conjuror that began just as her mother's had, and her gran's had, and her great-grandmother's before that—eager, ready for her to do more conjure work.

"It's opening up even more. I won't get to see the progress. But you'll write to me?"

"Yes, ma'am."

"And tell me everything?"

"Of course."

"And don't go wandering around those cities. It's unnatural to be up there like that. Bad things happen—"

"I know, Gran." Ella had heard the story about her mama's twin and how she'd gone missing the one and only time the family had ever gone to a Marvellian city. Her name added to the countless other Conjure folk who had never returned after traveling to the sky. But nothing like that would happen to her. "I promise I'll be safe."

Gran kissed her forehead and helped her pull one of her crisp white mantles over her clothes. "You do us proud now, you hear?"

Ella most definitely would.

"Don't let them give you any trouble," she said.

Ella winked. "Never."

"You ready?" Papa asked.

She took one last look around. Conjure skillets sat on the stove; the family altar blazed bright with tall candles and portraits of smiling ancestors. Shelves full of glass jars boasted twilight stars. The garden crept along the wall as if it too had come to say goodbye. "See you later," she whispered before darting into the courtyard.

Ella skipped under a massive live oak that grew out of the center, its ancient arms a canopy of wind chimes, blue glass bottles, and shimmering orbs. She gazed up and whispered goodbye to it too. The tree shook.

"Hurry, Ella," Mama called out. "A storm's coming."

Papa's red car sat in the carriage area.

Ella, Mama, and Winnie piled inside. The conjure emblem

on the house gates flared as it opened. Ella held her breath. This was it.

Papa eased through the streets of New Orleans. Fewels rushed here and there, never looking up or noticing how conjure families opened their windows and sang colorful parasols into the city sky to help hold back the rain. Their stomps and claps rumbled beneath the thunder. A chorus of voices trickled into the car: "Storm keep passing on. Let them journey on. Keep passing on!" Gran always said, "Conjure's like a really good song, one with a melody and rhythm only *we* can hear and feel."

The car inched along under the beautiful canopy. Ella spotted candles left in windows and galleries dressed in black, red, and green, all in support of her decision to go to the Arcanum Training Institute. Many folks wore their Sunday best and threw conjure-roses—the beautiful black flowers freckled with crimson that every Conjuror kept close for luck—as the car passed.

The petals rained down on them, and Ella's heart swelled as the well-wishes made their way through the car windows.

"*Good luck, Ella!*"

"*Praying for you and your success.*"

"*May the ancestors protect you.*"

"*Be safe.*"

People bowed and tipped their hats.

"The Duvernays don't have a candle in their window," Winnie pointed out. "The Beauvais either."

"Hush now," Mama replied. "Never mind that."

Ella was too excited to even ask what that meant as Papa passed the red gates of the Underworld at Congo Square, the gargantuan deathbulls towering over the city and keeping watch on those wishing to enter the Land of the Dead. She blew a kiss at them, and they each nodded their great heads in her direction.

"Will you miss them?" Winnie asked.

"I don't think so. Well, maybe not for a while." She had been so ready to leave home for so long that she couldn't even possibly think she'd be homesick.

"Will you miss *me*?" Winnie's eyes grew wide.

Ella tickled her little sister until Papa paused in front of Ella's best friend's house. Reagan Marsalis's whole family stood on their small lawn ready to greet them. Mr. Marsalis lifted his top hat, and Mrs. Marsalis blew kisses. Ella grinned so hard her face hurt.

Reagan raced over to the car, her brown cheeks sweaty from the September heat. Ella rolled down the window.

"For luck." Reagan held out a bright blue luck root from the Underworld. One of her favorite plants.

Ella reached for it, and the flower walked from Reagan's hand to hers. "Thanks."

"Write me?" Reagan asked.

"Every day."

Ella pressed her face to the window, watching as Reagan chased the car until Papa turned toward the dock. She wished Reagan would've accepted her invitation and come with her.

But just as a pinch of sadness threatened to squeeze her heart, a Marvellian water-zeppelin sat on the water waiting like a fallen star.

Ella's stomach flipped.

This was the most important night of her life . . . maybe of all their lives.

The Marvellian Times

THE ARCANUM TRAINING INSTITUTE TO OPEN ITS DOORS TO CONJURORS

OP-ED by Renatta Cooper

SEPTEMBER 20

A brand-new day at the Arcanum's Lower School—and not everyone is happy. So many angry people will be protesting outside those gigantic sky doors.

Why?

They've done the unthinkable . . . opening the 250-year-old center to the Conjure folk of the world.

After prominent American conjure-politician Sebastien Durand won his case in the Marvellian Courts of Justice, the ban was ruled unlawful and at odds with the Marvellian Constitution.

A magical edit was proclaimed. The Constitution amended. Now Conjure folk can come on in.

But only one little Conjuror enrolled . . . Sebastien's daughter, Ella Durand.

Stars, help her!

CHAPTER TWO
THE STARDUST PIER

The ride to the Stardust Pier felt like a lightning flash. One moment Ella and her family were skimming across the Gulf of Mexico and the next they were in the middle of the Atlantic Ocean, standing on the Stardust Pier, awaiting the arrival of the sky-ferries for the next leg of their journey. The late September heat clung to her skin.

Plump star-lanterns drifted overhead like ginormous glow-bugs. Other water-zeppelins peeked their heads above the water, dropping more families on the ever-growing platform. Ella could've sworn she felt it expand under her feet little by little to make sure everyone fit.

Dressed in all white, her fellow Level One trainees were doves ready to fly off with their marvel-valises. She glanced at her floating juju-trunks, strange in comparison. But she took a deep breath, then smoothed the front of her new uniform and tested pulling the hood up around her long twists. The excitement made her fingers quiver. No more quilted aprons or conjure jackets or family crossing rings. Something new. Something different.

"I expect weekly starposts, little girl," Mama demanded.

Ella looked up at her mama, the moonlight drenching her brown skin. She was still impossibly beautiful even when upset. "Yes, Mama."

"It's a huge responsibility to be the first. You don't just represent yourself, but all of us." Papa put a warm hand on Ella's shoulder.

"I know," Ella replied.

Winnie tugged at her. "Who are *those* people?" She pointed at the back of the woman nearest them.

"Security coppers," Mama whispered.

"What's that?" Winnie asked.

"Like Fewel police." Ella thought they looked like a bunch of angry toy soldiers. The liquid gold crests on their jackets glowed, and she wished she could reach out to touch the *M* symbol.

"Do they have to be with *us?*" Winnie leaned in closer. "I don't like their weird dogs." A few gripped the leashes of red-eyed wolves. "And their birds look mean too."

They sent black ravens into the sky above, and they surveyed all the arriving water-zeppelins.

"*Tsk.* None of that. Mind your business. They're here to make sure everything goes smoothly," Mama replied.

Ella wouldn't let herself think about what *not smoothly* looked like. She'd planned out every detail: choosing the outfits her parents and sister wore, making sure Gran twisted her hair and threaded it with charm ribbons, and tucking her best friend Reagan's trusty luck root into her pocket. She kept slipping her hand inside to tickle it, enjoying how its leaves reached up to meet her fingertips. It made her feel like Reagan was holding her hand.

The night had to be perfect. And she would be perfect.

Ella waved at onlookers on nearby platforms. She figured since they were staring so bad, she might as well say hello. People held up signs, but strangely she couldn't make out the words on them even when she squinted. The night air thickened and turned hazier each time she tried. Weird. Maybe it was a Marvellian thing. She still had so much to learn.

"Can you see those?" she asked Papa.

"No," he replied. "Must be nothing worth repeating."

Ella gave the crowds her biggest and brightest smile and tried to hold the grin for as long as possible. The press-ferries flew overhead with their cameras incessantly flashing as they sent their news-boxes out by the minute.

Papa pointed up at the moon. "I'm excited to fly!"

The Arcanum Training Institute's sky-ferries would arrive any minute. Ready to pick them up. Mama always said a watched pot never boils, but Ella was certain the thick clouds would erupt with light any second.

The excitement and anticipation bubbled up inside her.

The crowd headed toward a turbaned brown man on a dais.

"Welcome, welcome! What a glorious night . . . actually, a truly *marvelous* night if I do say so myself . . . and I do say so." The man waved his arms around. "The line starts here. Right over here. This way. Last names, please!" A glittering scroll floated just above his shoulder, and she knew her name was on it.

"Ella, Ella." Winnie slipped her hand into Ella's free one.

"Look—there's stars on your dress. When those things"—she pointed up at the floating star-lanterns—"get close, you can see them."

"It's not a dress, it's a Marvellian Mantle," Ella corrected, because big sisters didn't let little sisters go around sounding foolish.

Winnie reached to touch her mantle again, but Ella dodged her little fingers. "You'll get it dirty."

"I don't want to wear a white one."

"All Level Ones do," Ella informed her.

"I want blue 'cause it's my favorite color." Winnie's eyes filled with tears.

"Blue is for Level Threes. Besides, you're too little to come," Ella reminded her sister, although this time she felt a little sad.

Mostly, Winnie irritated Ella, getting into her room or whining about playing or wanting to always do everything she was doing. But as Ella stared out at the other kids on the platform, she wondered how many new friends she'd make and how long that would take. She already missed Reagan, but deep down she thought maybe she'd miss her little sister too. She could always count on Winnie to want to be her best friend forever, no matter what.

A gasp startled Ella, disrupting her thoughts. Whispers crackled in hundreds of different languages.

Mama's chubby alligator, Gumbo, slithered out of the water and onto the pier, slapping his tail with excitement.

"There you are," Mama said to Gumbo. "Getting old, eh? That deep water tough on you, old boy? Got here just in time to see our girl off."

Gumbo grunted.

A few kids scampered even farther away from them while others inched closer to have a look.

She'd read that most Marvellers had pets and sometimes monsters in their homes, but only Conjurors had companions, which were like your animal soul mates. It had always been so normal to Ella . . . up until this very moment. As she stood on the pier, all those *regular* things about her family seemed so different even among these very *different* people.

But she was ready to tell everyone about it all. She just knew everyone would love it.

✦　✖　✦　✖　✦

"LET'S GO CHECK IN, SHALL WE?" MAMA SAID.

"Oh, you're finally ready?" Papa smiled.

Mama clucked her tongue and placed a firm grip on Ella's shoulders as they made their way toward the turbaned man with the floating scroll. The coppers clung to them as they joined the line. Everyone stared. Ella winked just like Gran did when people were looking her way.

The man smiled at them; his long beard twinkled as if it were filled with stardust. His ornate turban changed colors, the folds cycling through peacock blues and sherbet oranges and butter yellows, while its tiny diamonds caught the moonlight. He wore a deep red Marvellian mantle, the black lapel covered in all sorts of mastery pins that Ella couldn't wait to ask him questions about. She knew from her research that he was an Arcanum instructor with at least an eighth degree in his marvel. The Arcanum Training Institute's crest—a five-pointed star—pulsed on his chest as if it were made of living veins.

He gazed down at Ella. "Last name . . . though I think I already know it."

"Durand," she replied.

The scroll opened on its own, each name shining as he read it. "Davidson, Delilah. Nope. Doumbouya, Hassan. Not you. Duca, Giulia. Not quite. Domen, Yuyi. Perhaps close. Ahhh . . . Durand, Ella."

She nodded.

"And I am Masterji Thakur, a Paragon of Taste with a spice marvel." He held out his hand to shake hers. She took it, and he wiggled her arm until she smiled. When he let go, a tiny star anise danced in her palm. "The tongue tells truth! Welcome. So glad you are here. Looking forward to getting to know you."

While Mama and Papa spoke to Masterji Thakur, Mama's alligator companion nudged her leg and smiled up at her with a full set of sharp teeth. Ella bent down to kiss Gumbo's wet nose. More people turned to look, and Ella supposed that maybe having a twelve-foot alligator beside you might be strange. A boy inched close to them, squinting and staring, followed by a little girl sneaking up to admire Gumbo's tail. Mama turned to say hello, and Ella began to explain, but the kids scuttled away.

The pier went silent.

The first sky-ferries sliced through the clouds, their brass noses radiating like suns. The sky-ferries' bellies held the initials A.T.I. Engines blazed bright with stars spinning in their gilded spheres. Ella thought it was almost as if a pod of whales had taken flight after strapping enormous glass carriages to their stomachs. She spotted plush sofas and fancy dining carts and twinkling lights inside them.

Ella gasped. "Papa, what's in those engines?"

"That's stellacity. You'll learn all about it." He rested a hand on her shoulder.

Ella held her breath and opened her eyes as wide as possible. She wanted to see every single detail: how they landed on the water with barely a whisper, how their bodies resembled a night sky full of stars, how clouds of steam hissed from their fins.

Out of the first one stepped a beautiful brown woman wearing a paper wreath of marigolds. Draped in a black Marvellian mantle, she held a cane that sparkled in the moonlight. Ella knew that she was one of the most important people at the Institute *and* the reason Ella was even here.

Headmarveller Paloma Rivera.

Ella had seen her face projected from the Marvellian newsboxes in Papa's office. She'd sneaked in to watch and listen to all her speeches about how the Arcanum had to be open to all, and how Marvellian society must make space for all magical human beings.

Ella stretched up on her tiptoes to have a closer look. She was even more beautiful in person.

Headmarveller Rivera greeted Masterji Thakur and directed the floating scroll to jump into her pocket. "Welcome, Marvellian families, to the most wonderful starry night. The start of a brand-new journey for our children." Her voice was as gorgeous as she, sweet and sunlit like a jar of honey. "I am just one of a dynamic pair to lead the Arcanum Training Institute for the coming year. Headmarveller MacDonald is awaiting our arrival."

With a flap of her mantle, a flurry of papel picado exploded from the folds. The tissue paper cutouts boasted little elephants, pigs, cows, snakes, and roosters. The tiny rectangles swarmed the crowd and burst with noise. She put her hand on her lapel, tapping an ornate pin. "I am a Paragon of Touch with a paper marvel. The hand has no fear!"

A few others repeated the phrase back at her, and Ella realized that they, too, were Paragons of Touch.

Ella glanced up at Papa. "I can't wait to have a marvel."

"Soon, baby girl, soon." He squeezed her shoulder. "You'll have your marvel and your motto, and take your place here."

Mama's eyes narrowed, and Ella heard her suck her teeth. But Ella couldn't wait to belong.

More papel picado rained down on them. A magenta elephant roared its tiny trunk at Ella. She tried to catch it, but the creature poofed into a ball of smoke.

The crowd clapped as the woman took a small bow.

"All the light to everyone. What we practice is no easy feat. It takes discipline, honor, and focus to develop the light inside you. So glad you all are here." Ella felt the woman's eyes land on her and her family. "Children, say your farewells, and let us fly, shall we?" She motioned her arm to the right. "It's time to usher in the next generation of great Marvellers."

The sky-ferry doors opened with sighs of steam. Kids kissed their parents and shuffled forward to line up. Ella turned to say goodbye to Mama and Papa.

"Ha, I don't think so," Mama said. "We'll be coming with you."

Ella started to pout, but Headmarveller Rivera stepped out of the crowd and made her way over.

Everyone turned to watch.

Ella held her breath.

"Would you like to ride with me?"

Ella stared up into the Headmarveller's warm eyes. The

woman had the kind of smile you could feel. Ella glanced over her shoulder at Mama, waiting for her to nod.

"I assure you, it's very comfortable," Headmarveller Rivera added.

"We would love to," Papa replied. "Right, Aubrielle?"

Mama's eyebrow lifted. "Yes. Yes, of course."

Headmarveller Rivera winked at Ella. The coppers escorted them into the largest sky-ferry while the other trainees and their families moved as far away from them as possible.

Mama looked nervous. Papa squared his shoulders. Ella beamed and felt special.

"Welcome!" Headmarveller Rivera opened her arms.

The sky-ferry spread out before them: lush velvet seats, brass buttons Ella wished she could press, and a constellation map glimmering with colorful animals.

"This way." An usher led them down the long aisle.

"All this room for just us," Papa remarked.

"Gumbo needs three seats anyways," Mama added.

"Your comfort is important to us." Headmarveller Rivera pointed Ella's parents to a booth.

Ella bounded ahead, looking for a spot with the best view. Winnie followed, then sat opposite her.

A woman in a pillbox hat held a tray of bubbling drinks. "Care for a fizzlet? We have all flavors. What's your pleasure?"

Ella took a purple one. Winnie took a green one.

"Be sure to drink it quick, otherwise it might just float away," the woman warned. "It'll also help your ears adjust to the altitude as we take off."

Ella guzzled it; the sweet bubbles burst on her tongue.

"Look!" Winnie pointed out the window.

Ella looked out. The sky-ferry door closed. The stellacity spheres burst with light as the engines began to hum.

The sky-ferry lifted in the air, and her stomach dropped like she was on a roller coaster. She grabbed Winnie's hand and squeezed it tight.

There was no turning back.

✦ ✱ ✦ ✻ ✦

ELLA GAZED DOWN, AND SHE COULDN'T SEE THE STARDUST PIER anymore. They were passing floating lighthouses, slicing through dark and stormy clouds. The minutes stretched to what felt like hours, and Ella worried they'd never get there. But just as frustration bubbled up in her chest, the grounds spread out beneath them like one of her gran's quilts stitched with threads of light.

The whole place held wonders: starfruit trees and moon-flowers, a vertical maze of wires lifting cable cars and trolleys to gilded docks, balloons dropping fireworks, and the gates of the Arcanum Training Institute for Marvelous and Uncanny Endeavors shining like sunrays fashioned into iron spindles and copper spires. The wild metals writhed, moving towers and turrets around like musical chairs. They stretched so high Ella couldn't see where they ended and began. The windows glinted as if welcoming her with a wink.

Ella gasped.

She desperately wanted to belong here.

She would do whatever it took. She would master every level. She would pass every test.

She would become a Marveller.

The very best one.

THE CONJURE EDICT

The League of United Marvellers hereby proclaims that the Conjure folk* of the world are granted citizenship to the Marvellian community. Amendments to the Constitution will end the Conjure Codes and ensure equality for all within Marvellian cities and Institutes.

*The term *Conjure folk* encompasses all congregations in the United Conjure Congress, including but not limited to delegations from North America, Central America, South America, Cuba, Cape Verde, and so forth.

THE CARDS OF
DEADLY FATE

Moments after Ella's arrival at the Arcanum Training Institute, a woman hunched over a *Marvellian Times* news-box, watching it all unfold from the comforts of her prison cell. The news hologram flickered bright, making her pale white skin even more ghastly.

The woman cackled, her unused laugh rough as sandpaper. "Well, star's teeth, they let her in." She leaned as close as possible to the black-and-white projection, reaching out to try to catch the tiny version of the first Conjuror to ever attend the prestigious school. But the little light version slipped through her fingers like a will-o'-the-wisp.

Headlines pulsed over the girl: HORNET'S NEST HEADED FOR THE ARCANUM LOWER SCHOOL–FULL BLOWN SCANDAL AS THE CHILD OF CONJURORS LET IN. The articles about the little Conjuror crawled above her tiny hologram.

The woman slowed the crank, so the sentences spilled out one by one and she could absorb every word.

"It'll be the greatest show in the sky." The woman smiled. "For now . . ."

A window appeared in the right-hand corner of her cage. She gazed out at all the other prison cells floating in a dusky abyss like sad, dimly lit stars in a hellish sky. The windows used to tease her like a messed-up funhouse. A grand trick that made her jealous, for she loved a good illusion.

The world would never know that she sat inside a deck of cards suspended in the middle of time, in the middle of life and death. Her eternal punishment. Marvellians loved their rules.

"Dinner," a voice shouted inside her cell.

She'd already eaten hours ago. There was a little brass lamppost near the food slot. A nice new touch. Inside the slot sat a little fluttering hummingbird cake stretching its wings. A brass skeleton key stabbed through its middle like a fork.

A smile broke out on her severe yet beautiful face. Finally. She'd been patient. She chased the treat with her fingers, catching it and plucking out the solid, weighty key. She licked off the frosting and revealed a delicately etched rose and the initials—C.B.—on the handle. The Aces had come through as they'd always done.

There were no doors in this place, but that wouldn't be an issue. This was just what she needed. Her fingertips tingled. It'd been so long since she'd felt her marvel hum inside her like a stellacity current. Eleven years. 4,015 days. 96,360 hours.

She laughed until her mouth went dry.

Something had been stolen from her, and she would take it back.

CHAPTER THREE
THE BOTTLE TREE

Ella and her three new roommates were having a staring contest. Each refusing to blink. Each waiting for the other to speak. Each wondering who would make the first move. Ella's words got stuck in the back of her throat. She didn't have this problem back home, and it always felt like she had more friends than stars in the night sky.

But here . . . she was on her own.

She opened and closed her mouth a few times, unsure of the best thing to say. She wanted it to be good, and she'd practiced in front of the mirror all summer and role-played with Reagan, but every one of those rehearsed lines disappeared out of her head like *poof!*

These girls looked so important.

The first one had a strange armor-wearing creature on her shoulder and expert bangs sweeping across her forehead like a black curtain. The second one wore the prettiest hijab cupping her rosy, brown cheeks, and she cradled a bejeweled lantern. The third one clutched a terrarium full of pixies so tight her white knuckles turned red. She hid under a mop of tangled hair, and her ruddy white cheeks made her look flustered.

Ella touched the luck root in her pocket, wondering how different this all would've been had Reagan accepted her invitation too.

She squeaked out a "Hi! I'm Ella."

"We know," the dark-haired girl replied in soft-accented English. "Do you speak other languages?"

"French, a little Spanish, but I'm learn—"

"No Mandarin or Cantonese? Shame." She exhaled her disappointment. "I'm Lian Wong . . . like *those* Wongs. My dad is the Supreme Head Judge of the Courts of Justice." She didn't wait for the other girls to introduce themselves before parading about the room as if she was ensuring she'd picked the best bed. Her little creature adjusted its armor, and Ella wondered if it was similar to her parents' conjure companions. "Jiaozi, be still, be still, will you?" she barked.

"What is that?" Ella admired the small animal.

Lian scoffed. "It's a fu dog, you know, like a Chinese guardian lion."

"Oh." Ella had never seen one before.

The fu dog trundled about, preening and showing off.

"I'll put you in your crate and lock it this time." Lian scooped Jiaozi up.

Maybe fu dogs and companions weren't the same after all. Conjure companions were never caged because it'd be like locking away your best friend, a part of you.

The hijabi girl stepped forward. "I'm Samaira."

Ella admired her beautiful lantern. "Is there a real genie in there?"

Samaira's nose scrunched. "We never call them that. There's a djinn. A nice one too. Comes and goes, but I like to carry this so she'll be comfy when she comes to visit." She stroked its sides as if Ella had insulted it. "And my 'umi is the *President* of the United League of Marvellers."

Ella gulped. She'd made another mistake. Oof.

"I'm Siobhan," the last girl whispered with a thick Irish accent. "And I'm nobody."

The other girls giggled, but Ella didn't know why.

Ella started to explain that she was a Conjuror, but Lian cupped her hands together, and a tiny ball of light appeared.

Ella's eyes widened; she'd never seen Marvellian magic before. She couldn't wait to be able to do something like that. It was so different than conjuring.

"What are your marvels?" Lian said in a haughty tone. "What Paragon do you think you'll be in?"

Oh no. Ella still didn't know.

"*I* come from an entire family of Spirits." Lian tossed around the tiny ball of marvel light from palm to palm. "My yéye has a weather marvel and loves working with storms. I think I'll follow in his footsteps."

Samaira craned forward. "How'd you learn to call your light already?"

"Been practicing for years." Lian flashed a smug smile. "Private lessons."

"One of my moms is a Touch like Headmarveller Rivera, but she has a gem marvel." Samaira pointed to the pretty ones on her headscarf. "They're infused to help me remember things. And my 'umi is a Vision with a wisdom marvel. Her legendary advice column in *The Marvellian Times* contains the best prophecies and predictions. But I want to be a Taste and have my own bakery. I'll make bursting basbousa. The whole world will be obsessed with my cakes."

Ella squirmed, wishing she could rattle off what marvels Mama and Papa might have, but she had no idea how conjure fit into all of this.

Lian and Samaira glanced at Siobhan next. "Ma's a Touch with a metal marvel. She can work with wild iron and make you anything you want. Pa's a Spirit. Can cross just about any veil," she mumbled.

"Didn't your mom go to jail?" Lian asked. "I saw that in the *Marvelous Tattles* news-box."

Siobhan's cheeks flamed.

Samaira gulped, then turned to Ella. "Do you really have bad light inside you?"

Ella bristled. "No, what's that?"

Before Samaira could answer, Ella's parents and Headmarveller Rivera burst into the room.

"Your parents are here?" Lian's nose crinkled.

Ella pursed her lips, not knowing what to say.

"Hello, petites," Mama said with her big voice. Gumbo lumbered in right after, leaving a trail of wet spots across the floor.

The girls shrank away from her parents. Ella supposed they looked peculiar: Papa with his long locs, top hat, tuxedo and tails, and a ribbiting frog on his shoulder; Mama in her flowy dress with a big alligator hovering behind her skirts, her big, beautiful storm of hair, and the most noticeable thing . . . the conjure mark on her brown skin.

"Very nice to meet you all." Mama waved.

No one responded except for Siobhan.

Headmarveller Rivera tried to make polite conversation.

Mama patted Ella's shoulder, and their eyes met. Her voice drifted through Ella's head like a lullaby. *Your room at home is much bigger, and the dorms at Madame Collette's are still lovely. I'd let you stay there instead of home this year if you want. You sure about this?*

Ella couldn't remember a time when she hadn't heard Mama's nosy voice in her head if she was close by, from whispered reminders to feed the orchids to sweet encouragement when she struggled to memorize the role of each conjure card to bedtime stories to help her fall asleep. Until Ella's conjure companion showed up and guarded her mind from pesky family members, Mama or Papa or Gran would be able to cross into her mind to communicate and (sometimes) read her thoughts.

"Yes, Mama," Ella whispered back.

"Fine." Mama leaned down and kissed her forehead.

Conjure folk tend to be friendlier. Mama's voice trickled inside her head again.

Ella nodded. Maybe they all just needed more warming up.

Papa removed his signature skull-rimmed top hat and greeted the girls and Headmarveller Rivera.

The girls gawked and remained silent.

Headmarveller Rivera smiled. "We are so glad you're here with us, Ella."

Papa glanced back at Mama. "I'll take Winnie on a walk while you get our girl settled." He winked at Ella before slipping out of the room.

While Headmarveller Rivera looked on, Lian, Samaira, and Siobhan turned to their corners of the room. Ella stared back and forth from her juju-trunks to their marvel-valises, and she couldn't wait to visit a Marvellian shop and buy hers. Covered in beautiful constellations, they unpacked themselves on command. Ella filled with embarrassment that Mama was the only parent here helping with the move in.

Mama tapped Ella on the shoulder. "These clothes won't put themselves away over here."

She shrugged, then helped Mama fill the bureau, hang five white Marvellian mantles in her private closet, and place a pot of conjure-roses on her bedside table.

Ella spread one of Gran's quilts over her bed, then fluffed the pillow. Her hand caught the edge of something. She lifted the pillow to find a conjure coin. The twinkling copper warmed in her palm.

"Bet I know who that's from," Mama said with a smile.

Ella flipped the coin, then pressed it to her ear. "See you soon, petit. Glad we're here together," the sweet voice of her godmother and Mama's cousin, Sera Baptiste, whispered. "Wish I could be there tonight. I'll come see you soon. Still putting the finishing touches on my Conjure Atelier. I hope you'll love it." Ella couldn't wait to see one of her favorite people, and she was pretty sure Mama only agreed to let her enroll at the Institute because Aunt Sera would be teaching the Conjure Arts for the first time.

"She's going to be giving you extra lessons so I can ensure that all this *Marveller* stuff won't mess you up." Mama's warm fingers found their way to the tiny mark on Ella's neck. "You mind what she tells you, you hear?"

"Yes, ma'am." Ella started to tell her that she'd be okay when Winnie skipped back into the room like a great, big interruption. Winnie tugged at Ella's mantle, pulling her away from the other girls. "Ella, you've got the best room. I looked at the other ones."

"What did you find out?" she asked, knowing that's what Winnie desperately wanted her to say.

Headmarveller Rivera smiled as Winnie fired off her report. "There's another Level One girls' dorm next door called Hydra, and the boys' ones are right across the hall called Canis Minor and Zepus. But there's more for older kids." She butchered the pronunciation.

"All of our dorms seek to meet all the needs of our trainees. We have quite a few more than that," Headmarveller Rivera said.

Winnie grinned at her, then turned back to Ella. "That lady downstairs said you should be able to see one of the towns 'cause you have the biggest glass."

"Window?" she corrected gently.

"Yes, that's what I said." Winnie darted over, pressing her little palms to it. Ella joined her at the wall of arched windows, her heart thudding. She'd seen maps of the floating Marvellian cities—the bustling canals of Astradam, the elegant streets of Celestian, the entertaining quarters of Betelmore—in Papa's office. But Mama never let her go with him on his trips. Not after her Mama's twin sister Celeste went missing in Astradam when they were young girls. But when the cities arrived close to the Institute, she'd take the first chance she had to visit each one and sail along the wires in the air-trollies headed to explore shops on every high street and low street and spend all the gold stellas and silver lunari her papa had given her. It would just be her little secret . . . and she'd be very careful.

"Thanks for the update, Cricket," Mama said. "Great sleuthing."

Winnie skipped around and reported more discoveries:

"You have your own bathroom!"

"Four closets. One for each!"

"The clock floats and has messages! I want one for my room at home."

Ella's new roommates gawked at Winnie like she was a fly let into the house, and Ella's cheeks warmed with more embarrassment.

"Cricket, sit on the bed and help match Ella's socks. The dirt dobbin must've gotten into the suitcase and made amuck," Papa said, but his attempts to distract her proved unsuccessful, so he took her on another walk.

Ella sighed with relief as she took out the supply list to double-check that she had everything: her satchel ready to be filled, an astrolabe, the glass weather cistern, a spice dubba, the mortar and pestle, her trusty Paragon chart to remember all five groups, the new peacock stylus Gran had given her.

She stacked her session manuals in order:

A History of Marvellers by Yves San Michel

What are Marvels and Why Do We Have Them? by Mae Lam

The Five Paragons of Marvelling by Ian Pearce

The Stars Above Us—Astrology from All Around the World by Riley Clayton

Notable Channellors and Determining the Right One for Your Marvelling by Tabitha Bledsoe

Ella pinned a picture she'd drawn of the perfect Arcanum uniform on the corkboard over her desk: a white Marvellian mantle, a neatly ironed skirt or pair of pants, a well-packed satchel, and the translation crystal around the neck. Then she set out her sketchbook and her Institute handbook and traced her fingers along its emblem—the five-pointed star.

She was ready.

✦ ✶ ✦ ✳ ✦

AFTER ALL ELLA'S THINGS WERE UNPACKED, MAMA LIFTED ONE OF the family brooms from Ella's suitcase.

"We aren't witches," Samaira called out.

Headmarveller Rivera shushed her.

"This is no witch's broom, sweet one," Mama informed her. "It's to sweep out bad spirits. A must-have for a new space. Much like how Lian is lighting incense on her new altar."

Lian flashed them both a weak smile, then her eyes found Headmarveller Rivera.

Ella smiled at her, and Samaira's expression softened.

Mama tapped her fingers on the bureau. "I'm putting the hoodoo-hot sauce in the top drawer. You know the food here isn't going to have the taste from home."

"I still want to try it."

Mama turned her nose up. "Marvellian food never has enough flavor for me."

"You've had it before?" Ella's ears perked up. "You never told me that."

"I haven't told you a lot of things." Mama opened the drawer. "Gran whipped this up special. It'll cross right through the bland and give it a kick. Be like you're in our kitchen." A sudden sadness crept across her face. "Time to conjure the bottle tree. The last thing. The sky-ferries will take us back to the pier soon, but I want to fortify it for you."

"I can do it," Ella replied, feeling both sad and excited that her parents were leaving.

"I know you can, my sweet, but your mama wants to help some too." Mama set out pale blue bottles from a special case and tied white string around their necks. She placed a few of the Durand family saints on the nightstand beside the conjure-roses. "Baby girl, I'm starting to regret agreeing to this," she whispered.

"It's *fine*."

The saints clapped their tiny porcelain hands.

"Blessings, always, upon your house! Thank you for taking us out of that awful darkness," one of the saint statues said.

Ella glared at the figurines. "Sssh, St. Phillip." She couldn't think with all their racket. Their glossy white faces wore smiles and cheerful expressions. They blew kisses (especially St. Valentine). They bowed. They saluted.

"Wonderful new room, Ella!" St. Catherine shouted.

"We're so proud," St. Christopher added.

"What are those talking things?" Lian looked up from arranging her fu dog's mini-lair. "Dolls?"

"They're saints," Ella answered.

"Passed down through our family. They give us counsel and protection," Mama added.

"They're lovely," Headmarveller Rivera replied. "Much like the living votives I have from Mexico."

These saints used to sit among a hundred more in the front parlor at home, doling out advice and blessings, and now they would watch over Ella as they'd done countless other generations of their family. Even if she didn't want them to.

Lian eavesdropped with curiosity. Samaira gawked with

awe. Siobhan grinned so wide Ella could spot most of her teeth. Headmarveller Rivera admired them.

Thankfully, Mama finally shushed the chattering saints. They exchanged huffed glances. Some clutched their rosaries and Bibles and performed the sign of the cross, then apologized and resumed their inanimate positions.

"Now get on with conjuring the tree." Mama handed Ella each blue glass bottle as she placed them in a circle on the floor. She'd fixed plenty of bottle trees with her mama and Gran in order to protect their home; it'd become a reflex. "You know the spell."

Mama gave her a jar of dirt and a seed. "Just like the one from home."

Ella groaned. She hated being rushed. "Conjure needs enough time to rise . . . like beignet dough," Gran always said, and Ella agreed. But Mama had her own way. Each Conjuror did.

"Untwist your face," Mama ordered.

"Fine," Ella mumbled as she made a tiny mound of dirt in the middle of the circle of bottles and placed the seed inside.

Ella remembered the first plant she'd ever made grow. She'd still been small enough to fit on Gran's hip, and she'd reached her pudgy fingers out to touch the black calla lilies in the greenhouse. Her favorite. They'd reminded her of Papa's beautiful dark skin. She'd been so surprised when they'd stretched back to meet her fingertips, and it took her years to understand how she was able to cross into their life force and bend their will to hers.

With all these Marvellians watching, she took a deep breath, closed her eyes, and called to the conjure inside her, asking it to wake up. Her head grew dizzy and light. Her ears filled with a creaky, stretching sound as she felt for the seed's root. Sweat coated her forehead. Her imagination filled with its possibility, the darkness turning to twilight. Her wish blossomed as she sang the spell and made her request: *Grow deep roots and protect us all from evil as we sleep.*

Her eyes snapped open, and she tried not to focus on everyone gawking. Papa had told her Marvellian magic was different than theirs, and she couldn't wait to keep showing off.

The noise of a tiny rapid heartbeat sounded. A little sapling sprouted from the dirt, then clawed along the floor like ivy. Its bud opened, and tubers escaped. They curled around each other like ropes and thickened into a tree trunk, its girth growing up to the ceiling. Branches exploded in all directions. Green leaves filled in the tree's skeleton. Now a huge live oak identical to the one in the Durand's courtyard sat in the corner, stretching out over Ella's bed.

"Last step," Mama reminded her.

"Bottles," Ella whispered.

Nothing happened.

"With gratitude and a little *oomph* in your voice. It can't hear you."

"Bottles, *please*," Ella said to the tree.

Its arms reached down to pick up the blue bottles by the strings, one per each, and then stretched back upright, and the bottles hung like colorful pendulums. Death moths fluttered around the tree.

Mama lifted Ella's chin. "Well done, baby girl. Even better than the ones I conjure." She kissed her forehead.

Ella turned around to shocked faces. Headmarveller Rivera cupped her hands over her mouth.

"Star's teeth! There's a TREE in our room!" Lian said as her fu dog scampered around the trunk, ready to climb. "Come back here!"

Siobhan's pixies shot out of her terrarium and swarmed the tree. "Don't do that!" she scolded.

"What kind of marvel is this?" Samaira gazed up at its branches. "This magic is different!"

Ella cringed at the word. It was one Mama hated . . . for *magic* felt too simple for what they could do.

Mama nudged Ella to answer the question.

"It's a bottle tree," Ella finally squeaked out.

"We conjure these to keep bad spirits out of a space. Any evil would get trapped in the glass containers," Mama added. "Then Ella could dispose of it appropriately."

They all circled the tree.

"It's beautiful," Headmarveller Rivera remarked.

"So amazing." Siobhan smiled at her.

"And you sing your . . . ?" Samaira asked.

"Spells." Ella nodded. She didn't realize Marvellers wouldn't know much about conjure.

"We say incants." Lian ran her fingers over the bark, then looked proudly at Headmarveller Rivera.

Ella couldn't wait to learn the similarities and differences.

"Marvellers can't make things grow." Samaira pursed her lips.

Ella gazed at her, puzzled.

"What she means is that we don't marvel from nothing. We manipulate what's already there. It's an art and a science." Headmarveller Rivera touched one of the tree's leaves.

Ella felt Mama's hand find her shoulder. "Well, we all have much to learn from one another."

Lian whispered to Samaira. "It's like the Aces."

"We don't speak about them, Miss Wong." Headmarveller Rivera's voice went stern.

"What's that?" Ella asked.

A tense quiet spread throughout the room.

Ella's stomach tightened. Was growing things bad? What did the Aces mean?

A bell chimed. The ceiling lanterns flickered. Papa and Winnie rushed back in to hug Ella.

A Level Three student swished into the room, her mantle an ocean of blue behind her and her shock of red hair in a bun. "Good evening. A star's blessings to you all. My name is Katherine, and I'm a trainee ambassador. Mr. and Mrs. Durand, your sky-ferry is ready to return to the Stardust Pier. Level Ones, it's time for our midnight assembly."

Mama turned to Ella. "You'd tell me if anything was wrong, right? If anything happened?"

"Yes, Mama. Always."

"You'll write?"

"Yes, Mama."

"You'll use the conjure-cameo?"

"Yes."

"You'll be safe and stay out of Marvellian cities?"

"Yessssssss."

Mama kissed her forehead one final time. Papa winked at her. Winnie sniffled and waved.

There was no turning back now.

The Arcanum Training Institute for Marvelous and Uncanny Endeavors

Welcome to the Arcanum family!

This handbook is designed to help new members of the Arcanum family learn the rules and expectations of our marvelous and spectacular center.

Marvellers practice the noble art of *marvelling*, channeling the celestial light within to manipulate the universe and display its grandeur.

Besides learning to use your individual marvels, trainees will also study many other skills that will help them throughout life in both the Marvellian and Fewel worlds.

THE TENETS OF MARVELLERS:

Integrity—Honor the elders, the marvels, and one's ancestors.
Self-Control—Positively control one's feelings and behaviors.
Perseverance—Show effort and persistence to walk a noble path.
Goodness—Only channel the light.

TRAINEE OATH:

I shall observe the tenets of Marvellers.
I shall respect the elder Marvellians.
I shall never misuse my marvel.
I shall be a champion of fairness and justice.
I shall only channel the light for good.
I shall never covet or desire another's marvel.

———————————————————————————————————

Trainee signature   *Star ink preferred

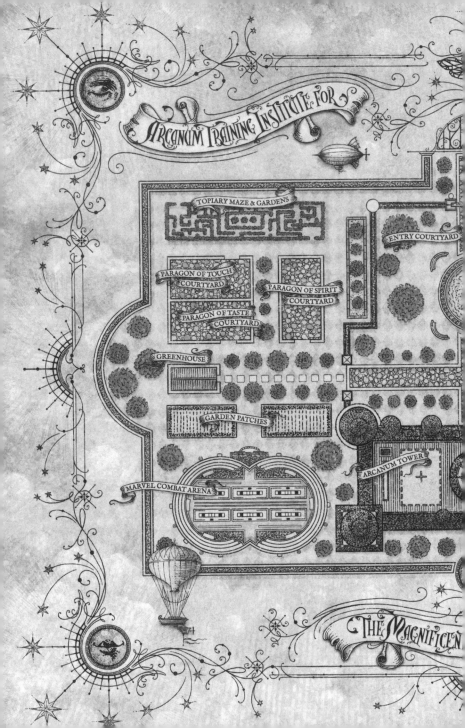

CHAPTER FOUR

MIDNIGHT LANTERNS

Ella stood in the Ursa Minor lounge soaking up everything around her: a marble fireplace carved in the shape of a bear's mouth sparked with blue fire, star-lanterns released glitter showers, and the little bear constellation skulked across the ceiling.

It was so different than Madame Collette's Conjure École back home. That blush-pink mansion in the Garden District with its wildflower bushes, wraparound galleries, and eccentric bedrooms had felt like the whole world . . . until now.

All kinds of girls zipped around like honeybees, some plopping into cozy armchairs, others perched on the spiraled staircases, and a few clustered around the worktables. They all looked so different from one another, a kaleidoscope of colors and shapes and sizes. She tried to guess who lived in which floating Marvellian city, or a Fewel city like she did, as she scanned everyone's name tags. A few of them stole glances at her. Some whispered. Most giggled. A few snickered. She smiled back. It reminded her of the first day she'd had at Madame Collette's, and she knew just what to do to make friends.

A woman waved her plump arms in the air. "Girls! Girls! Find seats, please. Get settled. There's much to be done." A teapot sat on her shoulder, making Ella wonder what the woman's marvel and Paragon would be. "I'm Ms. Paige, your Tower Adviser in charge of all Level One girls."

Ella found a small chair to squeeze into.

The woman pointed to her teapot, the beautiful porcelain as round and pale white as her. "I'm a Paragon of Taste with a tea marvel, dearies. British, specifically, but the pot can brew you any kind you like in an instant." She pointed at a nearby door. "Those are my apartments. I live between this tower and the next one, Hydra. I'm here for all the things that go bump in the night, and there's a lot of that here at the Arcanum, I suppose." She chuckled. "But when you miss your grown-ups or get sick or need anything, come ring the bell." She clapped her hands. "All right, time for translation crystals before orientation, little stars." The Tower Adviser handed out translucent stones threaded on strings. "This aids Marvellers from all over the world in understanding one another. Languages will be translated for you effortlessly as long as both people are wearing them. Be sure to keep them on."

Ella slipped the necklace over her head just as the others did. There was a click and pop in her ears. She tucked the crystal beside the conjure-cameo she wore, the carved medallion of her mama's and papa's faces.

Ms. Paige handed out cups. "Drink a little warm fizzlet." Her teapot poured the bubbly liquid. "Hold the cup tight so it doesn't drift off or explode. Have a deep belch."

Ella remembered the delicious drink from the sky-ferry and quickly chugged the liquid just before it could wiggle out of the cup. She added to the chorus of burps and giggles in the room.

"Please wear the crystal for safety reasons and community building," she added. "It should acclimatize in just another second. Keep expelling gas."

"Mouth farts!" a girl named Lizzie shouted, while trying to hide behind big, black curls.

"Now, now, mind your manners, as that is the Marvellian way."

Giggles filled the room.

The pressure in Ella's ears cleared.

"Turn to your neighbor. Share your name, where you're from, and maybe something you like. Don't be shy. Have a chat while I hand out your Arcanum ID cards." Ms. Paige made her way through the room. When she handed one to Ella, she leaned in and whispered, "Very glad you're here."

Ella replied with a big smile as the tiny portrait of her face filled in above her name and two blank lines awaited her marvel and Paragon. She couldn't wait to figure out where she belonged in this place.

She tried to join a group, listening along its edge.

"I'm Anh, and I'm from Hanoi," the smallest girl piped up, her black hair cupping her cheeks like a mushroom. "I have a paddy egg." She showed it off in her palm, twisting left and right as the shell changed colors. "My family grows them. We have reverie marvels. They hatch dreams. Sometimes wishes. But I've been getting some nightmares too. I don't like those."

Another girl turned to Ella, her curious hazel eyes full of

mischief. Her name tag read PILAR DIAZ. "Are you keeping that crocodile in your room?"

The group turned to look at Ella, their eyes scanning her from head to toe.

Ella laughed. "Gumbo's an alligator."

"You're not supposed to have pets," said a girl with a fat gray spider spinning a web on her shoulder.

"You have one," Anh pointed out.

The spider girl scoffed. "It's a family protector. An ancient being that's been with our bloodline since like forever." The girl sucked her teeth. "All premiere West African Marvellians have one, and I'm from a very *notable* family. You've probably heard of us, the Asamoahs, we're seriously *legendary*. The most famous. So, definitely *not* a pet."

"Gumbo is sort of like that. A conjure companion, really, or a soul mate," Ella said. "But he's with my mama. Mine won't come until I'm thirteen."

"Weird." Pilar's eyes narrowed.

"Or awesome," Anh replied. "I wish I could have something like that."

The spider girl did a lap around the circle, shaking everyone's hand. "Well, I'm Abina. I have an arachna marvel, a Paragon of Sound."

"What's that?" Ella tried to get a close look at the spider.

Abina barely shook Ella's hand. "I can speak to arachnids, including their king, Anansi, of course," she said with pride. "Paragons of Sound can communicate with all creatures. How do you *not* know this?"

Ella felt silly for not knowing, but nodded as if she did, and tried to push away her embarrassment. She knew the basics about the five Paragons of Marvelling—Papa and the griots had helped her with those—but she was still learning about all the different kinds of marvels. There were endless possibilities.

"We haven't had our Marvel Exam." Anh crossed her arms over her chest. "So how would she?"

"I heard it's not until the end of the year." Pilar whipped out the student handbook.

"But like, don't most people know from their families? I've *always* known my marvel and my Paragon," Abina boasted.

A chorus of *me toos* echoed from the group.

Clearly Ella didn't have all the information yet and needed to get to the Arcanum library as soon as possible. She wouldn't be caught not knowing something again.

"Now, where was I?" Abina said.

Ella didn't want this girl not to like her. Abina's gorgeous braids were threaded with jewelry and her smile reminded Ella of Reagan's, so she tried again. She reached into her pocket and retrieved Reagan's luck root. "Isn't this cool?"

The girls leaned in close to watch the blue flower stretch itself upright, stem coiling around Ella's fingers. She hummed, and its fluorescent petals wiggled and waved. "Each one helps you with something you need."

"Whoa," Anh said.

"How does it do that?" Pilar asked. "Where is it from?"

"The Underworld. They grow—" .

"Are you even allowed to have something like *that* in the dorms?" A new girl barreled through their circle, breaking it in two. Pale white and freckly, she glared with intense green eyes.

Her glittering necklace flashed her name like a lightbulb. Clare Lumen.

Lian followed with a smug grin.

Ella froze.

"Wouldn't want to get in trouble already. The whole world's talking about you. See?" Clare held up a news-box. Ella's name glimmered in big, bold letters as an image of her father tipping his top hat played like a tiny hologram right before their eyes.

Ella gulped.

"You're famous."

Ella hated that word. Everyone back home said the same thing because of the importance of her papa's job and Mama's notorious conjure skills. Her family couldn't go anywhere without being stopped, having to talk to so and so, or get hemmed up into having iced tea and pound cake on somebody's porch. But maybe at the Arcanum, it'd help her meet new people.

"Let's just hope it's the good kind of famous and not the *bad* kind." Clare smiled slowly, revealing a perfect set of white teeth. "Because no one—"

The ceiling flared and sparked, filling with golden stars, the noise cutting off whatever Clare was about to say.

Ella's heart leapt at the sight.

"Ooooh," Ms. Paige squealed. "Our first starpost mailing of the year."

Star-shaped letters rained down, zipping left and right, up and down, somehow knowing how to find their owners. Two stopped in front of Ella, backflipping. She plucked them out of the air. The envelopes were thick, made of celestial-blue paper, and her name was written in gold ink. Just like her Arcanum acceptance letter.

Ella pinched the stardust seal of the first one and yanked the paper out. A good-luck note from Mama and Papa, which made her smile even more as she tore into the second one. Her eyes soaked up the message:

Dear Ella,

I will be your mentor this year. I'm very happy to welcome you to the Arcanum and help you learn the great Marvellian Way.

Very glad you are here.

All the good marvelling to you.

Masterji Thakur

The nice man from the Stardust Pier. She pressed the post to her chest, happiness tingling in her fingertips.

Ms. Paige clapped her hands and drew everyone's attention back to the center of the room. "Okay, everyone. Put your starposts and IDs away. It's time. Orientation. Come. Come." She jumped and clicked her heels together. "This way; we don't want to be late. So much to see."

Clare flashed another smug look at Ella before setting the news-box on the table and jumping to the front of the line. Ella followed the other girls and tried not to glance back at the medley of headlines flickering above the news-box like a tiny living billboard.

What were they saying about her—and was it good or bad?

✦ ✖ ✦ ✖ ✦

ELLA HELD HER BREATH AS THE LEVEL ONE CORRIDOR EMPTIED into the biggest foyer she'd ever seen. It felt like three train stations sandwiched together.

"Welcome to the heart of the Arcanum, little stars!" Ms. Paige announced while trying to herd the group together.

Thousands of trainees whizzed past, their mantles a riot of colors: more Levels Ones in white, Level Twos in bright orange, Level Threes in sapphire blue, and Level Fours in plum purple.

"The night is marvelous." Ms. Paige waved her hands in the air.

Ella agreed. This whole thing felt like a spectacular.

While Ms. Paige spoke about the history of the Institute, Ella's focus drifted high above. Trolleys glided along suspension ropes headed to all the various levels. Piped in gold and paneled in bright colors, they reminded her of the streetcars from her home. The five Paragon symbols winked along their sides, and placards advertised their destinations: THE PARAGON TOWERS, THE LIBRARY, THE GRAND ASSEMBLY ROOM, THE SUPPLY STORE, THE INFIRMARY, THE DINING HALL, THE ARCANUM DOCKS, and more.

"Be sure to wave," Ms. Paige said, and they walked past living-busts of the founders. Olivia Hellbourne the Patient with her magical flute; Shuai Chen the Keen and the storm clouds swirling around his chest; Indira Patel the Brave and her beautiful gold daggers; Louis Antonio Villarreal the Sage with his twitchy handlebar mustache and glittering crystal ball; and Femi Ademola the Honest and his bowl of truth soup.

While Ms. Paige explained the varying corridors, Ella felt a familiar tug, similar to when she'd cross into the Underworld with her family. The tingle always started in her heart as she stood in front of the beautiful pit bulls that guarded the gate.

"What is happening?" she whispered to herself, breaking away from the group, letting the tug pull her in the opposite direction. She found herself moving down a darkened corridor, standing before an elevator that said RESTRICTED LIFT. Her fingers searched for a button pad like the Fewel ones, but there was nothing but a coin slot. Where did it go? Why did she feel the crossing tug here . . . so far from home?

"Lost from the group, are we?" came a voice from behind.

Ella spun around to find Masterji Thakur. Her new mentor. Oh no! Was she already in trouble?

"I am Masterji Thakur. We met earlier this evening, and I'm hoping you got my starpost." He smiled at her, his long mustache wiggling with glee. His gorgeous turban now glowed with beautiful shades of green and patterns of dancing pearls.

"I—I—" she stammered. "Yes, yes, I did."

"I'm headed to the midnight assembly; would you like to accompany me?" he asked.

She nodded and quickly followed.

"I'm looking forward to having you in my course this year and for our mentoring sessions." The warmth of his voice erased any worry she had about possibly being in trouble. "I'm here for all your questions as you learn the great Marvellian way, and how, really, to forge your own path here as a new trainee."

"Thanks," she said.

He opened a set of iron-wrought doors; they twisted and untwisted into versions of the Arcanum's motto—*Every stu-*

dent is a star!—in many different languages. Beyond them were thousands of eager people in the entry courtyard.

She gazed back once more at the restricted lift, but it was no longer there. Strange.

"Join the crowd of Level Ones. It's about to begin," Masterji Thakur directed. "You won't want to miss a thing."

Ella's heart fluttered as she looked out at the crowd. She abandoned her curiosity and found a spot beside her new roommate Siobhan.

The Headmarvellers stood on a platform above a great fountain. A white man with fiery red hair towered over Headmarveller Rivera.

A clock echoed.

Strike one. The kids roared.

Strike two. The stage under the Headmarvellers swung left and right like a great pendulum.

Strike three. It lifted into the air and circled over the crowd.

Everyone reached their hands up, trying to touch it.

Ella blinked in disbelief. "What is happening?"

"Everything!" Siobhan squealed, and her tiny pixie giggled.

"Cheers, my budding Marvellians, my little neophytes," Headmarveller Rivera's voice thundered.

The crowd screamed.

"For my new Level Ones, I'm Headmarveller Rivera, and I brought you up from the Stardust Pier." She gestured. "This is my governing partner, Headmarveller MacDonald."

He took a bow. "Welcome home!"

Headmarveller Rivera pointed up, then scowled, waiting for *The Marvellian Times* news-blimp to drift out of view before speaking again. "We are fallen stars. Each one of us containing the elements that make up the beautiful canvas above. Those blinking balls of light gave each of you your unique and precious marvels. And it's why we make our home here, so far up, and away from the rest of the world. To always remember. To revel in the endless light." She waved her hands in the air. "The sky binds us all together."

The older kids whistled. Ella watched how excited they were, how big their eyes grew, how much they seemed to love this place, and she realized that she wanted to be just like them, that she *could* be now that she was here.

Headmarveller MacDonald clapped. "This year will be a journey for us all. For our new Level Ones, it'll be a time of discovery, learning about your marvels and how each Paragon seeks to offer up a family of like minds and talents."

Ella grinned at the sound of his thick Scottish accent.

He held out his arms. "To honor that, we always begin with this tradition initiated by one of our great Institute founders, Indira Patel the Brave. We send our wishes up to the stars in hopes that they will be granted." He motioned to the left. "Level Fours, if you would please."

The oldest kids cut through the crowd in a storm of purple mantles. They toted baskets full of tiny lanterns, slips of parchment paper, and brass styluses.

While Ella waited for them to reach her, she looked around. With kids from every corner of the world, she tried to make guesses about where each one came from and what their marvel could be, but there were just too many to watch.

"Didn't she get the uniform guide?" Ella overheard Clare say.

Ella spotted the one girl who stood out from the rest: arms crossed over her chest, blond hair a mess, a poked-out lip, a strange clown doll peeking out of her hoodie pocket, doodles on her sneakers. The only person in the Level Ones' group *not* wearing a mantle.

Whispers exploded around Ella.

"*Must come from a bad family dressing like that.*"

"*Aren't those Fewel clothes? Yuck! Wonder if she is one and in the wrong place.*"

"*She's got a doll . . . maybe she thinks this is day care.*"

The girl's cheeks grew redder as each insult hit. Ella knew she must've come from a Fewel city like hers.

Ella squared her shoulders and stepped between the group and the girl, blocking their view. "Hi." She tucked all the bravery she had into her voice. "Instead of saying those things, why don't you ask her where she's from?"

Lian's eyes narrowed. "Who asked you?"

"No one, just offering my two cents," she answered.

"Your what?" a boy said. His name tag read PHILLIP DAVIS.

Ella started to explain, but Lian rolled her eyes and walked away with Clare.

"Aren't you that Conjuror?" a girl named Farah asked.

"Yes, that's me," Ella said.

The kids started to laugh and took off.

Ella gave the blond girl a sympathetic look, but she frowned. "I didn't need your help."

"But—"

A finger tapped her shoulder.

Ella whipped around to find the Tower Adviser, Ms. Paige, standing beside a boy with thick locs and deep brown skin.

"Ella, meet Jason," Ms. Paige said.

The boy gazed at her with eager eyes. She stayed tight-lipped and thought if she kept on frowning, he'd eventually go away. That's how she got rid of boys at Madame Collette's Conjure École.

"Jason, meet Ella."

He grinned at her, a slight gap in his teeth.

"He's going to be your guide here for a while. A trainee helper."

Ella scanned his white mantle, expertly ironed like hers. "But he's . . . a Level One?"

Ms. Paige put a hand on her shoulder. "He's from the Eugene family. Might as well be our most famous lot here."

His eyebrows lifted.

"I'll leave you two to get acquainted." She sauntered off.

Ella eyed him, trying to figure out what was so special about him aside from his last name and excellent hair.

"I just have a lot of siblings here and at the upper school," he replied, as if he could sense her question.

Ella and Jason stared at each other. She didn't think this boy would be any help to her. She already knew a lot about the Institute from her research, and she planned to live in the Arcanum library the first chance she got, and she definitely didn't need a fake friend given to her by an adult either. She was great at making friends back home and just needed a little time to meet people. But . . . a tiny part inside her betrayed her, whispering, *Maybe it would be nice to have someone on my side.*

But did they really think she needed a babysitter?!

He pulled a scroll from his pocket. "Want to sign my petition? I need a thousand names."

"For what?"

His hair jumped. "It's for Betelmore to come closer to the Arcanum this year. They've got Marchand's Mischievous Menagerie now. It's the best animal—"

A tall Level Four boy stopped in front of them. He had Jason's same brown face, but with a peach fuzz mustache, and even longer locs. "Jay, what are you doing?"

Jason froze.

"I know you're not annoying people about that petition. Not after I told you . . ."

Jason's eyes bulged. "Ummm . . ."

The boy turned to Ella. "I'm Wesley Eugene." The way he said his name let Ella know he was important. "Take one of each."

With quick hands, Ella plucked the items from his basket. The little ball-shaped lantern in her hands held a tiny candle.

"This is one of my brothers," Jason said with a sheepish grin.

"The best one," Wes teased.

"Want to sign still?" Jason showed him the paper, then Wes put him into a playful headlock until he squealed. Wes strode off, smiling.

Jason tried to de-wrinkle his mantle and pretend nothing had happened. His hair shook like it too was aggravated.

"Why do your locs move like that?" Ella asked, wondering if he used the black magic oil her papa did.

"My sister Grace put a wiggle-incant in my oil. Mama said it would wear off. But it's been like this all summer."

Ella tried not to laugh as he shrugged.

"It's almost time for our wishes," the Headmarvellers called out.

Ella watched the others around her. They seemed to know

just what to do: scribbling words on the paper, sticking it inside the candle wax, holding it up until the wick ignited on its own without explanation, and setting it free.

Jason held up his candle. "Watch me."

"How do you know?"

"Older siblings. Remember?" He pointed out two girls who shared his same smile and two boys with locs like his own. "There's Wes again, in Level Four, Allen and Beatrice in Level Three, Grace in Level Two. They showed me yesterday so I wouldn't embarrass them."

She let him help her even though she definitely didn't like it. But no one wanted to look foolish on their first day either.

"What are you going to write?" he asked.

"None of your business."

Ella wrote on her paper: *Everyone will like conjure—and me.*

THE ARCANUM TRAINING INSTITUTE FOR MARVELOUS AND UNCANNY ENDEAVORS

LEVEL ONE TRAINEE TIMETABLE
FIRST YEAR TRAINING SESSIONS

Name: *Ella Durand*

CORE REQUIREMENTS:

Introduction to the History of Marvels and Marvellers   Dr. Amir Zolghad

Introduction to Marvel Light   Dr. Amelia Bearden

Conjure for Beginners   Madame Sera Baptiste

Universal Incants and Their Origins   Dr. Guadalupe Perez

PARAGON REQUIREMENTS:

Future Forecasting I—Divining the Future Around the World   Dr. William Winchester

Global Elixirs   Masterji Raj Thakur

West African Oral Story Incants   Dr. Kwame Mbalia

Global Elementals— Water and Air   Dr. Anne Ursu

EXTRACURRICULAR ACTIVITIES:

Stardust and Exploration   Location: Observatory, Adviser: Dr. Meghan Cannistra

★—★—★— **STARPOST**—★—★—★

Hi Ella,

  Do you need help getting to the orientations tomorrow? We have a tour. I can meet you in the Level One dormitory hall. At breakfast, you should get a doubting doubles. They're so funny and so stressed out. You eat your worries. Sort of. They're from Trinidad. My dad's from Jamaica, but we still like them. You didn't ask for that information, but I wanted to tell you anyways.

From Jason (remember me? I'm
supposed to help you!)

★—★—★— **STARPOST**—★—★—★

Jason,

  I don't need help. I'm going to tell the Tower Adviser and the Headmarvellers that it's a WASTE to have you tagging along after me. I know what I'm doing.

From,
Ella

P.S.: I will try the doubting doubles, but I really want the flying hotcakes. I heard those are great too. But do you know if they have syrup?

CHAPTER FIVE

NEW BEGINNINGS . . . AND THE MARVELLIAN WAY!

"E lla!"

"Ella!"

"Ella Charlotte Baptiste Durand!"

"Get up! Right now, young lady. *Something's* going on." St. Anthony clapped. The family saints waved with upset looks on their porcelain faces. The bottle tree glinted in the morning light, casting shadows on her quilt.

"Petit." She heard her godmother's voice. "Wake up please."

Ella sat up and rubbed her eyes. Her beautiful godmother's face stared back. Aunt Sera. Her white kaftan made her brown skin look frosted. A matching headscarf held conjure-roses and swaddled her thick hair.

Ella dove into her arms. "Did I oversleep or something?" She glanced up at the clock. Its brass arms showed half past six, and the message—*Rest Time*—flickered. The word *Breakfast* would replace it in an hour.

"No, no," her godmother replied. "Not that."

Ella glanced around and panicked. She was in a completely different room. "What happened? Where am I?"

"The Hydra Tower." She pointed up. A snake made of starlight slithered through the ceiling licking its tongue out to greet them.

"But I was in Ursa Minor. Where's Siobhan? Or Lian and Samaira?"

Her godmother pursed her lips. Ella's heart skipped, her mind filling with a thousand questions about why they weren't here. Did she mess up last night at the midnight assembly? Did someone find out about her visit to that strange elevator? Would Mama and Papa be upset with her already?

"They felt you'd have more space in the Hydra Tower with one roommate instead of three. That you'd be more comfortable."

"But I was already comfortable." Ella gazed around at her new room: a tornado of clothes littered the floor; gigantic windows lined one wall; a desk and her own bathroom awaited her. "Besides, how'd I get here?"

Her godmother took her hand. "Baby, best not to ask questions you already know the answers to."

Ella tried to remember last night. She'd slept great, feeling like she was floating in her new bed. The dreamy memories washed over her: the sound of her godmother's voice waking the bottle tree with her song, *Southern tree, find the breeze. Lift your roots; pluck what we need.* She recalled the sensation of being lifted from her bed by its thick arms as it gathered her things and carried her into the hall.

"It was the least disruptive way," her godmother explained.

"But—"

Three knocks on the door sent the saints into a panic.

"I sense danger," St. Christopher said.

"There's mischief afoot," St. Ursula interjected.

"Ella? Ella, darling? The star that rises first gets the sky." Ms. Paige's soft voice found its way inside. "We have someone for you to meet."

Aunt Sera answered the door. Ms. Paige and Headmarveller Rivera ushered in a grumpy girl. Ella recognized her. The one from the midnight assembly yesterday. Her icy blue eyes found Ella and narrowed.

They all exchanged morning greetings, though the women seemed surprised to see her godmother.

The papel picado flowers in Headmarveller Rivera's hair waved. "Time for introductions."

"I've brought tea," Ms. Paige said. Three steaming teapots circled her like a tiny galaxy orbiting a sun. She patted a Paragon pin on her lapel; the golden mouth smiled back at Ella. "Care for a cup?" She waddled forward. "Can do chai, matcha . . . even sweetened and iced like you Americans from the South desire. I promise you, I have the very best. There are also biscuits. The English variety."

"No, thank you," Ella replied, unable to break eye contact with the girl.

"Well, Brigit, this is Ella." Headmarveller Rivera ushered Brigit forward. "And Ella, this is Brigit." She rested a hand on Brigit's shoulder. "She's from New York City, and she's having a tough time adjusting here like yourself."

"I am not having a tough time," Ella protested.

"Then maybe you can help her. Brigit's been raised outside of this world . . . much like you, but among only Fewels.

Which is so rare for Marvellians. Living with them and not knowing your heritage can be challenging. A shock to the system. So, she's struggling to adopt our ways, which you already know much about."

Ella did love to be helpful. Gran said it was one of her most noble traits. But she wasn't so sure about this.

"I don't care," Brigit snapped.

Ella frowned. Why was she so grumpy?

"Maybe a little tea would help." Ms. Paige's teapot wiggled.

"Maybe they both prefer coffee like me," Headmarveller Rivera said. "The Mexican way with cinnamon."

"Madame Baptiste, any for you?" The teapot turned to her godmother.

Her godmother waved it away.

Nervous dragonflies tumbled in Ella's stomach. She didn't understand why she needed to change rooms. Had her roommates complained? Did they hate her bottle tree? Had she snored that night? Did she even snore in the first place? Emotions roiled inside her: from pride at the beauty of the tree to bubbling anger at having to move to hot humiliation about what everyone must think.

"Go on. You must have something. It's only polite," Ms. Paige pressed.

"What did I do wrong?" Ella asked.

"Oh, nothing, dearie. Nothing at all. Don't fret." Ms. Paige patted her shoulder.

Aunt Sera crossed her arms over her chest. "It's the first day of term. This can't happen again. There will be one allowance—and one only. Neither her parents nor I will play this game all year. It's a transition for everyone involved. We cannot have any further chaos."

"It won't be a problem at all. Trust me." Headmarveller Rivera smiled.

"I don't," her godmother snapped.

Headmarveller Rivera's cheeks pinkened, and she sat straight up. "We, too, want a smooth process."

Aunt Sera rolled her eyes, took Ella's hand, and kissed it. "All will be well, petit."

Another knock shook the door, and in popped two of the starfolk. Ella was so excited to see one up close. They had kitten-like ears, tiny pairs of spectacles, and furry skin the color of night. She'd read about how they were born from the stars in *The Mythical Realms: Creatures Adjacent to Marvellers*. She couldn't stop herself from smiling at them. Hundreds of questions bubbled up inside her; she felt like Winnie.

"Two of our trusted caretakers are here to make sure you're all settled in. We've also ordered the automats to assist with *tidying*." Ms. Paige walked around inspecting Brigit's mess, the teapot following closely behind her. "This is Auriga and Aries. Meet Ella Durand."

They waved at one another. Ella noticed how Auriga kept smoothing her small pinafore and Aries kept stealing glances at Brigit.

"Oh my stars!" Auriga gasped at the sight of the tree.

An angry blush turned Brigit's face hot sauce red. "Ugh! I'm done with this." She leaped into bed and swaddled herself in the most beautiful quilt Ella had ever seen. The images glittered as the sunlight found them. Until now, she'd thought

Gran's quilts were the most amazing. Where did she get such a thing?

Brigit released three of the loudest and fakest snores. The starfolk giggled.

Headmarveller Rivera called Brigit's name a few times, then turned back to Ella. "I'll check in with you to see how you're settling in. Thank you for your flexibility and cooperation."

"Chin up, that's the Conjuror way." Aunt Sera kissed Ella's forehead before slipping out.

The ceiling rumbled and shimmered. A star-shaped letter sailed down and into her hands. Ella knew who it was from before she pinched the stardust seal.

Mama.

Ella,
    Please let us know that you are okay. Use your
conjure-cameo. I am not happy about this room change.
I might come straight up there and bring you home.

I'm not happy either, Ella thought.

She kept reading. There was also a note scrawled in Papa's handwriting.

Adore you, baby girl. I know you'll take this in stride.
Let us know you're okay.

                                    Love,
                            Mama and Papa

Ella tucked the letter away and tiptoed around the room. Ms. Paige had been right. It was twice as big, and her bottle tree stretched out to fill the open space. The big glass window revealed the glittering Cloud Nests encasing the Arcanum, and she hoped she'd have the best view of the floating cities. Maybe she could get used to this. Though part of her felt disappointed because it wasn't the dream she'd had all summer: being best friends with her new roommates, exploring the Institute together, staying up all night to talk and practice their marvels.

Ella glanced at Brigit's sleeping form, wondering if this messy, grumpy girl would be her friend. Did Ella even want a friend like that? The total opposite of Reagan, who'd give you her last conjure dollar if you ran out and who never let a bad day show up on her face.

Ella's eyes found the clown doll sitting on Brigit's nightstand. It didn't look like a regular one from a circus back home. It was dressed in a diamond-checkered costume with a pointed hat and a ruffled collar. Maybe a harlequin? The word *Feste* was stitched across its chest. It winked at her.

She yelped and turned her back to it. Was that real?

Ella decided to mind her own business for now and try to make everything perfect.

Again.

◆　■　◆　✦　✦

AN HOUR LATER, ELLA ATTEMPTED TO RIDE THE ARCANUM TROLLIES herself to the Vision Tower for her very first orientation on her very first official day at the Arcanum Training Institute for Marvelous and Uncanny Endeavors. She'd read about those who had vision marvels—people who could see into the past, predict the future, decode dreams and nightmares, decipher prophecies, and have special memories. They were considered wise. Gran could definitely fit in here.

She held the trolley map in her hands, studying the three lines. Blue, Black, and Gold. This couldn't be *that* hard. At home, she'd taken the streetcars with Mama all the time—and if Mama had been the kind of mother to let her go by herself, she could've gotten all the way from her house to Reagan's on the St. Charles Avenue line. No problem.

The moment she walked out of the dormitory hall, people began to stare, and she wished they'd mind their business. She made it to the nearest trolley platform, bypassing the elevator and taking the winding staircase up to wait, then pulled a rope overhead. A chime sounded. "Next trolley arriving in one minute."

She double-checked her timetable; the brass tablet in her palm flickered, reminding her to go to the top floor of the Vision Tower to meet her class at 8:30 sharp. She'd be early, deciding to skip breakfast after the room-changing incident, needing a little time to get her spirit right, as Gran always said.

Her stomach growled, and she slipped out a bag of sun seeds Mama had tucked into her bureau, quickly popping them into her mouth before they released their bright rays.

The Gold trolley approached. Its sleek panels sparkled as if they were made of stardust. The car was filled with Level Three and Level Four students and a few Arcanum instructors.

The door slid open and an automat smiled at her. "Welcome to the Gold Line. Arcanum ID out. Tap the pad, then find a seat."

Ella stepped aboard and followed instructions. She slid into one of the plush benches.

Three chimes sounded. "Moving forward," the automat announced. "Touch Tower up first."

The trolley sailed across glittering ropes, making lefts and rights as it stopped at each destination. Ella looked over the edge, down at Arcanum instructors fussing at trainees about their mantles or issuing demerits or carting all sorts of peculiar objects; starfolk pushed carts of supplies, and automats wheeled around, sweeping and shining every surface; bell-blimps floated about releasing their friendly reminders about the school day.

"Vision Tower ahead. Prepare to exit," the automat announced.

Ella grabbed her satchel and darted out. She walked down the platform staircase and into the Vision Tower foyer. A massive mechanical eye hung from the ceiling, blinking and turning to gaze in different directions. A gigantic heliogram of founder Louis Antonio Villarreal tipped his wide-brimmed hat. "Welcome to the Vision Tower, a place where you shall see more than you've ever seen before." His mustache twitched. "My bigote predicts the future. What can you all see with your mind's eye?"

Crystal balls floated about, whispering, "The eye is wise!"

Divination laboratories wore curious signs:

DO NOT DISTURB—READINGS IN PROGRESS!
SENSITIVE PROPHECIES ABOUT!
TREAD LIGHTLY, FOR TIME IS UNFORGIVING!

Scrying mirrors called out, "Have a glimpse of your future and revisit your past." One wall held doors, windows, knockers, and knobs that promised views into other places and times. Another contained portraits of great Marvellers who were Paragons of Vision: Reginald Rasbold and his prophecy marvel and his near perfect predictions; Pilar Ponce's reverie marvels and her famous Dream Workshop; Silas McGeary's famous Twisty Time Treasures of rare objects from past time periods.

Ella reached for one of the doorknobs promising a glimpse into the prehistoric world.

"I wouldn't go there."

Ella swung around to find Jason. He smiled and his locs wiggled.

"Who asked you?" she snapped.

"You okay?" Concern filled his eyes.

"I'm fine!" She turned back to the wall.

"My sister Bea has a timesight marvel, and she says dinosaurs aren't all that great. Very angry all the time. I've begged her to take me back there, but . . ." He shrugged.

"So, she's a Vision?"

"Yep."

"Is that what you're going to be?" Ella wondered what was marvelous about him other than having great hair.

"I think the Marvel Exam will say that I have kindred marvel—always been able to communicate with animals. It's a Paragon of Sound."

"What's the exam like?" Ella's mind churned with all the possibilities about where she might end up.

"My siblings won't tell me. They said it'd ruin the experience," he said. "But Grace said you can train in whatever you want. No matter what the exam shows. Though most kids let it—or their families—decide."

"So I have to wait *all* year?" she said, frustrated.

Jason shrugged. "Guess we have to learn about all the Paragons first."

"It's going to be tor—" Ella screeched and pointed at Jason's mantle pocket. "There's . . . there's a thing in your pocket." She swatted at him, but he jumped out of the way.

Jason's entire face lit up. "It's a friend. Don't worry."

"What is it?"

"She's a rottie. They're little marsupials who are misunderstood. Sweet Pea, this is Ella, and Ella, this is Sweet Pea."

The creature's ears perked up.

"They live in the Arcanum walls." Jason nuzzled his nose into her fur. "They love to have their pictures taken and hoard desserts in their pouches."

Ella cringed but stepped a tiny bit closer. Sweet Pea *was* sort of adorable, smiley, and had a long tail. Her night-black coat sparkled as if she'd been dipped in stardust. The way Jason cared for her reminded Ella of the way her parents and Gran loved up on their conjure companions.

Jason fed Sweet Pea a cookie. "They were rescued by Australian Marvellers and brought here. Aren't they cute?"

Two Level Three kids rushed into the foyer, dueling with long, glowing staffs. Jason pulled her to the side.

"What are those?" Ella watched in awe.

"Stapier sticks."

Ella let the funny word roll around on her tongue.

"They're for funneling light before we get our channellors. But we don't get them until we're Level Twos. My older sister let me use hers once, though." Jason's eyebrows lifted. "You've never seen one?"

"No." Ella realized there was so much missing from the Griotary's files on Marvellers.

"You also use them for Marvel Combat." He waved his hands in the air as he explained the game—two players from each Paragon team battling it out with bright stapiers until they reach the final rounds and get to use their very own channellors to best their opponent. "My brothers are champions. I'll be too scared to try out next year."

"Knock that off!" an automat shouted. "Put them away before I take them."

Ella and Jason giggled.

A bell-blimp skated into the tower, releasing three high-pitched chimes, and the voice of Headmarveller MacDonald boomed: "All trainees please report to your first-period sessions. You will earn two demerits for lateness. A reminder—if you reach ten in a week, you'll earn Saturday detention. All the light and good marvelling. Be well, and most importantly, prompt."

The ding of arriving trolleys echoed with footsteps following. The foyer flooded with trainees going this way and that way.

Jason said goodbye to the rottie as she darted out of view, then turned to Ella. "Ready?"

"Of course," she answered.

They climbed the twisting stairs to the very top of the tower. Half of the Level One class waited outside the Tower Meeting Room. Ella spotted her old roommates Lian and Samaira. Their piercing stares made her skin hot. Part of her wanted to march right over to them and ask why they had her kicked out of their room . . . but she didn't want to spend the rest of her day upset.

Siobhan waved, and her pixie blew Ella a kiss. Well, at least it seemed like Siobhan didn't dislike her.

Clare brushed past her. "I already know everything about the Arcanum. This is such a waste." She thumbed her flickering necklace and inched closer to Abina and Lian.

"Same," Abina chimed in. "My family gets a tour every year—especially in the first weeks when the building transforms."

"And I already know all the teachers," a boy with brown hair added.

"They know who I am." Lian primped, using a tiny comb to make sure her bangs were perfect.

"I just want my stapier," a boy with a face full of freckles complained. "I'm ready to compete in Marvel Combat."

"Some things have changed," Jason piped up. "New teachers."

Kids turned to stare at him. He gulped.

The doors snapped open. Masterji Thakur stepped out. He wore shiny blue pants and a long tunic, and his bejeweled turban matched. "This way, my newbies."

They filed into a large meeting room lined with benches. Arcanum instructors stood in the middle and called out to them.

"Good day, young stars!"

"Find a seat."

"Prepare for the adventure of a lifetime!"

Kids scrambled, trying to nab the best bench or to sit with their new friends. Ella spotted her godmother, Sera Baptiste, among the instructors, and they nodded at each other.

Ella, Jason, and his roommate Miguel sat together. Ella kept her eyes on the door. Where was Brigit? Her stomach churned with guilt.

"What's wrong?" Jason asked.

"My new roommate isn't here yet. Maybe I should've woken her up." She bit her bottom lip and scanned the room to be sure she hadn't missed her. She caught Siobhan trying to sit with Lian, Samaira, and Clare only to be shunned.

Ella motioned her over.

Siobhan ran in her direction. "Thanks."

"No problem."

Ella introduced her to Jason and Miguel.

"Is that a night pixie?" he asked, excited.

"How'd you know?" Siobhan's face lit up.

He pulled a book from his satchel—*The Mixed-Up Files of Marvellian Creatures*. "It's my favorite. I feel like faeries and pixies are misunderstood."

"Me too." Siobhan grinned, pulling out another book, *Mr. Jay's Pocket Guide for the Care and Feeding of Pixies*. "Latest issue. It's my favorite."

Jason grinned so hard.

The star-lanterns dimmed, and the room went silent. *Brigit, where are you?* Ella thought.

"Welcome, new training class." A man stepped out of the line of instructors. "I am Dr. Zolghad, a Paragon of Vision and from Iran. Though I make my home now in the great Marvellian city of Betelmore." Ella thought he looked like he'd just awoken from a thousand-year sleep. He held a peculiar news-box. "I will be your instructor in the Great Marvellian Way, learning the history of our wondrous society and how we all came together." A smile tucked itself into the corner of his mouth, and he chuckled to himself like he had a secret. "Today, you'll meet all your instructors for the year. But a little history lesson up first . . ."

Light illuminated his news-box, projecting onto the ceiling. "Attending the Arcanum is the initial step in joining our great community. This is the earliest footage we have pieced together from our very first Gatherfeast. Marvellian historians recovered images from excavated news-boxes and scrolls to piece together what it might've looked like on that cold January day almost three hundred years ago."

An image appeared, the first Marvellers sitting at a round-table covered with food.

"Can someone tell me why the first Marvellers did this?"

Ella's hand shot in the air, but Dr. Zolghad selected Farah.

"All the magical people of the world had to hide. They were tired of that," Farah answered.

"Yes, yes. And why did they choose to shed their own names and call themselves Marvellers?"

Ella almost jumped off the bench, the answer bubbling up inside her.

"Sae-Hyun Oh?" he called out.

"I don't know," she grumbled.

Ella waved her hand even higher. Maybe he couldn't see her in the dimly lit room.

"Chance Richardson," he said.

He shook his head.

"Youssef Doumbouya?"

The boy stuttered out, "Umm . . . to marvel . . . to marvel . . ."

"Yes, Youssef," Dr. Zolghad replied. "Go on."

He slumped back.

Dr. Zolghad tsked-tsked, and his eyes found Ella's excited hand.

He nodded. "Ella Durand."

"To *marvel* means to witness or to gander. The first Marvellers felt that all magical people"—Ella tried not to wince at using that word—"and their marvels were supposed to be celebrated. Everyone might speak a different language, look different, or have different gifts, but they all come from the stars and belong together. So they decided to make it official and form a community to protect themselves and embrace their gifts."

"Very good," he said. "You know the history. Impressive." He turned to another instructor, shocked. "Perhaps you'll have a memory marvel like me and end up a Paragon of Vision. The eye is wise!"

"Good job, Ella," Jason whispered, and she smiled in return.

"I didn't even know that," Miguel chimed in.

The doors snapped open, and everyone turned to look. Brigit skulked in, mantle disheveled, no satchel, and holding that strange-looking clown doll.

"So good of you to join us, Ms. Ebsen," Dr. Zolghad said.

Brigit grumbled in reply as she looked around for a seat.

"Isn't that Ella's roommate?" Clare announced, soliciting giggles.

"Hush, hush," Masterji Thakur called out.

Ella waved her hand at Brigit and patted the spot on the bench next to hers. Brigit hustled over and plopped down.

"Now that we have everyone, we can continue." Dr. Zolghad motioned to his left. "Dr. Mbalia, if you will."

The other instructors took a step back.

A tall Black man stepped forward, his bald head catching star-lantern light. "I am Dr. Mbalia." His deep voice boomed, making Ella sit up straight. "In my class you will learn the importance of the story incant and its connections to West African cultures. Where once upon a time is more than just a tale told to you at bedtime." The star-lanterns dimmed, and as Dr. Mbalia spoke, shadows poured from his mouth. "A spider is not just a spider."

The shadows turned to silhouetted shapes. Gasps exploded. Ella spun around trying to examine every light image moving throughout the room.

"Not when it faces a lion." Another shadow poured out of him, taking the shape of a lion. The two silhouette creatures dueled until the other instructors began to clap. The star-lanterns sparkled and the silhouettes disappeared. "Maybe one of you will have a story marvel like mine and be a Paragon of Sound. The ears listen well!"

The room exploded with claps. Ella swelled with excitement. She wanted to be able to do that.

Brigit muttered, "I hate this," under her breath. Ella couldn't imagine how anyone could see all of this and feel mad. Brigit took out a pair of knitting needles and a half-done quilt square and started stitching. It featured part of a woman's face, one Ella didn't recognize.

The room's massive chandeliers started to dip up and down, the noise of turning screws silencing the room.

A squat white woman bumbled to the center. "I am Dr. Bearden. I don't do anything fancy. That's not my schtick. Utility is the name of the game. I've got a cog marvel, and I'm a Paragon of Touch. The hand has no fear—and neither do I." She paced in a circle. "During my course, Introduction to Marvel Light, you'll learn about what's inside you." She turned left. "Someone bring me a stellacity sphere."

Excited whispers crackled among the students.

Another instructor wheeled out a golden object made of dozens of spinning rings. "Marvellers spend years refining their light," Dr. Bearden said, tapping the rings to make them go faster, "but first you must learn to pull it out."

A few grumbles about wanting to have stapiers and to be Marvel Combat champions echoed. Dr. Bearden spoke louder. "Just like stellacity powered the sky-ferries that brought you here, the light inside you is your current." A blazing ball of light appeared in her palm, and she threw it into the core of the rotating rings. It flared like a firework, the light almost blinding. "Then, and only then, might you be ready for a universal channellor, those stapiers you covet, or better yet, your very own unique channellor suited to your talent."

Ella joined the chorus of *oohs* and *aahs*.

"The best Marvellers understand command and control," Dr. Bearden added. "And most importantly, always channeling the light. Always seek what is good."

Everyone clapped.

Dr. Zolghad stepped forward. "Dr. Winchester is next."

No answer.

Dr. Zolghad's eyes landed on a sleeping man tucked into the corner. He said the instructor's name one more time.

The man startled. "Here! Right here! Not to worry."

Chuckles exploded.

"I'll teach you to see the past, present, and future. Very

exhausting work, seeing all those things," he mumbled. "The eye is wise! But a nap must come first." He fell back asleep.

The other instructors stifled their laughter.

Dr. Zolghad stepped forward again. "Dr. Guadalupe Perez, who is your Universal Incants teacher, is en route. Her flying llama needed to see a special veterinarian in the Andes Mountains, but she will teach you how all the various magical languages of the world came together to create our Marvellian incant-book. Dr. Ursu, who teaches Elemental Marvels, will also join us later; she had to help reset the Storm Nests over Betelmore. Too much lightning and not enough shielding us from Fewel-planes. Her legendary weather marvel will set them straight. She's practically a lightning rod herself." He turned to face the group of Arcanum instructors. "And last, but certainly not least, are Madame Sera Baptiste—our newest faculty member and head of the new area of study, the Conjure Arts—and Masterji Thakur, Elixirs extraordinaire. He makes our wonderful Elixir of Light that helps identify each of your marvels."

Ella's heart squeezed at the sight of her godmother. Everyone would love her as much as she did.

Masterji Thakur and her godmother stepped forward together. Masterji Thakur lifted his arms in the air, and with the gesture came a tornado of colorful powders and intoxicating scents.

"It's like Holi!" someone exclaimed.

Ella stared up in awe. How could he do that?

"I am Masterji Thakur. Your first introduction to the Paragon of Taste. I will be teaching you about elixirs, unlocking the power of three-thousand-year-old spices and how they aid in marvelling. The tongue tells truth!"

The room clapped.

He turned to face Aunt Sera, handing her a beautiful bushel of lavender. "Welcome to the Arcanum," he said. "So happy to have you with us."

"Thank you, Masterji Thakur." She sniffed the bundle.

Aunt Sera turned to face the trainees. Ella flashed her godmother the biggest smile. "I am Madame Baptiste, and I'm from New Orleans, Louisiana, a great conjure town in the Fewel-world, and I will teach you the Conjure Arts. We do not know yet which Paragon will be lucky enough to receive those with a conjure marvel, but I can't wait to teach you all that we can do." She threw the lavender into the air and started to sing. *"Pretty petals lend us your love and shade."*

The lavender exploded, growing into a massive canopy that reached out to every corner. A purple glow shaded the room. Ella watched all the other students look up with wonder, and she felt a surge of glory.

Whispers sizzled like popcorn in a skillet:

"Can I have a conjure marvel too?"
"How did she do that?"
"Marvellers can't make things grow."
"My mom says the way they practice . . . is uncivilized."
"Is it evil to control living things?"
"Why can't they start their own training center? And let it be in the Underworld where they belong."

Ella stiffened as she heard more of the bad versus the good. This was not the reaction she'd expected her godmother to receive. Jason's hand found hers, and he squeezed it. A pit burned in Ella's stomach. One she tried desperately to ignore.

Clare whispered into Lian's ear and glared in Ella's direction.

"Don't worry about them," Siobhan said. "If it makes you feel any better, they hate me too."

"Why?" Ella asked as Siobhan's pixie softly stroked her cheek.

"'Cause my ma does business with faeries."

Ella's eyebrow lifted. "Is that bad?"

"They don't always follow the rules," Jason informed her. "And their food is banned." More whispers crackled.

Masterji Thakur stretched out his arms. "SILENCE!"

The room froze. A jolt shot up Ella's spine.

"We welcome all who contain light *and* all who wish to train here at the Arcanum Institute. We will have none of this discriminatory behavior. In the press, many have expressed opinions about our decision to change . . . But it's just that, *our* decision, and we have made it. That bigotry is not to find its way into our walls."

Masterji Thakur scanned the room, a challenge crackling in the air, daring any naysayer to object.

Ella's heart now felt frozen. She was afraid to breathe.

"Our history has not been perfect. When we started living together as magical people, we ostracized many citizens of our own community. People struggled to find acceptance and understanding of their unique abilities. But that will end now. Conjurors are part of the Marvellian society. Officially. If I discover any type of un-Marvellian-like behavior, it will be escalated to the Headmarvellers, and I will recommend immediate expulsion from the Institute. Our community has no place for this any longer."

"Aces!" someone blurted out.

The entire room exploded with whispers.

Masterji Thakur put his hand up, then rubbed his mustache. His jaw clenched. "Let's get something straight—the Aces were a misguided group of Arcanum students. Many turned into criminal adults after being expelled. But we dealt with it as a community, and they were excommunicated from our cities and our society or rehabilitated and given second chances. Nothing to speculate about. There is no place for them here, and there's no parallel between the Aces and Conjurors. That word is nothing more than a slur." His gaze seemed to find every kid in the room. "Dismissed!"

The doors opened and the trainees started to leave. The teachers huddled, concerned expressions all over their faces.

Ella's stomach squeezed as people passed her whispering.

But she squared her shoulders and met every curious gaze with an equal stare.

★—★—★— **STARPOST**—★—★—★

Dear Reagan,

I hope my mama gave you the starpost box so
you can get letters from me. I had her order you one.
Everything is great here. I wish you could've come.

Love,
Ella

★—★—★— **STARPOST**—★—★—★

Hi Mama and Papa,

I'm okay. Please don't worry.

Love,
Ella

THE LADY WITH MANY FACES

The prisoner took several days to craft a version of herself to leave behind as a decoy. Upon regaining her marvel, she had discovered that her gift felt rusty, so she used it only a little each day until she could trust it to do what she needed again. She'd open and shut her eyes, letting the objects reveal their true selves, the strings of matter that made them. From the apple on the food tray to the quilt on her bed to the mirror on her wall, all were stitched with gray threads.

When she'd trained at the Arcanum as a kid, no one appreciated her particular marvel. The ability to see the threads of the universe and manipulate them was labeled dangerous. Rare. Scary. Chaotic. A monstrous marvel. It didn't fit neatly into the categories Marvellians love. Placed in the Paragon of Vision, she found that even her fellow trainees distanced themselves and nicknamed her the Ace of Anarchy, a troublemaker.

But her father had thought it extraordinary, and the two of them had put on grand plays where she'd transform into every character, and she'd helped him turn his struggling commedia dell'arte theater into the greatest Marvellian show there ever was, the Trivelino Troupe's Circus & Imaginarium of Illusions. She could still see the beautiful heliograms projecting from the billposters and hear the noise of the crowds. After he'd died, she was left alone with a mother who wished she had a simpler marvel or was a simpler person.

"Be different, Gia," she muttered as she put finishing touches on her inanimate double. "Be nicer, Gia. Be more gracious, Gia. Be more serious, Gia. Stop all that laughing, Gia." She cackled, thinking of her mother. "I will be very different. I will now be the worst thing the world's ever seen."

CHAPTER SIX

JUMPING JOLLOF

The rest of the day, Ella's thoughts spun like the crank of a news-box. She couldn't stop thinking about the Aces and who they were and why people thought they had anything to do with Conjure folk. Masterji Thakur's words buzzed through her: *"There's no parallel between the Aces and Conjurors."* But why were people saying that in the first place?

She knew exactly the place where she'd find the answer. The place she'd been so eager to get to since she'd arrived.

The library.

Ella skipped her free period time and stood before gilded double doors and a massive sign sparkling with THE GREAT ARCANUM LIBRARY. The look of it reminded Ella of a jewelry box she'd spotted on Gran's dresser with writhing filigree, twisted threads of gold on its lid. Her heart hammered as the doors parted like the opening of a book.

A labyrinth of never-ending shelves soared up the walls. She craned her neck to see where they ended, but she couldn't. Brass spindles curled into balconies, and small elevators toted visitors to and from the levels. Striped balloons carried books from one shelf to the next, finding eager patrons or red-cloaked librarians awaiting them, and others held banners with rules: NO TALKING. NO RUNNING. NO TEARING, BENDING, SMEARING, SMUDGING, DEFACING, OR MISTREATING OF ANY BOOKS. AND DEFINITELY NO EATING. YOU WILL REGRET IT!

Ella twirled around. The Griotary back home was so tiny in comparison. The three-story building always moved when Fewels felt the need to terrorize the neighborhood. Here at the Arcanum Library, she thought, every question she'd ever had in her whole life might be answered.

Chubby blimps dragged displays advertising different books to read:

JUST IN! R. WEATHERSPOON'S LATEST ROMANCE— *THE YOUNG AND THE MARVELOUS*—TWO STAR-CROSSED MARVELLIANS FROM DIFFERENT PARAGONS FALL MADLY IN LOVE.

CRIME WRITER LAMAR GILES'S *FAKE MARVELS* ARRIVED THIS MORNING. BE PREPARED TO ENTER THE DARK SIDE OF ASTRADAM'S LOW STREET.

SEVERAL NEW BIOGRAPHIES ABOUT OUR NEW PRESIDENT, MADAME FARAH AL-NAHWI, CIRCULATING FROM LEGENDARY JOURNALIST DAYO P. LEARN HOW SHE KEPT MARVELLIANS SAFE IN FEWEL CITIES.

At the very center of the cavernous space there was a desk occupied by a small Black woman with cat-eyeglasses. She was

the sun at the center of this vast universe. Over her volumi-
nous Afro floated a bright balloon with a flashing sign—HEAD
LIBRARIAN AND ARBITER OF ALL INFORMATION, MADAME
MADGE.

"Can I help you?" Her nose crinkled like a molasses cookie.

"Madame Madge, I want to know about the Aces and why
people think they're the Conjurors, and I want to know about
why people think growing things is bad and why—"

"Star's teeth, slow down, young lady." She placed a hand on
Ella's shoulder. "I can't help you if you're all tangled up like
this."

Ella took a deep breath. "I want to know about the Aces."

"Now, why would you want to learn about a thing so terrible?"

"I have questions."

"Ella Durand, yes?"

"Yes, ma'am." Ella gulped.

Madame Madge's eyes narrowed as her glasses slid down
her nose.

Ella pursed her lips. Maybe she shouldn't have asked.
Maybe she should've sneaked around and looked first. But
she didn't know where to begin.

"You're the little Conjuror, aren't you?"

Ella nodded.

"People won't like you going around asking those questions,"
she warned, leaning forward to take a closer look at Ella. "Not
at all what I was expecting. The way the news-boxes stirred it
up. You look . . . as normal as any Marveller could be. So much
fuss for nothing." She sucked her teeth. "You know they did
the same to the Caribbean folks when we got here, too, many
decades ago. Everyone was vexed. Always had something to say

about our steel drums and water marvels, and the barrels our mamas sent up. Took forever to get them to add a jerk pan to the dining hall here. But *they* always make it seem like we all came together like missing puzzle pieces. That the big Gatherfeast we celebrate was so easy."

"Oh," Ella replied, not knowing exactly what she was talking about. She felt like she had so much to learn about how all these very different people had decided to come live together in the skies.

Madame Madge hummed, then looked back down at her book, and Ella knew that meant, like Gran, she was done talking.

Ella turned to walk away.

"Miss Durand," she called out.

Ella whipped back around.

"Those curious like yourself often look upstairs in the back of the Arcanum History section." She winked.

Ella looked up, spotting the huge sign. She darted to the nearest staircase, passing more wizened librarians toting armfuls of books, automats leading sullen trainees with detention slips, and people browsing.

The Arcanum History section felt tucked into the back, neglected and unused. A gauzy veil stretched around the perimeter like curtains on a four-poster bed. She looked left and right before slipping into that section.

The area was chock-full of things—not only books but old files, card catalogs, leather map tubes, gramophones and older news-box editions, dusty albums, photographs, and so on— displayed in glass. Book spines glowed as she passed. Faded letters spelled words Ella had never seen before—Cardinals,

Stellacity, Marvel Code. Some thin, some thick, and many too heavy to hold in her hands.

She plucked a book called *A Thousand Years of Light: An Arcanum History* and scanned the contents, finding a chapter titled "Evil Marvellians Throughout the Ages." She flipped to the section to read about notorious criminals like Phineas Graham, who'd attempted to track the movement of the bank and rob it; Milton McAllister, who sold Fewels Marvellian food to make them delusional; and Gão Sousa, who'd created a prophecy lotto to make people bet on each other's futures. Her eyes scanned the page, finally finding what she'd been looking for . . . the word *Aces*:

> *The Aces formed in the Arcanum's Lower School. Five trainees with rare marvels experimented, learning to share their talents unnaturally. Each one had a monstrous marvel that did not fit neatly into the Five Paragons, leading them to reject the categorization system. Over the course of their studies, they developed an elixir that allowed one to borrow another person's sacred marvel light and—*

Sharing marvels—how was that possible?

The words scrambled, morphing into one big word on the page: REDACTED.

She shook it. "What's wrong with this book?" The words scattered, then reformed, and the same word flashed. Ugh! She was just getting to the good parts.

She put it back on the shelf and plucked another one, called *Bad Light: A History of Criminality in the Marvellian World.*

She'd read faster this time in case something strange happened again. She flipped to a chapter called "The Aces."

>Throughout time, many Marvellians have fallen into evil, using their ancestral gifts for unsavory means. Many laws have been passed to make sure everyone stays on the right path, but Marvellers, like Fewels, are susceptible to the Fewel qualities of pride, greed, lust, envy, gluttony, wrath, etc. But the notorious Aces took their desires to the darkest place in Marvellian history. Led by a woman who called herself the Ace of Anarchy, Gia Trivelino, and—

The words dissolved, replaced again with the word REDACTED.

Ella shoved the book back, frustration welling up inside her, and stomped to another aisle. Why would Madame Madge send her up here if she couldn't read anything?

"All these books are weird."

Ella jumped, then turned around to find Brigit sitting on the floor with a lap full of yarn. "I didn't see you there," Ella said.

"I know."

"What are you doing here?"

"What does it look like?" Brigit held up her knitting needles. Gran would've said Brigit's hands moved quick as a cricket, looping and stitching the thread. Ella couldn't keep up as the beautiful new quilt grew longer and longer by the second, spreading across Brigit's lap. She thought about asking her to make one for her. Maybe they could have matching ones in their room, but Brigit wasn't exactly friendly yet.

"I know . . . ," Ella started, but stopped. "Do you know what's wrong with these books?"

"I tried to read one, but it kept messing up, so I don't care anymore."

Ella tried a few more, and the same thing happened. She would have to talk to Madame Madge about it. Was she doing something wrong?

A bell-blimp found its way into the section: "The dining hall is open. Chef Oshiro has created three new sushi constellations. Please make your way and see what the savory galaxy has in store for you. Level Ones, we look forward to welcoming you."

Ella sighed and put the book back. "Want to go eat with me?" She hoped Brigit would say yes. It was their first official dinner at the Arcanum. Earlier, she'd skipped breakfast and they'd eaten lunch in class. She didn't really want to walk into the dining hall alone and didn't have time to send Jason a star-post to meet her.

Brigit didn't look up from her knitting needles.

Click-clack.

"Brigit?" Ella stepped closer, noticing how Brigit threaded with her eyes closed.

How was she knitting like that? Ella touched Brigit's shoulder. Her eyes snapped open; the blue of her pupils had turned snow white.

Ella scrambled back. "Are you okay? Your eyes—"

"It's nothing." Brigit blinked and the blue appeared again. "What do you want?"

"How can you knit like that?"

"I don't know. Always have been able to." She glanced back down at her creation: the completion of that strange woman's face.

"Who is that?" Ella pointed.

"I don't know," she snapped.

Ella made a mental note not to repeat that question. She tried again. "Sure you don't want to go to the dining hall?"

"I don't like the weird food here."

"But it's fun."

"I just want a hot dog from home."

"Where'd you come from?"

"New York City." Her hands slowed.

"I'm from a Fewel city too. New Orleans."

Brigit scrunched her nose. "I don't like that word."

"Which one?" Ella eased closer but stopped when Brigit's eyes narrowed.

"Fewel," she said, re-looping her needle. "Everyone keeps calling me that. Sounds like *fool*, and I'm not one."

"Just means someone who can't see magic." Ella winced at that word again. "A non-Marveller."

"Guess you're one too."

"Not really. I'm a Conjuror," Ella corrected.

"So, you're basically like them?"

"Not that either."

Brigit's cheeks pinkened. "Then what are you?"

"Something else." Ella didn't know how to explain why Conjurors were left out of the Marvellian world. Gran had told Ella that Marvellers felt their talents were *too* different. But Ella never fully understood why. Papa said Marvellers had always needed Conjurors—to look after their dead and to work in their cities. Plus, she could do marvelous things just like the others at the Institute.

Ella took a sun seed from her pocket and tossed it at Brigit. Its glow made her jump. "How'd you do that?"

"It's from home."

Brigit inspected it. "You have weird food there too? I can never go to New Orleans now."

"It's not. Taste it."

Brigit sniffed it, licked it, then popped it into her mouth. Her eyes opened super wide as she chewed. "It tastes . . . tastes like how I feel like the sun would."

Ella grinned. "Just a conjure trick."

"But how did you *know* how to do that?" Brigit pressed. "Have you always just known how to do magical things?"

Ella winced at the word. "It's not magic, or at least that's not how Conjure folk see it."

"Then what is it?" Brigit crossed her arms over her chest. "Everyone here can do things . . . things other people can't. They just seem to know."

"It's just our way. Who we are. It's the work that we do." Ella didn't know how to really explain it. "Did you not know . . . you were different?"

"What does that even mean?" Brigit sighed. "I live in New York City. Everybody's different there."

"But like different *different*—a Marveller?"

"One day I was hanging out with my guardian, Ms. Mead, knitting mittens to sell on the subway, and the next thing, I woke up here." She squeezed her knitting needles tight.

"Never heard of a Marveller not knowing they were one, and I've always known everything about Marvellers."

"Why do you want to become one so bad?"

Ella bit her bottom lip and thought of all the times she'd overheard her papa justify why she should go to the Institute. That Conjurors deserved the opportunity to safely live away from Fewels and to be accepted as just as powerful and respected as those of Marvellian ancestry. Other groups had integrated and become part of the community over time. Why not them? They should at least always have a choice. "I want to be marvelous too."

"But you already are."

Brigit's compliment felt like a rare jewel.

"You sure you don't want to come?"

"Too busy." Brigit lifted her knitting needles again and tapped the curious box beside her. "Got snacks."

Ella craned to have a closer look. She guessed it had once been the color of licorice, now faded, and she spotted the outline of stars and faint Arcanum initials. "That's a pretty pocket-box."

"A what?"

"A pocket-box," Ella repeated. It was the sort of thing she'd seen in one of the Marvellian vintage catalogs Mama pretended not to order from—*Victoria Valerino's Vintage Vanguard*. "I can show you."

"Whatever," she grumbled.

Ella tried one final time to get Brigit to come. "You sure?"

"Sure as the first time you asked." Brigit turned her back.

Ella was on her own.

✦ ✕ ✦ ✧ ✦

ELLA STOOD IN THE DINING HALL ENTRANCE ALONE. A ROOM large enough to fit every person at the Arcanum buzzed with movement. Canopied tables held the instructors, then trainees by level, and she gazed around for those in white. Level Threes chased recently hatched milk dragons who escaped from their cream eggs, while Level Fours faced off with shortbread stapier sticks, pretending to be Paragon champions engaged in Marvel Combat.

Clare sauntered by. "No friends, huh? Must suck."

Ella scowled. But a warm hand found her shoulder. She gazed up at the beautiful brown face of her godmother.

"She has the best friend a girl could ask for." Aunt Sera waved.

Clare scampered away as Ella hugged her godmother.

"I've missed you." She planted a kiss on Ella's forehead. "It's been a little chaotic here. So many rules about what you can and cannot teach." She mimicked Headmarveller Rivera's voice. "'We don't sing our incants; that would be inappropriately emotional.' 'We could never do a field trip to the Underworld, as that would be terrifying for our pupils.' 'We must adhere to all rules and push forth rule-based learning in a controlled environment.'"

They both laughed.

"Sorry I haven't seen you much." Her godmother kissed her cheek. "It's been quite the adjustment, and I had to go back home to get conjure glass. My plants kept dying, so I had sweet Headmarveller MacDonald build me a special greenhouse for our plants."

Ella hadn't thought about what it might've been like for her godmother to teach all the things she grew up learning.

"And by the way, I've been sending your parents updates and asked them to relax as you settle in here."

"Thanks, Aunt Sera. They keep sending me a million star-posts. What are you doing? Did you have a good day? Did you eat? How's this and how's that?"

"It's all that good love."

Ella laughed. "They could love me a little less."

"Impossible."

They walked into the dining hall.

Menu-balloons whizzed around like miniature sky-ferries, and they held placards advertising tonight's specials. A sushi conveyor belt oscillated over different tables while ornate food carts looped in and out of the aisles toting all sorts of wonders: pizza towers floating one over the other, forever noodles stretching by the second, teasing tamales opening and closing their corn husks, glass boxes churning out rainbow popcorn, laughing latkes and spinning samosas, a chocolate fountain with shortbread stapler sticks for dipping, and more. Ella felt like she'd stumbled upon the most amazing, magical food trucks.

Ella couldn't wait to try it all.

Headmarveller MacDonald waved at her godmother.

"Ella!" Jason rushed up to her. "Saved you a seat—" He swallowed the rest of his sentence after spotting her godmother.

He squeaked out a tiny hello.

Aunt Sera kissed her cheek again. "We'll get our time soon. Go on and eat with your friends." She sauntered ahead, sitting with the other instructors.

Ella walked beside Jason to the Level One section. The tables looked full, and she didn't recognize many faces from her first day of classes.

"Did you get my note?"

"What note?"

"Ugh, the rotties tricked me again. Took the sugar and ran." Jason slapped his forehead. "I need to give them a treat after."

"What?"

"Never mind." He led her to a long table where mostly Black and brown Level One trainees sat. She remembered a lot of their names and was grateful many still wore their name tags.

Everyone looked up. Abina frowned, the fat spider in her hair blinking its eyes at her. Conversations stopped.

"Hi." Ella earned a few grumbled responses and some slight smiles. Many took off their translation crystals and spoke all different kinds of languages, making it impossible for Ella to understand them now.

Ella and Jason found seats. Nerves started to flutter in her stomach, but a starfolk approached with a food cart. "Hi, Ella, remember me?" It was Aries, the starfolk who'd tidied her room after she was moved. "Dim sum! Dancing dumplings. Take your pick—steamed or fried! Want to try one?"

Jason took a bamboo basket. "My brother Wes said they do a different routine based on what's inside them. The chicken ones are wild. The pork ones kind of lazy."

Ella shrugged, indecision flooding her. She wanted to try everything.

"Start with this one. I'll be back." Aries gave her one.

More starfolk and carts approached.

"Hot curry! Indian—all regions! Jamaican, Trinidadian, Guyanese, Japanese, Vietnamese, Malaysian, and more . . . take your pick. Get it while they're crying hot, otherwise you will be."

"Eat these jerk wings before they insult you."

"Pirate puri, hot and ready to attack any masala."

"Funny falafel tell the best fart jokes!"

"Watch the frijoles face the habichuelas. A battle for bean name begins! Pick your side!"

Ella couldn't make up her mind, partly because there was so much to taste, and the other kids at the table kept staring at her. She ended up using her chopsticks to pluck four sushi rolls from the air when Chef Oshiro's sushi belt hovered over the table.

"Everyone ready?" Abina announced with a clap. "The jollof cart is here."

Colorful pots of rice wiggled, their lids sliding left and right as if eager to release their contents. Tiny flags flashed on their bellies.

The starfolk chuckled. "I guess you've learned the tradition."

"I have an older sister," Abina replied. "Time to see which jollof is best."

"What about rice and peas?" Tiffany called out.

"Next time." Abina crossed her arms over her chest like she was preparing for battle and grabbed the pot with the Ghana-ian flag. Abina challenged the others. "What you got?"

"What's happening?" Ella whispered to Jason.

"I don't know," he replied in the middle of battling a jerk wing.

"Ghana has the best jollof," Abina boasted.

Tochi jumped up. "Nope, Nigeria." He plucked a pot from the cart.

"We all know it's Senegal." Ousmane grabbed another.

"Tuh, Sierra Leone." Namina grabbed a third.

"Always, Mali." Boubacar took a fourth pot.

"Côte d'Ivoire!" Claudie shouted, grabbing one.

Limnyuy, Fatu, and Daré took the last three, representing Cameroon, Gambia, and Togo.

"We'll see. We'll see." Abina clutched the sides of hers, barely keeping a handle on it. "Rules are, whoever is the first to get their rice to jump the highest wins."

The table cheered. Ella wished she could participate. She'd never had jollof rice but thought maybe she could use jambalaya.

"Youssef, you have the longest arms. You judge," Abina ordered.

He stood, stretching his long brown arms over the pots.

"Ready?" Abina grinned. "Set . . . GO!"

The competitors snatched the lids off and started singing to their rice. A jolt went up Ella's spine. Their songs reminded her of conjure spells. Were they similar?

The kids rapped their fingers along the table, the vibration rippling. The rice grains started to jump, one by one. As their voices grew louder, the grains leaped higher and higher. Ella's heart thudded with excitement.

One of Tochi's grains hit Youssef's arm first. Tochi leaped from his seat. A big grin consumed his face. "Naija no dey carry last!"

Other trainees high-fived him and chanted, "Nigeria! Nigeria!"

Abina plopped into her seat, defeated.

"That was amazing," Ella said. "You sing like we do. Like Conjurors."

Abina's eyes narrowed, and the table went silent. Jason froze mid-chew.

"We aren't the same," Abina snapped.

"But—" Ella's heart lodged in her throat.

"We have different experiences," Tochi added with a hopeful smile.

Someone mumbled the word *Ace* under their breath. Ella searched for the culprit.

Abina turned her back. "No, we *are* different," she said before laughing and speaking a language not even Ella's translation crystal could decode. Her stomach churned. She felt like a mountain had grown between them.

Those words raced over and over again in her head.

We are different.

★—★—★— STARPOST—★—★—★

Hi Ella,

I have some tips for you. My sister Beatrice told me.
The Blue line runs late on Tuesdays.

Always go to the Institute Store on Mondays
because that's when the new things are put out. If you
want new styluses and ink pots or cloud erasers, they
have everything.

If you send Chef Oshiro a starpost, they will make
you something special.

From,

Jason

★—★—★— STARPOST—★—★—★

Hello Jason,

I don't need help. Okay? Well, not really. Like not a
lot of it.

From,

Ella

P.S.: I heard that the pancake cart makes Japanese
souffle ones on Sundays. Is that true?

★—★—★— STARPOST—★—★—★

Hello my petite,

I miss you. Sent you JuJu Bees and MayPops. You

know I don't like you having too much penny candy,
but I figured you probably missed home.

Love,
Mama

★—★—★— **STARPOST**—★—★—★

Brigit,
 You forgot to do your homework. I left the notes on
your desk. Let me know if you need help.

From,
Ella

★—★—★— **STARPOST**—★—★—★

Ella,
 I don't care.

From,
Brigit

★—★—★— **STARPOST**—★—★—★

Hi Ella,
 I've never sent a starpost before, so I hope this
makes it. Home is fine. Madame Collette thinks
you'll lose all your conjure by being up there at the
Arcanum. But I told her that wasn't true. Send me a list
of everything you're eating. Miss you.

From,
Reagan

CHAPTER SEVEN
SPICES & DEATHBULLS

As the days tumbled from late September into October, the weather balloons turned orange and marigold to match the trees. Tiny pumpkins hung from brass lanterns, and even the automats wore sweaters and scarves. Kids from warm climates took bets about when the first snow would arrive, and Ella could hardly believe that she'd been at the Institute for two weeks and knew which trolley to take to each one of her sessions, which automats would report you and which ones would tell jokes, and which instructors would answer all your questions and which ones would shoo you away.

Ella wandered through the Taste Tower foyer with Brigit as they headed to their first Global Elixirs class with Masterji Thakur. Paragon training had begun, finally. Brigit had started to warm up to Ella, and now they often ate and went to classes together, and sometimes even stayed up late to gossip. Mama had reminded Ella of their Durand charm. "We could melt an iceberg, baby," she'd always say. It'd been nice to be around someone who was also an outsider and didn't judge her for not knowing all the Marvellian things.

"We could've stayed at breakfast longer," Brigit complained.

"I wanted to see this tower without the crowds. Isn't it cool?"

A mechanical mouth hung from the tower dome like a gigantic chandelier, and every few minutes the heliogram of founder Femi Ademola smiled, presented his bowl of truth soup, and said, "The tongue tells truth. Have a sniff and a taste." Delicious smells flooded the air.

Cloud nougats floated by, and Ella popped as many as she could into her mouth before they turned stormy. She peeled fruit stripes from the wallpaper, the stickiness coating her fingers. "It's like the whole place is edible."

"Who cares?" Brigit grumbled in response.

"Me! C'mon, it's so cool. You can't eat New York City! This has to be better than that."

"New York has the best food in the world." Brigit perked up.

"I used to think that New Orleans did . . . until I got here." Ella gazed all around. "There are so many new things to taste." She walked over to a wall of memory-atomizers and squeezed a pump. The bright blue liquid swirled around her, the scent reminding her of hot beignets from home.

A sweet-balloon whizzed by. "Help me get it."

Brigit complained but jumped to her feet. They chased it. Ella wanted to taste its sugar tuile basket and cotton candy belly. "Hey, stop!" she shouted at the balloon. "Wait for us!"

"You have to use the secret word to make it freeze." Jason stood in the entrance, a rottie perched on his shoulder. Ella smiled at him. She'd gotten used to him, too, discovering he wasn't so bad.

"Eww." Brigit pointed at him. "A rat."

Jason turned to the tiny creature. "Forgive her insult, Brownie, and meet Brigit." He turned back to her. "Brigit meet Brownie. He is *not* a rat."

"I think I'd know. We have plenty where I'm from," she challenged. "Who names a rat Brownie, anyways?"

The rottie whimpered.

"They're not rats. Brownie is just visiting to bring me news about how—" He gulped down the rest of his sentence. "Actually, never mind." He rubbed his nose against the rottie's tiny black snout.

"You can talk to them? How?" Ella asked.

"You're going to think I'm weird."

"We already know you're *weird*," Brigit replied.

Ella laughed until Jason smiled.

"My momma calls it my sonar," he said. "I could always hear them in my head, all of their tiny voices asking me to help them with this or that. They talk at different frequencies, depending on the creature. I . . . I . . . could show you how it works . . . but it's a secret."

Brigit's ears perked up. "I like secrets."

A jolt shot up Ella's spine. "Me too."

"Skip lunch, and I'll let you see it," he said.

"Okay," Ella and Brigit said in unison.

The sweet-balloon whizzed by again. Ella and Brigit took off again.

Jason chased behind them, yelling, "Ladha! Brownie says that's the word this month."

The sweet-balloon froze, then plummeted until it hovered right above their heads. Up close, Ella marveled at how the sugar stripes knitted across the cotton candy like the most beautiful basket weave.

"What did that mean?" Brigit asked.

"*Delicious* or sometimes *taste* in Swahili," Jason replied, then tickled Brownie. "I think."

The bottom opened like a hatch, and three gold coins dropped out. They each caught one.

"Paragon coins! I got a heart." Ella ran her fingers over the tiny thumping emblem before unwrapping and devouring the rich chocolate.

"Maybe you're a Spirit," Jason said.

"I got a hand," Brigit said.

"You might be a Touch." Jason motioned at her knitting needles.

"I don't want to be anything." Brigit threw her coin at the trash can. The rottie leaped from Jason's shoulder, catching the coin midflight, and skittered away.

"Never waste sweets," Jason said with a laugh.

"Everything's weird here," Brigit said.

"I got Taste"—he showed her his coin. A tiny mouth emblem smiled—"but I'll be a Sound."

A bell-blimp skated into the tower, reminding them to get to class.

The ding of arriving trolleys echoed, and the noise of footsteps followed. Trainees climbed the stairs and piled into elevators, heading to their first classes. Orientations were finally over!

They raced up the stairs to the top floor. Masterji Thakur waited. "It's time to test your tongue at last. Follow me!"

Abina and a boy named Pierre argued. "Ghanaian spices are finest. Everyone knows that."

"No, the French only need salt, pepper, and butter," Pierre challenged.

"Everyone knows India has the best," a girl named Aparna shouted. "Every region has something different. Masterji Thakur will agree with me."

"Vietnamese spices are the most amazing," Anh said. "Nothing is better than rau ram."

Ella tried hard not to roll her eyes or laugh.

"How about we take our seats and find out?" Masterji Thakur said.

They filed into the room. A domed ceiling held the rich blue color of a peacock's tail trimmed with gold. Ella felt transported to a decadent palace in the northern states of India. The walls were choked with glass jars of every spice imaginable. Ella tried to read all the labels—tarragon, fae rose, fennel, wombie gold, saffron, cinnamon, star tears—but gave up after losing her place. She wondered how Masterji Thakur was able to get things down without a ladder.

Desks were piled high with embossed session manuals, *A Beginner's Guide to Spice Elixirs from India, Pakistan, Bangladesh, and Nepal* by Riddhi Parekh; a golden scale; sets of porcelain spoons; and metal tins.

"It's time to learn the rules." Masterji Thakur led them through the various rooms: elaborate kitchen laboratories where trainees brewed elixirs; an apothecary that would rival Gran's conjure pharmacy with all its bottles; the equipment counter to borrow tools and vessels needed to mix powerful ingredients; a gigantic wiggling nose and flicking tongue ready to sniff and taste your creations for accuracy; and curing rooms for elixir aging.

"Be sure to adhere to the allergy guide when you handle ingredients. Also, the goggles on your desk are to be worn at all times when mixing."

Ella took copious notes, her new stylus feeling like it moved too slowly to keep up.

Masterji Thakur walked the group back into the lecture room.

"Now we're ready for business." Masterji Thakur sent them to their assigned seats.

The tiny bright balloon tied to Ella's stylus holder flashed her name. It danced left and right as if it were happy to see her as she slid into the two-seater desk. She glanced at the other balloon—her desk mate would be her former roommate Lian. But soon, all the two-seater desks were filled up while Ella's remained empty.

She gazed around and found Lian squeezing between Abina and Clare. Her chest tightened. She was now the only kid in the entire room without a partner.

Masterji Thakur paused before Ella's desk. "You're missing something here. Yes, yes. Incomplete. And we can't have that." He plucked the balloon beside hers. "Lian Wong!"

Lian jumped to her feet. "Yes, Masterji Thakur."

"Why aren't you in your assigned seat?" he asked.

"I like this one better," she replied.

"I went to great lengths to sort you all properly. Two is the perfect set—not three."

Lian stood up. "I do think, sir, with all due respect, that my father, Dr. Wong, the Supreme Marveller Judge, would want me happy."

"All students are supposed to be comfortable," Clare chimed in. "Says so in section nine of the Arcanum Handbook."

"The most important part of the handbook is the section on being a good citizen and having proper manners. That is the Marvellian way," Masterji Thakur said. "Please make your way to your assigned seat."

"I'll sit with her," Brigit called out. "No need for Princess Lian to trouble herself."

Ella covered a smile as Lian scowled.

"We must all watch our citizenship-like behavior. We don't do name-calling," Masterji Thakur said, and Ella could tell he was holding back a smile. "But thank you. Lian, move into the empty seat next to Evan, please."

Masterji Thakur had easily just become her favorite instructor at the Arcanum.

Brigit snatched her name-balloon and plopped down next to Ella.

"Thanks," Ella replied.

"I'd rather sit with you than Evan Gannon any day. He keeps farting."

Ella tried not to laugh.

"Time to get to the fun stuff." Masterji Thakur retrieved a cart from behind his desk and wheeled it down the long aisle that split the desks into two sides. It held a series of glass orbs on a tiered tray. He tapped each one and they took off, whizzing around like birds preparing to land. "Inside these containers are some of the oldest spices known to the world. Each has certain properties that can be used."

Ella tried to watch every single one, but they moved so

quickly from one table to the next. She wondered how he could do that, how his marvel worked.

"In our study of spice elixirs, we shall tour the world—continent by continent—learning regional spices. First up is my home country, India. I'm from Rajasthan, specifically, and you will learn about all the states as well as India's neighbors, Pakistan, Bangladesh, and Nepal too." He sent another glass orb into the air. "That one is saffron. It has more than a hundred and fifty aroma compounds. Comes in many different threads you'll have to memorize. Must be handpicked and used carefully in incants." He pointed at another full of golden orange powder that glittered like a tiny pulverized sun. "And here, this is probably my favorite, turmeric. Good for many things requiring cleanliness and getting rid of bad omens and spirits. And always used in my favorite timewarp tarts."

Another glass orb lifted from the cart.

"This tricky one is cumin. Good for cunning elixirs. Along with dried unicorn poop."

The class snickered.

Masterji Thakur cleared his throat. "And honey dust."

As the glass orbs continued to lift from Masterji's cart, Ella's heart lifted and settled like she was on a carousel. She wanted to taste each one. She wanted to ask Masterji Thakur a thousand questions, just like she peppered Gran with questions when they'd collect herbs from the conjure garden.

"Those with Taste marvels center on how food, tonics, poisons, elixirs, spices, and the like can be used to channel the light. Maybe one of you in this room might have a confectionary marvel, creating the greatest candy our world has ever seen. Or another might have a healing marvel, mastering the use of spice incants to soothe ailments, or invent rapturous perfume—yes, yes, the nose and the tongue work together." He raised his arms as if he were conducting a grand orchestra. "Repeat after me—the tongue tells truth."

He grinned as the chorus of voices echoed. "By the end of the year, we shall see who among you will join us."

Ella's heart squeezed. She didn't know what Paragon she wanted to belong to or where conjure would land, but she was excited to find out.

He lifted a metal tin from his cart. "But inventory first. You must always know what you possess in order to know all possibilities. Your spice dubba will be your best friend in this course." He tapped the tin in his hands. "The place where you'll keep ingredients stored neatly. Nothing worse than needing materials and not being prepared. I'll be grading your weekly tidiness. Always be ready."

The glass orbs dove back to his cart and nestled themselves into their containers.

"Everyone open your containers," he instructed. "Quick, quick. Place your metal spoon to the side."

Ella's fingers worked so fast to pry hers open that she almost dropped the lid. Brigit thumped at the metal tin and ignored him.

"It opens easily," Ella said to her.

"I know, and don't care."

"Okay." Ella turned back to hers, shocked.

Masterji Thakur continued: "Every Marveller skilled in spice work will have base ingredients. You must be adept in the flavors of the world. My homeland is a big part of that puzzle."

As he spoke each spice aloud, canisters left the enormous

shelf, floating over each trainee and sprinkling three scoops into their tiny metal tins.

"Coriander . . . dhaniya."

"Turmeric . . . haldi."

"Green cardamom . . . hari elaichi."

"Cumin in both powder and seed form . . . jeera."

"Red chilis . . . lal mirchi."

"Pay close attention! You must know all the names for the spices and the correct pronunciations. These vary from region to region, but we shall start here."

Ella felt a tiny lick on her arm. She looked down to find one of Siobhan's pixies gobbling up grains of cumin. She shooed it away, but it cackled in her face. Siobhan giggled until Masterji Thakur tsk-tsked.

Ella panicked, swatting it with her notebook, then sat upright, eyes fixed on Masterji Thakur. She didn't want to get in trouble. Not in his class. Not ever.

"How can you do that, Masterji Thakur?" a boy named Brendan asked. "How do they fly like birds?"

"Only Marvellers who turn bad control things," Clare blurted out. "Like the Aces." She turned around to stare at Ella. "Or," she coughed, "Conjurors."

Whispers spread through the class.

Ella sat up straighter, returning the glare. Why did Clare think she was bad?

"Enough of that, Miss Lumen. One demerit for not following instructions. I warned you about bringing them up." Masterji Thakur took a long pause. "There are many things that might make Marvellers do bad things with their marvels." He rubbed his beard. "But my spice marvel isn't about control. I can't make spices from scratch or influence the plants they come from. I can use the light inside me to interact with them, to understand their properties, and to, at times, encourage them to move. There's nothing *bad* about that." His eyes landed on Clare. "But we should all be careful with these terms, good and bad, and dark and light. Makes us nothing better than the Fewels."

Clare's face turned pink, and she grumbled, "Whatever," under her breath.

Ella tried not to smile when Masterji Thakur winked at her.

"Now, everyone listen up! We must encourage the spices to settle. One of the universal incants used is *shanti*. When Marvellers came together, each community added incants to our global lexicon. Everyone repeat after me."

A chorus of voices butchered the word.

"Not *shannn-ti*. *Shaan-thee*. Try again."

Ella whispered the word just as Masterji Thakur had said it. The first incant she'd ever used. Her tongue struggled, the word rolling over it. She almost sang it, her reflex to sing conjure spells ever present. But she took a deep breath and closed her eyes, saying the word firmly.

Her spices nestled in their tiny containers, and the lid of her dubba container shut and sealed.

She beamed. That's right. She could do it.

Masterji Thakur smiled at her, then addressed the class. "I see some of us are struggling." He put his hands in the air and took a deep breath. "Shanti! Peace."

The rest of the lids shut at the same time.

Maybe she'd be a Paragon of Taste.

AFTER LUNCH, JASON DRAGGED ELLA AND BRIGIT TO SEE HIS secret. "We should've taken the Black Line. It'd put us closer to the Arcanum menagerie. Now we got to walk through the Headmarveller's Wing instead," he admitted while squeezed between Ella and Brigit on a trolley bench.

"But I *like* the Gold Line. You can see Headmarveller Mac-Donald's waterhorse through the windows over there. The Cloud Loch floats right beside it." Ella rolled her eyes. "You act like you've seen a *thousand* of them."

"Well, actually, Headmarveller MacDonald has me feed Edi on Wednesdays," he reported.

"Why are we going to the menagerie, though?" Brigit asked with a sigh.

"You'll see." Jason grinned, and his locs wiggled.

Three chimes sounded.

"Moving forward," the trolley automat said. "Touch Tower up first."

They sailed through the belly of the Institute. Jason and Brigit argued about the best kinds of animals while Ella eavesdropped on the other trainees.

A bunch of Level Ones burst into an argument about the Paragons.

"Everybody knows Sounds are the best. They're always super chill and relaxed. Have the best lounge with all the instruments in it," one said. "And they get to learn all the animal languages."

"I think I'll end up a Spirit, but I really want to be a Vision because I don't want to be rivals with my older sister. Spirits and Visions *hate* each other," another added.

"Bad things happen to Visions. All the bad Marvellers had

those kinds of marvels. They see too much of the future. They get greedy, arrogant," one replied. "My dads warned me."

"No, that's Touches. Like the Aces. I think their leader was one, you know? Gia Trivelino. That's what my aunt said."

Ella leaned closer. That name. She'd seen it in the library book before it was redacted.

One kid turned to look at Ella before saying, "But nothing's as bad as *some* kinds of magic."

"What are you looking at?" Brigit barked back.

Ella loved how Brigit didn't think twice about yelling at someone when they were being mean.

"Don't listen to them," Jason whispered. "They don't know what they're talking about."

Ella pursed her lips. "But why do they think the Aces are the same as Conjurors?"

Jason looked at the ground. "Ever since Madame Baptiste made that lavender grow, everyone's talking."

Ella's eyebrow lifted with suspicion. "Why?"

"My sister Bea said Aces had monstrous marvels. Those are illegal. Ones that didn't fit into the Paragons," Jason said. "They didn't like the groups or . . . the rules."

Ella's thoughts took off in a hundred directions: Who wouldn't want a Paragon? What kinds of marvels did they have?

"Sound Tower ahead. Prepare to exit," the trolley automat yelled.

"That's us." Jason stood.

They ambled off and down the platform stairs.

Ella stopped abruptly, a deep tug pulling her in the opposite direction. Brigit crashed into her. "What the heck?"

"Wait!" Ella walked forward to an elevator marked

RESTRICTED LIFT. The same one from the night of the Midnight assembly, but it was now in a different place.

The doors opened with a chime, and Ella felt pulled inside.

"What are you doing?" Jason asked. "We're late for my secret."

But Ella was already inside. "I feel like I'm supposed to be in here."

Brigit followed. "This is weird. There's no buttons." She ran her fingers all over its velvety walls. "C'mon, Jason. You scared?"

Jason shrugged and skulked inside.

They gazed around.

"Now what? How does it work?" Jason inspected the levers and unmarked buttons.

Brigit searched the walls.

Ella squeezed her eyes shut, and thought, *What are you trying to show me?*

The elevator wiggled left, then right, and the doors snapped closed.

"Oh my god." Brigit pressed herself into a corner.

Ella grabbed the nearest railing while Jason cowered.

The elevator dropped. Down, down, down, then left and right, and diagonal. Layer upon layer of the Institute flew by so fast, Ella couldn't even get a good look. But one thing was for sure—this place was bigger than she could've ever imagined.

"Where are we going?" Jason shouted.

"How do we make it stop?" Brigit tried to yank the lever.

"I don't know!" Ella's stomach jumped up and down with each elevator jerk. Maybe this was a mistake. Maybe they'd never get out of here.

The elevator stopped. The three of them gazed out of the window. A glittering sign said FOUNDER'S ROOM. Ella felt pulled forward. The crossing tug again. How could she feel that so far away from home? Was something wrong with her?

"I just wanted to show y'all the animal menagerie." Jason pouted, as the elevator doors started to open.

The doors slammed shut again, and the elevator wiggled as if responding to Jason's request.

It shot back up, then left and right.

"WHAT IS HAPPENING?!" Brigit said. "I'm over this."

"I think it listens." Ella thought that could be the only reason.

It opened across from two gold columns and a sparkling sign: ANIMAL MENAGERIE & AQUARIUM.

They poured out of the elevator.

"Ugh, I'm never getting in there again." Brigit glared back at the strange elevator.

"Hurry." Jason led them forward. "We're late."

Ella rushed ahead through the golden gates, then glanced over her shoulder to find the elevator gone. What had just happened?

"C'mon." Jason grabbed her hand. Exhibit after exhibit spread out before her, stacked like hatboxes. Animal sounds both familiar and strange filled the entire space with an odd melody. Automats and starfolk climbed rolling ladders and used pulleys to lift food high up to the ceiling cages.

"Whoa," Brigit said.

"Awesome, right?" Jason watched their expressions.

"Hello, Jason Eugene. Very nice to see you." An automat tugged a wheelbarrow of rotties. "The wombies are waiting. Been asking for you."

He grabbed three smocks off wall hooks. "Quick, put these on. That elevator made us late. They must be starving."

Ella and Brigit pulled the smocks over their heads and

almost had to run to keep up with Jason. "Who?" Ella called out, but Jason was too far ahead of them.

"I've never seen animals like this before," Brigit said, awe tucking itself into her voice, to Ella's surprise. It was the first time Ella had seen her enjoy anything Marvellian related.

"Me either." Ella couldn't stop trying to peek at everything as they snaked through the hallways. She spotted all kinds of animals she'd never seen before: wary birds with signs warning of their deadly horns and dagger-like toes, gryphons sharpening their claws, tiny rainbow piggies, and impundulus making lightning with their wings. There were so many to visit and learn about. It made her think about what kind of conjure companion she might get on her thirteenth birthday—and whether Marvellian creatures were now eligible.

Jason shooed Brigit and Ella along. "No time." Jason made a left and stopped in front of a sign—WOMBIE BURROWS. "They're probably already upset." He picked up two lanterns and handed one to Ella and the other to Brigit.

"They prefer soft glows." Jason led them forward. "No sudden movements until I introduce you, okay?"

"Introductions?" Brigit's eyebrow lifted.

"They're suspicious of new people."

"They're animals," Brigit replied.

Ella thought of Gumbo and Paon and Greno, her family's conjure companions, and how they, too, usually held skepticism. She elbowed Brigit's side.

"*Oww,*" Brigit yelped.

Jason gave her a look and walked into the dark and cool habitat. A network of tunnels covered the wall behind a fenced area.

"Who's there?" came a small gruff voice.

Ella smiled, loving the sound of their voices.

"It better be Jason with the appetizers," came another.

"All you can think about is food. That's it. All you discuss. Tidy up your burrow, why don't you?" came a third.

"Will you sing us the lullaby before bed?" said a fourth. "The babies need it today."

Ella lifted her lantern, and thousands of furry round faces stared back, little button noses turned up with suspicion. "They talk?"

Jason shushed her. "Don't be insulting. Of course they do. But they'll speak in their own language if you make them upset, and only I will be able to communicate with them."

Ella couldn't stop smiling as they sniffed her, their little wet noses tickling her forearm. "Where did they come from?"

"Marvellers rescued all magical creatures from Fewel cities," he informed her.

Jason rattled off facts about wombies—like their favorite grass to put on the barbecue, how they like their coffee, and how they appreciate a good joke above all. Apparently, they used to live in Australia until the Fewels discovered them, and then the Marvellians brought them up above. Now they were almost extinct in the Marvellian world because they pooped gold squares.

Ella tried not to laugh at them or how Jason treated each one like a person. She followed his precise instructions to arrange their food in the proper place and pour the right amount of coffee into their cups. Brigit sat with the babies, getting roped into reading them a story from their extensive little habitat library.

Jason showed Ella an alcove beside the tunnels that looked

like a secret room. The corners spilled over with styluses, ink pots, paper, jars of this and that, tools, and journals.

"Is this your—"

"I come here when I get overwhelmed." His gaze dropped to the floor. "The wombies look after it for me. My mom talked to Headmarveller MacDonald about it."

Brigit nosed around. "Who's this?" She pointed at a heliogram perched on a tiny shelf. It projected a man Ella had never seen before.

"Only the most famous Marvellian veterinarian ever, Kiyota Murakami. His kindred marvel allowed him to talk to all living creatures, and he wrote down all their languages. Even ant dialects. I want to be like him."

Brigit leaned forward, squinting at the projected image. "He wears hearing aids."

"What does that have to do with anything? There are lots of ways to listen when you're a Sound." He stared at her puzzled, and she blushed.

"Jason!" A chubby wombie trundled to the fence. "We're having a bit of trouble with the you-know-what."

The others nodded.

Jason flinched. "Let's not talk about her right now."

"About what?" Ella asked.

"Sweetie has been eating everything, Jason. You must do something," another pushed.

"Many are afraid of her. She's getting too big."

"I'll check on her later. Not now," Jason said, as he collected the golden squares and placed them in a special jar.

A tiny whimper cut through the room, followed by the heavy pad of feet as the burrow vibrated.

"Oh no." Jason darted to the entrance, but a big creature bounded out, sending the wombies scrambling in a thousand directions.

As the animal got closer, its wet snout and big jaw and boxy shoulders sharpened into view.

"That's a . . ." Ella stepped forward.

Jason's locs jumped, and sweat poured down his cheeks.

"A baby deathbull." A pair of these beautiful massive pit bulls sat at the entrance of the Underworld back home ready to stare into the pits of a person's soul. "Where'd you get him?"

"I found her."

Ella's eyes narrowed. "You can't just find—" The deathbull tackled her, licking her cheeks and sniffing her hair. Ella ruffled her ears and sang the song her parents did whenever they went through the gates. *"We're crossing over yonder, crossing over yonder . . . to be with those we love."* The baby deathbull calmed in Ella's lap, her big eyelids getting heavy as she fell asleep.

Jason smiled, starting to hum along.

Ella looked up at him. "How do you know the song?"

He hiccupped and stopped. "Heard it once."

Brigit raced out of the wombie habitat. "Ohhhh! Its paws are almost as big as my face!"

Confusion swirled inside Ella. Why would a deathbull be all the way up here? Why would Jason have one? These divine creatures were born and raised near the Underworld Gates.

Did everyone have a secret . . . or was everyone hiding something?

★—★—★— **STARPOST**—★—★—★

Papa,
  Random question . . . can deathbulls survive
outside the Underworld?

Love,
Ella

P.S.: And tell Mama to stop worrying. I like my new
room. I'm fine. I know Aunt Sera is also letting you
know how things are.

★—★—★— **STARPOST**—★—★—★

Dear Masterji Thakur,
  Can I ask you some questions about the Institute?

Please.
Ella

★—★—★— **STARPOST**—★—★—★

Dear Ella,
  Of course you can. I will send you an appointment
card for our first mentorship meeting. I can answer all
your questions then.

Masterji Thakur

★—★—★— **STARPOST**—★—★—★

Aunt Sera,

I can't wait to see you again. Do you feel that crossing tug sometimes here? I can't figure it out.

Love,
Ella

POCKET DOORS

Gia cocked her head, glancing at the copy of herself one final time. Dark hair. Very blue eyes. Big sloping smile, a harlequin grin, her father used to call it. She took one last look out her window at the other floating prison cells. She vowed never to return to this place. No matter what.

The key rattled on the table. "Time to go." She grabbed it and knelt before the lamppost. She got to work plucking at its iron frame like it was nothing more than yarn on a loom. Her hands twisted each iron thread until a door stood before her. The most beautiful door she would ever make. One leading to freedom.

She fashioned the keyhole perfectly for the key she'd been given and shoved it in. The key turned on its own with a deep click and the door opened. The Underworld spread out on the other side: a glorious landscape with roads leading in millions of directions, massive gates, and countless doors to different eternal destinations. High Walkers in top hats used their canes to shepherd souls to their proper resting places, while

Low Walkers drove cages full of skeletons. Twilight stars shimmered over tombstones and crypts and endless graves. And at the center of it all lay a turreted mansion and a stretch of mountains that had never been more beautiful.

The noises of the Underworld greeted her.

"This way to the Elysium Fields. Keep left," a High Walker called out.

"El Otro Lado two leagues ahead," another shouted.

"The gate to Diyu is through the forest," a third hollered.

"Those wishing to visit loved ones make your way to the right. His Excellency Baron Durand, the Grand Walker, is back in the office. Join the line nearest the Cardinal."

The key melted into a silver staircase that stretched to the nearest road. She took one careful step after the other. The door closed behind her and disappeared. The Ace of Anarchy was free.

Now the show would begin.

PART II
CONJURE LIGHT

CHAPTER EIGHT

LIGHT AND WORLD-EGGS

Ella paced in her dorm room waiting for Brigit to pull on her mantle and brush her hair so they could get to their first session of the day. "We've got to go."

Ella liked to have a lot of time to get to their classrooms because even as October passed quickly by, she was still learning the peculiarities of the Arcanum Institute. The trolleys ran backward on Wednesdays and the towers shifted positions on Sundays. Some of the automats liked to send Level Ones on wild goose chases when the building moved just to see the trainees end up in the wrong places, and the starfolk were always too busy to help.

But she'd found her rhythm and had learned there were a lot of rules to marvelling. They examined fallen stars and charted the constellations every Monday night in the observatory. They spent two mornings a week in the library with Dr. Perez and her flying llama translating all the different incants used by Marvellians from around the world. On Thursday afternoons, Dr. Ursu, her amazing hair always full of static, took them to collect lightning from the Cloud Nests. And Ella was often the only student awake in Dr. Zolghad's History of Marvels class while they looked at artifacts. The only class that hadn't started was her godmother's Introduction to Conjure, and she couldn't wait for that to join her Friday schedule. The best part, Mama had stopped asking her to use her conjure-cameo or send starposts every two seconds.

Brigit stomped out of the bathroom. "We still have five minutes."

"If you're on time, you're late." Ella pointed at the clock-lantern flashing red with reminders. After she'd first moved in, Ella often left Brigit behind, but now she felt like being a good roommate, a good friend, meant you waited.

"Who ever said that?" Brigit yanked on her mantle.

"My papa." Ella paced in front of their glass windows, watching the bright orange and red leaves whip past.

Brigit rolled her eyes, pulled her hair into a ponytail, and stuffed yarn balls in her satchel. "Seeee . . . I'm ready!"

Ella grabbed her session manuals off the floor, and they darted for the door.

"Wait!" Brigit turned back around. "Forgot Feste." She plucked the clown doll from her bed.

Ella shuddered. Something was still odd about that doll. It felt like the ones back home with spirits trapped in them. She never forgot how it winked at her, but figured she better not call it weird to Brigit. She never went anywhere without it.

They ran all the way to the Touch Tower, nearly earning a demerit from Dr. Weinberg for scaring her golem and causing it to molt some of its clay, and narrowly missed receiving another from Dr. Stone for aggravating her emo-stones and disrupting their absorption of daily feelings.

The girls tumbled into Dr. Bearden's Channellors Chamber covered in sweat, out of breath, and embarrassed. Well, at least Ella was. Dr. Bearden had already begun her Introduction to Marvel Light lesson.

The room felt like a museum of random ordinary objects; the walls held glass cases boasting keys, pendulums, coins, oven mitts, ropes, even teakettles, and more.

A chandelier made of cogs, gears, and lightbulbs trailed Dr. Bearden, bathing her in a bright halo. "One demerit each for lateness, you two. The rules are the rules, and the new Headmarvellers and their Dean of Discipline are quite strict this year," she called out. "Fold in, fold in, and follow along."

Clare and Abina snickered.

Ella's heart sank. Her first demerit, a first at the Arcanum she'd never wanted to experience. The upset filled her up from head to toe. She bit back tears. Jason flashed her a supportive smile as she plopped down across from him at their worktable. Brigit sat beside her, grumbling.

"Historically, Marvellers have used many things to channel their light," Dr. Bearden said. "Items as unique as the vast array of countries Marvellians descend from."

Ella had seen advertisements in Marvellian newspapers about the best place to buy channellors—*Curtis & Claude's Channellor Consortium*—with catalogs full of all kinds of things Ella never thought you could use.

"But first, they all had to learn to control it using—"

The sound of *click-clack*s interrupted Dr. Bearden. Everyone's eyes followed the noise straight to Brigit and her knitting needles.

"Excuse me, young lady," Dr. Bearden said.

Brigit didn't look up. She began rocking back and forth with her eyes closed and her hands moving lightning fast just as she did in their bedroom.

"Brigit Ebsen, is it? You need to join us." Dr. Bearden snapped her fingers, but Brigit didn't move. "Participation is an essential part of this course and your overall marks. Did you hear me?"

No response.

Ella's cheeks flamed with secondhand embarrassment. She tapped Brigit on the shoulder. Why wasn't she listening? Didn't she hear Dr. Bearden talking to her? They'd already been late. Why make it worse?

"She's a weirdo." Clare looked over her shoulder at Ella. "I guess birds of a feather live together . . ."

"Hush, hush." Dr. Bearden swatted at Clare. "Brigit!"

Ella felt a flash of fear on Brigit's behalf.

Brigit's eyes snapped open.

"Give me that." Dr. Bearden held out her hand.

Brigit handed Dr. Bearden the knitted square. Dr. Bearden's cheeks turned apple red and she jammed it into her mantle pocket. "You think you're the next big Marvellian comedian, eh? See me after class, Miss Ebsen."

Brigit slumped forward.

"You okay?" Ella whispered.

"Fine."

"Where was I? Ah yes, marvel light is with us from birth,

but it takes years of practice to channel it effectively. This year, you'll learn to pull the light out of you."

"Ugh! Why can't we use stapiers?" Anh said a little too loud. "I want a Sabrewhizz. My sister has a Dueluxe."

"I want a channellor now," Miguel added.

"That's for Level Twos and Threes, respectively. Let's see if you last long enough. If you can't channel the light, then you can't remain here." Dr. Bearden wheeled out a cart full of stellacity spheres; their spinning rings catching the star-lantern light. "Your first primer. You must learn control and precision, getting your light to stabilize inside this before you can venture into more advanced territory."

She set one in front of each student. Ella marveled at hers, staring at the empty core ready to receive her light.

Dr. Bearden wagged a finger in the air. "You've seen these vessels your whole lives . . . from the engines of our sky-ferries to our house generators to our cities' air-trolley pistons. Some of you might even be lucky enough to have stellaric cars at home, too."

"We have three," Lian chimed.

"My father has four," Clare added.

"Quiet, quiet!" Dr. Bearden rolled her eyes, then cleared her throat. "The rings transform starlight into energy. Spend some time taking a look. We'll go over its parts in a few minutes."

Ella quickly pulled the stellacity sphere close, holding her breath until she'd seen each part—its beautiful celestial etchings, the five main rings, the small brass sphere at its center, and the thick stand. She didn't have a clue how she'd get her light inside this amazing object, but she was excited to try.

Siobhan sneaked up beside her. "The room sucks without you." The pixie on her shoulder nodded in agreement. "Lian and Samaira make all the rules, and they're always hosting parties. All the snobby girls come over to gossip."

Ella laughed. It felt good to be missed. "You can come visit me and Brigit in the Hydra Tower. That is, if she ever stops . . ." Ella shot a look at Brigit, who grunted in response, returning to her knitting needles.

"Really?" Siobhan's eyes grew big. Her pixie climbed on top of her stellacity sphere, and Ella and Jason laughed. "Night pixies are daredevils," she said.

"You think this is going to be hard?" Ella asked. "I've never channeled the light before. Well, I mean, that's not how we do it. Or what we call it."

"Ma says I don't have an ounce of light in me. That it's all bad."

Ella flinched.

"I don't mean like that. Just that . . ." Her white face turned red. "She thinks I'm a bad seed is all."

"Yeah. Okay," Ella replied, not knowing how to deal with how the word *bad* always felt attached to her like a constant shadow that would never leave.

Clare, Abina, and Lian walked past Ella's worktable, each taking turns to "accidentally" knock something off. Jason started to pick up the objects until Dr. Bearden called him to the front of the room.

"We're not ghosts, you know!" Siobhan barked at them.

Clare laughed. "Might as well be."

"Have you even met one?" Ella asked.

Lian scoffed. "Isn't that your job?"

"Yes, it is." Ella puffed out her chest. Then she parroted something Gran always said about the noble service provided by Conjurors as stewards of the Underworld: "Ensuring that your ancestors make it home to their resting places is important work." Ella let her eyes sear into Lian's until she looked away.

"I don't know why that girl Brigit even bothers with class if she's going to do *nothing*," Abina snarked.

"Might as well go back to whatever Fewel city she came from." Lian flicked her hair.

Ella glanced at Brigit, who was still knitting away as if she couldn't hear their taunts. It was another picture of that strange smiling woman.

"A Marveller who doesn't love marvelling is worse than a *Fewel*." Clare let the word draw out so it sounded like fool.

"How many Fewels do you even know?" Siobhan challenged.

"Have you even been to a Fewel city?" Ella asked, tired of their meanness.

"Whatever." Clare traipsed off with Abina and Lian.

Ella and Siobhan broke into a giggle fit. Brigit finally looked up.

"Aren't the stellacity spheres great?" Ella pointed at Brigit's unopened box.

"I don't care. I'm biding my time."

Her words gave Ella a hot flash. "I know, but if you did care"—Ella chose her words carefully as Brigit's pinkish nose crinkled with irritation—"I think you might like the stapier next year. It's sort of like a fatter version of one of your knitting needles." She pointed at the nearest glass case, displaying the long blades.

"I won't be here next year." Brigit looked away.

Ella didn't want that to be true.

Dr. Bearden clapped, getting everyone's attention. "Now, to practice. Put your hands together and make a little cradle by interlocking your fingers. Think of the light inside you. Call it to your fingertips as if you were getting ready to use it." She closed her eyes, and a ball of light appeared in her palm like a tiny sun. "The goal will be to place your ball of light in the stellacity sphere, and we'll be able to measure its current."

Ella put her hands together and stared into her palms. This was so different than conjuring.

Clare's ball of light shot into the air like a meteor and she cursed. Brendan's hands turned as red as his hair, almost igniting in flames. Samaira's floated off like a soap bubble.

"Gentle. Gentle. I didn't say shove it," Dr. Bearden shouted. "Using light takes control—and balance."

Ella squared her shoulders and whispered the word: "Light." Nothing.

She glanced around. Anxiety flooded her stomach.

Lian and Abina achieved perfect balls of light and smiled smugly at each other. Dr. Bearden cheered at their progress.

Jason squealed, and she glanced behind her. A bouncing ball of light sat on his palm. He caught her looking. "Yours work yet?"

"No." She kept staring at her hands as hard as she could. Maybe her glare would make it appear.

"Use the light! Draw it up like a well," Dr. Bearden called out. "It's waiting inside each one of you . . . eager to emerge. Focus! Focus!"

Ella shut her eyes and strained.

The light.

She tried to think of sunrays and candle flames and lamps. Anything that glowed.

Nothing.

Again.

It all felt so foreign, so difficult in comparison to conjure. She would close her eyes, and the darkness would've filled with possibilities, her wish laid out before her, ready to be sung into existence and into the twilight.

"You look like you're about to poop," Jason teased.

Ella's eyes snapped open. "And you're annoying."

He laughed, and then she laughed too.

"You'll fart if you keep it up," he added.

"Gross," Brigit mumbled. "But probably true."

Dr. Bearden walked from table to table, adjusting postures and hand positions, and giving tips.

Ella whispered to Jason. "How do you *actually* do it?"

He bit his bottom lip. "When I use mine, I just tell it what to do. That's what my dad does."

Ella looked at him puzzled. "That's not how we do it. We sing, we ask."

"I know," he whispered.

"You do?" Her eyebrow lifted.

Jason gulped down his response as Dr. Bearden paused in front of their worktable. "Go on, let's see it. All in the will. Command it."

Ella took a deep breath. All eyes turned to watch her. Dr. Bearden's curious gaze sent a tremor across her skin.

She yanked at her gift like a cord and demanded it obey.

Her hands glowed, then a ball of light appeared. But not bright—instead a black light with a violet and white core. Like a sky at twilight. Ella jumped with surprise. What was this?

The whole room scampered away. Ella heard the words *bad* and *light* whispered in various combinations.

"I've never seen anything like this before." Dr. Bearden inched forward to inspect it. "Natural talent. Great control. There's some sort of light inside you after all."

Ella clapped her hands to disperse the light. She didn't know if that was a compliment or something else.

✦　✳　✦　◼　✦

ELLA'S SKIN FELT HOT AND PRICKLY AS SHE PACKED UP HER SATCHEL and prepared to leave class. The lingering stares and the crackle of whispers about her marvel light gave her a headache. She ignored Jason's worried questions about her feelings. Frustrated, she popped up from the worktable and straight into Clare.

"Watch where you're going," Clare said before turning back to Abina. "My older sister said they're coming today. We *have* to be the first Level Ones to get one."

"Get what?" Ella asked.

Clare's nose scrunched up. "None of your business."

Ella rolled her eyes. Brigit walked up. Clare scampered off with her crew.

"Everyone's going to the school store," Jason reported. "Betelmore docked while we were in class. There's going to be a ton of new stuff."

"What?" Brigit asked.

"Each town comes close to the Institute every year so we get a chance to visit them or our parents can come see us here." Jason packed his satchel. "But Clare and Abina probably want a malyysvit. My brothers haven't shut up about them. Only released once a year."

"What?" both Ella and Brigit said.

"A *molly-sveet*. The world-eggs. Hatches a mini-universe. You never know what you'll get. My brother Wes had one years ago. His had hurricanes, and the storms lasted all night. Momma threw it out. Now he wants another one. They're only the most popular thing in the Marvellian world."

Ella had never heard of them.

"I'll show you."

"Not so fast, Ms. Ebsen, please stay behind," Dr. Bearden called out.

"Meet you there, I guess." Brigit shrugged.

Ella flashed her a sympathetic smile before leaving with Jason. She wondered what Brigit had knitted that made Dr. Bearden so upset. How much trouble would she be in?

Ella and Jason followed behind a small group of Level Ones into the Institute's supply store. The space buzzed with Level Twos and Threes and Fours. The whole school felt like it'd crammed into the space, all vying for a malyysvit.

Arcanum balloons sailed above, boasting the wonders in each aisle:

ANIMATED AND DIMENSIONAL INK POTS FROM
IGNATIUS IACOBELLI'S INCORRIGIBLE INK SHOP
HERE STRAIGHT FROM ASTRADAM!

CONSTELLATION MAPS, AISLE THREE.
NORTHERN, SOUTHERN, AND HIDDEN SKIES OF
PARALLEL DIMENSIONS. GUARANTEED!

STORM JARS, DUBBAS, AND ALCHEMY BOXES BROUGHT
STRAIGHT FROM CALDWELL'S CHARMING CO-OP.

Her mouth hung open so wide Gran would've asked if she was looking to catch flies. Aisles spilled over with every object a trainee would need. They weaved through a row of twinkling starpost stationery, which waxed and waned like the stars themselves. The postcards sat in rows, their heliograms projecting images of the Arcanum or celebrating the Marvellian holidays—Halloween, the Gatherfeast, Founder's Day. Brushes swept along the interior of glass jars eager for ink and paper. Gold incant pots glowing like bowls of sunlight sat on shelves ready to be filled with ingredients.

Ella thought she could easily spend all the money her parents had given her in this store alone.

Jason nudged her arm. "Look," he whispered.

They watched Siobhan's pixies swiping self-twisting hair ribbons, charm-yarn, and emo-gems while Siobhan admired the starscopes and astrolabes. Uh-oh! She wondered if Siobhan knew about it. "Should we tell her?"

"I mind my business," he mumbled.

Mama would've said the same thing.

"The counter opens in seven minutes," a Level Three boy shouted. "There's already a line. Grab a ticket. Quick!"

Ella stopped spying and grabbed Jason. They spilled out of the aisle and stood in front of a closed window that wore the sign ARCANUM SPECIAL ORDERS. A clock ticked down the minutes. A ticket machine spat out red slips to anyone who pulled its lever.

Ella spotted Brigit's blond hair and put her hand up. Brigit moved through the crowd, finding her way over.

"Everything okay?" Ella asked.

Brigit grunted. "I guess."

The Level Ones clustered together.

"It's a lottery this year," Anh said.

"Ugh, that's not fair," Clare complained.

"My 'umi wouldn't get me one even though she's the President," Samaira chimed in. "I begged her."

"Let's each get a ticket," Jason said.

"I don't know if I can afford it." Brigit's cheeks reddened.

"You won't win anyways," Lian said as she sauntered up to the machine.

Brigit scowled at her, then followed, yanking the lever. "We'll see about that."

Tochi and Ousmane high-fived before grabbing theirs. Ella took one, too, then stared at the *Mischa's Original Malyysvit—#1 World-Hatching Eggs* poster. Eager kids pressed the heliograms to watch the pictures project into their hands. They admired the decorated shells, taking guesses about what sort of universe would hatch from each one. The poster voice repeated its slogans:

"ONLY THE BEST PRODUCTS COME FROM
HORBACHEVSJY'S HOUSE OF INVENTION!"

"NEW AND IMPROVED COSMO-GROWER!"

"I don't even know if I want it—but how much, just in case?" Brigit retrieved a small plastic card from her pocket. It had her picture beside neon numbers.

"What's that?" Jason's eyes grew big.

"What we use to buy stuff in New York City."

Brigit let Jason examine her money card. "You can't use that here, though. Fewel money isn't accepted," he told her.

Brigit looked confused.

"You'd have to exchange it at the Marvellian Mint in Celestian City," Jason explained. "The bank."

"My parents have those cards too. In case we do business with Fewels," Ella said. "But conjure dollars and coins are so much more fun." She opened her bulging coin purse, showing her black dollars and large colorful coins.

"You've got a lot of money," Brigit said, shocked.

Ella smiled shyly and let Brigit thumb each fat coin, admiring how thick and heavy the gold stellas felt and how the silver lunari would wiggle if squeezed too tight. It made her wonder more about Brigit's life before the Institute. She knew her family was fortunate. Mama reminded Ella every chance she got, pressing upon her that not everyone shared her blessed circumstances. Conjurors tried their best to take care of their own.

They waited eagerly. Brigit took out her knitting needles and started up again.

"How could you possibly do this right now?" Ella threw her hands up.

Brigit's face pinkened. "Sometimes I can't help it. I get this weird urge."

In an instant, Ella felt terrible. This was the first time she'd seen her like this, and she started to apologize, but Brigit was already in her trance, hands moving, a beautiful tapestry developing in her lap.

The kids around them were too fixated on the store window to even see Brigit, so Ella's embarrassment subsided.

The clock chimed and the window blind snapped open. A round-faced woman smiled at them; her peach hijab made the brown of her skin almost glow. "Settle, little stars. I'm Madame Kazem."

Everyone clapped. Shush-balloons swarmed overhead.

"I can't call the numbers with all this racket." She waved her hands in the air. Everyone went silent. "Now, listen up. There's a lottery every week to keep it fair. I've ordered a set number, and when we're out, we're *out*. You'll have to wait until next year. No whining." She turned the machine lever and started to call the numbers. Lucky Level Three and Four trainees screamed as their numbers were announced and their friends flocked to them.

Ella pressed her ticket to her chest, hoping it'd absorb her wish. She wanted a malyysvit badly. Maybe not so much to see what would hatch from one of the beautiful eggs, but rather for everyone to be excited for her.

"Last one for this week," Madame Kazem called out. "Ticket #7298."

"That's me," Brigit whispered.

Jason let out a whoop, and Ella squealed in excitement.

An older trainee overheard and shouted, "This Level One's got it."

Brigit's needles dropped, and her latest quilt square slipped to the ground as she was ushered to the front of the crowd.

Madame Kazem turned over her ticket and checked the ledger. "We'll charge it to your account." She handed her the beautiful dusty-rose egg. Its gold garlands and sparkling jewels advertised the promise of a desert world.

The other kids swarmed Brigit like a kicked beehive. There were pats on the back and hundreds of congratulations and so many smiles. Surprisingly, Brigit lapped it up, and it was the first time Ella had seen her smile, a real deep-down grin. Winning this world-egg seemed to make Brigit happy.

Ella reached down to pick up the knitted square—a picture of the egg and the winning lottery ticket number stretched across it. How had Brigit made this before Madame Kazem announced the final winner?

But as Ella watched Brigit, her own excitement began to fade. It seemed like everyone wanted to be Brigit's friend, wanted to talk to her, wanted to see what was inside her egg. At one point, Brigit looked up, and Ella tried to flash Brigit a supportive smile, fighting off the secret pit burning in her stomach.

Dear Ella,

All is well at home. You are missed. To answer your question about deathbulls . . . they're drawn only to Conjure folk. Hope that helps.

Love,
Papa

CHAPTER NINE

THE CARDINALS AND STARPOSTS

The next day, Ella clutched a pulsing appointment card from Masterji Thakur.

TIME: **Just before lunch**

WHERE: **Arcanum entry hall**

Ella was so excited to talk to him that she'd counted down the hours. She'd written a starpost to Papa telling him all about the color of her marvel light and done her homework twice just to be sure she'd memorized everything. Then she'd made a Masterji Thakur question list: *Could he give her more books on spice marvelling? Did he think she was blending in well? Did he know what Paragon the marvel exam would place her in at the end of the year?*

"You're happy," St. Catejan said. "Must be good news."

"All smiles. We love to see it." St. Phillip clapped.

Ella couldn't even be annoyed with them. Not today. "I

get to see my mentor. Masterji Thakur. Maybe he can tell me which Paragon conjure will fit in."

"Wishing you the best luck." St. Catherine waved.

"Your mama will feel more settled now that you're finding your way," St. Christopher said.

"But always keep an eye out," St. Lucy warned. "Especially of your roommate. She's up to something."

"Okay, whatever you say." Ella blew them a kiss, and they settled.

Noise echoed from the lounge. Ella packed her satchel and left the room. She might as well be early for her appointment.

Voices and squeals filled the space. Ella spotted Brigit surrounded by both the Hydra and Ursa Minor girls. They oohed and aahed over the beautiful world-egg and its instructions. The advertisement played over and over again, shouting about the malyysvit's unique qualities. Brigit's eyes lit up as the girls quizzed her about it. Even Ella's old roommates were there, and Abina smiled excitedly at Brigit.

Ella hadn't been able to get that pit out of her stomach since the day Brigit won it. She'd wanted one of those eggs badly, and even though Brigit now had one, and more people were visiting their room to gawk at it, it didn't feel like they were the least bit interested in her.

Brigit stood and called out her name.

"What?" Ella's anger felt loose.

"The egg's already changing colors."

"I hate that thing!" Ella lied.

Brigit's happy face turned sour, her blue eyes filling with hurt.

Ella burst out of the dormitory. If she heard one more thing about that malyysvit, she might scream. Fighting back tears, she made her way through packs of Level Fours in their purple mantles, headed out to the greenhouses, and Level Threes exiting their star labs.

She whizzed past Dr. Winchester.

"Excuse me, Miss Durand, that's one demerit for running." He pursed his wrinkled lips and scowled.

"But—" Ella started to protest.

"That's another for insubordination. You must do better to fold into our ways or you won't make it very far." He skulked away, leaving Ella speechless and even more frustrated. There were other kids running in the hall that he didn't stop.

Ella finally made her way to the Arcanum entry hall, planting herself on the Institute's golden seal—the five-pointed star. She tried to shake off her irritation, gazing up at the gorgeous ceiling; the constellations tumbled in and out of animal shapes. She started naming them. "Orion, Vulpecula, Lyra, Cygnus, Boötes . . ."

"Well done, Ella. You know the Greek ones, and in no time you'll move on to the Chinese Lunar Mansions and beyond." Masterji Thakur's warm smile greeted her. "So glad you could meet me." He waved her forward to the Arcanum entrance doors. "This way. This way. We're headed out for an adventure."

"Where?"

"I want to show you something, you'll see . . . but first, how are you liking the Arcanum?" They walked outside and along the main path.

"Everything is fine," she replied quickly, not wanting to seem like she couldn't handle the work or that she'd just had a fight with her roommate. She picked up her pace, afraid she might blurt out more. She craned her neck to see all the topiary mazes of moonflower hedges and starfruit trees. She wondered if there'd be snow all the way up here as they got closer and closer to December. She'd read when the Institute was positioned over tropical places, the grounds were littered with palm trees.

"A new pair of shoes can be fine or okay, Ella—but this is the Arcanum. It's supposed to be marvelous."

Ella perked up. "Oh, I meant—it is. I love it so much. I feel so lucky to be here."

He rubbed his mustache. "Hmmm," he said in the way Papa did when he felt like she wasn't telling him the entire truth. "Well, I felt just the same way when I first came here. Never wanted to leave. Though it wasn't always easy as Marvellers from different countries started to live together. There were some growing pains. All those different traditions becoming one." He chuckled. "How are your sessions?"

"I love all my classes, but yours is my favorite," she replied as they passed the Founder's Fountain.

"You flatter me." He paused and pointed at all five legendary Marvellers holding up a platform. "Truly unnecessary. If I was a trainee, Dr. Mbalia's class would no doubt be my favorite. Seconded by Dr. Ursu's. I've always found story and elemental marvels fascinating."

Ella's back straightened. "I'm not just saying that to butter you up! I promise. I love spices. Back home, I help my gran in our garden a lot. I'm good with plants. Aren't spices just dried up plants? I could be a Taste. Conjure could fit there."

"Yes, yes. We have some time to figure that out."

Ella felt a squeeze deep down at the bottom of her stomach. Sometimes when she caught someone staring at her or accidentally caught a snippet of a nasty whisper, it made her wish she already knew her Paragon. She felt like a puzzle piece desperate to find its place.

"But the administration has begun discussions. Everything here requires so much talking and coordinating with the upper school . . . This rule and that rule must be followed; this tradition and that tradition cannot be altered. After our very first Gatherfeast almost 300 years ago, it took us 50 more years to open the Arcanum and agree on what it'd be." He rolled his eyes. "It'll take all year to work out where conjure belongs. And I have no doubt my Elixir of Light will determine the right place for you. But in the meantime, I figured you'd have many questions, so I want to show you something that might ease some of your worries for now."

They passed the celestial-blue Stariary, the Institute's post office, where star messengers transported envelopes and parcels and packages throughout the Marvellian world. Ella couldn't wait to start bringing her starposts out here instead of using the starpost boxes inside the Institute. "It's even prettier than I imagined."

"It is. It is. Getting a good starpost can brighten your day." Masterji Thakur led the way forward. "This way."

The entry path ended at a massive column stretching from the ground and into the clouds. The five Paragon symbols decorated its massive body, twinkling like molten gold.

"The Arcanum Cardinal." Masterji Thakur gazed up in awe at the tower. "Did you know that there are four of these columns in the world?"

"No." Ella stared, trying to figure out why it looked so familiar. Was it just because she'd seen it in all the books she'd read about the Arcanum? Or was it something else?

"One in each city and this one here, of course. They all look a little different. But this one might be my favorite. Just so magnificent."

Ella walked around its colossal base and she felt that familiar crossing tug again. The one from the elevator. The one from home.

"Does New Orleans have such things?" he asked.

The entrance to the Underworld Gates popped into Ella's head. She pictured the deathbulls resting their backs against two great columns, and the large one in front of her papa's office, the Mansion of Death. She told Masterji Thakur all about them.

"Very interesting. I hope to see them one day," he said.

"I can show you everything." The thought of her favorite teacher coming down to a Fewel city to visit made her heart jump.

"I would be honored." He patted her shoulder. "Do you know anything about how the Arcanum came to be?"

Ella riffled through her satchel and retrieved a book almost the size of her. "I took *A Thousand Years of Light: An Arcanum History* out of the library."

Masterji Thakur tapped the book. "The Marvellian world has many secrets, Ella. Ones that haven't found their way into books—"

Ella put a hand to her chest as the pulling sensation overwhelmed her.

"Are you okay?" Masterji Thakur paused.

"The Cardinal makes me feel strange."

"How?" His bushy eyebrows lifted.

Ella wasn't sure if she could explain it to a non-Conjuror, but around Masterji Thakur, she felt safe enough to try. "When my family goes into the Underworld, I feel a tug. The crossing tug. Like I'm being pulled through the veil." Ella placed a hand at her heart. "I also feel that now. It's so strong."

He stared at her curiously.

"Papa says it's because of the twilight stars, the ones in the Underworld's sky." Ella gazed up at the Cardinal again. She was probably just too far from home, her body still adjusting. Maybe this was what Gran meant when she said being up here was unnatural.

"That is curious. Very curious." He opened and closed his mouth strangely. "We can end our meeting early today if you need to."

"No, no. I want to know everything about Arcanum history."

He smiled. "Just know that history is like a palimpsest manuscript. Know what that is?"

She shook her head no.

"It's a document or a book in which words have been written on top of the original text. Our society is a bit like that. But under a mag-scope . . . you'll find all the things others have tried to cover." He handed her two books, *Let Them Tell It— The Truth About Conjure Folk and Marvellers* by Valerie Peaks, and *A Secret History of Conjurors in the Marvellian Universe* by Edward Clayton. "These are from my library, and ones you might not find in our Arcanum one."

Ella ran her fingers over the covers, buzzing with questions. "Why wouldn't these be in the library?"

Masterji Thakur opened his mouth to answer, and his voice garbled, then squeaked. "Don't ask that."

Ella's stomach squeezed. Had she said something to upset him?

Sweat beaded across his forehead, and he cleared his throat a few times. "I must go." The words almost strangled him.

Ella's heart thudded. "Are you okay?" she shouted after him.

Masterji Thakur wiped his forehead and waved, then hurried back to the entrance.

Ella watched until Masterji Thakur was out of sight. What had just happened? She couldn't help but feel that somehow Masterji Thakur's sudden departure was all her fault.

✦ ✖ ✦ ✖ ✦

ELLA TRIED TO SLEEP. BUT HER MIND JUST WOULDN'T SHUT OFF. SHE replayed what happened with Masterji Thakur over and over again, stuck in a loop. The weird cough. The way he'd shut her down. She'd gone to his office, but nothing. She'd sent over a dozen starposts.

Nothing.

And now, all the questions and worries were aggravated honeybees in her mind. Had she messed up? She thought about telling Brigit what happened . . . but Brigit was looking at her world-egg, absorbed and still mad at Ella for how she'd acted earlier. Jason had been too busy to hang out, his siblings celebrating his sister Grace's birthday. She was on her own.

Ms. Paige peeked her head into the room and turned the

lights out. "Sleep well, Level Ones. Dreams full of marvel light."

The night-balloons puttered into the room next, their tiny candles casting small halos over everything like pairs of eyes.

Ella yanked her gran's quilt over her head, the patches threaded with light ribbons releasing a tiny, comforting glow.

"Sweet dreams," St. Raphael cooed.

"You look troubled, child. Nothing rest won't fix," St. Catherine whispered.

She shushed them. *Go to sleep*, she told herself. She thought about sending a starpost or a note to Aunt Sera to see if she knew why Masterji Thakur might've gotten upset with her, then shook her head. She didn't want her to know anything was wrong.

Ella stared up at the bottles in her tree as they caught the night-balloon light. The branches bloomed with belladonna, a sign of danger to come. She wondered what, though . . .

The sound of feet hitting the floor made her turn over. Her heart fluttered as she watched Brigit get dressed in the dark and grab her satchel. What was she doing?

Brigit gazed around and shooed one of Siobhan's pesky pixies from her bathroom before tiptoeing over to Ella's bedside.

Ella squeezed her eyes shut, pretending to sleep, but she felt Brigit lean over her. "Goodbye," Brigit whispered gently, then Ella heard the sound of her walking toward the door.

Where was she going?

As soon as Brigit left the room, Ella counted to ten, then kicked off the quilt.

"Back to bed with you," St. Christopher commanded.

"I told you she was up to something. The saints know, Ella," St. Maria added.

Ella ignored them and followed Brigit. A cold breeze and a night-balloon trailed her down the tower's spiral staircase.

"Go away." She swatted at the pesky balloon, but it clung to her like a watchdog.

The Hydra constellation twinkled from the ceiling, bathing the wood beneath her slippers with tiny light freckles.

Ella eased into a long corridor. She spotted a streak of Brigit's white-blond hair in the distance. Ella followed. She raced past gigantic windows, dim star-lanterns, and silent automats. The whole building felt asleep like the Institute itself needed to recharge.

She bit her bottom lip, knowing she should be tucked in bed and not this far away from her dormitory tower. Papa would've said, "The rules land on you a little harder, baby. Always know that." But she needed to see what Brigit was up to. Brigit was her friend, even if she hadn't been acting like one lately. What if Brigit was in danger?

She approached the entry foyer. Trollies sat high above on platforms, their destination cards blank. Night-balloons illuminated the glass ceiling now absent of its constellations and revealed glimpses of a starless sky. The soft hiss of lampposts echoed.

Brigit slipped into the Touch Tower, skittering under the massive mechanical hand now frozen in a wave. She passed the heliogram of Indira Patel the Brave, her daggers perched above her head.

Ella kept trailing.

Art and dance studios lined the left side and lapidary labs

the right. Origami cranes whizzed just overhead. Suddenly, a light appeared, the glow from one of the Institute's automats. Brigit turned. Ella ducked behind a cabinet display boasting the best knives for vanquishing. She quickly turned a corner to catch Brigit slipping through an open side door.

Ella walked down a stone path beside the topiary garden, inching past the Founder's Fountain and ducking straight into the Stariary.

The place felt like the cross between a birdhouse—well, a house for a thousand birds—and a post office. There were so many small doors opening and closing, closing and opening, and out of those windows came envelopes held by tiny, wiggly stars. They shot left and right and up and down, headed in a million directions before disappearing into the dark sky overhead.

Ella wished she could shrink herself down and peek into the tiny alcoves. Striped balloons and plump golden dirigibles clustered in the center with baskets ready to receive parcels and packages. A large clock tower soared up to a glass dome. Its face held numbers and directions, and a map of the world flickered in the background. Ella gazed up in awe. "Wow."

"Why are you following me?"

She whipped around and met Brigit's angry blue glare.

"What are you doing?" Ella asked. "Are you okay?"

"Why do you care? You didn't earlier." Brigit frowned.

Shame pooled in Ella's stomach. "I didn't mean . . . I'm sorry."

"Too late." Brigit wore a strange harness and a stuffed Arcanum satchel, and had a parachute bunched in her arms.

"Where'd you get that?"

"I made it. Turns out there's an endless fabric room in the Touch Tower supply rooms."

Ella started to ask where she was headed, but the thousands of tiny doors of the Stariary reopened and a flurry of letters shot out, drowning her voice. They ducked together, both looking up and watching the tornado of sparkly letters swell like a swarm.

Ella whispered the word *wow* again as the noise died down.

"Well, I'm leaving." Brigit jammed her hands against her hips. "I don't care if you tell on me."

"I'm not a snitch. But why?" Ella's papa had done so much to make sure she could be at this special place. She couldn't imagine not being here.

"You wouldn't understand." Brigit's eyes narrowed. "You can have the room all to yourself now."

Ella's heart squeezed. "What if I like sharing a room with you?"

"Why are you staying? You should go too. I've heard the things people say about you, about your family."

Ella flinched, the sting of Brigit's words ringing true. Too true. "Sometimes, I feel the same way. Like I don't belong."

"I don't belong here either. People call me a Fewel . . . or even an Ace," Brigit added, biting her bottom lip. "It was a mistake." She tightened her harness, then looked up at Ella, eyes softening. "Leave with me. The package slide will get us out." She lifted the parachute. "Bet I could carry both of us down to that pier."

"The Stardust Pier?" Ella tried not to be shocked. "It's not that easy."

"Tell me how, then."

"You've got to take one of the Arcanum cable cars down to Betelmore. After that, you can catch a sky-ferry to the different piers. That's what my book said."

"Have you done it before?" Brigit asked.

"No, but my papa has. He comes in and out of Marvellian cities."

Brigit's eyebrows lifted. "I just want to go to New York City. Ms. Mead is probably still looking for me."

Ella had never been to that great vertical city of skyscrapers with its orange taxi-lifts taking passengers up and down. She'd only seen images on the Fewel television Gran hid in her room to watch strange stories in the afternoon.

"If you mess up, you could end up in the water. And with sharks," Ella replied.

"Before the sharks . . . both of you will have to serve DETENTION!"

Ella and Brigit turned around.

It was Aries, the starfolk. He wore a long tunic, and his ears were perked up.

"Oh no—*you* stay away from me!" Brigit exclaimed.

The creature put his furry paws in the air. "I was *just* following orders."

"From who?" she spat back.

"The Headmarvellers."

"What's going on?" Ella waved her hands around.

Brigit wagged her finger in the creature's face. "You kidnapped me. You're the reason I'm here."

He shrugged his shoulders and turned to Ella. "Nice to see you again." He extended a soft paw, and Ella shook it.

"Stay away from her!" Brigit hollered.

"You never told me any of this." Ella's eyes volleyed back and forth between the two of them.

"You never asked!" Brigit said.

"Both of you should be back in bed this instant. The photo-balloons have probably already caught you and sent their reports," Aries said. "Dean Nabokov is not one to play with. Rumor has it, she used to captain a pirate ship before coming here. Heard she's banished kids to different time periods until they learned their lesson."

"How'd you find me?" Brigit yelled. "You following me?"

"How dare you accuse me of such a thing. It's my nightshift this week. Not my job to babysit runaways. I tell the star messengers what to do and make sure the compass rose tower is functioning." He pointed at the large, beautiful clock in the center of the Stariary.

Brigit adjusted her harness. "You can't stop me."

"Maybe we should just go back to bed," Ella said to Brigit.

"You can," she said. "This is my chance."

The harlequin doll climbed out of Brigit's satchel and tapped her on the shoulder. "Brigit." His voice squeaked.

"Feste . . ." Brigit's face turned bright red.

"Brigit, please calm down," the doll said.

"You can talk?" Brigit stumbled back.

"Your doll is alive?" Ella remembered when it winked at her.

Feste sighed. "I'm not a *doll*, I'll have you know. I'm a protector. Her protector at that. Been with her from birth." He stood a little straighter with hands on hips. "I am very important."

"What . . . who . . . I can't believe—get away from me," Brigit shouted.

"Feste T. at your service." He took off his tiny hat and bowed; the tiny bells on it chimed.

Aries riffled through his pockets. He dug out a small satchel labeled *The Nostrum Nook's Sleepy Time Powder* and stepped closer to them. "I hate having to do this again. Ella, sorry you're involved. Only supposed to use it under the direst of circumstances."

"I'd say this is one," Feste replied to Aries.

"Don't come any closer!" Brigit backed up.

"Just listen to us, Brigit," Feste said. "You'll love this place, I promise. It's everything you ever wanted and would talk to me about. You'll get to learn things and go on adventures and have real friends. Not everything will be perfect all the time, but there's always something good here."

Brigit's face turned a deeper red, edging on purple.

"What's going on?" Ella asked, her panic rising.

Aries rushed toward both of them, blowing dust in their faces. It fell against their cheeks like soft baby powder and smelled just as sweet. Ella's eyes drooped, and she couldn't make them stay open no matter how hard she fought. Her arms and legs filled with tiny tingles and that lightness you feel when you're dreaming. Before she knew it, she was fast asleep.

The Arcanum Training Institute for Marvelous and Uncanny Endeavors

October 27

TO: Dean of Discipline

Two Level Ones spotted out of bed post-lights-out curfew! See photo-balloon evidence attached. Several heliograms captured.

Demerits and detention slips will be sent via automat. Saturday detention required.

★—★—★— **STARPOST**—★—★—★

Ella,

    The rotties told me you got in trouble. Are you okay?

From,
Jason

★—★—★— **STARPOST**—★—★—★

Jason,

    Ugh, so much happened. I got detention. I'll tell you everything at dinner.

From,
Ella

★—★—★— **STARPOST**—★—★—★

Ella,

    Young lady, what is this I hear about you out of bed after curfew? We must discuss. Come to my Conjure Atelier early, please. I need to lay eyes on you.

From,
Aunt Sera

THE ARCANUM TRAINING INSTITUTE FOR MARVELOUS AND UNCANNY ENDEAVORS

+ ———————— ARCANUM MEMO ———————— +

TO: Arcanum Faculty
FROM: Masterji Thakur

Dear all esteemed Arcanum Faculty,

Just a quick note—I know you've all been discussing our newest student's ability to adopt our ways. I assure you, this'll be her home soon enough. Let us welcome her wholeheartedly. She's a lovely trainee and deserves our benefit of the doubt and open-mindedness. For she profoundly respects each of you, and thus we should offer her the same.

                                        Best,
                                        Masterji Thakur

THE GREATEST SHOW
IN THE SKY

The city of Betelmore hadn't changed much in the eleven years since Gia had been away. She looked out on it from the air-trolley's window. They always flew along the wires of this place like a kettle of jeweled hawks, cresting over the rooftops of turreted houses and quaint shops all stuck together like assorted taffies. There used to be heliogram billboards lighting up the skies, projecting all the entertainment this city had to offer. Her show used to have the largest one. An entire city quarter dedicated just to her. She could almost hear the applause again.

The air-trolley headed for the last stop on the Crimson Line. Only those with enough courage would be venturing to the low street entrance this late.

A few Marvellian coppers stood on the platform, lifting their stellaric-lights to have a closer look at exiting passengers. The crowd thickened like homemade pudding as she slipped past them.

"What's your name?"

"Where are you headed?"

"What is your business here?"

The chorus of their interrogations bounced off the station's walls, and the lies she fed them rolled out with ease. She mimicked the voice of one of the nannies that took care of her after her father died. Soft, warbly, almost fragile. Then she giggled to herself as they let her pass.

Gia ambled down the great iron steps connecting the upper decks of the air-trolley platforms to the streets below. Her feet almost broke into a dance as they hit the cobblestones. She took a left and disappeared down the nearest staircase leading to the second layer of the city.

The low street had a pass-me-by appearance, which clearly whispered, "Move on unless you know where you're going." Its ramshackle storefronts leaned at odd angles, like bones knocked a little out of their sockets. A trickle of brass melodies greeted her from a nearby speakeasy as Conjurors played music for a joyous crowd, and her nose filled with the glorious scent of fae sweets. Fat fall pumpkins sat in windows as late-night shoppers slipped in and out of Ignoble Incant Imporium or the Wicked Warehouse of Wonders or into the open-air Mischief Mart full of trinkets offering dark promises.

It'd been so long since she'd walked this road, but her feet remembered the route. There used to be diamond-shaped signs leading the way. There used to be a line down the block. There used to be her favorite busker bringing curious visitors to their Commedia Close. This all used to be hers.

Gia stood before the gate. The Trivelino Troupe's Circus & Imaginarium of Illusions sign had faded, the letter blocks a chipped blur now. Beside it the poster's heliograms were now frozen, the projections of her different characters and acts silent and still. A government warning poster flashed its threat:

WARNING: DO NOT TRESPASS.
This area has been declared a restricted area in accordance with Title 2356 under Marvellian Unlawful Acts. Entry is forbidden. Penalty fine up to 3,000 gold drams and 2 months hard labor in the Cards of Deadly Fate.

Gia cackled. "Bet they couldn't keep my fans from coming, waiting for my return." She looked left before digging a pincushion from her coat pocket, then pricked her finger and let a drop of blood hit the jagged cobblestones. A thin halo stretched before her like the skin of a bubble, and she stepped through into the Close. Her father's illusion had held up over the years. No one could see through the shroud unless she wanted them to. Only those with Trivelino blood could ever reveal its secrets.

The beauty of it shined. Red, black, and white diamonds, a grand piazza boasting her ticket booth and a gondola waiting to take her inside.

All was just as she'd left it eleven years before the accident: the entry canal of mirrors, the waterway surrounding the big top, the walls of attractions tucked into the circular amphitheater, and the floating stages.

Once inside her dressing rooms, she ran her fingers over everything: her various faces still on hooks, smiling brown ones, gorgeous black ones, angry white ones, eager tan ones, all premade and ready at her disposal; tins of chalk-white face powder and bloody lip paint on her vanity; her father's mimicry potions on tiered shelves, shimmering the darkness; and her stage name poster—*the Ace of Anarchy*—staring back at her.

She sat at her desk, her legs finding the grooves still in the seat, and glanced at a family portrait of her mother, her, and a chubby toddler playing peek-a-boo between her legs. It felt like a hundred years ago, rather than eleven.

"I've been expecting you," came a voice from the ceiling.

Gia looked up, spotting a starfolk's white gaze in the rafters.

"It's time to open the vault so we can unleash chaos," she said.

Ella!
Do not open my closet!
Under zero circumstances.
I locked our "problem" in there. We will deal with him later.

Brigit

★—★—★— **STARPOST**—★—★—★

Dear suster,

I wuv you.

I miss you.

I want to come.

Tell me everything.

Winnie

★—★—★— **STARPOST**—★—★—★

Ella,

Do you really have bad light inside you?

From,
You'll Never Know

CHAPTER TEN

CONJURE MARKS
AND HAINTS

E lla stood in her godmother's conjure room in the Spirit
Tower before their first ever lesson for the year, waiting to
be fussed at for landing herself in detention.

"Tell me what you think? Feels like home, right?" She
watched Ella's every move. "They made me redo it a thousand
times until they felt it fit with Arcanum 'culture.' I wanted a veil
so we could practice crossing. I'd have rings forged for every
student. But no. They weren't ready for all that. Instead, they
delayed everything. 'Everything must be preapproved.' Now
I'm almost a whole month behind all the other instructors."

"You get to start on the best day of the year—Halloween."
Ella gazed all around.

It felt like she was in the cozy den of a Conjuror. Three large
trees grew in the space, their thick arms crisscrossed over her
into a thatched ceiling. Glass bottles hung like colorful stars
from the branches. A trio of boudoirs held oils and powders
and dried roots. A quartet of obsidian cabinets boasted plants

and herbs from the Underworld. Tiny doors lined the walls, each marked with a symbol and a name, entrances to offices of spirits ready for offerings to do one's bidding. A tiny part of her felt homesick for Mama and Gran and Papa . . . maybe even Winnie.

A six-foot boa constrictor dropped from one of the bottle trees' branches and licked its tongue out at Ella.

She jumped back.

"Echi, play nice," Aunt Sera cooed. "She's so happy to see you." She let the snake lick her cheek.

Ella was used to all different sorts of conjure companions, like roosters and dogs and lizards, but snakes always terrified her a little at first. Until she got to know them.

"Your mama and I are wondering what yours will be. We've got bets going. She just doesn't want a mouse showing up," she said with a chuckle.

"Don't be mean about mice," Ella replied. Mice were helpful if you made friends with them. They enjoyed a bargain. Cheese and sugar cubes usually did the trick.

"Where are the worktables?" Ella pointed at a circle of fluffy cushions.

"Put them away until we need them. They clogged the energy. Everything is already so stuffy here."

"What about Halloween decorations? All the other teachers have them."

"Ah, yes. Knew I was forgetting something." She clapped her hands. "Close your eyes."

Ella obeyed and heard her godmother take a deep breath and begin to sing. Ella's whole body warmed, and she felt like she was home again, the music of her family all around her.

"Okay, baby, open."

Ella inspected her additions, tiny skulls and pumpkins scattered about.

"So, you approve? I want to make the best impression possible—for the both of us."

Ella nodded and smiled.

Aunt Sera reached her hand toward a trellis of conjure-roses, stroking the beautiful black petals. "They don't love being outside of the Underworld or away from the heat."

Ella inhaled their musky scent.

"Speaking of which," Aunt Sera continued, "while I have you here early . . . help me move this baby Quassia to the back corner before all the commotion comes when your class shows up." She lifted a pot from the table like a delicate egg. "This one is giving me trouble."

The plant's stem curved into an upside-down smile out of the soil. Red triangle-shaped flowers were dangling bells. They hissed and writhed with volatile energy. Gran called these dangerous and irritable plants "hot plants" and kept them in a separate area of the garden and greenhouse, each one inhabiting its own personal cage like petulant birds in a quarantined aviary. Mostly, they weren't supposed to leave the fields of the Underworld except for serious conjure work.

Ella didn't like these plants. They made her afraid, their energy and will hard to cross and work with.

"Quassia," she whispered. "It can be used as a threatening root to control a spouse, mate, or child. Not very nice."

"Indeed. A nasty one," Aunt Sera replied. "But necessary to learn and classify all the Underworld plants. We will be working on these in November."

Ella helped her godmother cradle the plant, and they took tiny steps together.

Echi dropped down from the tree, startling the Quassia. The plant's flowers multiplied, then stretched into massive fingers trying to grab hold of Ella's hand.

She leaped back.

The hot plant grew to the ceiling.

"Aunt Sera!" Ella dodged its viscous flowers.

"Let's control it together," she shouted. "Cross into its will."

Ella tried to clear her mind of the fear long enough to hear the plant's life force. The plant snapped its red claws at her.

She stared it down.

"Focus," said her godmother.

The warmth of the conjure filled her, the volatile energy of the plant existing alongside it. "I can't," she stammered, and began fumbling through the song.

Aunt Sera began to sing, and Ella parroted her melody.

The hot plant's fingers recoiled, shriveling back to the size of chili peppers. The stem shrank down into its pot, curving away like a dog's tail tucked between its legs. The hissing turned into a whimper as if it was sorry.

Aunt Sera kissed Ella's sweaty forehead. "Good girl, my Conjuror. Now, should we discuss you out of bed? Detention?"

Ella's whole body still hummed from dealing with the Quassia. She didn't want to talk about anything.

"Or the fact that you've racked up quite a few demerits?" She tsked disapprovingly. "What's going on?"

Ella never imagined she would've gotten even a single demerit. "Please don't tell Mama and Papa."

Her godmother's strong gaze felt like a hot comb whisking too close to her ear. "That will depend."

"It was because of my roommate, Brigit."

"Did she tie you up?"

"No, ma'am."

"Did she put a Simon Says spell on you?"

"No, ma'am."

"Then you can't blame nobody but yourself. Shouldn't have been out of bed. So why were you sneaking around?"

Ella stared at the floor. "Just being nosy."

"Umm-hmm."

"But maybe they forgot. I haven't gotten a slip yet to serve it."

"You wish, baby girl. I got them to delay it so we could talk first and I could figure out what was going on with you. That slip will show up any day now." Aunt Sera kissed her finger and touched Ella's nose. "Speaking of nosy . . . your Mama wants a report on your conjure mark."

"Already?"

"She's worried about missing everything. The bargain was I'd send her regular reports and she'd back off, which she has." Aunt Sera flashed her own mark; the beautiful black roots slithered across her skin. Ella traced a finger along one, feeling its warmth and puffiness from her conjure work.

"It hasn't changed." Ella pivoted around. The Baptiste women didn't take *no* for an answer.

Her godmother swept up her hair and inspected the mark on Ella's neck.

"That's because you're not practicing. The more you do, the more it'll open and cross your skin. Plus, you should be casting tricks and working spells on your own, too, in your room."

"I just didn't want everyone to ask questions or stare." Ella bit her bottom lip. "You think the other students will like learning about us?"

"If they're open-minded. Our skills aren't so different. Not as much as they make it seem. They just don't understand it. Label it bad without knowing anything."

"In their handbook, it says to only channel good light. And someone sent me an anonymous starpost asking if I had bad light inside me."

"They're afraid. Short-sighted."

She told her godmother what happened in her channellors class with Dr. Bearden, describing the black light and its violet and white core.

"A beautiful twilight. It's powerful. They try to label us. Try to make us ashamed. When we were enslaved, our talents and skills adapted under brutal torture, and after freedom, there was more terror. Enduring that leaves a mark. Conjure is a bittersweet cross between rage and hope, but yet still full of love. We lived suspended. Every Conjuror from New Orleans to Havana to Cartagena to Bahía knows that. A bruised fruit is still sweet, baby."

"But it feels different to do things the way they do," Ella said. "Like when you stretch your muscles too hard. I don't know how to explain it."

"Don't do it like them; keep to the way we do things." Aunt Sera closed the gap between them. "Just know today's gonna be fine." She lifted Ella's chin. "We got blood at the root, and ain't nothing wrong with it. The only thing bad about it is what happened to us. We will find our place here. Any of these Paragons will be better for having you in it."

Her godmother's words warmed her, filling in the tiny holes left behind by all her worries and questions.

A bell-blimp floated into the room, releasing a tiny chime.

"Please don't tell Mama."

Aunt Sera nodded. "Ready?"

"Always." Ella smiled for the first time that day.

✦ ▪ ✦ ✖ ✦

THE SPIRIT TOWER HALLS SPILLED OVER WITH EXCITEMENT AS trainees moved between sessions and chased the new Halloween decorations popping up all over the Institute. Skull-covered balloons dropped chocolate Paragon coins, stormy cloud nougats, and spiraling ginger stars. Pumpkins held caramel boxes filled with wiggly animal cookies.

The heliogram of founder Shuai Chen welcomed everyone. His lightning-filled clouds swirled around a massive mechanical heart hanging from the ceiling. Its chambers spilled over with spinning cogs and gears. "The heart beats true! Enter the Spirit Tower, a place to feel more than you have before." His chaotic laugh echoed.

Her godmother hustled trainees out of the hall. "Welcome, welcome. Everyone find a cushion and claim it as your own," she called out.

Ella created a little trio in the middle and waved Jason over. Brigit hovered in the doorway.

Ella darted over to her. "Hey."

"Hey." Brigit pursed her lips and looked away.

"I'm sorry, okay?"

"Same," she replied, then cupped her hand to Ella's ear. "Did you get my note? We need to deal with that *thing* in my closet.

✦ ✦ 175 ✦ ✦

While you were gone earlier, I pretended like I wasn't mad at him and trapped him inside."

Ella thought about Feste locked away. She didn't know what they were going to do. "Sit with us?" Ella pointed to the open cushions beside Jason, and Brigit plopped down.

The room devolved into chaos despite Aunt Sera's commands.

She wished her godmother would use the shush-balloons that other instructors did. But deep down ... she really wished the other kids would respect her godmother enough to be quiet when she asked the first time. Ella knew better than to talk when grown folks were talking.

Aunt Sera clapped her hands. The candles went out, bathing the entire room in darkness.

The trainees screamed.

A candle ignited beneath Aunt Sera's face, casting an orange glow over her brown skin. "I see I've gotten your attention."

No one made a sound.

"Since today's All Hallows' Eve to some, Halloween to others, and the day before el Día de los Muertos to many, we shall begin our first conjure lesson of the year with a discussion of the Underworld." She opened her arms wide. One of her conjure maps lifted from her desk and floated above the seated group, stretching over their heads like a massive black blanket threaded with starlight. "The Conjure Arts are about crossing. Movement. Work. The crossing of waters which led to a crossing between life and death, and through pain."

"Water? Are you a secret mermaid or something?" someone shouted out.

Jason rolled his eyes, and Ella hid her grin.

Aunt Sera chuckled. "I wish. Ella, wouldn't that be an amazing new conjure talent?"

Ella flashed her godmother a smile.

"But no, unfortunately, the crossing of West Africans to the New World, the Caribbean, and South America during the Transatlantic Slave Trade is what I meant. That period and the hundreds of years after it applied pressure to our gifts, changed our marvels, so to speak. Some of us were able to restore our gifts to what they once were, while others weren't able to."

"My momma said Jamaicans aren't Conjurors," a girl named Charisse said.

"There are Conjurors everywhere," Aunt Sera corrected. "Shall we continue?"

The map illuminated. Excitement rippled through the room. Ella's anxiety lessened.

The map unfurled its contents: the souls, tiny as match flames, on their way to doors to each afterlife location, the twilight sky and its stars, all the roads of the dead filled with High and Low Walkers on their routes, the two deathbulls at the main gate, fields of plants, and more.

"Wow," she heard a nearby whisper.

"So cool," Jason replied.

"You get to go there?" Brigit leaned close.

"It's pretty amazing," Ella whispered back.

"This area of the Underworld is the suspension. It's between life and death. A place souls begin their journey to their final resting place. A very, very long time ago, the non-Fewel folk, as everyone used to be called, outsourced the divine responsibility of deathwork to Conjurors, and their gifts built this place. Think of it like a very large transit hub." She used a long glowing pointer. "There are many entrances and exits, and doors to every after-death destination."

Ella couldn't fight the big smile on her face. She surged with pride listening to her godmother talk about a place that was so important to her. A place where their ancestors lived. A place her papa was in charge of.

"Why those silly hats?" Abina asked.

Anger flashed through Ella. "They're not silly."

Brigit shot Abina a dirty look, but there were still a few chuckles.

"We don't use that word," Aunt Sera gently corrected. "Those with short top hats are Low Walkers who train to become High Walkers—the ones with the bigger top hats. The High Walkers are in charge of guiding souls to their final stops and maintaining those doors to Hades, the Elysian Fields, Annwfyn, Yomi, Mictlan, Guinee, and more. There are millions of doors to take care of and patrol. Make sure nothing or no one escapes."

"What is that big building in the center?" Samaira asked. "The one with the column in front of it."

"The Mansion of Death. The place for the Grand Walker, the man in charge of the Underworld—"

"Who?" Evan interrupted.

"His Excellency, Mr. Sebastien Durand, the father of one of our very own, Ella Durand."

Ella's cheeks warmed as her entire class stared. For the first time, she saw some awe mingled in with the suspicion and wariness.

"Isn't he evil?" Clare called out. "That's what all the news-boxes say."

Jason snorted. "Do you believe everything the news-boxes say?"

Ella tightened her fists, wondering how anyone could ever think her papa was evil.

"There's nothing bad about this place or anyone who inhabits it," she spoke up.

"Ella is right," her godmother said, tone measured. "The Underworld isn't evil or bad. It isn't hell. Though some of the doors lead to different versions of that eternal punishment—"

"But wasn't the prison made there? The Cards of Deadly Fate? And those are for evil people?" Samaira asked.

"Yes—"

"But where?" she continued to press.

Aunt Sera took a deep breath and explained: "Marvellers who have committed crimes exist inside this powerful set of conjure cards. They're made from the threads of death and act as vessels, or containers. Once sentenced, you cross into the card and are held there in perpetuity or until you're released."

More hands shot into the air with rapid-fire questions.

"I'll teach you all about it, and we'll be there soon enough. Patience. Patience." Aunt Sera used her pointer to highlight the Underworld mountain ranges.

"Maybe if you'd explain things clearly, we wouldn't have so many questions," Clare muttered.

Ella felt hot again. "Ignore them," Brigit whispered, but Ella knew she couldn't understand.

"What was that?" Aunt Sera's eyebrow lifted. At last, it seemed her patience had worn thin.

Ella braced herself. There was no response.

"I'll continue, then." She turned back to the map. "These mountains are filled with twilight stardust that's fallen and hardened into rock over millions of years. The transmuting of them has led to lots of amazing technology—"

"That's a lie," Lian challenged. "My father says you have an agenda."

"Mine said the same thing," Evan added.

Ella jumped up, feeling like she'd swallowed lightning. The map lifted higher to avoid her. "You're all wrong."

"Ella," her godmother said. "Thank you, but that's enough." She turned to look at Lian and Evan. "I have no agenda but the truth. Happy to talk to you about it anytime."

Aunt Sera clapped her hands. "I think that's enough of the map for today." She placed a hand on Ella's shoulder. "Instead, a scary story is in order. It is Halloween, after all. Ella, would you please grab that calling jar from my desk?"

Ella tried to calm down as she followed her godmother's instructions. On holidays, Ella had seen Gran create these calling jars to place on porches and altars and windows. Her skillets smoked with dandelion, tobacco, aloeswood, and devil's bit, ready to welcome the spirits to cross over for a meal.

An uneasy silence had settled over the room. Jason flashed her a thumbs-up, and Brigit glared at anyone who whispered.

"I'm not *just* going to tell you a story. What's the fun in that? And there's always several sides to one . . . and the truth." Aunt Sera took the jar from Ella's hands and motioned for her to stay put beside her. "Will it be the Lady of the Bayou in New Orleans? Or the Hungry Man, who knocks on every door until someone lets him in to eat? Maybe Murderous Mabel, who lures Mardi Gras partiers to their death in the French Quarter? Any of these spirits would have something to tell."

Everyone shouted names.

Aunt Sera winked at her and whispered, "Who should it be?"

"The Lady," Ella mouthed.

"The Lady of the Bayou, rumored to tame all the swamp beasts." She held up a slip of paper. "Who has great handwriting?"

She chose Ousmane to write the Lady's full name, then took it, dipped the edge of it in a nearby prayer candle, and watched it ignite. "Ousmane, will you assist?"

He stood.

Aunt Sera handed Ella the mason jar as she dropped the flaming slip inside. "Screw the lid tight."

The jar's ingredients heated, sizzled, and swirled into a tiny dark storm.

"What's happening?" Clare called out.

"She's coming," Aunt Sera replied.

Ella's heart jumped in her chest, her excitement bubbling over.

The dark storm settled. Aunt Sera took the jar from Ousmane. She unscrewed the lid, releasing smoke that took the shape of a Black woman dressed in white.

"Lady of the Bayou, we humbly request a story on this All Hallows' Eve. Set the records straight about all the things they say." Aunt Sera bowed.

The woman spread out her arms and took a deep breath. "Let them tell it and I'm a whole villain . . . but you haven't heard what really happened. Open your ears."

★—★—★— **STARPOST**—★—★—★

Ella,

    White light is right and yours isn't.

From,

You'll Never Know

CHAPTER ELEVEN

DETENTION

ANovember frost coated the big windows in Ella and Brigit's room. Ms. Paige dropped off a float-fire. It blazed bright, crackling with warmth as it drifted around. After showering and wrapping her favorite scarf around her wet hair, Ella retrieved the braid-hands Mama had packed. She plopped onto her bed.

Brigit looked up from the late assignments piling up on her desk. "What are you doing?"

"My hair," Ella answered.

"Are those . . ."

The lid sprang open.

"Yes." Ella plucked a vial of coconut oil and a tub of gel from another compartment. She sprinkled a few drops of oil on the braid-hands and they startled awake, stretching and cracking their knuckles.

"I've never seen you do that before." Brigit eased out of bed.

"Then you haven't been paying attention." Ella removed

her scarf, and a perfect replica of her mother's beautiful brown hands darted straight to her thick hair, sectioning and combing through her zigzag curls.

Ella ignored Brigit's staring, taking out the latest starpost she'd gotten from Masterji Thakur.

Dear Ella,

Thank you for checking in. All is well. But it's best that we hold off on meetings for now.

I hope you are enjoying those books I gave you. I look forward to discussing them with you soon.

See you in class.

Masterji Thakur

She felt worried despite his message.

Brigit eased onto the edge of her bed, still watching. Ella wanted to tell her that it was rude to sit on other people's beds . . . well, according to Gran. It was also rude to stare. She sighed and set the starpost down. "Never seen anybody get their hair done before?"

"I have, but not . . . with floating hands."

"Just a conjure trick. You can cast copies at a braid shop or beauty salon. Then Mama trained them. That way my hair is always neat." The whole process made her miss Mama. The oil smelled like her, and the sensation was so familiar she expected to glance back and find her there.

A tiny smile found its way into the corner of Brigit's mouth.

Ella tried to change the subject. "Are we going to deal with"— Ella pointed to Brigit's closet—"*that*." She'd been thinking about what they'd do about Feste. She'd been feeling bad about him being locked in there for weeks.

"He can't be trusted. I tried to talk to him. But he lies." Brigit crossed her arms over her chest. "Maybe we should leave him in there forever."

"Or maybe we should ask him some questions?" Ella craned to look at the closet door, but the braid-hands popped her scalp as a reminder to sit still. "We could find out who gave him to you."

Brigit stood, starting to pace. "I don't know."

The braid-hands finished Ella's hair and zipped back their case.

"Your hair looks nice." Brigit stared at her two fat cornrows.

"Thanks. You ready?"

"No."

"C'mon."

Brigit took a deep breath. "Fine."

They tiptoed to the closet and pressed their ears against the wood.

"You hear anything?" Brigit asked.

The door shook, and a tiny chime sounded. "Let me out!" a voice squeaked.

Ella and Brigit jumped back and exchanged glances.

"Wait." Brigit grabbed one of her blankets and held it up. "If he tries to run, I'll throw this on him. You open the door."

"Okay." Ella held her breath and turned the knob.

The door creaked open.

Feste barreled out with his hands up.

Brigit started to drop the blanket.

"Let me explain!" He backed himself into a corner. "Give me a chance to tell my side of the story!"

"We're listening." Brigit glared at him.

"I was sent with you by your grandmother, Clara."

Brigit froze, dropping the blanket at her feet. "But I don't have a grandmother. I grew up with only Ms. Mead."

"I know this comes as a shock to you, and we probably should've told you sooner, but Ms. Wilhelmina Mead was one of your grandmother's most trusted friends. A very powerful Marveller living there. The perfect guardian for you."

Ella watched shock wash over Brigit's face. "Are you okay?"

"I always knew New York CITY was a weird place . . . but not weird enough to have Marvellers there." Brigit's eyes widened.

"There's Conjurors, too, in Harlem and Brooklyn. That's what Papa says."

A look of surprise consumed Brigit's face. "Keep going, Feste. Tell me everything."

They sat on the ground as Feste paced back and forth in front of them.

"Some Marvellers live outside Marvellian cities, but it's very rare." He put a tiny stuffed hand on her knee. "I only know what she told me and what I saw after famed toymaker T. Deonn brought me alive to serve and protect a little girl." His little stitched mouth stretched into a smile.

"Where is my grandmother now?" Brigit asked.

"She used to visit you once a month when you were smaller. Remember the lady in the hat?"

"The one with the golden roses on it." Brigit nodded.

"She charged me with watching over you, alongside Ms.

Mead, and instructed me to travel with you wherever you went. Once your marvel started to show itself, we knew it was time for you to come here. The Fewel-world is cruel."

"Conjurors hate having to deal with them," Ella added.

"What is my marvel?" Brigit pulled her knees to her chest as if she was ready to curl into a little ball.

Feste touched her knitting needles and gave her a look that seemed to say she already knew the answer.

"But why would she send me away? Who is my mother?" Brigit's cheeks flushed, and tears welled in her eyes.

"I don't know. But there are some things in your pocket-box. Your grandmother tucked them away for the right time." He pointed to her nightstand.

Brigit jumped to her feet and grabbed it.

"I can show you how to open yours. They're all different." Feste did a lap around the box. With a gentle push, he flipped open the lid. Inside sat Brigit's money-card and a few knitting needles. Brigit removed the items to reveal faded illustrations of the Paragons in its base. Feste climbed inside and jumped on them, then waited.

"What are you doing?" Ella asked.

"Just wait," Feste replied. "There's a few secret compartments. They don't all open at once. Only if and when the pocket-box decides to trust you."

Nothing happened.

"Let me try," Ella offered.

Feste backflipped out and Ella thumped them again, but faster this time.

The box rattled left and right.

Brigit reached for it. "What did you do?"

"We asked it to reveal its pockets." Feste pointed into the belly of the box. Now there were dozens of stacked compartments, enough to fit at least a hundred knitting needles and more. Ella thought Brigit could fit a small library in there, too, if she were the reading kind. Some pocket-boxes even fit people.

Brigit gasped.

Ella held back a smile because she felt like Brigit was a little like her pocket-box. Full of secrets and hidden compartments that took time to open up.

Brigit ran her fingers through it. "Ms. Mead said it was my birth mother's." She touched the A.T.I. acronym. "I used to make lists of what the letters stood for. I thought it might be her name."

"Arcanum Training Institute," Ella replied.

"Yeah, I figured out that much."

Ella reached inside, feeling around for additional clasps. "You can open each one . . . and see if there's stuff hidden. Some of these have up to a hundred different pockets." Ella coveted such a treasure. "It's awesome. They don't even make these anymore. Would cost at least two hundred stellas in a vintage shop."

"How did you know how to get it to open?" Brigit asked Feste.

"There's six grooves near the outside lock. That's the knock key," he informed her. "But many use incants to hide pockets too."

"Sometimes it takes years for it to show you all its secrets," Ella said, remembering what she'd read.

Brigit riffled inside and retrieved old styluses, a moldy Marveller-bar, and a huge skeleton key imprinted with a diamond and wrapped in thread. "Weird," she said, setting the objects to the side, and fishing for more. Ella inspected the huge key, long and heavy in her hands. It reminded her of the iron keys Conjure folk put on their altars for protection or to make way for new things. *Must unlock a very old door,* she thought. But the thread around it puzzled her.

Lastly, Brigit pulled out a torn heliogram of a woman in a hat.

"That's your grandmother," Feste said as Ella showed Brigit how to press the picture and make it project. The torn projection struggled to glow, colors bleeding and fritzing, the shape struggling to animate, but Brigit didn't take her eyes off the beautiful lady tipping her hat.

Ella noticed the woman's sparkling blue eyes and peculiar smile. Brigit had the same ones.

"Where is she?" Brigit asked.

Feste bowed his head. "She died some years back, sadly."

Ella reached out and took Brigit's hand. She couldn't imagine what it was like to all of a sudden go from hearing about having a grandmother, the excitement, to having her so quickly taken away.

They sat together, watching the broken heliogram struggle to keep its shape. The woman looked like she was hiding something—like she knew something that no one else did. Ella knew there had to be more to the mysterious lady. And certainly, more to Brigit.

✦ ★ ✦ ★ ✦

THE NEXT MORNING, ELLA PULLED HER MANTLE OVER HER HEAD, preparing for detention, when she heard a tiny squeak. She yanked her hood back and spotted a tiny rottie slipping through the door. She'd come to recognize them individually by the tiny handmade collars she'd helped Jason make for them. This one was Sugar Bean.

She crouched low and said hello.

The little creature sniffed her, then pulled a piece of paper from her pouch. Ella opened it, finding Jason's scrawled handwriting.

I'll see you during detention today. It's in the
Arcanum menagerie, and I have to help the birds.
I found out about that weird elevator too.

Jason

Ella went to her desk and retrieved one of the conjure candies Mama had sent her as payment to the rottie for delivering Jason's message. She handed it a MayPop gummy. "Make sure to eat fast or else they might get angry with you." The tiny rottie zipped out the door with a flash. She turned to Brigit. "Let's go. Jason will be there today."

"Oh, good. I have something for him." Brigit grabbed a knitted square from her desk and jammed it into her pocket, then followed Ella out of the room.

An automat waited for them outside the dormitory door.

"This way, little stars!" it said.

The trollies whizzed overhead like honeybees headed for a hundred different flowers, and Ella wished she were riding one of them instead. Even on a Saturday, the Institute still exploded with activity.

"We should just take off running," Brigit teased.

"Isn't that what got us in this mess?" Ella reminded her, even though she loved seeing Brigit happy. The torn picture of her grandmother seemed to have softened her.

"I am programmed to go up to thirty miles per hour," the automat replied. "I can also lengthen your stay in detention if you'd like."

Brigit walked a little slower. "I can't try to escape again even if I wanted to." She held up her knitting needles. "They did something to them. Said if I tried to go, I couldn't take these with me. I even tested it. Walked to one of the border walls. It yanked me back so hard, I skinned my knee."

Ella spied a strange symbol on her needles. Three hash marks. "Oh!"

"I'd never leave these behind." Brigit held them to her chest.

The automat made a turn into the Arcanum menagerie.

"Your detention location," the automat ordered.

They headed to the back; a terrible smell choked the air.

"Eww!" Brigit covered her nose.

A mix of other students, some Level Twos and Level Threes, waited before a door labeled DUNG COLLECTION. She gazed around at the other unfortunate trainees who had ended up here. Siobhan and her pixies waved.

A starfolk caretaker ambled over with an armful of shovels. "Welcome to detention. I'm Deneb. You'll be removing all poop from the animal cages today. Names please." She held up a scroll.

"Brigit Ebsen."

"Ella Durand."

"Ji-hoon Kim."

"Justin A. Reynolds."

"Siobhan O'Malley."

"Greg Andree."

"Norah Richmond."

"Tochi Onyebuchi."

"If you need me, I'll be checking in on all the habitats." Deneb gave everyone their assignments on slips of paper. She turned to Ella, Siobhan, and Brigit. "You start in the aviary. Those phoenixes and impundulus got into it last night. Feathers everywhere. Get them cleaned up. Follow the sign." She pointed down a long corridor. "You can leave when it's complete. Use your best effort or you'll be doing it all over again. Neatly, completely, and with pride. That's the Institute motto. That's how mastery is done."

She pivoted and snapped her furry fingers at a Level Three girl. "Mary Pender, you're going to spend your entire third year in detention if you don't get it together. Put that Marveller-bar away before it's mine and get into that unicorn lair this instant. Their poop has to be collected and processed first."

The grumpy girl sighed and frowned. Ella didn't want to be like Mary. She didn't want to be here for detention ever again.

"And Angela Thomas, I see you trying to sneak out. Get that bucket and clean up the dragon slop. Japanese ryū get fussy when the lair isn't tidy. We don't want them to leave," Deneb barked. "I will call your mother. Ms. Julia will come up here, and we both know that's not the trouble you want. Not after last year."

The girl grabbed the bucket, her groans echoing.

Ella and Brigit held back giggles as they headed for the aviary with Siobhan. They walked down the corridor, following the signs.

"What did you do?" Brigit eyed Siobhan's pixie hanging out in the hood of her mantle.

Siobhan pointed behind her. "Pixies got me in trouble. They were stealing in the store."

Ella remembered seeing them take self-twisting hair ribbons, charm-yarn, and emo-gems.

The pixie ducked in shame.

"Now I have all these meetings about if they can stay with me or if I have to move rooms too."

"Like me?" Ella perked up. "Why?"

"Lian and Samaira complained. Then their parents called."

"Snitches," Brigit said.

"But I didn't do anything." Ella's mind combed through everything that happened the night she moved into the room.

"You didn't have to. They didn't like your tree or your saints . . ."

"Or anything." Ella felt an angry squeeze in her chest.

"You got a better roomie now." Brigit smiled at her, and Ella thought, *yes*, she definitely ended up in the best place.

The aviary spread out before them. Gilded cages held all sorts of birds she'd never seen before.

Jason dragged a bucket of feathers behind him. They were everywhere, poking out of his locs and covering his mantle.

Ella and the girls laughed.

He looked up, smiled, and waved them over. "I've been dealing with them all morning."

"What happened?" Ella gazed into the basket. It looked like an entire bird had molted all its feathers.

"I had to help Dr. Silvera negotiate a treaty between the Avian elders." He wiped the sweat from his forehead. "They hate sharing space."

"Plants are like that too." Ella thought about the red Quassia.

Siobhan's pixie darted into the aviary, and she took off after it. "Oh no! Styxie, you come back here."

Ella and Brigit laughed.

Jason led them into the aviary. "Did you get my note?"

Ella held it up. "Spill it. What did you find out about that elevator?"

"I asked the impundulu." He smiled as if what he'd just said was the cleverest thing ever.

"Huh?" Ella said.

"The what?" Brigit said.

"The lightning bird. She's the oldest inhabitant of the Arcanum Lower School. I was thinking out loud about how I could make it up to the wombies for being late, complaining about the elevator, and she overhead me," he reported. "And she likes me because I got Dr. Silvera to move them farther away from the phoenixes. It took hours."

Ella thought about Jason negotiating back and forth with birds, and it made her chuckle to herself. He was probably really good at it, like dealing with all his siblings and being stuck in the middle.

"Izulu said the elevator was made by the original architect of the Arcanum. That it either takes you where you want to go or takes you where *it* wants you to go."

"How can an elevator do that?" Brigit scratched her head.

"I don't know," he admitted. "I don't know what kind of marvel could create that, and she didn't either."

The starfolk Deneb passed by the aviary. "I hear a lot of talking and not a lot of work."

Brigit scowled and Jason jumped to work. Ella tried to distract herself by cleaning up the cages and greeting the different birds, but her thoughts swarmed in her head. Why had the elevator made her feel that tug? Maybe she'd been secretly homesick? Maybe it was a reminder that she was far away from home? And why had it taken her to the Founder's Room? Maybe it'd been a mistake?

"Jason!" a voice echoed through the space.

They all looked up, finding one of Jason's older sisters, Beatrice. They shared the same round brown face. A fat bumblebee sat atop her pretty hair bun, and Ella couldn't tell if it was fake or real.

Jason tucked into himself like a turtle. Sweat flooded his temples. "What are you doing here?"

"Mom sent—" She stopped, and her eyes found Ella, who waved, but Bea's face hardened. "You're that conjure kid?"

"Yes," Ella replied proudly.

"Jason." Bea said his name like a firework. "Let me talk to you for a second." She pulled him to the side. Ella's stomach flip-flopped because she wanted Beatrice to like her, and she didn't know why Beatrice seemed upset.

Brigit looked up, staring at Beatrice and Jason talking. She took out a quilt square from her pocket and stepped out of the cage, interrupting them. "Jason, I sort of . . . like, made this, and your sister is on it too. Well, your whole family. It's a portrait." She handed it to them. "I don't know what it means, exactly."

He reached for it. "Thank y—" He swallowed the rest of the word, his smile turning to a frown, his eyes bulging.

Bea snatched the quilt square from Jason, her teeth clenched.

"You think this is some kind of joke?" She balled the fabric and threw it in Brigit's face, then yanked Jason away.

"What's wrong?" Ella rushed to Brigit's side.

"I don't know what I did."

Ella spotted tears in Brigit's eyes as she picked up the crumpled quilt square. Ella took it from her and smoothed it.

"I . . . I . . . didn't mean to hurt his feelings. Is something wrong with me?"

Shock rippled through Ella as she examined the beautifully stitched portrait of Jason's gigantic family. Why would Brigit knit this? How would she know?

"But what is this? I've never seen it before." Brigit wiped her cheeks.

A pinch squeezed Ella's heart. Why would Beatrice and Jason get so upset? A reason she didn't want to believe bubbled up inside her.

"It's the conjure symbol." She traced her fingers over the black skull filled with diamonds and conjure-roses. "It's drawn on every door so we can find each other." Ella nibbled her bottom lip as she stared at Jason's family members, each with the conjure symbol in the center of their mantles. Her pulse raced.

Did Jason secretly hate her?

★—★—★— **STARPOST**—★—★—★

Jason,

Are you okay?

From,
Ella and Brigit

THE VAULT

Gia left the Close with a new face today. Her hair night black and her sun-kissed skin the color of warm sand. She resembled a woman fresh from the Polynesian Prefecture or somewhere equally warm. She tightened her neckscarf and wandered through Augusta's Automat Mart on Betelmore's high street, inspecting an automat. "These have gotten so much fancier since I've been gone."

"I'm a Minder Model 6800. The best there is," the tinny voice answered.

She glanced at her starfolk helper. "You think this will work?"

"Yes, madam," he replied.

"I need it to be better than the best. I need it to be perfect. I need it to follow instructions." Gia shined the very top of the automat's head.

The starfolk opened the machine's cavity, rearranging its insides. "I've programmed it to feed you the information you need and do whatever you need done. It will obey your every command."

The automat bowed.

Gia smiled. "First errand done. Please see that our new friend arrives at the Arcanum's Lower School without a hitch."

The starfolk nodded and rushed off with the machine.

Gia stepped back on the street. Thick storm clouds shifted overhead, threatening a cold autumn rain. She pulled up her hood. It would turn to snow soon. People buzzed around, zipping in and out of stores, wondering aloud if the afternoon tempest would delay their shopping.

The storm ushered in the dark by the time Gia arrived at the graveyard. She laughed to herself. "All these empty graves just for show. Marvellers scared of death, scared of their own shadows," she said, thinking of the proper burial grounds in the Underworld.

The last time she'd come here was to pay respects to her father right before the accident, before she was sentenced to life in prison. Her feet found the right path.

The Trivelino family vault rose above her, its emblem pulsing after detecting her presence. She traced her fingers over the sock and buskin masks—one sad, tragic face and one happy, comedic one—waiting for the door to open. But it didn't. She tried again. She'd seen both her mother and father do it so many times during her childhood, squirreling away money from their business to avoid the prying eyes—and pockets—of the bankers of the Marvellian Mint. "What is happening?"

She looped around the stone, looking for signs of damage or

forced entry. Nothing. She tromped back to the front and tried one final time.

The emblem sparked, then a message appeared in the stone:

THOSE WHO SEEK ENTRY MUST BE PAIRS BONDED BY BLOOD. ONLY TOGETHER SHALL YOU CLAIM WHAT YOU DESIRE.

"Pairs?" Gia shouted. "There is no one else but me! I am the heir . . ." Her voice tapered off, and she thought about the family portrait on her desk, the tiny toddler clutching her leg. Gia squeezed her eyes shut. "Mother, what have you done?"

She punched the stone. Her hand found its way to a locket she always wore—one that held a tiny portrait of her late daughter.

"The child is dead."

CHAPTER TWELVE
SMILE FOR THE NEWS-BOXES!

After dinner, Ella and Brigit spilled out of the dining hall with the rest of the students headed back to the dormitories.

"Jason never showed up," Brigit said. "You think we should go check on him?"

"Maybe I can send a rottie or we can find his roommate, Miguel?" Ella felt desperate to talk to Jason before they all went home for winter break in a few weeks. She wanted to know how he really felt about Conjurors, how he really felt about her.

Brigit shrugged as they made their way to the dormitory halls. "I just want to tell him it was an accident. I don't know why I create half the things I make."

The ceiling overhead sparkled, and a starpost dropped down into Ella's hands. She quickly broke the seal:

Dear Ella and Brigit,
    I can't talk about that thing right now, okay?
Everyone is watching.

I'll get in trouble.

Jason

P.S.: I'm leaving for winter break today. My family is taking a trip to the Mer-Kingdoms of Polynesia. My father was appointed diplomat to all magical creatures still living outside of the Marvellian cities. Can you send me my classwork and homework please?

Ella and Brigit exchanged glances. Why would Brigit's knitted square get him in trouble? Or was he ashamed to be even associated with something conjure related? The thought made her sick to her stomach. He was supposed to be her friend.

"Curfew approaches. Two hours until lights out. Make your way to your rooms," the Tower Advisers shouted through the halls. Level Ones and Level Twos scampered toward their dorms.

Ella and Brigit headed for the Hydra Tower when Headmarveller MacDonald called out Ella's name.

It felt like a thunderclap.

Ella whipped around. Both Headmarvellers stood at the hallway entrance. "Can we speak to you, privately?"

Everyone went quiet and turned to stare at her.

"I'll meet you back in the room." Brigit flashed her a supportive smile, then darted into the Hydra Tower.

Nosy onlookers watched as Ella approached the Headmarvellers.

Headmarveller MacDonald motioned for her to walk with them. "We'd love to take a few heliograms together to commemorate and document your time here with us."

"Okay," Ella replied.

"We'd mail one to your parents, of course. We've been sending regular correspondences as requested." Headmarveller Rivera led the way to the entry hall, where dozens of reporters clustered.

As they were spotted, the camera clicks echoed, blinding Ella with flashes. "Is there something going on?" Ella was ushered in front of the crowd.

"Just a few local reporters from Betelmore. Everyone is so excited that you're here, Ella." Headmarveller MacDonald walked ahead to dole out instructions while Headmarveller Rivera moved on top of the Arcanum seal, orchestrating a pose.

"You do like it here, right?" Headmarveller Rivera fussed with the papel picado on her collar. "We've been good to you, yes?" Her eyebrow hitched.

"Yes," Ella said, pretty sure Headmarveller Rivera didn't actually want to hear the truth.

"That's very good. Throughout our history, many communities have struggled to acclimate to the Marvellian way. They each faced their unique set of challenges, but our global society has become more welcoming, more open over time. We hope you feel that way. We hope that the Arcanum represents the best of our community."

More clicks, more flashes. Ella wasn't sure why Headmarveller Rivera was telling her these things.

Headmarveller MacDonald rushed back over and stood to Ella's left. "Ready? Big smile for the news-box reports, okay?"

Ella nodded and cheesed for the cameras. The reporters shouted her name, asked her to look left and right, up and down, smile with more teeth, give a silly face. Her cheeks almost hurt by the end of it. She watched how quickly they loaded their film into the news-boxes, sending out tiny projections of her throughout the Marvellian world.

"How are you faring?" one reporter asked. "Have you been able to keep up with the sessions?"

"I love all of them," she replied with the Headmarvellers smiling on.

The questions piled on top of one another.

"What Paragon will conjure fit into?"

"Looking forward to your first Gatherfeast after the New Year?"

"Any interest in Marvel Combat? Think you've got what it takes to be a champion?"

"Do you feel safe? Even with the threats?"

Ella's jaw dropped. "Threats?" Ella looked up at Headmarveller MacDonald. "What threats?"

"That's enough for tonight." Headmarveller Rivera ushered the reporters out the front door and into the night.

Ella watched as they pressed their cameras to massive windows, trying to take more pictures. A few starfolk and automats rushed them toward the Arcanum docks.

Headmarveller MacDonald smiled at her. "Before you run off to bed, shall we have a wee chat?"

Ella gazed down the Headmarveller's Hall, not wanting to go to their offices, not wanting this whole thing to feel like she was in trouble, but a weird tingle in her stomach made her think otherwise. "Why were they asking me about threats?"

"It's not an issue, Ella. We didn't want to worry you or your parents. There will always be people who try to thwart change,"

Headmarveller Rivera said. "This Institute is the safest place in the world, I assure you. So many great Marvellians lent their marvels to fortifying it."

Ella didn't quite understand what she was talking about but followed Headmarveller MacDonald. Photo-balloons swarmed overhead, zipping in and out of the Dean of Discipline's den.

The wrought-iron doors opened as Headmarveller Mac-Donald approached.

Ella froze. "I don't want to." What if people thought she was in trouble?

The Headmarvellers exchanged glances.

"We can talk in the hall," Headmarveller Rivera replied. "We just want to make sure you're feeling like the Institute is a good fit for you."

"Are you making friends?" Headmarveller MacDonald rubbed his red beard.

"Yes."

"Are you enjoying your sessions? Not just your godmother's?" She nodded.

"Good, good." Headmarveller Rivera pursed her lips.

Headmarveller MacDonald took a deep breath. "We need to ask you a question . . . and it's of a sensitive nature, so we hope you understand."

Headmarveller Rivera's warm brown eyes found Ella. "This isn't an accusation, and we will also be asking other students, but your old roommate Samaira Al-Nahwi is missing her lantern. Remember the one on her nightstand?"

The question surprised Ella. "I remember." Her pulse hummed. What exactly was she asking her?

"It's a family heirloom. Samaira is very distressed, as you can imagine," Headmarveller MacDonald added. "Have you been back into your old room in the Ursa Minor Tower?"

"No," Ella replied.

They exchanged glances again.

"Are you sure?"

Those three words burned. Ella's cheeks flamed. "Do you think I took it?" The only thing Ella had ever stolen in her whole life was a dollop of raw cookie dough when Gran turned her back in the kitchen. She knew what part of the Underworld thieves were sent to, and she wanted no part of that. "I didn't."

"It would be okay if you were curious. I know the Marvellian world is new to you and you're getting used to all its wonders." Headmarveller Rivera's crown of papel picado animals smiled at Ella.

But anger exploded inside Ella. Her hands and feet tingled with rage. "I didn't take it!"

She darted down the hall. The Headmarvellers called out to her. She ran as fast as she could before the tears rushed out. She didn't want anyone to see her crying. Tears blurred everything in her path.

But she didn't stop running.

MEMORIES LONG FORGOTTEN

Gia stood outside the fae teahouse Éire & Seel. Tucked away at the edge of the low street, it was marked only by a single flower on the door. Each Betelmore quarter used to be filled with all sorts of entertainment before Marvellians turned cold and dry. They used to love a good show, but laughter seemed banned now. Perhaps she'd caused the end of it all.

She lifted the knocker, ready to step through the veil and enjoy herself.

A squat woman opened the door; shabby garments almost swallowed her. "You know the price."

Gia filled the woman's gnarled hands with shiny trinkets and plenty of gold stellas.

"Very nice." The woman flashed a toothless smile, then let her enter.

As Gia trailed her down a long hall, the woman transformed step-by-step into one of the most beautiful women she'd ever seen. Iridescent skin, bright eyes, and ears elegantly pinched at the tops.

The room unfolded; cozy alcoves held luxurious cushions and curious visitors. Servants whizzed in and out, slipping behind silk screens or pushing out papered wall panels. They wheeled in carts brimming over with fae rose creams, persimmons and pomegranates, honey croissants, and sticky saffron cake.

Her stomach growled, and her mouth watered; it'd been days since she ate a full meal. Thick perfume swirled in the air, relaxing her muscles instantly.

"What's your pleasure tonight?" The woman ushered her into a luxurious booth. "Beautification treatment? Care to join a gambling table and test your fate? Or have you come to forget?"

"I need to remember."

"Ah, then I have just the thing for you." She plucked a fat teapot from a nearby cart and set a cup before Gia.

The peculiar porcelain changed color as the hot silvery liquid steamed; tiny primrose-pink tulips bloomed, winking and stretching their petals along the white curves of the handle.

Gia sipped, waiting for the tea to do its work, to allow her to remember the night that she'd lost everything. She had to remember the time of death of the child. That was the only way to enact her plan to get into the family vault.

The Cards of Deadly Fate had dulled her senses, erasing the edges of memories while she'd been suspended between life and death.

Her vision went black, and she let herself tumble forward into darkness. Back onstage, she'd given the performance of her life. The nauseous hum of the crowd rushed back, eleven years later . . . and the sound of his bones snapping as she pulled the threads of life from Phineas Astley.

Her rival had challenged her to a duel in order to show the Marvellian world who, in fact, was the best ringmaster of them all. A contest comprising three acts of marvelous magic. The victor won the other's fortune—and glory. She'd won the first round, lost the second, and struggled with the third.

She rewatched the scene as if it were happening again.

His incessant laughter drove her to the very edge. "Women are no ringmasters. Stick to the sideshow. Your father did it better."

Her rage bubbled up, her marvel out of control. She muttered an indefensible incant. The light burst out of her, ripping him in two. The crowd was soaked in blood as if a sky of red paint had rained down. Her mother held her pint-size daughter in the front row. The toddler's very blond hair now crimson.

The screams overpowered the big top's clock chiming. Gia gazed up: it was 9:22 p.m.

Gia's eyes snapped open. The memories fresh, so tangible she could almost taste the blood.

She'd spill more this time.

CHAPTER THIRTEEN

BLUEPRINTS

Ella darted into the empty Taste Tower and tucked herself behind one of the puffy couches. She thumbed her conjure-cameo, thinking about squeezing it to contact Mama and Papa. But she didn't need Mama nosing around and making everything worse. She could solve her own problems. Or at least try.

She tried to calm down, wiping away her tears and swallowing down all the anger she felt.

Someone called her name.

Ella peeked out from her hiding place.

Masterji Thakur waved.

She wiped her cheeks and came out. "Are you mad at me too?"

His face softened. "Now, why would I be?"

She shrugged, thinking back to their last meeting.

"Headmarveller MacDonald said you got upset, so I came to find you. Is that all right?"

She nodded.

"What happened?"

The warmth of his gaze freed Ella's tears. "They're trying to make me feel like I did something . . . like I don't belong here. Why?"

"But you do belong." Masterji Thakur gave her a big hug. "And I can prove it. Come with me, Ella."

Masterji Thakur put his arm around Ella, and together, they walked down the corridor. Big windows revealed towers trimmed with ribbons of November snow. The two sky lakes were frozen solid, and the trio of glasshouses glittered with a light sheen of ice.

Ella felt the familiar tug starting again as they approached the RESTRICTED LIFT. She thought about telling Masterji Thakur that she'd been inside before but decided against it.

Masterji Thakur inserted a special coin into the elevator and the doors shut.

It shot straight down, then left and right. Layer upon layer of the Institute flew by so fast it made her light-headed.

"The Institute is a palimpsest all its own. Remember that word I taught you?"

"It's where words have been written on top of the original text." She'd written out the word in her notebook over and over again, loving the way it sounded and the idea of words crossing over and under one another.

"Very good." He pointed out of the elevator window. "The real Arcanum heart is buried."

The elevator stopped before a large black door. THE FOUND-ER'S ROOM. The place the elevator had tried to take her before.

"This way." Masterji Thakur fished a key from his pocket.

The door creaked open to reveal a small hallway flanked by portraits.

"Wow." Ella felt that bone tug again. "Where are we?"

"The very first space ever built at the Arcanum Institute." Masterji walked ahead to the first portrait. "I used to come here a lot. Trying to understand the founders. Trying to understand their ultimate desires when forming this place."

Ella's heart hammered. The tug grew stronger as she surveyed the room, visiting each founder's wall portrait.

"Whose mustache is better?" Masterji Thakur put his face beside the portrait of Louis Villarreal to compare twitching mustaches. "Back home in Rajasthan, I used to win competitions."

"Definitely yours." She stretched on her tiptoes to look into the eyes of Indira Patel, and she spotted three hidden daggers in her hair. "Did they all get along?"

"They were united in their purpose, but of course, there was tension. Whose customs got to be followed? Whose protocols were the best? They had to figure out a way to blend. To take the best everyone had to offer and turn it into something new . . . marvelling." Masterji Thakur led the way down the hall. "But you haven't seen the best part."

Ella followed him into a hexagonal room filled with a circular table and five chairs. Thick, glowing paper hovered over it. "What are those?" she asked.

"The Arcanum blueprints," Masterji Thakur replied.

Her heart fluttered as she stepped closer and closer to the floating blueprints, her eyes widening as the stark white lines on the iron-blue paper flickered every few seconds. Each miniature tower stretched high, each little trolley snaked along its route, and each corridor boasted its session rooms. "They look like . . ." Ella looked up at Masterji Thakur, perplexed.

Masterji Thakur's mustache quirked, and his eyes held a spark that gave her the courage to say it.

"Conjure maps."

"See, my dear? You belong—" Masterji's words garbled and he started coughing. The same terrible sound escaped his throat like that day at the Arcanum Cardinal.

Ella panicked, rushing to his side. "Oh no! Are you okay?"

Masterji Thakur's eyes bulged, and he took a handkerchief from his pocket, trying to cover his mouth. The squeak in his voice sent a shiver through her. He grabbed at his jacket pocket before yanking out a stylus.

"Should we go to the infirmary?" Ella scrambled.

He shook his head and doubled over. "Paper," he rasped.

Ella's hands shook as she searched for loose paper. She found a sheet in a nearby drawer.

Masterji Thakur started to scribble, then fell to his knees. Ella filled with more panic. She put a hand to her chest, afraid her heart would leap out.

Sweat soaked the edges of his turban, the colors cycling in rapid succession. His throat spasms grew louder and louder. He scratched messy words on a page:

CONJURORS WERE HERE!

"But . . . but . . . I don't understand!" Ella said. Inside her head grew a massive web of questions in need of untangling.

Masterji Thakur broke into another coughing fit.

Ella raced to the wall and grabbed a circuit-phone. The tiny buzz filled her ears, and she thought she might not be able to hear the other speaker over her thundering heart.

"Arcanum Operator, how may I direct your call?" said a voice on the other end.

Ella blurted out what had happened to Masterji Thakur.

"We're sending help right away."

The line went dead. Ella rushed back to Masterji Thakur's side. His throat spasms grew worse with each passing second.

Moments later, the doors snapped open and three Arcanum doctors marched in. She recognized only one, Dr. Winchester. His ancient gaze found her and he scowled.

"Mitha!" one of them said.

Masterji Thakur crumpled the paper and slipped it into her pocket before falling to the ground.

They ran over to him.

"I am Dr. Choi." The woman put a hand on her shoulder. "Are you okay?"

"Yes," Ella squeaked out, unable to keep her eyes off Masterji Thakur. Dr. Choi nodded, then darted back to Masterji Thakur.

Dr. Winchester's eyes narrowed. "I hope you weren't down here meddling in Arcanum business, young lady."

Ella started to defend herself, but the other Arcanum doctor stepped forward. "Ella, is it? Come with me."

Ella reluctantly left the room.

"I am Dr. Slade." Her red hair was a wild tangle around her shoulders.

"What's happening to Masterji Thakur? Will he be okay?" Ella's worries jammed all together. "What's wrong with him?"

They entered the RESTRICTED LIFT. Dr. Slade kept her hand planted on Ella's shoulder. She stared at Ella for such a long time that Ella waited and waited for her to say something, anything, but she didn't. Ella started to feel sick to her stomach.

The elevator doors slammed shut, and it zipped left and then bolted up.

"What happened before we arrived, Ella?" Dr. Slade asked. "What were you doing in the Founder's Room?"

Ella slipped a hand into her mantle pocket, where the crumpled paper lived. "On a tour."

"At this hour? After curfew?" Her severe frown was a straight line. "The Founder's Room isn't a place for trainees."

"Masterji Thakur is my mentor."

The woman dug her fingers into Ella's shoulder.

"What did he tell you?"

"Nothing."

Dr. Slade held her gaze. Ella felt like she was trying to pry into her thoughts. Finally, she let her go and turned away.

"Have a good night, Ella," she said, teeth clenched.

Ella began to respond, but something told her this wasn't the time to be polite. She shot out of the elevator. What had Masterji meant—and how did Conjurors get there?

One thing was certain: Conjurors weren't new to the Arcanum. She belonged there just as much as the other students. Ella felt a familiar spark rising in her spirit. It was the feeling of home.

Now she had to figure it out.

CHAPTER FOURTEEN
KNITTING VISIONS

Two weeks later, Ella walked down the hall toward the Hydra Tower, clutching her conjure-cameo, thinking about summoning Mama to tell her about what happened to Masterji Thakur. She still hadn't been able to make sense of what happened. He wasn't answering her starposts or teaching classes. Headmarveller Rivera had reported that he'd come down with a bad cold. But something nagged at her, and she couldn't quite believe it. Mama would know what to do and how to help him. Maybe she could send a spell to help him get better.

She ducked past kids dragging their marvel-valises from the dorms. Was everyone leaving early for winter break? It made her think of how much she missed Jason and how desperate she was to talk to him.

"Stop running!" an automat shouted at her.

Ella ignored it, eager to get back to her room. She rounded a corner, smacking straight into Clare and her news-box. It sailed in the air, then crashed and cracked.

"Star's teeth!" Clare tried to gather the pieces. "Look what you did!"

"I'm so sorry." Ella picked up the crank and the now broken bulb. "I didn't see you."

"Ugh, now I have to get Daddy to send me another one." She cradled the busted news-box. "He's going to be so mad."

"Tell him it was my fault. I can pay for it." Ella's heart raced, the guilt swirling inside her.

"Do you even have Marvellian money?" Clare inspected her from head to toe.

Her words felt like a slap. "Of course."

"Daddy wouldn't take it anyway. He doesn't even want me to *talk* to you. But I'll be telling him what you did." She strode off.

Ella didn't have time to think about Clare's threat and resumed running. She climbed the Hydra Tower staircase two steps at a time, then barreled into the room shouting, "Brigit!"

But she found a frazzled Brigit throwing things at Feste.

"What's going on?" Ella ducked behind the trunk of her bottle tree, eager to avoid being hit by a flying object.

"Someone's been spying on me."

Feste hid behind the foot of her bed. "Calm down!" He waved his tiny stuffed hands in the air. "It wasn't me."

"What happened?" Ella said. "I thought you forgave him." She'd seen such a change in Brigit since discovering the heliogram of her grandmother. They'd stay up late listening to Feste's stories about her. Brigit had started to pay more attention in class and ask more questions about marvels and Marvellians. It'd seemed like she was sinking into the fact that she belonged here.

Brigit kept hurling objects. "I thought he was telling me the truth!"

"I am! I am!" Feste waved an appointment card at Ella. Popsicle red and blinking like a siren. A mandatory meeting.

Ella plucked it from Feste but maintained her distance, still skeptical about the talking doll.

Her eyes scanned the message:

Dear Brigit Ebsen,

It has been brought to our attention that your knitting has revelatory information, and thus we must investigate. Please bring your needles and the latest quilt you've been working on to Dr. Karlsson's office immediately. She's expecting your arrival. If you are more than ten minutes tardy, an automat will escort you.

LOCATION: **Vision Tower, seventh floor, office #8**

Thank you for your cooperation.

Good marvelling,
Dean Nabokov, Dean of Discipline, Arcanum Lower School

Brigit paced. "I bet it's that starfolk kidnapper. I swear I'll lock him in a closet too."

"The starfolk can change their sizes and would easily slip beneath the door," Feste informed her.

Brigit lobbed another shoe in his direction, and he cartwheeled out of the way, the little jingles on his hat tinkling.

"You're going to be late," Ella said.

"I'm not going."

"You have to." Ella put a hand on her shoulder, and Brigit startled out of her rage. "I'll go with you."

"But I don't want to."

"They'll probably take your knitting needles if you don't."

Tears filled Brigit's eyes, and she tried to quickly sweep them away. Ella hugged her.

Brigit's appointment card turned an angry red.

"We have to go," Ella said.

Brigit sighed, then turned to Feste. "You stay put."

Ella and Brigit ran the entire way to the Vision Tower, arriving without a minute to spare. They dodged trainees pouring out of forecasting labs, talking about their moon prophecies. Brigit accidentally bumped into a tall older boy.

"Watch it, onesie," he barked.

Brigit grumbled. "You ever want to scream in their faces? Use your marvel to shrink them? If I could knit a spider's web, I'd trap them just to see them freak out."

Ella giggled.

"You could do it. Punish them. Send them to the Underworld or something."

Ella swallowed the rest of her laugh. The warnings her gran always issued drummed through her: *Whatever is conjured with an ill heart will backfire.* "I can't. I mean, I wouldn't."

"I'd send them to the worst hell if they made me angry."

"We're not allowed to be angry," Ella replied.

Brigit scoffed. "I'm angry all the time."

"You don't get in trouble for it."

"Oh," was all Brigit managed to say as they took the elevator to the seventh floor.

Dr. Karlsson's office door glowed. Stags made of silver galloped along its perimeter, and tiny snowflakes fell.

Brigit lifted the large knocker and let it drop with a thud.

"Enter!"

The door creaked open.

They walked into a cave-like room. Jagged brown walls sloped overhead; bright murals boasted more stags and a few trolls. A woman sat at a large desk surrounded by looms making their own tapestries and blankets. Baskets upon baskets of wool and yarn were stacked in perilous towers. Spindles spun thread on their own. She rocked in her chair, her back to Ella and Brigit.

"Dr. Karlsson . . . it's me, Brigit Ebsen." She eased closer, then glanced back at Ella.

Ella urged her forward. "And me, Ella Durand, her roommate."

The woman's chair swiveled. Her eyes were fogged over, the pupils the color of a stormy sky. Just like Brigit's when she knitted. She worked yarn around needles. *Click-click-clack.* That tiny familiar sound sent a ripple through Ella.

"Just one second, girls. The universe is transmitting." Her hands moved so fast; Ella felt sick trying to watch them. Even faster than Brigit's hands could. The cloth under her needles exploded in length.

Brigit and Ella exchanged terrified glances.

The woman's eyes finally cleared, revealing a brilliant crystal blue, and she set down her work.

"Ah, yes, Brigit . . . and Ella." Dr. Karlsson smiled.

Brigit handed the woman the appointment card.

Her bright eyes combed over both girls. "I am Dr. Karlsson,

and I work with the Level Fours who have forecasting marvels. But Headmarveller Rivera asked me to speak to you. Can you tell me a bit about the things you knit?"

Brigit shifted her weight left and right before answering. "Sometimes it's nothing . . . you know . . . like images of things I'll be doing the next day or like warnings of things I might get in trouble for."

Ella was shocked. She'd had no idea these were the things Brigit was knitting.

"How long have you been doing it?"

Brigit took a deep breath and looked over at Ella.

Ella flashed her an encouraging smile.

"I fall into, like, these dazes, almost like falling asleep with my eyes open. But I never knew why. My guardian said I made my first pair of knitting needles out of two sticks when I was five, and then my second from two pencils at seven." She bit her bottom lip. "I sometimes even knit in my sleep. It was always something I could just do. The only thing I'm good at."

"Very interesting." Dr. Karlsson rose from her chair, her red Marvellian mantle trailing her as she stepped closer. "Do you see things as you create? Or are they always surprises afterward?"

Brigit jumped. "How'd you know? Someone is spying on me. That must be why I'm even here in the first place."

"Calm yourself, child. No need to get defensive." Dr. Karlsson chuckled. "Sounds like you might have a timesight marvel, and it shows up in your knitting."

"What's that?" Brigit's eyebrow lifted.

"You have the ability to see images of the past, present, and future as you knit. Events left on the threads of the universe. Like the Norns of old."

"Norns?" Ella said.

"Don't worry much about that. Just means that you will be a Marveller with a Paragon of Vision. My very own group. We'll be proud to have you. The eyes are wise!"

Brigit gazed at her.

Ella's stomach pinched with surprise envy.

"Can I see some of the things that you knit?" Dr. Karlsson asked. "You sent Dr. Bearden into quite a tizzy. I was very delighted."

Brigit laughed.

"What did you make that got her so mad?" Ella asked.

"Dr. Bearden has a farting problem—"

"*Flatulence* would be the nicer word," Dr. Karlsson added.

"I knitted her with all the beans she loves to eat and the stomachache she was about to have that day." Brigit smiled. "I didn't mean to." She dropped to one knee and dug through her satchel. She handed Dr. Karlsson a bundle of small blankets and quilt squares. "I've been knitting the same thing over and over again lately, though. A woman's face. And I don't know why."

Dr. Karlsson unfolded the bundle. Each one held the face of a woman wearing clown makeup and a strange, sinister smile.

Ella had seen the image on Brigit's blankets before and assumed it was someone Brigit knew. Seeing these up close made Ella's stomach twist with equal parts fear and curiosity.

"Do you know who she is?" Dr. Karlsson ran her fingers over the threads.

"No," Brigit answered.

"Is she bad?" Ella craned to have a closer look. The knitted portrait looked almost real, as if any minute, the woman would burst out laughing.

Dr. Karlsson pursed her lips. "I'm more interested in why you might be knitting this particular face."

"Who is it?" Brigit asked in desperation.

"Gia Trivelino, the Ace of Anarchy. A once bright student who fell into evildoings." Dr. Karlsson rubbed her hands together. "Very misguided. Didn't fit in."

"I've seen that name in the library," Ella admitted.

"She was very damaging to our school—and our community."

"What did she do?" Brigit asked.

"It doesn't matter," Dr. Karlsson said. "She's far, far away now. Locked up in those cards. Where she belongs. Never you mind. Nothing to worry you."

"But why am I knitting her?" Brigit asked.

"I've heard the kids whispering about the Aces now that . . ." Dr. Karlsson's eyes found Ella. "Sometimes images can get lodged in our brain as Paragons of Vision. We are influenced by those around us. Must certainly be a mistake."

Brigit and Ella exchanged a look.

"You're very talented." Dr. Karlsson patted Brigit's shoulder. "I'll be glad to have you in my sessions come your fourth year."

Ella felt another pinch. Both Brigit and Jason knew which Paragon they'd end up in, knew where they belonged, and Ella was still trying to figure it all out.

But she tried to swallow it down. To be happy for Brigit.

As Ella and Brigit walked back to the Hydra Tower, Ella listed out all her theories about why Brigit might really be knitting this woman. "Maybe you saw her face in one of the library books, or maybe you saw an old news-box."

"I haven't seen any of those things." Brigit's shoulders slumped. "I feel like this is a bad thing. I used to just know small things . . . like the right numbers for Ms. Mead to play in the Quick Pick lottery or if it would rain or when I'd have a bad day. Then it started to get worse. I guess that's why I'm here."

Ella took Brigit's hand. Brigit stopped. Her lip trembled. "But seriously, why am I knitting this person? I don't believe what Dr. Karlsson said."

"Come home with me for winter break." Ella squeezed Brigit's hand. She knew she should've asked Mama first, but she felt like it was an emergency and she'd understand. Hopefully. "We'll figure it out. I promise."

The Arcanum Training Institute for Marvelous and Uncanny Endeavors

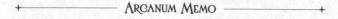

TO: Headmarvellers MacDonald & Rivera
FROM: Doctor Karlsson

Dear Headmarvellers,

I've spoken with Brigit Ebsen and find her to be a prickly pear of a delight. The images she's knitting puzzle me. I never thought I'd see Gia's face again. Why would she be knitting this criminal, this stain on our society? But I'll investigate and report back. May I ask who alerted you to Brigit knitting these images?

All the good light to you both and happy winter moon!

Best,
Freja Karlsson

★—★—★— **STARPOST**—★—★—★

Dear Mama,

Can Brigit come home with me for the winter break? She doesn't have anywhere to go. Pretty please?

Love,

Ella

★—★—★— **STARPOST**—★—★—★

Ella,

Yes, she can come home with you. But don't spring things like this on us, baby. You know I don't like last-minute company.

Love,

Mama

P.S.: I hope you have a plan for her because we all know houseguests are like fish . . . they go bad after three days, and I want no fussing during the holidays.

★—★—★— **STARPOST**—★—★—★

Dear Masterji Thakur,

Are you feeling better? I came by your office and they said you left early for winter break.

I am worried. I hope you're okay.

From,

Ella

CHAPTER FIFTEEN

THE RED BOOK

Three weeks later, Ella was back home and folded up in her grandmother's arms.

"You don't even look like my baby anymore," Gran said. "Don't smell like her neither. Been up in the sky too long." Ella hadn't even made it across the threshold before she got caught in a big hug. "Learn anything worth repeating up there?"

"Let her breathe," Mama fussed at her own mother. "Been a long journey from the pier."

Gran looked over Ella's shoulders, spotting Brigit. "Who you brought with you, baby?"

Brigit's face turned bright red.

"This is my friend from school." Ella pulled Brigit closer so Gran could do her usual inspection. "Brigit, this is my grandmother."

She wrapped her arms around Brigit, squeezing her tight. "Welcome!"

Brigit's eyes bulged with a startled yet happy shock.

Ella gazed all around at the Mississippi farmhouse where they spent most Christmases. It smelled and felt like home, even if there were some changes. The plants had grown in the windows, and one of the black cats had had a litter, and the wallpaper had changed from slate gray to haint blue. There were new saints from the New Orleans house on the mantel now, cheering and clapping at her, and protection orbs hung from the ceiling. The Christmas decorations had already been arranged without her.

She'd missed everything.

The tree twinkled in golds and reds, the prayer candles were nestled with holly, the stockings wiggled with glee, and the ceiling held fake snowflakes ready to shower down.

"Ella! Ella!" Winnie barreled down the hall and into Ella's arms. Her sister had grown a little and now had plaits all down her back. A surprise pinch of sadness hit her. She'd wanted to go away so badly, and now she didn't get to see everything.

Winnie paused and stared at Brigit. "Who is that?"

"My roommate, Brigit."

Brigit waved at her.

"But you had three roommates." Winnie gazed at Brigit with big, nosy eyes.

"Well, now it's just Brigit and me. Which I like better anyways."

Winnie didn't hear the second part of her sentence because she'd already skipped over to Brigit, cooing over Feste, taking Brigit's hand to drag her off to play.

"Wash up for dinner," Gran ordered. "And make sure your room is ready for your guest."

While Winnie monopolized Brigit, Ella went to her bedroom and opened her little red door to find the family's dirt dobbin perched on the canopy of her bed. His usual dust storm rained down on her blanket. "Couldn't even let me have one night here before you made trouble," she said with a smile, having to admit to herself that she'd missed him a little.

He stared back with big droopy eyes, then let out a wail that sent another storm of dust through her room. "You're not Ella. You don't even smell like her. You're somebody else. I want my Ella back."

"Shoo . . . shoo," Ella hollered even though she usually loved it when he'd appear in her room or chase her around, making tornadoes together until Mama fussed about the mess.

He disappeared with a poof.

She was still *herself*. Or so she thought.

Everything in the room looked in order—her tiny desk still had her undisturbed knickknacks, and her replica of the Arcanum Institute still floated over her worktable perfectly assembled. No evidence of an unauthorized Winnie visit.

A trundle bed had been set up for Brigit. She fluffed the pillows, then checked her tiny bathroom and set out a towel. She wanted Brigit to be comfortable. She wanted Brigit to like it here. She wanted Brigit to think Conjurors were clean and nice.

The door burst open. Winnie dragged Brigit by the hand. "This is where you'll be staying even though my room is better."

"Leave her alone," Ella told Winnie.

"It's fine." Brigit smiled down at a grinning Winnie.

"Gran said get ready for dinner." Ella turned Winnie around. "So wash your face. You've got a chocolate mustache."

"Brigit gave me a chocolate Paragon coin. One with the blinking eye on it." Ella closed the bedroom door in Winnie's face and locked it.

"She's cute." Brigit did a loop around the room.

"Or annoying." Ella's stomach squeezed as Brigit inspected her space. She wondered what she thought of it.

"You got a lot of stuff." Brigit plopped down on the trundle bed.

"Yeah." Ella didn't know if she meant that in a good way or a bad way. "Mama says I'm a pack rat."

"At Ms. Mead's, we weren't allowed to have a lot of stuff. We lived in dorms. Sort of like at the Arcanum, but with rows of bunk beds. Only one bathroom. But Ms. Mead made me a pod."

"A what?"

Her blue eyes lit up as she described it: a tiny playhouse on stilts, shaped like a honeycomb, with the best view of New York City.

"I miss it sometimes." Brigit took out her knitting needles. Ella gaped when she saw the binding symbol was no longer there. "What? You're staring."

"Your needles."

"Yeah, so?"

"It's just . . . I'm surprised they took off the incant."

"Said they trusted me to come home with you." Brigit looked away. "Didn't think I'd run away from your house."

Ella picked at her quilt. "Is that true?"

"Maybe. I don't know yet. Only takes twenty-three hours by bullet train to get to New York City. I looked it up."

Ella nibbled her bottom lip. She most certainly didn't want

Brigit to make her escape when the Headmarvellers were trusting her and her parents to look after Brigit. But most of all, she didn't want her to leave and not get to laugh with her every day or see her scowl at this thing or that.

Winnie banged on the door and shouted through it: "Dinner! Gran said Brigit could sit next to me."

Ella sighed, opened the door, and let Winnie lead the way to the dining room. A chandelier of half-burnt candles cast a warm glow over their long table. Another large Christmas tree sat in the corner.

"Everyone sit, sit," Gran said.

Gumbo stretched under the table waiting for any wayward piece of chicken or lost sausage to come his way. Brigit jumped at the sight of him.

"He doesn't mean any harm," Gran said. "A big kitten."

"But he's an alligator." Brigit eased into her chair beside Winnie.

"It's just Gumbo," Winnie replied. "And this is Greno." She pointed to the frog sitting in a nearby teacup.

Gran shooed Paon off the table. The rooster squawked.

"Conjure companions, right?" Brigit asked.

"Yep." Gran looked pleased, and Ella felt proud that Brigit remembered her godmother's lesson.

Gran patted Ella's hand. "Go help your mama and papa with the food. I've got plenty of stories to keep our houseguest entertained."

Ella slipped into the kitchen but paused when she realized she had caught her parents in the middle of an argument. She ducked out of sight and craned to listen.

"She's different now, Sebastien. I can feel it. That little spark we love inside her is dimming. I never wanted her going up to that school. I knew it would wear her down." Mama wiped her clean hands over and over again on her apron. "We should've told her."

Ella's pulse raced. *Told me what?* she thought. A deep cold dropped into her stomach. She didn't realize the real reason her parents were fussing and fighting all the time. That it was about her attending the Arcanum Institute. She'd always thought Mama wanted her home because Mama wasn't good with change.

"And saddle her down with it? No, my love, why not let her enjoy it until all the mess shows up." He reached his hands out for her, and she moved away from his touch.

Nerves and curiosity bubbled up in Ella. What were they talking about now?

"Her heart will be shattered. Chewed up by *those* people up there who have always felt they were better than us. The right kind of gifted people. It isn't okay. They're already sending us threats now that we have a starpost box. And you know what happened to my family, my twin sister. She never came home after we visited Astradam. Poof, gone, like the others." She crossed her arms in front of her chest. "And we've sent our baby into that lion's den. I should've never agreed to this." Her bottom lip trembled. "This experiment of yours will have consequences. I will not lose her like I did Celeste."

As she watched her parents, Ella felt the heartbeat of the storm between them. Its arms squeezed her like a monster.

Worry lines creased Papa's dark skin. "Conjure communities are under attack, Aubrielle. I had to do something. The Fewels burn down everything we have. Always. We've had to hide. We deserve to escape too. Freedom to showcase our gifts without fear of discovery." He pulled Mama into his chest, wrapped his arms around her, and began to rock until she softened. "Our children need to know our world *and* theirs. That's the only way they'll be truly safe. To be able to survive in both."

Mama let her head drop back on his chest and took a deep breath. "Tell me they won't break her? I worry they'll never accept that she belongs there."

Ella stood up. "I do belong there. I'll be okay."

Mama flinched. "Now, look here, little girl, what did I tell you about eavesdropping and nosing in grown folks' business?"

Ella ran to Mama, hugging her as tight as she could to reassure her. "I promise, I'll be okay. I'm strong. Masterji Thakur told me so." She'd been waiting to talk to them about Masterji Thakur and the Arcanum blueprints and everything that had happened to her so far. But it tumbled out, unraveling like yarn.

When she finished, she braced for her mother's reactions. Would Mama even let her go back to the Arcanum?

Mama pursed her lips and Papa paced, all while Gran hollered about bringing the food out before it got cold.

"I don't know anything about Conjure folk being at the Arcanum before you, baby." Papa rubbed his thick beard. "But I know they have a lot of secrets—and I promise to look into it. We'll get to the bottom of this."

"Too many." Mama stroked Ella's cheek. "We just wanted to protect you."

Ella thought back to the Stardust Pier. "Papa, what were on those signs, you know, the night we went up to the school?"

He looked sheepish. "Nothing worth repeating."

"You changed them, didn't you?"

He kissed her forehead. "I did what papas do. Now, let's enjoy your few weeks home. No more talk of this, okay?"

Ella nodded.

"Grab one of those platters and let's eat."

They carried everything to the dining room: a roasted chicken with crispy skin, a porcelain bowl bubbling with filé gumbo, stuffed bell peppers, fried oysters, seafood dressing, mac 'n' cheese, a stack of golden cornbread, and a flying hummingbird cake from Conjure Cake's Bakery for dessert.

"Does any of the food do anything weird?" Brigit asked.

Gran laughed. "It sticks to the bones and warms the soul."

The plates were passed around, and Papa started a round of jokes.

Ella sat back watching how much Brigit laughed with her family. She'd never seen her smile that wide.

She hoped that it was enough to make her stay.

✦ ✖ ✦ ✖ ✦

AFTER CHRISTMAS AT THE DURAND FARMHOUSE, BRIGIT HAD FULLY adjusted to living with them. Ella loved having a person to share scary stories with late at night, a friend to help her feed the chickens without making a mess, someone who would make sure the cats stayed out of the coop, and a buddy to wander the woods behind the farmhouse. They filled a journal with reasons why Masterji Thakur might've given her the note and what it could possibly mean. They even tried several unsuccessful attempts to send Jason starposts in Celestian City with non-Marvellian stationery, and Brigit spent time with Mama working in the family conjure room.

But a tiny shadow seemed to follow Ella. She woke up early each morning to make sure Brigit was still in the trundle bed beside her. She checked to make sure Brigit's clothes were still neatly tucked away in the drawers she'd set aside for her. She made sure to ask her every single day if she was having a good time, thinking for sure that one of these last few days before they headed back to the Arcanum, she'd wake and find that bed empty and Brigit gone, run off again.

On New Year's Eve morning, Ella paced in front of the family conjure room while Brigit was still asleep, trying to drum up enough confidence to interrupt her mother's sunrise work.

The door eased open. *Get on in here before you put a hole in my floor and wake this house*, came her mother's voice in her head.

She reluctantly entered. The conjure room spread out. There were two doors—one to welcome the living, and the other, the dead. The ceiling held a canopy of Underworld plants, flowers peeking through the foliage, appearing and disappearing in a game of hide-and-seek. The walls were covered in wooden cabinets full of her gran's dried divination herbs and blessed candles. A large table sat in the very middle, draped with a purple cloth, a wax pillar in its center.

Mama had her hands deep in root mixtures. "Make yourself useful and bring me the bloodroot from the cabinet. The powdered version, please."

Ella riffled through the cabinet of herbs, eyes scanning over all the little drawers of dried roots and plants, the labels in

Latin: *trillium grandiflorum, viburnum, eugenia pimenta,* and so on.

She brought her mama the root.

"Thank you." Mama kissed her forehead. "Okay, out with it, baby girl. I don't want to have to nose around in there."

"Mama!" Ella protested.

"So what is it? You truly happy at the Arcanum? Now it's just you and me, and you can be honest." Mama took Ella's hands and replaced hers in the soupy herb mixture. "Knead it well."

"Yes, I promise," Ella said. "I really do love it."

"Is that so?" Mama pinched Ella's nose. "Then if it's not the Arcanum, what *is* bothering you?"

"I'm worried," Ella admitted, swishing her fingers in the liquid, chasing the conjure-rose petals as Mama sprinkled in the bloodroot. "Masterji Thakur wanted to tell me something, about Conjurors and our history. I just know it."

"That's one part of the puzzle. Now, what's part two? I know my child." Mama plunged her hands back into the bowl alongside Ella's and continued to mix. "You will comb through every library until you get the answer about those blueprints. So, I'm not worried about that. What else is going on?"

"Brigit," Ella whispered.

"You ready for her to go home? She's a lovely girl. Hasn't been a lick of trouble or a burden."

"No, no . . . it's not that. I just think she's going to not come back to the Arcanum."

"What do you mean?" Mama's eyebrow lifted.

"She hates the Institute. She hates being a Marveller. She wants to go back to New York City . . . and I don't want her to go." Ella bit her bottom lip to keep it from quivering. "I don't want her to run away."

"People will end up where they want to be, baby. You can't reverse a tide. Especially not with someone who has a will as strong as Brigit's. She will make her own way . . . as will you."

Ella clenched her teeth. Mama never told her what she wanted to hear. "But—"

"I *think* you should give her a little more credit. Give yourself a little more too. She's changing. When you've been on your own for so long, it's hard to know how to count on folks to be who they say they are, to show up for them. But she has you, the best of us, my loyal love." She kissed her forehead again. "And she's a good friend too."

Ella smiled.

"Now get Brigit up and packed, then meet me in the kitchen for breakfast. We'll leave shortly after. I'm certain our trip today will be a reminder to stay put. She'll love our New Orleans house and the conjure pharmacy."

Ella grinned and ran off to wake Brigit. She thought about calling Reagan too, and letting her know they were coming to New Orleans, but she felt weird. Would her and Brigit get along? Reagan had never met a Marveller before.

Once everyone was out of bed and stuffed with breakfast, Brigit and the Durands stood around the table.

"Where are we going?" Brigit asked.

"You'll see." New Year's in New Orleans was Ella's favorite holiday tradition.

The kitchen bubbled over with commotion.

"Sebastien, did you move them? The Louisiana one isn't in

here." Mama combed through her *Red Book: A Compendium of Conjure Maps*.

"I haven't been in that trunk, beloved. I know better," Papa said with a chuckle.

"How long is the drive?" Brigit asked.

Winnie giggled and slipped her small hand into Brigit's. "We're not driving, silly."

Brigit glanced questioningly at Ella, who just smiled.

"Takes about three hours by car, and no one wants to deal with those Fewel police." Gran pinched Brigit's cheek. "You'll see." She plucked the missing map from the back of another and handed it to Mama. "If it had been a snake, it would've bit you. Moving too fast, can't see nothing."

Mama kissed her mother's cheek and spread a map of Louisiana across the table. An outline of the boot-shaped state pulsed on the thick paper, its sprawling cities and sleepy towns and rural outposts gleaming and glittering. Tiny midday suns glowed over safe places to visit and setting suns over dangerous ones. She waved her hands over the paper and it lifted off the table. Her quick fingers plucked at the city of New Orleans, magnifying it; the ink-outlined buildings and little moving trollies and beautiful houses stood straight up like a miniature dollhouse version of the city.

"Let's go to Congo Square. I need to dip into the pharmacy before heading to the house," Mama told Gran and Papa.

"Everyone ready?" Papa put on his tall hat.

"How does this work?" Brigit clutched Feste tight.

"Ah . . . our network. Yes, yes. I suppose my cousin hasn't taught you that yet." Mama took a cushion from her pocket. Little golden pins, one for each family member, imprinted with their names poked out of it. "I made this for you last night." She held one up; the glittering metal sparkled with Brigit's first and last name. "When you place it onto the map, you'll travel."

Ella leaned over to Brigit. "Feels a little like a roller coaster at first, but you get the hang of it."

"But why?" Brigit asked.

"Hasn't always been safe for us living among Fewels. If I'm honest, it still isn't. We had to make our own ways. Conjure affords us that. We can move more easily this way without harassment." Mama pulled on her gloves. Her purse floated beside her. She handed each one of them their pin, then retrieved her own, and winked at Ella and Brigit. "Suitcases in one hand and pins in the other. See you in New Orleans, babies."

"All together now," Papa replied as they each prepared to stick the pointed end into the map.

"Ready?" Ella held her breath and hooked arms with Brigit, and they stuck in their pins at the exact same moment.

They dissipated. The drop felt like a warm ocean wave had hit Ella and she'd been dragged under.

When Ella reopened her eyes, they were standing on the edges of Congo Square in New Orleans.

Ella always loved her first moments after arriving in this city. The sizzle of it filled her with excitement. The square bustled: musicians played their horns and people danced; fortune tents freckled the cobblestones with each Conjuror bragging about who had the best conjure tarot; vendors shouted about their piping-hot beignets, early King Cakes, fresh conjure candies, and sun seeds with the promise of tasting bright.

Ella heard Brigit gasp as she saw the gates to the Underworld towering behind them and their gargantuan deathbulls keeping watch on the line of those waiting for a ticket to enter. People tended to the altars at their feet.

Papa kissed Mama and told them he'd meet them at the house in a bit. The crowds parted for him as he walked through the square.

"Is your dad famous?" Brigit's eyes grew wide, taking in everything.

"Kind of." Ella grinned, relieved to see Brigit's excitement.

Ella, Brigit, and Winnie followed behind Mama and Gran through the streets. Rows of shops boasted holiday lights and displayed all manner of things: magical headscarves wrapping themselves in pretty patterns, floating wigs fluffing themselves, the latest model of braid-hands, parasols promising to block humidity and heat, nail art to guard against jinxes and hexes, and more.

Gran took Winnie into the toy store while Ella pointed out everything to Brigit.

Passersby nodded at them. Others whispered. A few stopped to talk. The only person she hoped to see was Reagan.

"Hey, baby girl Durand, how's that school in the clouds?" Mr. Boudreaux tipped his hat before slipping into McKinney's Mojo Mansion.

Ella smiled. "Fine."

"Glad you still looking like one of us, sugar." Ms. Morrow called out her beauty shop.

A beautiful woman with a crimson parasol stopped Mama. "Madame Durand, did you hear? Is it true? *The Conjure Picayune* says so."

Mama's delicate features tensed with worry. "What is going

on? We've been in transit." Mama glanced at the girls before she and the woman stepped away.

Ella and Brigit pressed their cheeks against the glass windows of Evangeline's Edible Enchantments shop and watched tiny hummingbird cakes fuss and fight, flaming cauldrons of bananas foster, spiraling snowballs soaked in syrup, jars of shining sun tea, and bourbon honey bread. Then Ella dragged Brigit to the Conjure Creole Creamery, where attendants pulled levers making decadent concretes and malted mischief milkshakes full of pralines and petit fours and pieces of pecan pie.

They sat on a bench and ate their sweets. Kids in a nearby park jumped double dutch in the air, almost floating off.

Brigit could barely focus as she gazed around at the other buildings. Crowds moved in and out of the conjure bank counting their colorful coins and black dollars. "There are trees!" Brigit pointed at the money trees behind the tellers.

Ella used to love watching her family's money tree being brought out from their vault and trimmed when her mama or papa made a withdrawal.

"It's so . . ."

"Awesome," Ella finished her sentence.

"Yeah." Brigit took Ella's hand and squeezed it.

"Maybe too awesome to leave?"

"Yeah, definitely."

Ella dropped a dollop of ice cream on her shoe. "Ugh!" When she looked down, she found a tiny rottie licking it clean. "Brownie, is that you? How did you get here?"

"Jason!" Brigit jumped off the bench, giving him a surprising hug.

"What are you doing here?" Ella's stomach knotted. The day

in the Arcanum menagerie rushed back. Brigit's quilt square of his portrait and the conjure emblem blazing on his chest. His face as he and Beatrice rushed away. Did he secretly hate her?

"I've been looking for you. Sending you starposts. Did you get them?" His voice almost quivered.

"We just got here from Mississippi." Ella eyed him. "We don't have a starpost box there."

He scooped up the rottie and stuck it in his backpack. Ella thought he looked different in Fewel clothing: a hoodie, jeans, and sneakers. "I came with my mom, and to return something," he said. "The deathbull." He nodded in the opposite direction at the woman talking to Ella's mother.

"*That's* your mom?" Ella asked. "How does she know my mom?"

Jason looked at the cobblestones. "She's a Conjuror."

Ella's eyes widened with shock. "And you didn't tell me? You let me think I was all by myself." The hurt washed in furious and hot. "That's why you had the deathbull in the first place. That's why Brigit knitted the emblem on your mantle."

Brigit gulped.

"I wasn't allowed to. Sworn to secrecy. Our family doesn't talk about it. They even hide their companions. No one in the Marvellian world knows." Guilt flooded his eyes, then tears. "I'm sorry."

"Like the bee in your sister's hair," Ella almost barked.

Jason nodded sheepishly.

The three of them stood there silent. Ella felt hot-grease mad, as Gran would say, and she wanted to yell even more at Jason, to stop being his friend.

Fat tears rolled down his cheeks. "But I told my family I was going to tell you. I stood up to them."

Ella gulped, thinking about how nervous he often got and how hard that must've been.

"I understand if you don't want to be my friend anymore." More tears poured down, and Brownie stared at Ella with big, pensive eyes.

Ella threw her arms around him. She didn't know what it meant to keep secrets like those, ones that belonged to many others besides just yourself. "I—"

An alarm sounded. Then came the sound of barking dogs. People started to run. Papa appeared at the top of the street and Mama rushed toward them. "Let's go, quick, quick."

Marvellian coppers and their wolves appeared on the streets. Fewel folks walked past them as if they were ghosts. Ella felt like all the Conjure folk took a deep, collective breath.

Brigit took her hand. "What's happening?"

Jason's momma dragged him in the opposite direction. They all shouted their goodbyes.

"The Cards have been breached," a paperboy shouted. "A criminal has broken out. They're blaming us. Take cover."

Ella felt frozen, a knot twisted in her stomach, and she knew something had to be *very, very* wrong.

The Starry Chronicle

BREAKING NEWS:
CONVICT ON THE LOOSE!

Patrick Diaz

JANUARY 1

The Cards of Deadly Fate are reporting a breach. The entire prison is on lockdown. The disgraced yet legendary circus performer Gia Trivelino has escaped. Serving time for the murders of both her circus rival and her infant daughter, she is considered very, very dangerous.

We'll keep you updated with the latest. Keep your news-boxes on!

★—★—★— **STARPOST**—★—★—★

Hi Masterji,

I sent you several starposts. Did you get them over break? Are you feeling better?

I also have some questions about what you showed me.

See you soon.

Ella

★—★—★— **STARPOST**—★—★—★

Dear Ella,

I hope your break was as wonderful as mine. I am excited to discuss your questions with you. I'm including an appointment card. Please come see me when you arrive back at the Arcanum.

Safe travels. See you soon.

Masterji Thakur

TO: His Excellency Sebastien Durand, Grand High Walker
Mansion of Death
Underworld
Congo Square, New Orleans

Dear His Excellency Sebastien Durand,

I'd like to inquire upon your services. This is an unusual request, though you probably get many. I need a soul reaped from the Underworld. She died on June 18 at 9:22 p.m. I'll pay the top price—name it.

Let me know the cost.

It is imperative.

Best,
G.T.

PART III
ARCANUM SECRETS

FOURNIER'S CURIOUS CLOCKWORK

Gia ran her fingertips over the pocket watches on the counter of Fournier's Curious Clockwork Shop in the glitziest area of Betelmore's high street. A cacophony of *tick-tocks* and *cuckoos* filled the space, and she felt like she was inside a clock itself. The shop was round, its walls covered in a plethora of weights and pendulums and cogs and gears, all trimmed in buttered brass. All manner of clocks were for sale, some with hands that ran backward and others with hands that ran forward, some that promised to stop time, some that promised to steal time.

Gia wasn't certain any of them could deliver on those promises, but she was certain the man behind the counter could.

His black mustache twitched like the second hand on a clock as he stared back at her curiously. "What was it you were looking for again?"

"Time is a funny thing."

"Indeed," he replied. "I've always had an affinity for it." He obsessively fingered a pocket watch.

"What kind of bugs live in your clocks?"

"Excuse me?" His back straightened. "My instruments are of the highest quality."

"Not ticks, right?"

His grimace broke into a smile.

She released her favorite laugh—one with a high pitch like a tinkling bell—and pointed to the shop's sign. "You must be *the* Fournier."

"Guilty. I'm Fabien." He nodded. "And what about yourself?"

"Colombina," she replied, the name of her favorite character to play. "I can't create anything as wonderful as these clocks."

His pale white cheeks went pink. Gia could sense weakness in the way someone might catch the scent of a person's shampoo. It made her adept at making others feel comfortable just long enough to get what she wanted. Her father had taught her that. A staple of the theater.

"What's in that pocket-box of yours?" He pointed at the box she'd strategically placed on the counter.

"The world," she joked, teasing the opening of it. "I've heard you like to make trades."

"That depends on what you have to offer," he replied.

"Do your watches really stop time?" She flashed him a smile.

"Only create tiny hiccups. All in good fun." He winked at her. "So, what do you have for me?" His heart-shaped face reminded her of her ex-partner, and for a fleeting moment she felt sorry for what she was about to do.

Gia's fingertips warmed. She blinked and the room transformed; the threads of the universe rippled out before her like a grand tapestry made of starlight. She pulled a thread and forced the door to lock and the OPEN sign to change to CLOSED, but he was too busy entranced with her pocket-box.

She wrapped a watch chain around Fabien Fournier's wrists before he realized what was happening.

"What are you doing? Let me go," he hollered.

"Calm down. You won't die. At least . . . I don't think," she replied. "We shall see."

"Take the money from the safe. Take whatever you want."

"I am not here for money. You don't remember me, do you?" He trembled.

"You had so much to say during my trial. So many choice words for the judge. 'She's narcissistic. She's not a rule-follower. She's an anarchist.' You provided special clocks for my father. You were part of the family. How dare you not remember what you've done?"

His face drained of color. "Gi—Gia. Gia Trivelino?"

"Well, at least, a version of me. The eyes give me away . . . but no one ever pays attention. If you looked close enough, you'd see beneath the veil; you'd see the lie. No one really wants to, though. They all want to believe the fantasy." She laughed and removed a small vial from her pocket-box. The red liquid flickered like flames in the glass. "Now drink this."

He thrashed around. "I will not! Put me down."

"So stubborn." She uncorked the last of her father's mimicry solutions and pressed it to his mouth. She just needed to see if it still worked. If she could take enough of his marvel to mimic it.

He turned his head left and right, fighting her. "The coppers will find you, and you'll go back to where you belong." He fought her grip. "You have bad light in you. Always knew that."

Gia tsk-tsked. "Where exactly do I belong? Back in a cage?" She cackled. "There's no good and bad, Fabien. No light and dark. We're all one awful day away from becoming the world's worst nightmare."

Fear flickered in his green eyes. "Let me go."

"Now, do we have to do this the hard way?" she whispered into his ear, then flashed him a wicked smile.

He opened his mouth and she fed him the flaming liquid. "Swallow," she ordered. "All of it."

He obeyed. Immediately, his white skin turned red, his veins bulging, and sweat poured down his cheeks.

It was working. Or so she hoped.

His mouth opened, and a brilliant ribbon of light trickled out. His light. His marvel.

Gia had an empty vial ready to catch it and tuck it away.

★—★—★— **STARPOST**—★—★—★

Ella,

Please let me know when you and Brigit get back to the dorms. I'm still feeling nervous, baby girl. Though you might be safer all the way up there while we deal with Marvellian pressure on the ground.

I'll keep you posted and you do the same.

Love,
Mama

CHAPTER SIXTEEN
EXTENDED VACATIONS

E lla caught sight of the Arcanum in the sky-ferry's grand windows. Its towers were trimmed with snow, and its banners wished returning trainees New Year's greetings in every language imaginable. The two sky lakes were still frozen solid, and the sky-ferry platforms glittered with perfect snowflakes. Ella's heart lifted with excitement as they landed and the stellacity engines turned off.

Starfolk helpers doled out instructions.

"The sky-ferry will resume its route in fifteen minutes," Aries called out as trainees lined up to disembark. "Trainees, suitcases will be brought to your room. As a new safety protocol and precaution, coppers will be checking them. Don't be alarmed. Keep the line tidy on the stairs."

Ella's stomach clenched. She pressed her face to the window, looking for the coppers. She remembered the note they'd sent home about them, the quote haunting her for days—*If you have nothing to hide, they will have nothing to find.* But she was eager to be back in the comfort of her room. And she was eager to talk to Masterji Thakur.

Papa smiled at her and Brigit. "You both ready?"

Brigit nodded. "Thank you for having me."

"You're most welcome." Papa tipped his hat. "Anytime."

Brigit stood. "I'll meet you inside."

"Okay," she said before turning back to her father. "Bye, Papa."

"Not so fast, baby girl," he replied. "You sure you ready to go back to the Institute?"

"Yes."

"What if I'm not?" He lifted his arm so Ella could tuck herself under it.

Ella loved snuggling up on her father because he was always warm, carrying heat like he'd swallowed the sun. She rested her head on him, and he held her hand.

"You have your mother's hands," he pointed out.

"I do not," she protested.

He chuckled, the deep boom of it rattling through her. "Same fingers and freckles along the knuckles. Powerful hands that will cast dynamic spells. Perfect for conjure." He kissed her forehead. "I want you to be safe, okay? There's a lot going on."

"I know."

"The breach of the Cards of Deadly Fate has turned the Marvellian world—and ours—topsy-turvy." He rubbed his beard.

Mama and Papa had sat her and Brigit down after the news broke, explaining how the breach of the prison had put a spotlight on the Conjure community. Ella didn't understand how or why Marvellians came to use their cards for their jails in the first place, and the answers to questions like those never showed up in library books.

"You know Mama didn't want you returning after winter break, but I thought you could handle it. I feel confident between your godmother here and that teacher you love so much, Masterji Thakur, you'll be in good hands. With all that's going on"—his voice dropped an octave—"Mama and Gran will be stressed. On high alert. Let's not give them one more thing to worry about. I need you to be safe. Okay?"

"I will. I promise." Ella fussed with her mittens. "Do you know anything about the person who broke out . . . Gia Trivelino?"

Papa's eyes softened. "Just that she did something unforgivable and used to be the most famous performer in the Marvellian world."

Ella's mind whirled.

"A penny for your thoughts?" Papa pinched her nose.

"It's nothing."

He squeezed her hand. "Promise me one more time you'll be safe?"

Ella nodded.

"You're my baby," he said. "I need you be careful."

Ella folded deeper into his arms, tracing her fingers along the intricate conjure marks that wrapped around his forearms. "Winnie's your baby."

"You are my firstborn." He held her chin and lifted it. His deep brown eyes bored into hers. "Pay attention to your surroundings. Pretend your head is a swivel. Always look behind you. Every shut eye ain't sleep. You know that." He tapped her nose again. "And keep a lid on that curiosity."

She gave him a kiss on the cheek. "I promise," she whispered. "No trouble."

Those words felt a little like a lie.

Ella scampered out of the sky-ferry. She caught the tail of trainees walking through the main entrance and into the foyer. Trollies adorned with snow caps, twinkling lights, and New Year's stars skated overhead. They spilled over with happy students headed to their dormitory towers. She joined the line to board the one marked URSA MINOR AND HYDRA TOWERS.

The girls jostled inside, sorting themselves into the plush seats.

"Find your spots. Buckle up," the trolley automat directed.

Ella walked down the aisle looking for Brigit. Other Level One girls quickly put satchels in empty seats or slid over to block Ella from sitting next to them. Her stomach knitted as she inched closer and closer to the back of the trolley. If she was unable to find a seat, she'd have to exit and walk or wait for the next one.

"Settle everyone," the automat announced. "Leaving in thirty seconds."

Ella tried to plop down into a seat with a girl named Ilse.

"You can't sit here," Ilse said.

"The seat's empty," Ella replied.

"Don't sit on Walter."

"Who?"

"He's a kobold . . . you know, invisible. Gets very upset when people assume he's not there. So, you can't."

Across the aisle, a series of laughs exploded.

"People would rather sit beside monsters than you." Abina stroked the tarantula in her palm. "Bad luck."

Ella gritted her teeth.

"I know from *personal* experience rooming with you. I had to go to a temple in Shanghai to be cleansed of it over winter break," Lian chimed in.

"The only bad luck comes from your terrible breath," quipped a voice from behind.

Ella pivoted.

It was Brigit. She immediately smiled.

Clare leaned forward. "And nobody asked you. I can't believe you're still here. Thought you failed out. I saw her grades. They were terrible. Worse than terrible. Horrendous."

"Oh, like your face?" Brigit shot back.

"How dare *you?*" Lian barked.

Abina, Clare, and Lian stood like they were preparing for a fight.

"Seats! Seats!" the trolley automat hollered.

Ella plopped into the booth beside Brigit.

The trolley jerked forward.

The girls tumbled to the floor while Brigit and Ella burst with laughter.

Abina crawled after her tarantula, cursing and fussing. Lian tried to fix her hair and get her fu dog to calm down. Clare smoothed her mantle like nothing had even happened. They glared at Ella and Brigit, which made them laugh even harder.

The trolley sailed through the belly of the Institute along glittering ropes, headed for the Level One dormitory towers.

"Thanks," Ella said to Brigit.

"Was nothing. They make me so mad."

Ella and Brigit whispered all the naughty things they'd do

to that trio of mean girls if given the chance . . . frogs in their beds, never-ending glitter in their hair, sending Feste to scare them at night.

A quiet smile crept into the corner of Ella's mouth, and she felt so good to be back.

✦ ✕ ✦ ✕ ✦

ELLA BARELY UNPACKED BEFORE GOING STRAIGHT TO MASTERJI Thakur's lab. Sugar snowflakes drifted from the sweet-balloons in the Taste Tower, but Ella didn't pause to try to catch them on her tongue. She held her appointment card tight along with a notebook, almost bursting with questions. His peacock-blue door glittered in the distance.

"Masterji Thakur," she called out.

A sign flickered through a series of messages:

MASTERJI THAKUR WILL BE ON AN EXTENDED VACATION. HIS TASTE COURSES WILL NOW BE TAUGHT BY DR. AHLU-WALIA IN THE INTERIM IN THE FOURTH FLOOR FLAVOR LABS. PLEASE SEE HEADMARVELLER RIVERA FOR ANY QUESTIONS. GOOD MARVELLING AND HAPPY NEW YEAR.

"An extended vacation?" Ella said, then she tried to open the door.

The knob wouldn't budge.

Something didn't feel right. Ella couldn't shake a sense of worry.

An automat approached. "Do you need help? Are you in distress?"

"No, I'm fine," she replied.

"Your heart rate is accelerated and you're sweating. Your

adrenaline is high. All indicators of stress," it replied. "Do you need to see Nurse Peaks? Or one of our noble Headmarvellers?"

Ella gulped; her mind felt like a shaken fizzlet bottle as she tried to calm down and to think of a good lie that would get it to leave her alone.

"Ella! Thanks for waiting on me." Another Level One trainee that Ella vaguely recognized walked up, holding a swollen glass bulb. A magnifying glass perched above it like a leaning umbrella. A strange plant glowed inside it. "We have appointments."

Ella nodded, pretending, until . . . the automat moved along.

"Thanks," Ella replied.

"No problem. I'm Bex." The kid had a curly mohawk and freckly light brown skin. Tiny rainbows were painted in the corner of their eyes.

"Ella."

"I know." Bex smiled.

"Right." Ella felt silly. "Thanks for helping."

"Heard that automat grilling you as I came up the stairs." Bex's eyes combed over the note on Masterji Thakur's door, and they showed Ella their appointment card. "I came up here to see him too."

"Why would he give us these and not be here?" Ella pressed her ear to the door.

"It's weird. We're working on a special project. I'm trying to regrow sunspice, which will bring the sand-dragons back home. This week is seed extraction. He knows that." Bex looked puzzled. "We have a strict flowering calendar."

"What is that container?" Ella stepped closer.

"It's a vivarium. Helps grow things."

"You have sand-dragons at home?"

"In Dubai, a Fewel city, like where you live."

Headmarveller Rivera popped out of the elevator. "I knew you two would be the first up here looking for our lordship Masterji Thakur."

Ella flinched at the sight of her, still upset after being accused of stealing. She didn't know how to feel about her anymore.

Bex held up the pulsing starpost. "He sent us appointment cards."

Ella clutched her notebook of questions to her chest.

"I'll make sure you're both the first to know when he's back. I think the two of you might be his favorite students this year . . . Not that we play favorites," she teased.

Ella searched her eyes for whatever it was that she wasn't saying. She didn't trust her the same way now. "He never misses appointments."

"It happens to the best of us, and I don't think we should hold it against him, Ella. Sometimes vacations extend. Everyone loves a long holiday break. Now, have either of you tasted the snow? It's quite delicious this year. Much sweeter." Headmarveller Rivera stepped under one of the taste-balloons and opened her mouth like a baby bird, catching a sugar snowflake on her tongue.

Bex squinted at her.

"Come now. Let's take a little stroll, shall we?" Headmarveller Rivera led the way back down the Taste Tower staircase, her cane clicks echoing as she yammered on. First about how the saltwater pools were still open and Dr. Vainikolo would be introducing new surfboards. Then she continued on about how permission slips had just gone out for the latest star expedition, but Ella's mind was squarely on Masterji Thakur.

They paused at the dormitory halls.

"Get some rest, the two of you. Sessions will be underway tomorrow morning bright and early." Headmarveller Rivera walked away.

Ella waited until Headmarveller Rivera was out of earshot. "Do you believe her?"

"Of course not." Bex smiled.

"What should we do?" Panic started to rise inside her again.

"Continue sending him starposts and keep an eye out. I'll go by his office every day. I'll let you know if I find out anything."

Ella and Bex walked together down the hall. "Do you live in Lepus or Canis Minor? My friend Jason lives in Lepus. Can you get him for me?"

"I live in Chimera." Bex pointed to the left.

Ella craned her neck to look. She'd never heard of that dormitory tower. "There's nothing there."

"Only those who need it know where it is," Bex said. "See you at the Gatherfeast."

Ella watched as Bex walked forward and disappeared. Now she had even more questions.

★—★—★— **STARPOST** —★—★—★

Jason,

    Masterji Thakur wasn't there. I need to talk to you.
Meet me and Brigit before the Gatherfeast?

From,

Ella

The Conjure Picayune

WILL HISTORY REPEAT ITSELF? THE CONJURE INTEGRATION CONUNDRUM

Margeaux DuBois

JANUARY 15

Conjure folk go missing in the skies. That's what they say. Look over your shoulder when you move through the Vellian Port. Hold your breath while you ride their sky-ferries and air-trollies. Keep your head on a swivel when you walk their streets. Mind your manners to avoid the ravens who will pluck out your eyes and the wolves who will eat your hearts!

The Griotarys in every conjure town keep records of missing folk: those with permits to work in Marvellian households, those sent to collect the dead, and those who hoped to be ambassadors of peace. The most famous of the lot, Celeste Baptiste, never returned at the tender age of eleven.

Now our Grand High Walker of the Underworld, His Excellency Sebastien Durand, has changed the rules . . . but the question remains: Should we venture high above?

What will happen to the little girl sent into the clouds? Will her light go out? Will she become our next fallen star?

CHAPTER SEVENTEEN

THE GATHERFEAST &
RETURNED STARPOSTS

Lunar decorations filled the halls, and everyone greeted each other with "Happy Gathering" and "Good marvelling" every few seconds while Ella and Brigit waited in line to enter the assembly hall for the Gatherfeast. The entire Institute hummed with excitement . . . and coppers. They were posted in every corner, and Ella worked hard to avoid their eye contact. Several kids hovered over news-boxes, turning the crank slowly to watch the latest headlines about the Cards of Deadly Fate and the criminal on the loose.

Ella tried to keep her eyes forward despite the feeling that people were staring at her.

"This way, Level Ones; the Gatherfeast shall begin shortly." Headmarveller MacDonald ushered them inside.

Brigit cupped a hand to Ella's ear. "Did you find Masterji Thakur?"

"He wasn't there, and I'm pretty sure Headmarveller Rivera lied to me about it."

Brigit's eyebrow lifted. "What do you want to do?"

"Investigate." Ella filled with resolve. "I sent Jason a starpost too."

"I'll help."

While the rest of the Level Ones speculated about the Gatherfeast—some said that it was just a big party and others said that you got to see the older trainees show off their marvels and a few said everyone got presents—Ella tried to get excited, but her hand found Masterji Thakur's starpost in her pocket again, and she couldn't shake the feeling that something was wrong.

Clare cut them off. "Watch where you're going," she barked. "And I got your little note, Ella. You'll pay for that."

"What?" Ella asked, confused.

Clare flipped her hair over her shoulder, then turned back to Lian to yell more. "I'm not going to be late just because Abina can't get her hair together. I want the best seats."

Ella stopped. What note was Clare talking about?

"Abina will just have to come to the Gatherfeast looking terrible. I don't even care. I'm still mad at her for not coming shopping with us in Betelmore." Clare led the way forward.

Ella felt a twinge. She didn't know why she felt compelled to go see if Abina was okay. "You wait for Jason, okay? Save me a seat. I'll be right back."

"What are you doing?" Brigit called out, but Ella ran back down the hall headed for the dormitories.

Ella slipped through the Ursa Minor door behind another student. The lounge looked just as it had before she moved: the cozy yellow chairs and the big bear constellation skulking across the ceiling. She climbed the spiral staircase. The sound of muffled crying slipped from Abina's room.

"Abina," she called out softly.

No answer.

Ella knocked.

The door eased open, and Ella spotted two eyes glaring back at her.

"Go away," she barked.

"You okay?"

Fat tears streaked Abina's cheeks. "I don't need your help."

"Why are you crying?" Ella said.

Abina's bottom lip quivered, and she burst into tears. "My braid-hands aren't working. Now I can't do my hair the way my momma told me to. And my sister is already at the Gather-feast. She can't help me either."

Abina opened the door and reluctantly let Ella in. Her hair was swaddled in a beautifully printed scarf tied the same way Ella wore hers at night. Bright Ghanaian cloth created a pretty canopy over her bed, and a glass container sat beside her table. Inside twigs, grass, and a little pool of water surrounded her fat spider.

The malfunctioning braid-hands spun in a circle, its dark brown fingers balling and un-balling.

"I don't know what happened." Abina crossed her arms over her chest.

Ella took the braid-hands and tickled the palms in the way she'd seen her mama do. The fists squeezed, then stretched, trying to escape Ella's grasp.

"I didn't realize you had them too," Abina said.

"Of course." Ella blinked at her strangely. "We have the same kind of hair."

Abina looked up, examining Ella's twists, and mumbled,

"Yeah . . . might be the only thing we have in common with Conjurors."

Ella rolled her eyes. "There's more than you think."

Abina pursed her lips.

"My gran says we're just cousins separated by water, time, and different experiences."

Abina looked down at her quilt. "I mean, I know about what happened and everything. It's just . . ."

"Different." Ella stretched each finger and massaged the palms of the braid-hands until they reset. Then she plucked a vial of coconut oil from Abina's hair kit and sprinkled it over the long fingers. They were ready again.

"Voilà!" Ella smiled triumphantly at Abina.

Abina fought a smile as she started to unwrap her scarf. "You don't have to wait for me."

"I don't want to go into the assembly hall alone," Ella replied.

"Me neither," she admitted.

Ella sat at Abina's desk while the braid-hands got to work transforming Abina's hair into pretty cornrows threaded with beads. Conversation stretched between them like beignet dough, rising and falling and turning into something new and unexpected. She met Abina's spider protector, Kwaku. She learned about how Abina traveled with her family to Accra when they weren't in Astradam. And Ella shared stories about her home in New Orleans and her gran's farmhouse in Mississippi. She heard all about Abina's mother's cloth marvel and all the animated dresses she made in her shop.

"Your hair looks nice." Ella loved her zigzag parts and how the beads sparkled.

"Uhh, thanks." Abina smoothed her mantle. "You ready?"

They ran to the assembly hall, and right before stepping in, Abina stopped Ella from going inside. "Just want to say thanks, you know, for like, helping me and everything. I know I haven't been . . . you know . . ."

"You're welcome." Ella felt like maybe this might change something between the two of them.

Ella and Abina slipped inside in the middle of Headmarveller MacDonald's speech about the important Marvellian holiday of the Gatherfeast.

". . . Sacrifice. Their will to live together in safety rather than danger. This is our yearly reminder. Our 299th one. Next year will be the three hundred year anniversary. Our ancestors came from all over the world and brought their traditions with them," Headmarveller MacDonald said. "So, we honor this memory by coming together when the Wolf Moon shows itself in the sky. The wolf is a lucky animal who always adapts for winter. We are like the wolf. We evolved and prepared for life away from Fewels. Now all the magical people live in harmony."

All the Marvellian instructors clapped.

"Let us eat!"

"Happy Gatherfeast." Headmarveller Rivera motioned to the starfolk, and they began food service.

"Happy Gatherfeast," the room shouted back, then exploded with claps as the food carts filled the aisles.

Ella quickly found Brigit and Jason, slipping into the seat they'd saved for her.

"Where were you?" Jason asked.

"Abina needed help." Ella reached for one of the spinning samosas.

"I don't know why you were nice to that girl." Brigit scowled. "She wouldn't have helped you."

"Yeah, but it's fine." Ella actually didn't have a solid answer for why she'd helped Abina. Maybe deep down she wanted Abina to one day be her friend. Or at least not hate her.

Brigit cut into her patois patty, then pressed her napkin in it when its reggae tune started. "I still hate the food here. Can't we just have your gran send some of her cooking?"

Ella laughed, then leaned forward to whisper, "Okay, we need to track down Masterji Thakur. He was trying to tell me something about"—she gazed around to make sure no one was listening—"the Arcanum and now, suddenly, is not here, and Headmarveller Rivera is lying about it."

"I don't trust her." Brigit scowled.

"You don't trust anyone," Jason said through a mouthful of jiggly japchae, the noodles bursting out of both corners of his mouth, trying to escape.

"Okay, you're not wrong, but they lie to make everything seem like it's fine all the time, and we know it isn't." Brigit's jaw clenched.

Ella's stomach flipped and flopped. "Like the time her and Headmarveller MacDonald asked me about Samaira's lantern. I haven't lived in that room for months. Why me? It was so embarrassing."

Jason's eyes bulged. "Maybe you should just ask your mom or dad or even Madame Baptiste about it?"

"Ella's mom will yank her out of here so fast," Brigit said. "I heard her say how much she hates Marvellian cities."

The truth crashed in. Ella imagined how her already nervous and upset parents would respond to her going on a rescue mission with conjure spells while the entire Conjuror world was being watched. Ella couldn't ask anyone for help and risk being taken back home. Papa had just said he felt happier about her being at the Arcanum because Masterji Thakur and her godmother were here. What would he do if he found out Masterji Thakur was missing—or hadn't returned?

"Like what if he really is on vacation? First, let's try sending him another starpost after the Gatherfeast. He answered yours over the break, so I don't see why he wouldn't answer another one," Jason said.

"I think we should go back to his office," Brigit said.

"Both are good ideas." Ella plucked a blank starpost from her satchel and quickly wrote a brief message:

Dear Masterji,
    You missed our appointment today. Will you be back soon? Is everything okay?

From,
Ella

Writing that message made her instantly feel better. She was taking things into her own hands. She breathed deeply, put the starpost in her pocket, and prepared to send it after the feast.

The dessert carts arrived, and she loaded up with more food than she could fit in her stomach—a dynamite dulce pot to eat before it detonated, giggly gulab jamun, ridiculous rum cakes doing stunts, and meddlesome mochis trying to wiggle their way into your satchels and pockets.

After the feast, Ella, Brigit, and Jason headed to the dormitories.

"Let me send the letter." Ella darted to the nearest starpost box and dropped it inside. Each time she used it, she thought it was so much more interesting than the plain blue mailboxes on city corners back home. The floating box shuffled left and right, then glowed as it stamped and processed her letter, ready to send it straight to the Stariary.

"Hopefully, he'll get back to me soon." Ella started to walk away.

"He will," Jason assured her.

"Definitely," Brigit added.

The starpost box flared, then chimed strangely.

Ella whipped back around. Its beautiful surface had gone blank, and it spat back her letter. She scrambled to grab it before it hit the ground.

On it thick black letters stamped over Masterji Thakur's name said: RETURN TO SENDER.

Ella's heart crashed into her stomach. What did that mean?

Make the Marvellian World Light Again!

Our government has lost its way
and forgotten its core values.

Clean up the skies!

Get rid of Conjuror
influence and sympathizers.

PUT MARVELLERS FIRST!
Integration is not the answer!

—Jefferson Lumen

TO: General Marveller Assembly

FROM: Security Council

See attached reports. Betelmore Infirmary reports
three people admitted with missing marvels. They
cannot use them. Their gifts have disappeared.

CHAPTER EIGHTEEN
THE ROTTIES & HOT MAPS

Ella, Jason, and Brigit stood in the dormitory hall staring down at the big black letters: RETURN TO SENDER.

"Maybe's something wrong with the mail?" Brigit took the paper from Ella and held it up to catch the light.

"Or this starpost box." Jason started to inspect it.

Ella's hand shook. "I think something bad has happened to Masterji Thakur."

Jason put his hands up. "Whoa, whoa, we don't know that yet."

"*Return to sender* means they can't find him—"

"Children, it's time to clear the hall and go to your dormitories for nightly curfew." Dean Nabokov strode through the halls, shooing everyone to their proper places.

"But it's an emergency—" Ella gulped down the rest of her sentence as Dean Nabokov strode toward them. She gasped at the sight of the woman up close. The lady wore an old-fashioned frock coat and her long black dress swished back and forth like a church bell. Her black hair was swept into a bun similar to the one Mama always wore to church on Sundays.

The woman rocked back and forth on her heels. Most Marvellers had something peculiar about them, but something about Dean Nabokov made her hard to place. Ella didn't know where someone like her belonged, but it surely wasn't here at the Arcanum. Maybe she belonged to another time period.

Ella figured it would be best not to mention anything . . . especially not to her.

"Let's make a plan tomorrow," Jason whispered as Dean Nabokov towered over them. He scampered away.

"Is there a reason the two of you are still in this hallway?" She pointed a gloved finger at them.

"No, ma'am," Ella lied. "We were just going to bed."

Brigit glared. "Yeah, right now."

"That's what I thought. You wouldn't want to continue to make trouble during your first year here, now would you? That might make it your first and only one with us at the Arcanum." Dean Nabokov's eyes burned into Ella.

Ella swallowed hard, almost tasting the sourness of Dean Nabokov's threat. She hooked arms with Brigit and scrambled down the hall, not stopping until they'd rushed through the door to their dormitory. Ella's heart thudded, and her breath caught in her throat. She was sure of one thing: the woman's gaze had passed through her, down into her heart, and its trail burned. She had not known that one person could be both beautiful and terrifying.

Brigit led the way to their room, complaining about Dean Nabokov and her attitude while Ella couldn't seem to stop staring at the RETURN TO SENDER message on her starpost.

She got ready for bed and took it with her, tracing her fingers over the black ink, worries making them wobbly. *What happened, Masterji Thakur? Where are you?*

Ella's dreams filled with plans, all the things she could do to find Masterji Thakur, and all the things that could go wrong.

The next morning, she woke exhausted and rushed Brigit to breakfast. In the dining hall, Ella made them sit far away from the other Level Ones so they could discuss what to do about Masterji Thakur without anyone overhearing.

"So, what's the plan?" Brigit asked.

"I want to do a hot foot," Ella said.

"A what?" Brigit stared at her, puzzled.

"It's a spell where you can track someone."

"Or poison them with a jinx," Jason added, "'cause that's what my momma always said."

"That's only if you're using it to cross into someone's will. If you're trying to change their actions or send them away," Ella corrected. "This is a different version of the spell. The hot foot can trace your footsteps."

They looked at her, confused. Ella wished that she had a book that explained it all so they could see pictures of what she meant—the map, the powder, the spell. But Conjurors didn't pass down grimoires or spell books or magical tomes of knowledge. Conjure families passed down their memories. There were no manuals to guide them. "Okay, let me explain." She took a deep breath and turned to Jason. "Let's say you lost a wombie."

Jason started his usual spiel. "They have a natural sense of direction and would never be—"

Ella put her hand up. "Let me finish."

Jason giggled. "Sorry."

"Okay, so let's say, you were missing a wombie, right? If we did a hot foot spell, we'd go to the wombie burrow and try to retrace its steps. Try to see where it went."

"But how?" Brigit questioned.

"By creating a hot foot map. We take a few of the wombie's things as locators of sorts. Things that have essence-traces is what my mama calls it."

"You can make a map just from that?" Brigit's eyes opened wide.

"Well, we can make all kinds of maps . . ." Ella swallowed the rest of the answer as Aries approached their table with a lunch cart. "Chocolate fizzy fondue? There's lightning lollies to dip. Anyone want one?" The fountain gurgled.

They all shook their heads no.

Aries lingered. "You all look like you're up to something . . . sitting all the way over here."

Brigit glared. "What're you going to do? Use more of that sleepy powder on us?"

"You should really learn forgiveness."

She hissed and he jumped, quickly moving on to the next table.

"We have to go see my godmother and get ingredients from her room. I can get her talking about the spell. I know what's in it, but I want to make sure I have the right steps."

"There's no way. She'll spot us." Brigit put her hands up. "Plus, we don't even know what to look for."

Ella thought for a long moment. She was right. They would waste so much time not knowing what to get, they'd easily be caught. Especially with her godmother's conjure companion, Echi, watching overhead in the bottle tree.

Jason slammed his hand on the table.

Ella and Brigit jumped.

"Oh, sorry. Got too excited," he said shyly. "But I know what we should do."

"What?" Ella and Brigit said in unison.

"The rotties."

"The rats," Brigit replied.

"They're not rats. They are little marsupials—"

"Yeah, yeah, yeah, you've only told us a gazillion times." Brigit rolled her eyes. "Just teasing."

"Wait, hear me out. They're quick and almost unseen." Jason ruffled through his satchel and retrieved a small cookie box; the wiggling animal crackers were fighting to get out. "I'll ask them to help." He handed them to Ella. "Leave tiny pieces near where they need to grab ingredients. I'll tell them what to do."

"Brilliant." Ella's mind churned, the plan clicking into place like gears in one of her papa's compasses, pointing her in the right direction. This could work. "Brigit, I need you to distract anyone trying to come into her room, and Jason, you direct the rotties and then keep an eye on Echi. That snake sees everything. I don't want one of them eaten."

The three of them scarfed down the rest of their breakfast, then darted to the Spirit Tower.

"We still have forty minutes before first sessions start." Ella pointed up at a nearby clock-lantern.

They hovered in the stairwell.

"I'll call them now." Jason knelt to the ground and put his

hand to the wall. He drummed a tiny beat and took out one of the cookies.

Ella and Brigit exchanged looks. This had to work. Ella started to count to ten, but before she got to five, she heard the *pitter-patter* of tiny feet and spotted the big black noses of several rotties peeking their heads out from behind columns.

"They're here." Brigit jumped. "They're here."

"Stay calm," Jason warned. "If they get too excited, they'll just want to play. I told them we were on a serious mission. A rescue mission." He lured them close with little bits of the cookies. "Ready?"

The tiny rotties squeaked and nodded.

Jason looked up at Ella. "Let's do this."

Ella took a deep breath and walked into her godmother's Conjure Atelier. "Aunt Sera," she called out.

"Yes, baby girl," she answered. "I'm in the back. Come on in."

Ella found her godmother pruning belladonnas inside her dark cabinet of Underworld plants. "What is it?"

"I wanted to ask you some questions about the assignment you gave us. You know . . . those." Ella pointed at the cabinet.

Aunt Sera's eyebrow lifted. "You know all of this already. That should be easy for you."

Ella glanced over her shoulder, spotting the quick flick of one of the rotties' tails. "I wanted extra work. You know how I like to know everything."

Aunt Sera smiled warmly. "Yes. Always so curious. I told your mother that I feel like your conjure companion will be a cat."

Ella rolled her eyes.

"Come help me with this first." She held a pot of warty and

hairy mushrooms. "These keep starting trouble in here. I have to find a new space for them."

Ella recognized them; she'd always thought they looked ugly. The mushrooms stretched up in the dirt, as most plants did when a Conjuror came near.

"What are these?" her godmother asked. "Correct pronunciation, please."

"Easy. They're stro-bli-o-my-ces. The Old Men of the Woods." She traced a clockwise circle in the soil as a sign of respect and reverence, a technique she'd seen Gran do. The mushrooms bowed their knobby heads in her direction.

"What can they do?" Ella hoped the rotties were quiet enough to avoid alerting Aunt Sera.

Ella had never cast a trick or spell using them, but she'd seen Mama and Gran fix plenty and use these ugly mushrooms for customers who complained about other people causing trouble in their lives. "For enemies," she answered. "But can I ask you about something else?"

"You can ask me anything." Her godmother pointed to a spot for her to tuck the plant.

Ella fingered the cookies in her pocket and tried to draw out her question, adding a lot of *umm*s and *ahh*s to buy herself some time. "Can you tell me about the hot foot spell? In our Future Forecasting session, we're learning about how you can use tools to find missing people, and I thought maybe it was the same." It wasn't quite a lie.

"Oh, very good question—and a well-spotted connection between *us* and *them*." Her godmother turned her back to continue her plant rearrangement in the tiny greenhouse.

Ella eased to her godmother's herb cabinet of bundled

ingredients, each premeasured for quick use. She placed fragments of cookies in the chili powder, salt, black and white pepper, chili flakes, and sulfur drawers. Now all she needed was a black candle and conjure paper.

Echi's eyes snapped open and found her. Ella looked away. avoiding the snake's sharp yellow gaze.

"The hot foot is simple. The candle does all the work once you dress it with the proper herbs. Heat is always last; you know that." She pointed. "First, turn down that tele-box so I can explain."

"Yes, ma'am." Ella turned the knob so the projections of *The Secret Marvellians of New York City* flattened and became a dull whisper. Quick as a cricket, she detoured to her godmother's desk, where a stack of conjure paper sat, slipping a piece of cookie there and into the candle drawer labeled NOIR.

Sweat appeared on her brow. She looked at the door and flashed Jason and Brigit a smile. Thankfully Aunt Sera couldn't see them from where she was standing. All the cookies were placed. Her aunt explained how to lay everything out for the spell and reminded her of the words to sing.

The first part of their plan had been a success. Now Ella had to hope the rotties didn't get caught.

Aunt Sera kissed Ella's sweaty forehead. "Good girl, my Conjuror. Check in with me later. Now, run along."

"Yes, ma'am." Ella scampered out and caught up with Jason and Brigit.

"Nice job." Jason patted her back. "The rotties will take things slowly throughout the day. I told them to bring it all to Masterji Thakur's room and meet us tomorrow."

This would work, Ella was certain of it.

★—★— **ARCANUM-WIDE STARPOST**—★—★

All trainees in Masterji Thakur's Introduction to Spice Elixirs, Indian Spice Alchemy, and Spice Genesis classes will report to Dr. Khan and Dr. Ahluwalia. Any pupil found evading new procedures will be escorted by the automats and receive automatic Saturday detention.

THE ACES

Gia sat in the very back of the air-trolley as it soared over Betelmore doing its slow tour about the city. She pulled up her fur-lined hood, making sure it shaded her eyes. Curious onlookers would only cause trouble. No, tonight only the right sort of folk would find her. She leaned forward, flicking two bloody ace cards on the pair of seats facing her. The most valuable cards in any deck. The crushed velvet blue looked lovely alongside the crimson red of the card. Easy to spot.

She laughed to herself.

People came and went at the various stops, and stewards in pillbox hats pushed carts and carried trays of drinks and snacks.

Gia glanced into her satchel at the three other faces she'd packed: the man with the curling mustache and button chin, the cherub blonde with rosy cheeks, and the deep brown woman with a constellation of freckles on her cheeks. Just in case.

"Is this seat taken?" a man asked.

She looked up and smiled. "Good to see you, Benjamin Mackenzie."

"It's been an age—" He suddenly cut off, as though strangled, when he attempted to say her name.

She smiled, reveling in how her gag still worked so many years later. They wouldn't be able to say anything she didn't want them to. He removed his hat. Sunburn streaked his pale white forehead.

"Hate to have called you out of the sun so soon," she said.

"I've been waiting for you. Came straight up from Havana, and it wasn't easy. They're still watching us." He loosened his cravat as if that would help him speak what she did not want spoken.

"I know, I know. Have a laugh. Bet you could use it." Gia smiled at her old friend. She'd missed how his nose wiggled when he got nervous. It'd been the same since they'd met at eleven years old as Level Ones.

Before she could make fun of Benjamin, a gloved hand snatched the other card, and a woman took the seat beside him. The most gorgeous woman in the world, Gia had always thought. Gia secretly kept a version of her face tucked away in her closet. Linh Nguyen stared back, long dark hair hitting her waist and lips pursed so tight they were a straight line.

"Good to see you again," Gia said. "It's been so long."

"Not long enough. Now what do you want?" her whisper was a bark.

"To watch the world burn."

The woman scowled. "I'm not here to play your games anymore."

Gia tsked. "Settle down. The night is young, and we don't have our final passenger yet." She patted the empty seat beside her.

"*He* would never come," Linh spat back.

Gia grinned. "Oh, I know. Trust me. I'll find a way to make him sweet on me again, though. And he's not our final guest . . . the shadow, of course."

Benjamin and Linh glanced at each other.

The air-trolley stopped at its final station. "Passengers, please disembark," an automat called out.

The trolley started to empty, passengers grabbing their bags and hustling out.

Gia raised her arm, trying out her new marvel. She spotted the clock-lantern high above in the ceiling and fixated on its moving hands. The noise of the *tick* echoed through her, and she wrestled with it, willing it to stop. Willing *time* to stop.

Wall sconces flickered. Everything paused.

The door slid open with a chime.

Gia spotted her long, vibrant skirts first. Still so unlike the stiff petticoats most Marvellian women chose to wear. Then her beautiful dark skin glowing in the light.

"What's happening?" Linh asked.

"I'm trying on something new," Gia said.

"I thought you said you'd never do that again." Linh's brow furrowed.

"I'm ready to resume the game."

Their new visitor slid into the seat beside Gia with the largest grin. "You miss me?" A hint of her Fewel accent still lingered.

"Always, Celeste Baptiste." Gia left a kiss on her beautiful face, the red lipstick a bloody smudge against the woman's brown skin. "Did you bring what I need?"

"Aces never disappoint." She placed a handful of vials on the table between them. "Good to see you all again."

"It's been an age, Celeste." Benjamin grabbed one of the vials.

Celeste nodded.

Linh fingered the bottle. "This will remove it? You promise?"

Gia let out an annoyed breath. "I am nothing if not loyal. You have maintained yours to me. Never speaking ill against me. You may have your true tongue back."

They each took the tonic and guzzled.

"Now, there's work to do."

The Marvellian Times

A CALL FOR PEACE!
LETTER TO THE EDITOR

FEBRUARY 1

Dear Fellow Marvellians,

The time has come for peace and full integration of the Conjure folk of the world into our society. If we return to our history, there are so many aspects missing, so many mischaracterized details.

It's time to right this wrong. It's time to shine the light—our marvel light—together so that the truth will be revealed.

We are stronger together.

Best,
Natalie Parker
Fifth Degree of Weathering,
Doctor Marvellian of America, Paragon of Spirit

CHAPTER NINETEEN

MASTERJI THAKUR'S LAIR

The next morning, Ella was jerked awake.

"Get up!" Brigit barked.

"What?! The alarm hasn't gone off." Ella rubbed the sleep from her eyes and found Brigit perched on her bed with Feste. "Did I oversleep?"

"Look at what happened to our room!"

"It's terrible," Feste exclaimed. "So rude. I need to patrol all night now."

Ella sat up. The entire room was in shambles: Chairs were overturned, toilet paper littered the branches of Ella's bottle tree, instruction manuals and books and parchment notebooks and styluses were scattered everywhere, and worst of all, their night-balloons wore nasty messages scrawled in red ink.

CONJURORS AREN'T REAL MARVELLERS!

GO HOME, YOU DON'T BELONG HERE!

NO BAD LIGHT, NO CONJURORS ALLOWED!

YOU LET THAT CRIMINAL OUT OF THE CARDS!

A hot flash hit her. The messages felt like a punch to the stomach. The saints on her bedside table burst with angry chatter.

"This is such an unfortunate disgrace," St. Agatha said.

"How did we not see them come in? We must stand vigil at all times now," St. Joseph replied. "Take turns staying awake."

"People, especially children, ought to be taught acceptance and peace," St. Francis protested with an angry clap of her porcelain hands.

The room exploded with noise. Ms. Paige appeared in the doorway, and behind her, many of the other Hydra girls peered in, all gasping. A flurry of gossip poured into the hallway. News traveled fast, and even the Ursa Minor girls had come over to take a look. She heard Clare's laugh and Lian's surprise.

A stone sat in Ella's stomach.

"We will get statements," Ms. Paige said, trying to reassure Ella and Brigit before she turned to the nosy girls at the door. "Back to your rooms with you all. Your sessions start in an hour, dearies. Get bathed and dressed. On with you. Shoo! Shoo!"

Ella jumped up and started to clean. Blood rushed to her head, and she felt like it would float off. Little white spots blurred her vision, but it didn't stop her determined hands from gathering the chaos of items strewn all over the floor.

Brigit slammed the door, shutting them all out, then started to help. "Why would they do this?"

"Because I'm a Conjuror." Ella looked at the destruction again, the weight of it like heavy bricks sitting on her heart. "I always just thought Conjurors and Marvellers didn't know each other well. That we were just a little different."

Feste scrambled to help grab small things he could fit in his tiny hands.

"Aren't these people *different* too?" Brigit cleaned the night-balloons. "How can they even tell you're a Conjuror? Couldn't you, like, have kept it a secret?"

Ella lifted her hair scarf to show Brigit her mark.

"It could be a freckle."

"But it won't be forever. You saw my mama and gran." Mama said there'd been many Conjurors throughout the years that did hide from Marvellians and Fewels alike, used makeup to cover their conjure mark and pass into Marvellian society. But her mama and papa's pride would never let her do that . . . and she would never want to. "I would never do that."

Ella swallowed the angry lump in her throat. No tears. That's what they wanted. And more importantly, for her to go home. But she didn't know how to explain it to Brigit.

A light knock rapped against the door. Brigit stomped over and yanked it open. Abina stood there.

"What do you want?" Brigit's eyes narrowed.

Abina pursed her lips, then took a deep breath. "I heard what happened. Can I help?"

Brigit whipped around to face Ella. "Can she?"

Ella nodded.

As Ella, Abina, and Brigit cleaned up the room in silence, her heart found its normal rhythm again. She climbed into her bottle tree, checked on the death moths, and collected the toilet paper. The branches bloomed with belladonna, a sign of danger to come. She wondered how things could get any worse. Masterji Thakur was missing, her room had been trashed, people whispered about the prison breach and Conjurors . . . Everything was falling apart.

Abina plucked the toilet paper from the low-hanging branches. "I'm sorry about what happened. It's not okay. I don't know who did it, but I'll help you figure it out."

Ella gazed down at her. "Thanks."

A bell-blimp drifted into the room. "Morning, future Marvellers! This is your daily reminder to get to your sessions on time. Let's keep our demerits low this training cycle. This is your five-minute reminder to get moving."

Ella scrambled out of the tree. Abina said she'd come back later if needed. Brigit locked the door behind her.

"Maybe we should skip?" Brigit offered. "Bad morning. Don't think anyone would blame you."

"I don't want anyone to know. I don't want anyone to think they got to me."

"Nobody's allowed to treat you like this. Not when you're my friend."

Ella smiled at her, then grabbed Reagan's luck root plant from the pot on her nightstand and slipped it into her mantle pocket. "Help me out today, okay?" she whispered to it. "I really need it."

As they barreled out of the Hydra Tower, commotion filled the halls. The starfolk carried several marvel-valises from dormitory towers. Six sulking kids filed out with their angry-looking parents. The Headmarvellers and Dean Nabokov tried to disperse the crowds.

Whispers exploded. Theories that these kids were being expelled for this thing or that.

Ella spotted Bex. "Hey, what's happening?"

"The news-boxes are calling for families to pull their kids out. Said it's not safe here anymore after the Cards were breached," Bex replied.

"Why?" Brigit asked. Bex didn't say anything but looked at Ella, their eyes flickering with a strange sadness.

"Because of me," Ella answered. Heat spread across her cheeks as she felt the weight of all the eyes on her.

Conjurors were being blamed for everything.

✦ ✖ ✦ ✖ ✦

"ALL FIRST SESSIONS WILL BE DELAYED BY TWENTY-FIVE MINUTES. Everyone please make your way to the Grand Assembly Hall this instant." Headmarveller MacDonald's voice echoed from a series of bell-blimps.

Ella and Brigit found Jason outside the Lepus dormitory. "You ready?"

He nodded.

Ella, Jason, and Brigit pretended to head for the emergency Institute-wide meeting, then scurried off to the Taste Tower. She knew she should behave, not draw any more attention to herself. That's what Papa said to do . . . but she had to go through with the plan.

Brigit went left to investigate the hall next to Masterji Thakur's classroom. "No one's up here. All clear," she reported.

Ella headed to the right. "No one down here either."

Jason pressed his ear to the door and tried the handle. "We have a problem. It's locked."

Ella and Brigit raced back.

"I've got something." Ella reached into her pocket, retrieving the luck root. It shimmied in her palm, then craned to inspect both Brigit and Jason.

"A plant?" Brigit frowned.

"Whoa." Jason leaned close to it, and it stroked one of his locs.

"Not just any plant, it's from the Underworld. Brings good fortune. Each petal will help you with something you need." She plucked one of the blue petals and squatted in front of the lock. She began to sing, *"Pretty petal, pick this lock. Release your luck to us . . ."* It leaped from her fingertip, pushing its way into the keyhole.

A deep click echoed, and the door opened with a whisper.

Ella grinned back at Jason and Brigit. They slipped inside, where the rotties eagerly waited for them with the ingredients.

Jason knelt, letting them jump all over him while Brigit looked around and Ella went to Masterji Thakur's desk. Everything was in its place—his spice dubba, glitter wax for his mustache and beard, a stack of notebooks, and a book called *Conjuror Conspiracies: The Real Truth*, by Kazz Stewart, with a note attached that said *Don't Forget to Give to Ella After Winter Break*. She grabbed both and brought them to Jason and Brigit. "Look!"

They thumbed through the note and the book.

"See!" Ella said. "Why would he have this if he didn't plan on coming back?"

All three of them exchanged glances.

Jason broke up more cookies, letting the rotties feast in exchange for their help. "Keep an eye out, okay? Guard the door."

Ella got to work. She grabbed one of the carved elephants from Masterji Thakur's desk, laid out a large piece of parchment, set the black candle in the middle, and opened up each herb cloth bundle to make sure she had everything.

"The heat is last," she reminded herself. "Gran used this to track Winnie once." Last summer, Winnie had decided she wanted to be an explorer and set off into the French Quarter on her own—until Gran had tracked her down at Córdova's Confectionary Cornucopia on Royal Street.

"Your gran could do anything." Brigit sat to her left, watching Ella's every move. Her compliment filled in the worried parts of her. She'd never done one of these spells before, and if she messed it up, they might not be able to figure out what happened.

Jason sat on the other side of the large conjure paper, his eyes growing wider and wider as Ella got to work.

"Okay, Brigit, you sprinkle the black pepper. Jason, you do the white pepper. Cover the map. Rub it in good. Then add the salt and the sulfur."

They rubbed their hands all over the paper while Ella did what her gran always did, mix the hot ingredients together, ensuring the right balance. The chili powder and chili flakes made her eyes water, but she wiped her cheeks with her sleeve. She rolled the black candle in the fire-red powder and set the candle in the middle of the map.

Ella sang to it, *"Little wick, let me borrow your light."* Her will crossed into the thin rope. A tiny tendril of smoke curled out of it before the candle ignited.

Brigit clapped with delight. "That was awesome."

Ella nodded shyly.

"What's next?" Jason asked.

"I ask the spirits to help me. To help us track what happened to Masterji Thakur." Ella handed Jason the carved elephant. "Put it beside the candle."

He gulped. "What's going to happen?"

"If it works, the candle will melt and reveal the path." Ella reached for their hands, and they made a circle around it.

"How?"

Ella shrugged. She really didn't know how it actually worked. Well, not all the details. She took a deep breath and sang the spell her gran always did: *"Show me the way to find what's lost."* Jason joined in and then Brigit. Their voices braided together.

The candle melted, and the elephant started to walk in circles. The three of them watched as the flames ate through all the powdery ingredients and the wax spun out like rich black ink, creating a map.

Ella gasped as the conjure paper filled in with an outline of Masterji's lair and lab. Tiny black dots showed his footsteps going round and round, then stopping. Another set of tracks snaked the perimeter. Not footsteps, but long snaking lines. "What are those?" She traced her finger along them.

"Automat wheels. Have to be." Jason inspected them.

"Where did he go?" Brigit leaned closer.

"The footsteps stop near the window," Jason replied. "What does this all mean?"

"He couldn't have disappeared into thin air," Brigit whispered.

Ella's heart did a flip. "He didn't. Masterji Thakur never left this room."

The Celestian City Chronicle

MASTERJI THAKUR SPOTTED ON THE OLD MARVELLERIAN SILK ROAD!

Mildred Fitzgerald

A flurry of reports are coming in that missing instructor Masterji Thakur has been spotted in the bazaars of Afghanistan. Pictures of him have surfaced in and out of spice stalls in search of a very rare ingredient.

FORBIDDEN PLANTS

Gia stood outside Alaoui's Apothecary and Nefarious Plant Nursery on Betelmore's low street. People skulked down the iron staircases and slipped out of shadowy elevators headed for the shops. They were often the sort of Marvellers who had trouble only channeling good light and following rules.

She stared at the WANTED posters of her face splashed over the shops' windows. The heliograms struggled to project, frozen in a sheet of ice while shuffling through her previous "faces" before she'd been sentenced to life in prison. The reward for her capture was one million gold stellas. That would make one a very rich Marvellian. A smile tucked itself into the corner of her mouth, and she admired her latest look before entering the shop. Today she wore flame-red hair and freckled skin as if she'd escaped a farm somewhere in the Empire of Greater Scots Ireland.

A bell struck as she walked inside the obsidian glass greenhouse. Warmth enveloped her, the humidity a glove sticking to her skin. Brass blimps carried miniature false suns and tiny rain clouds over a maze of plants. Black shelves held curious bottles of tonics and powders and tinctures that on any other day would draw Gia's attention.

But she weaved through the aisles, ducking to avoid the rain, and on the hunt for a peculiar plant that would most likely be hidden from display. She found the store clerk in a back corner.

"Excuse me, sir," she called out.

"It's Bassam, and I'm the owner," he replied. An oil lamp made his deeply tan skin glow. He sat on a velvet chair made for a giant, but was barely anything more than a skeleton. He pruned a strange flower. A lattice of climbing ivy hooked around him like an arbor.

"I'm in search of a rare plant, and I'm not sure you have it," she said.

"I have all plants," he barked without looking up. While he worked, hysterical gnats buzzed around him. He let them whiz in and out of his ears and nose, not bothered by their tickles. His focus was singular—the little flower leaves demanded attention. His gnarled fingers worked to untangle them. "This poor bugger got caught in the vines of a nightshade. It can be quite nasty at times."

"Do you have any red Quassia?"

The man dropped his scissors, startled. He looked up. "It's illegal to sell that line of the species now. The General Marveller Assembly just passed decree 8759 in the matter of Underworld Plants, and *that* particular one has been moved to the illegal list. We aren't supposed to carry any conjure plants." He gazed at her with curiosity. "Do you know much about them?"

"A bit."

"A plant marvel?" His forehead crinkled as he examined her. "Not quite."

"Asking for a powerful, deadly, *and* illegal one such as the red Quassia suggests to me that you have some skill . . . or you're a fool."

She laughed. "I have many skills. They will remain my business. And I've never been a fool. So, do you have it?"

"Indeed, and I can count on you not to tell anyone that I still have some in my possession. The law just came to pass. They shouldn't expect us to be able to get rid of it so fast."

She smiled at him, and he smiled back, revealing a set of rotten teeth.

"But it's very expensive . . . and as you probably already know, this particular species doesn't work for everyone. It's temperamental. Very few non-Conjurors can earn its full allegiance. I cannot guarantee it will behave. It's very stingy with its spice and nectar. Once sold, there are no refunds. The risk is yours."

Gia set a fat coin purse on his table.

His eyes bulged, then he tapped a bell to his right. The vines above his head moved, one sinewy cord wiggling loose and snaking along the floor. "Just a moment."

Gia watched as the train of ivy disappeared.

"That'll be two hundred gold stellas and twelve silver lunari."

She plunked her fingers in her purse and counted the money. She stacked the coins on the table where he could see each one. He tapped the bell again, and the train of ivy returned, now holding a clear bell jar and in it, the red Quassia plant. Its triangular petals looked like pulsing rubies. Gia felt its danger and smiled. Just the reactant she needed.

"Very misunderstood plant," he said while signaling the ivy to place the jar in Gia's hands. "No receipts. You never received this purchase here, and I will never see you again."

She nodded.

"Be careful," he warned.

Careful was not something she'd ever be again.

CHAPTER TWENTY
DEAN NABOKOV

The days turned into weeks and the weeks to months. February came and went, and not even the March winds could bring news of Masterji Thakur's whereabouts. She tried to busy herself with perfecting putting her marvel light inside her stellacity sphere, learning the rules of Marvel Combat, and reading everything she could about the origins of the Arcanum. As April rains soaked the Arcanum grounds, Ella's determination sharpened, and she tried everything she possibly could. During her Future Forecasting session, Ella peered into a massive looking glass, trying to will it to reveal a message, any message about what happened to Masterji Thakur and what he might be trying to tell her. Her mind was a flurry of worries, each one piling on top of the next. The hot foot map leading to nowhere haunted her. As did the fact that kids were being taken out of the Institute because of her.

"Open your minds, little stars," Dr. Winchester called out, raising his wrinkled hands in the air. "Try all the different objects."

Beside her, Jason grimaced into his scrying bowl. The water

refused to fill with clouds or reveal a message. Ella abandoned the looking glass and dropped the bundle of fortune sticks, holding the question—*What happened to Masterji Thakur?*—in her brain.

She thumbed through the interpretation guide.

The answer: *Outlook uncertain.*

Brigit scattered coins on the table, yelling at them in hopes that they'd work.

"Are you all getting anything?" she whispered to them.

"No," Jason said.

"I don't know how to actually *make* my marvel work when I want it to. It always does what it wants." Brigit shrugged. She'd been trying for weeks to use her timesight marvel to track Masterji, but they'd had no success.

Dr. Winchester surveyed the room. "Write down how you feel using your instrument. It might not be the right one for you, but you must test them all. It's the only way to discover if you're a Paragon of Vision." He pointed at the wall chart of different divination methods. "I hope to find those with litho-manic marvels. My crystals and stones get ignored every year."

Ella gazed up at the chart wondering if she'd be good at any of these. Dowsing with rods and pendulums seemed inter-esting, but only if she could learn to use one of the massive ones that were the size of the door. Astragalomancy and all the different lettered dice seemed fun, but she wasn't interested in pyromancy and playing with fire messages. Looked like trou-ble. Conjure folk already used necromancy to talk to spirits for many reasons, so maybe not that one, because she already knew how to do it. She wanted a challenge.

"Time to share before you move to another object," Dr. Winchester's voice cut through her thoughts.

Ella bubbled over with nerves. None of the objects she'd experimented with worked; she had nothing positive to say. The others shared their success stories.

"Brigit," Dr. Winchester said. "It's your turn. Tell me about the fortune coins. What did you see?"

"Ugh, I hated them. I won't be using any of this junk." Brigit shoved them away.

Dr. Winchester pursed his lips. "Oh, really?"

"My knitting needles work just fine." Brigit held them up.

"Tell us how they work?"

Brigit opened and closed her mouth, but no words came out. Her cheeks flushed pink with embarrassment. "I—I . . ."

Ella felt her hesitation. "Don't the messages come out in the yarn?"

Brigit nodded, starting to add to Ella's sentence.

"Ella, I didn't ask you. I asked Brigit." Dr. Winchester's severe eyebrows knitted into an angry caterpillar.

"I . . . I was . . ."

"I won't have outbursts of any kind." He pointed the rule-banner that floated around the classroom. "We don't interrupt. We don't talk out of turn. We speak when spoken to. This is the Arcanum standard."

Ella's stomach dropped. "I was just . . ."

"Enough." Dr. Winchester raised his hand.

Brigit grimaced. "She was just trying to help me. I didn't know how to explain it."

"Not another word. Ella, you can go see Dean Nabokov." Dr. Winchester glared at her.

"But—"

"Now!"

Ella swallowed the angry lump in her throat. Everyone stared at her. Clare hid a laugh behind her hands. Ella held back the tears until she got to the hallway and started her walk to the Dean of Discipline.

What had she done wrong? Couldn't she have just apologized? What would her punishment be?

She turned into the Headmarvellers' Hall.

A long bench sat beside the entrance to the Dean's room. On it sat Siobhan and her pixies, heads down, looking glum. The little pixies made noise as she approached, and Siobhan looked up. "What are you doing here?" she asked.

"Guess I could ask you the same thing." Ella plopped down on the bench beside her.

"Dr. Weinberg said my pixies were upsetting her golem." Siobhan scowled at her three pixies, causing them to hide. "You?"

Ella took a deep breath and swallowed the hiccup in her voice. "You know, my roommate . . . and friend . . . Brigit? She struggles sometimes. So I tried to help, and Dr. Winchester threw me out."

Siobhan's brow furrowed. "Weird."

The door snapped open, and out wheeled an automat. "We'll see Ella Durand first while we wait for Dr. Doyle to arrive and translate pixie languages."

Ella gulped and stood. Siobhan flashed her a supportive look as she walked into Dean Nabokov's room. A chalkboard held lists of students' names and their demerit reports. A truth-glass swirled sand from one side to the other as it measured the lies being told in the room. Ella imagined the closets full of torture instruments.

The woman watched Ella's every move as she settled into the massive armchair across from the desk.

Dean Nabokov combed through papers, her peculiar gloves leaving behind stamps. Her long black hair tumbled across her shoulders this time, and her skin had the gray-white color of a fresh corpse. Even still, she was strangely beautiful and terrifyingly tall.

"Ella Durand, is it?" A Russian accent flavored her words.

"Yes," Ella stammered out.

This was the last person she ever wanted to spend time with at the Arcanum. She'd heard other trainees whisper about her in the dining hall. How she'd punish kids. Make them clean the floors with tiny toothbrushes or pick every lint ball off every single pillow in the Paragon lounges or send them off through her punishment portals to work and learn lessons.

"I've received a report about your behavior in Dr. Winchester's Future Forecasting course. You were being disruptive—"

"I was just trying to help. I promise." Ella shifted to the edge of her seat.

"You just disrupted me." Her wire-rimmed glasses slid down her nose.

"I..."

"Should be silent until asked for a response."

A bead of sweat skated down Ella's back.

Dean Nabokov took her glasses off. Her eyes scanned Ella. "Do you like it here?"

"Yes. I love the Institute. It's my most favorite place. Well, aside from New Orleans. But yes, I love it," she babbled.

Dean Nabokov cleared her throat. "It doesn't seem like it. You're getting many demerits. There are complaints. I do wonder if this is . . . in fact . . . the place for you."

Ella didn't know what to say. Her face flamed, and she

clamped her lips tight. Uncontrollable tears brimmed in Ella's eyes. What was Dean Nabokov really asking her? Of course this was the place for her.

"You are a very bright and articulate girl. I thought maybe . . . just maybe this could work."

Ella's fists balled. "But it can work. My grades—"

"There you go interrupting me again. We don't do that here. We aren't so loud. We wait until someone is finished. We favor pleasant and measured conversations."

"I'm sorry." Ella gazed into her lap, trying to calm down.

Dean Nabokov tsked. "Sometimes we come to discover that the things we so desperately wanted aren't actually meant for us. There's much evidence that this might not be the right fit for you." She pressed a button on her desk. A photo-balloon rushed in and dropped a set of heliograms.

The projections showed her out of bed with Brigit that night at the Stariary and then her outside Masterji Thakur's lair yesterday. But she leaned closer to the little heliogram, looking for Jason or Brigit, and they weren't there. It looked like she was talking to herself and going in and out of Masterji Thakur's lair on her own.

"But . . . but . . ." Ella wouldn't rat on her friends. But she knew something was wrong with that photo-balloon since it erased Jason and Brigit out of the image. She couldn't defend herself without getting her friends in trouble.

"There are no buts here at the Arcanum. No *buts* in our work. That is not the Marvellian way. You must learn it if you want to remain here with us."

A storm swirled inside Ella. Back home, she'd seen Fewel folk be rude to her papa at times, especially when he was stopped by police officers while driving, or sometimes in cities without a large Conjuror presence, they'd call him names, say his clothes were funny-looking, or ask him a million questions about where he was going or what he was doing. Dean Nabokov's words felt just as sharp.

"Dr. Winchester also reported finding you in an unauthorized room before winter break. I don't even know how you got yourself to our Founder's Room in the first place, but it's off-limits to trainees. We don't snoop here. It's disrespectful."

Ella started to defend herself, but she didn't think Masterji Thakur would want her to mention the blueprints.

"Nothing to say for yourself?"

"I'm sorry. I was just trying to help Brigit this time." She gritted her teeth.

Dean Nabokov's eyebrow lifted with suspicion. "And it landed you here. It would be a shame if your parents or your godmother knew about your behavior." She pressed a button on the desk, and a tiny bell chimed.

"Please don't tell them," Ella pleaded. "I'll do better." The words felt like sand between her teeth.

Dean Nabokov pursed her lips, giving careful consideration to Ella's words. "I'll keep this between us for now, but I don't want to see you in here again."

"Yes, ma'am, you won't. I promise." Ella's heart thundered.

An automat whizzed inside. "Yes, Dean Nabokov."

"Please assign a Minder Model to Ella Durand for six weeks." Her eyes found Ella's tearful gaze. "Six weeks. Either we see an improvement, or perhaps decide once and for all that this place is not for you."

Her words walloped Ella like a punch.

THE ARCANUM TRAINING INSTITUTE FOR MARVELOUS AND UNCANNY ENDEAVORS

Dear Mr. and Mrs. Durand,

This letter is to inform you that there's been an incident pertaining to your child Ella Durand.

Overnight, in her room with fellow student Brigit Ebsen, a prank occurred where pesky Arcanum rodents called "rotties" got inside and created a mess.

We apologize for any distress and have taken measures to clean up the room and exterminate the rodents.

If you have any questions, please send a starpost to the attention of Dean Nabokov.

Dean Nabokov
Dean of Discipline,
Arcanum Training Institute,
Lower School

CHAPTER TWENTY-ONE

SECRETS & GAGS

S hould we discuss what happened?" Aunt Sera said as Ella stomped into her conjure room.

A news-box played, shouting headlines about the breach of the Cards of Deadly Fate and rumored Conjuror involvement. Ella's minder automat hovered at the door.

Ella would've rather done a hundred other things than talk about her trip to Dean Nabokov's office and her room being turned into a mess. She drowned in a wave of embarrassment and shame and hot anger.

"We'll find the culprits," her godmother said.

"It's fine."

Everything was fine.

She didn't want to discuss something she was trying very hard to forget. She just wanted to find Masterji Thakur.

"It's not." Aunt Sera tsked disapprovingly. She pulled out the chair beside her. "I can feel the tension here too. Someone is sending me mean notes. The cowards. So, I know you must be dealing with a lot too. Talk to me."

"I don't want to talk about it, and please let me figure it out. Don't tell my parents." Ella never imagined attending the Arcanum would include getting in trouble or messing up in her sessions or getting anonymous hate notes or having people stare at her.

"Well, if you don't want that, then you're gonna talk to me about it." She felt her godmother's strong gaze. "Now, fix your face and out with it."

Ella's hands shook, and she launched into her questions: "What really happened to Masterji Thakur? I know something isn't right. It feels like something . . ." She didn't want to use the word *bad*. She didn't want to speak it out loud. Gran said words had ways of taking shape.

"It is a little strange, I'll admit. A few news-boxes say he ran away. Others say he was fired. Is that what's distracting you, baby? I'm sure he'll be back. I know you've grown fond of him."

"But you must know something." A thread of stubbornness took hold of Ella, and she wasn't going to stop pressing her godmother until she gave her some answers. Real ones. No one seemed to have any. "A person can't just disappear like magic."

Aunt Sera winced at her use of the word. "I don't want to hear the word *magic*, Ella. It offends me. I hate the sound of it. The syllables, even. Grating on the nerves."

"You know what I meant." Part of her wanted to blurt out what they'd discovered in his classroom. Come clean about the hot foot. But she knew deep down that her godmother would tell her to stop investigating and be patient.

"Yes, but always be precise in what you call things." Aunt Sera rubbed her temples. "The world is chaos right now. Between the breach in the Cards and kids being taken out of the Arcanum and you being targeted . . . it's all a lot." She stood up and walked to the bottle tree. "We have to be careful."

Ella fussed with her mantle, then walked to her desk, where a set of conjure maps sat.

Her godmother looked up. "Out with it. I can sense the question tickling your tongue."

"Masterji Thakur showed me the Founder's Room," she said. "The place where they all used to meet and discuss the school."

"That was lovely of him." Aunt Sera touched her cheek.

"There were conjure maps there."

Her godmother sat up straight. "What do you mean?"

"I don't know. They looked like blueprints, though. Nothing I've ever seen before. When he tried to tell me, he started coughing badly and then choking. The first time it happened, we were near the Cardinal statue outside. I thought maybe he was sick or had swallowed wrong, but it happened again."

Aunt Sera began to pace with a look of horror on her face. "It's the muzzle."

"The what?"

"A gag. A way to silence you. I'd heard rumors about how the Marvellian government makes sure that certain things are never spoken of. They don't like their secrets out. They silence those they don't want talking."

Ella put her hand to her chest, fingering her conjure-cameo, and couldn't help being a little afraid. Goose bumps covered her arms. "Why wouldn't they want Masterji Thakur to talk about Conjurors? Why would they do something so horrible? What was he going to say?"

Aunt Sera rapped her fingers on the table. "It's awful." Her godmother glanced up at Echi, and she knew they were communicating. "This place has a nest of secrets like a mother bird squatting on her eggs. They tend to them with fierce protection." She bit her bottom lip. "But now, with us here, that carefully constructed nest is showing its edges, and they're scared of it unraveling. Some things might fall."

Ella didn't exactly understand what her godmother meant, but she was worried that Masterji Thakur might be one of those things. "I haven't heard from him since January, and tomorrow it'll be April fifth."

Her godmother kissed her forehead. "Don't you worry. What's done in the dark doesn't stay there for very long."

FUSSY REACTANTS

Gia gazed at the angry red Quassia in the bell jar. Each time she removed the glass hood, it hissed and flared, ready to spit its poison at her, and refused to part with the precious and valuable nectar inside its petals. It was as if it knew her intentions and had set its mind to go against her wishes. She couldn't be rash and risk getting poisoned, because a hospital visit would delay her plan. And she would have nothing come between her and her destiny.

Gia thumped the glass, and the plant hissed again.

"It only responds to a few," her prisoner called out.

She frowned. "And you're one of those people."

The prisoner didn't answer.

She glared. Her prisoner swayed, chains creaking, and he reeked like a foul monster buried in a forgotten dungeon. The Marvellian prison hadn't been like this. But her guest had put up such a fuss and refused to help. She did what had to be done. She'd never intended to treat her old friend like this. But she guessed her visitor probably didn't even think of her as a friend anymore. Apparently most people didn't want to be friends with a convicted murderer.

"As soon as you help me, I'll let you out of there. You will be free to go home. I'll even arrange transport. No hard feelings," she said.

"No hard feelings? You kidnap me, trap me in this cage for months, and then assume that I'll help you and go on my merry way?" the prisoner spat out. "I won't."

"Then you'll stay until you do, my sweet."

The prisoner scowled.

"You used to help me all the time, my Ace of Hearts. All the experiments we conducted to uncover the nature of our light. We spent our childhood together. That ought to count for something." She drummed her fingers on the glass. "I don't need you to make anything for me this time around. Just help me draw out the properties."

"Why?" The prisoner's eyes burned into hers.

"I learned hard lessons about telling people too many things." She gritted her teeth. "It gives them ammunition to turn on you." She remembered all the faces and voices of the people who'd testified at her trial. "I need the Quassia's spice nectar to mix into the Elixir of Light you make."

"Only if you tell me why," the prisoner replied.

"Just give me what I *want*!" Her scream shook the entire room. Gia used to be good at persuasion with her fellow Marvellers, and especially Fewel folks. Generally, she could persuade people into liking her, goad them into trusting her confidence, and manipulate children into abandoning their instinctive suspicions of strangers.

"If you get what you want, then what?"

A maniacal smile slid across her face. "Nothing will ever be taken from me again. I will be the most powerful Marveller in the whole world. Never to be imprisoned again. Never to be underestimated."

CHAPTER TWENTY-TWO
YARN PROPHECIES!

During Ella's Stardust and Exploration club meeting, she could barely focus on the spring star map she was supposed to be creating. She ground her teeth, and a headache punched her temples as she messed up the charts for the twenty-eight lunar mansions in the Chinese constellation system. Conversation swirled around her.

"So many people are leaving," Anh said. "I heard Evan might go and that Abina's parents want her to come home too."

"My older sister said something bad is going to happen. That more criminals will escape the Cards," Clare added, finding Ella's gaze.

"*The Starry Chronicle* said the cities will go on lockdown soon," Tochi interjected, taking a news-box from his satchel.

"My 'umi said they'll close the Institute if the prison isn't reset. It's too dangerous." Samaira's cheeks reddened. "But I don't want that to happen."

"My dad's been working a thousand hours. The judges are trying to help fix it, but I think it's an inside job. That a Conjuror let that murderer out." Lian flicked her hair over her shoulder. "I barely get to talk to him anymore."

Ella flinched. All of it made her wish Masterji Thakur were here. She tried to reason like Papa. "A problem is nothing more than a tiny machine whose insides are all bungled up needing repair," he'd told her once. "And how does one fix a machine?" He'd put a finger on her nose, claiming the distraction helped focus the mind. She remembered saying, "By taking it apart."

But each part of this complicated answer felt out of reach.

Brigit poked her. "Did you hear what I said?"

"No, sorry." She'd been so in her head, she'd forgotten Brigit was right there beside her.

"I'm ready to try my timesight marvel again. My extra classes with Dr. Karlsson are working."

Ella felt hopeful for the first time in weeks.

"I told Jason to meet us in the wombie burrows." Brigit flashed the new yarn in her satchel. "I can concentrate there."

After dismissal, Ella and Brigit went to the Arcanum menagerie. Ella's minder automat fussed at her the entire way, but both she and Brigit ignored it.

Jason was waiting for them outside the wombie habitat. "They're all napping, so it should be quiet."

"You ready?" Ella turned to Brigit, putting a hand on her shoulder.

"No, but I should do it anyways." Brigit dropped to her knees and unpacked her satchel, setting out the balls of yarn and her knitting needles. She took a deep breath. "I've never, like, purposefully done it. Dr. Karlsson said I should try thinking of questions or images or feeling."

"Maybe start with a question." Ella plopped down beside her.

Brigit took a deep breath and closed her eyes. She started to rock back and forth. Her eyes snapped back open. "But what if I can't?"

Ella patted her shoulder. "You can."

"If it doesn't work, at least we tried." Jason sat on the other side of her.

Brigit closed her eyes again.

Ella's heart drummed as she watched.

Brigit's hands moved so fast that Ella started to feel nauseated from staring too hard. The threads quickly transformed into a small quilt decorated with an image of Masterji Thakur. The brown figure held vials of liquid in one hand and a key in the other.

"Whoa," Jason said.

Brigit's eyes snapped open. "He's trapped somewhere."

"How do you know?" Jason ran his hand over the small quilt, inspecting every single knitted image.

"I could see him. He was mixing this and that. But sweating. He looked upset. Like he didn't want to do it. I've never seen him look so angry. Not since that day at orientation when he yelled about the Aces."

Ella started to pace in circles. "Could you see anything else?"

"There were chains around his wrists. He's in a messy room. There were weird faces on the wall."

"Faces?" Jason blinked, confused.

"I don't know what they were. Maybe they're masks." Brigit shut her eyes again.

A cold panic dropped into Ella's stomach. "What was on that table?"

Brigit's eyelids fluttered and Ella knew she was combing through everything. "... like vials and tools and one of those weird pocket-boxes ..." Brigit shook her head as if the answers might tumble out. "I wish I could see more." Her eyes snapped open.

Ella chewed the inside of her cheek as she thought about what to do. The fact that he was in a room wasn't much to go on.

Brigit dug into her satchel looking for more yarn. "Maybe I can try again. Shoot—I'm out."

Ella jumped to her feet, pacing the perimeter of the alcove, but the size of her problem remained the same: They weren't any closer to finding out where Masterji Thakur actually was and how to rescue him.

"What are we going to do?" Brigit asked.

Ella didn't know.

The Marvellian Times

COPPERS HEADED TO THE ARCANUM!
By Kate Milford

Despite the coppers' best efforts, convict Gia Trivelino remains on the loose. All three Marvellian cities have been on high alert for unusual activity and have enabled extra security precautions until she has been caught. Astradam and the Celestian City are in transit toward the Arcanum, which will help with security plans, but a special unit of coppers has been deployed to popular Fewel cities with Marvellian populations—New York City, Cairo, Paris, Accra, London, Mexico City, Tokyo, Beijing, and more. Turn to page 7 for a full list.

The Arcanum Institute is installing powerful incant bars on all windows at the training center to keep the students safe.

CHAPTER TWENTY-THREE
ALIBIS!

The days passed like the slow trickle of sand from one side of an hourglass to the other as Ella, Jason, and Brigit tried to figure out the cryptic message within Brigit's image. A rainy April had turned into a warm May. Brigit kept trying to knit more details related to Masterji Thakur's whereabouts. Ella thought about trying another conjure spell to get more information.

She stood beside the lamppost outside Dr. Mbalia's West African Oral room, waiting for Brigit and Jason with her minder automat.

"You've been good today. I shall give you an excellent report," it said.

Ella ignored its metallic smile, staring up at the black iron column and its glass box, trying to ignore the whispers of passersby. The column boasted a warm, flickering light, the stellacity current almost blinding. She wished and hoped that one day, she'd be able to conjure such a light.

"Beautiful isn't it," came Headmarveller MacDonald's voice from behind her.

She jumped. "Um, hi, Headmarveller MacDonald."

"Do you have a moment to talk, Ella?"

"I have class with Dr. Mbalia. He doesn't like it when we're late."

"I'll be sure to let him know it's for something important," he replied. Ella still loved the sound of his voice, the rhythm of his Scottish accent.

"Okay." Ella walked beside Headmarveller MacDonald. He asked her simple questions: Was she looking forward to celebrating Founder's Day? Was she excited about the Marvel Examination and being placed in her Paragon family? Was she looking forward to watching her first Marvel Combat match?

She tried to remain calm. She tried to make up reasons for why he wanted to chat. She tried not to panic.

They turned into the Headmarvellers' Hall. Photo-balloons swarmed overhead, zipping in and out of the Dean of Discipline's den. Bronze statues of former Headmarvellers waved as they passed, while imparting wise sayings.

"Always listen for messages from the stars. They're all around you."

"Never sour yourself with lies. Let there be a truth within you."

"The Marvellian way leads to the good light. Always follow it."

The office doors sprung open as they approached. A double staircase split in two, soaring up to a balcony holding two massive desks. Large glass windows revealed the Cloud Loch and

Headmarveller MacDonald's beautiful silver waterhorse Edi poking its head inside to eat from a bowl. A golden orrery consumed a massive table: the gilded model of the heavens detailing the locations of each Marvellian city and the Arcanum. It clicked slowly through its positions as Ella gazed into its complex innards of pendulums, cogs, and gears.

He motioned to the tea table. "Have a seat."

A chair scooted forward, presenting itself to her.

"Don't mind the comfort incants the old Headmarveller left. They mean well." He rubbed his chin. "Headmarveller Rivera will be down in one minute."

As she sat, the chair's cushions snuggled her in. "Am I in trouble?"

He put his huge hand to his chest. "We have a few questions—"

"I'm here." Headmarveller Rivera descended the staircase slowly, her glittering cane helping her with each step.

A cold twinge flickered over her skin.

Headmarveller Rivera sat in her big armchair across from Ella and took a deep breath. "There's been an incident, and I must ask you for your side of things."

"My side of what?" Her stomach twisted into a messy knot.

"Clare Lumen says you attacked her. She didn't report it right afterward because she said you've been sending her starposts full of threats and trying to make sure she stayed silent about it." Headmarveller Rivera sighed.

"What?" Her breathing tensed like she'd been chased by her next-door neighbor's old dog. "I didn't attack anyone. I didn't send any mean starposts."

"Clare has a flair for the dramatic, and I do wonder why

she's come forward all of a sudden . . . as this was many months ago, but her parents are making a fuss, so we have to take it seriously." Headmarveller MacDonald took a record-box from his desk and wound its side. It fluttered between them. A tiny recording poured out. Ella heard her own voice saying words she'd never said before, then Clare screaming in response and the sound of fists.

Her mouth hung open. "That's not me."

"It sure sounds like you."

"I've never been in a fight my *whole life*. Ask my parents." Ella felt like her heart might leap out of her chest. "I didn't do that."

"What am I supposed to do in my position?" he asked. "That is your voice."

"Yes, but—"

"Clare gave a statement. She says you broke her news-box too."

"That was an accident—"

Headmarveller MacDonald put his hand in the air. "Her father is a very important politician. Jefferson Lumen. He will not let this rest."

Cords of anger and sadness wrapped themselves around her heart. "I didn't do this. I didn't do this. I swear!"

"It was the last day before winter break. Can you tell me what happened that day?"

Her mind turned like sped-up clock gears, trying desperately to remember the details of that day. "I wasn't there. I promise you." Ella bit her lip. Her head thrummed. "I had a meeting with Masterji Thakur."

Headmarveller MacDonald held sympathy. "But Masterji

isn't here to give a statement right now. I'll need yours, as we must follow our Arcanum policies and procedures. Clare's parents are coming in for a meeting. Yours will have to attend as well. The incident will be brought before the Arcanum Lower School Disciplinary Board. Dean Nabokov will oversee it, and all evidence will be presented and reviewed to determine if you're fit to stay with us."

"But . . . but . . . but—" Furious anger swirled in Ella.

"I'm sorry, Ella. We must follow all the proper procedures and protocols. What are we without them? Chaos," Headmarveller Rivera said.

Dean Nabokov appeared in the doorway. "Clearly monitoring hasn't deterred your behavior."

Headmarveller Rivera pursed her lips. "Until then, you will be placed at isolation desks in all your sessions, and you're not to engage with Clare Lumen under any circumstances. You're to keep this confidential for your own sake."

"But I didn't do anything," Ella said over and over again as the tears fell from her eyes.

PART IV

THE ACE OF ANARCHY

THE HIGHEST HIGH
WALKER OF THEM ALL

Gia set out black coffee, a rum cake, roasted nuts, and platters of grilled hot peppers. Conjurors enjoyed being entertained. Never turned down a party with the right food and good music. She'd learned that much from Celeste Baptiste.

She expected her guest any minute now. Her fingers drummed against her finest lace. She'd draped it over a tea table and set it out in the Close's courtyard. The May weather was perfect.

She stacked four towers of golden stellas in the very center of the spread, and she planned to add a few extra if the news was good. He was a busy man with much to attend to. Her matter would be a chore. But he was the only one that could help. Every soul would be in his ledger.

Her heart squeezed with hope. Something she hadn't felt in so long. Good news could be headed her way today. Conjurors could've located her daughter's soul.

She would have her back.

The gate-bell rang.

She stood and smoothed the front of her brand-new dress.

Her starfolk helper opened the gate. "Your guest, my lady."

The most powerful High Walker of the Underworld strode in.

Sebastien Durand.

He was more handsome than he looked in the Marvellian news-boxes.

"Welcome. Please sit and thank you for coming all this way." She waved her hand to a nearby seat. "How was the journey?"

He obliged and removed his signature top hat. "Marvellian towns lack"—he waved his hand around as if to pluck the word from somewhere—"flavor, if you will."

She offered him a slice of rum cake and coffee.

His mouth broke out into a smile. "Your hospitality is . . . targeted, and very un-Marvellian-like."

"Conjure folk have been kind to me. I've always considered them allies, and hopefully still friends."

He took a slow sip. The steam circled his deep brown face like billows of smoke. "The travel coins you provided were extraordinary. Arriving right at your doorstep and without the hassle of customs was . . . dare I say, marvelous."

"Happy to provide more." She took the flat discs from her pocket. Their etchings writhed with forbidden travel incants. Then she added more gold stellas to the stack and motioned at it.

"Marvellian money doesn't interest me."

"It used to."

"I don't do things for the Aces anymore. Conjurors are done with that."

"But we aren't done with you." Gia flashed him a perfect harlequin smile. "We've supplied you with information all these years to help you achieve the Conjure Edict. We've blackmailed and disposed of things that needed to disappear. Brought things to light to sway hearts and minds when together we should've burned these cities to the ground. We helped you play your game."

Sebastien rubbed his beard. "That's the only reason why I'm here."

She nodded in agreement. "And now, you will play mine. Is there news for me?"

"No. I sent several trusted Walkers looking for your daughter. No soul is ever unaccounted for. If she were in my Underworld, I would've found her."

Gia gritted her teeth. A flare of anger consumed her, the memory of her mother's vault and twisted riddle. "What does that mean? I gave you her full name and the time and date of her death. Is that not enough?"

"Your daughter is not dead."

Gia sat up straight. "You're lying. I saw her covered in blood." Her mind toggled back to that fateful night.

"I thought you would be happy to hear this."

"I was never suited to be a mother."

The last thing she remembered before they'd carted her away was the way her daughter's blonde hair had been stained red.

"Gia? I know this is a shock, but there's no other explanation." He set the coffee mug down.

Gia laughed. "I saw her die. I need her essence brought back. I know there are those that have escaped before."

He edged forward in his seat with irritation. "Accidentally only."

"This will be *no* accident." She pushed the pile of coins closer to him.

"We don't play with the dead." He sucked his teeth. "Bringing a soul out of the Underworld has consequences—and I'm telling you she's not there anymore. You should be worried about where she is now."

"Nothing worries me," she replied. "I will find her if you cannot."

CHAPTER TWENTY-FOUR

THE POCKET-BOX

Ella ran to the animal menagerie. It was closer than the Hydra Tower, and she needed a friendly face right now. She hoped Jason was there. She darted past a crowd of Level Twos who held news-boxes and whispered about her papa and Conjurors. She felt the cold glare of several security coppers. Her minder automat warned her to slow down, but instead, she rushed through the doors, zipping around the exhibits, trying to hold back tears.

When she rounded the corner to the wombie burrow, she started calling Jason's name. The automat whizzed behind her shouting its instructions to keep her voice soft, but she continued to ignore it.

The wombies scurried out.

"What's wrong, Ella?" the largest wombie asked.

She barreled into his small alcove and gazed around. "Is Jason here?"

"Not yet. But soon. It's almost time for tea. Will you be joining us today?" This one held up a teapot.

She couldn't even answer the sweet wombie, afraid she'd burst, so she tucked herself into the corner and buried her face in her knees as the hot tears streamed down.

"Ella?"

She looked up. A trio of wombies stood before her, outside their habitat. They gazed at her, their furry round cheeks drooping, a sadness filling their bright eyes. One curled into her lap, and another wiped away her tears.

"What happened?"

"It's terrible. Too terrible," she said with a sniffle. "People think I did something I didn't do."

"That happened to us too. Very unfortunate. That's why people want to hurt us. And they love our golden poop," the large one said.

She couldn't even laugh. She felt so isolated.

The automat started to fuss again, and the sound of footsteps made the wombies hide.

But Jason and Brigit rushed in, dropping their satchels and diving right to the floor beside her.

"We've been looking for—" Jason started.

"Are you okay?" Brigit put a hand on Ella's shoulder.

The story tumbled out between tears. "Clare accused me of attacking her, but someone must've impersonated me somehow. I was with Masterji Thakur in the Founder's Room that day. There's going to be a trial with the discipline board, and my parents will be told any minute now. They're going to probably yank me out of the Institute. I just feel like I'm losing everything."

"Not us." Jason took her right hand and Brigit took her left.

"What should I do?" Her voice broke. "I have to fix this before my parents arrive. I can't leave the Arcanum."

A pack of rotties rushed into the room. A chaos of squeaking set off the wombies.

"What is it? Calm down." Jason crouched low and they climbed all over him, excitedly jumping and chittering. "Relax, please." He looked back up at Ella and Brigit with a huge frown. "The rotties overheard the Headmarvellers talking." More tiny squeaks. "The coppers have been secretly searching rooms and interrogating automats. They took Feste."

"What?" Brigit said.

Jason turned back to the rotties. "They're looking for a pocket-box. Feste was trying to protect the room."

Brigit jumped to her feet.

"*My* box." Brigit yanked it from her satchel. The lid sprang open, spilling yarn balls, session manuals, candies, and more.

Ella scrambled to help Brigit gather everything up while Jason tried to calm the wombies. She picked up the skeleton key. The thread looped around its body felt soft to the touch. She inspected the diamond etched into its handle. "Wait! Brigit! Jason! Look! It's from your vision of Masterji Thakur. The same key you knitted."

Brigit pulled the quilt square from her satchel. They compared the two.

"But what does it open?" Jason squinted at it.

"Should we check the pocket-box again?" Ella picked it up. "Maybe it opens a hidden compartment."

"After you showed me the knock-code, I went through all of them. Or I thought I did."

"Let's try again," Ella urged.

Brigit ran her fingers over the grooves just as Ella had shown her. The pocket-box wiggled left and wiggled right.

More compartments revealed themselves inside the seemingly small box. All three of them stared down into it.

Brigit ruffled her hands around. Mostly removing dust or old styluses.

"Keep reaching in," Ella encouraged.

"It's like there's hundreds of little spaces. Even more than before." Brigit's entire arm was inside the box now. She grimaced. "Wait. Hold on. There's paper." She tugged out a long rolled-up poster fastened with a threadbare ribbon.

The three of them worked to unroll it.

The paper was filled in with the slow precision of an artist's paintbrush, each line thick and bold with fresh ink.

Ella gasped.

In the distance, the great white tent of a three-ring circus appeared on a small island. It floated in a strange canal. Red, black, and white trailers appeared and snaked along the edge of the page like a colorful locomotive.

"What is this?" Brigit whispered.

"A vintage heliogram. Has to be," Jason said.

On the page, red diamond-covered trailers passed by first, and each one advertised its contents: roaring lions and tigers, charging rhinos and furious hippos, and a majestic white elephant at the very end. The animals peeked out their cages, and a sapphire leviathan poked its head above water. Ella heard feline roars and the trumpet blare of an elephant's trunk.

Jason kept saying "Wow" under his breath. "I've always wanted to go to one. My parents used to tell me about all the shows and circuses they used to go to, but they're all banned now."

White trailers came next, carrying people in sequined outfits and feather headdresses. They jumped from trailer windows, somersaulting across the procession's rooftops. The last set of vehicles chugged around the poster perimeter, and their black frames flashed the strangest oddities.

Ella felt the energy of the page beneath her fingertips. In the poster's foreground, a woman marched out, climbed on a striped platform, and hollered into a megaphone. Her voice echoed. Ella felt each booming word in her chest.

A portrait appeared, flashing strange characters and their Italian names: the Zanni, Vecchi, Capitani, Pierrot, Pantalone, and more. But they all seemed to be the same person dressed up in different costumes. Lastly, a long banner announced: *The Trivelino Troupe's Circus & Imaginarium of Illusions has come to play. Will you join?*

The address flickered:

COMMEDIA CLOSE

THE LOW STREET

BETELMORE

"Trivelino . . . like Gia Trivelino, the woman who broke out of the Cards of Deadly Fate." Jason's voice quivered as he stared back into the pocket-box.

"The Ace of Anarchy," Ella said, the realization rattling her.

"The woman I've been knitting," Brigit whispered.

Jason took out another object from the box, another old heliogram. The projection showed a group of Arcanum students posing together. A flickering banner stretched over their heads: THE ACES. "Look, it's that woman." Jason pointed.

Ella gulped, staring at the waving image a young Indian

man. "And there's Masterji Thakur right beside her. Well, a young version of him."

"They were friends?" Jason asked, puzzled.

"More than that . . . he was an Ace." Brigit's eyes filled with shock.

Ella couldn't even say a word. He couldn't have been. Masterji Thakur, a bad person? A criminal like that woman?

Brigit picked up the circus poster again. "You think he's there?"

Resolve surged through Ella. She didn't know how Masterji Thakur and Gia Trivelino were *really* connected, but she was determined to find out. "We have to try."

THE TRIVELINO TROUPE'S CIRCUS & IMAGINARIUM OF ILLUSIONS

Beware of strange magic under the great striped tent of a circus. From your seat it might look like nothing more than a few brightly colored clowns and twirling acrobats, hand-spun candy and roasted peanuts, twinkling lights and extraordinary human eccentricities, but a circus can be something more than just the greatest show in the sky. In fact, it can be something dangerously mysterious: a carnival of chaos, a mirage of make-believe, a resplendent reverie. But most often, it's a world where the watcher loses the line between the real and the fantastic.

But don't let us scare you, for we're known to jest. Come one! Come all! See with your own eyes!*

—Opening of the Trivelino Troupe's Circus & Imaginarium of Illusions Official Program

*Disclaimer: Management is not responsible for injury, loss of life, or any other peculiar circumstance as a result of attendance.

★—★—★— **STARPOST**—★—★—★

Ella,

I am on the first sky-ferry headed to the Arcanum tomorrow. Papa is already in Betelmore on business. He's coming in the morning.

Please be safe. We will be there soon for the hearing. Don't worry.

Love,
Mama

CHAPTER TWENTY-FIVE

THE COMMEDIA CLOSE

I n the dark of night, Ella eased out of her soft pajamas and into real clothes. Brigit tiptoed around trying to make as little noise as possible.

But the saints still woke up.

"You shouldn't be out of bed, young ladies," St. Anthony complained as Ella packed her satchel. "You know the lengths we went to in order to help you? The both of you? We've already worked so many miracles."

The bottle tree bloomed with watch-over flowers courtesy of Mama, and its branches held tiny protection lanterns that checkered her bed with light.

"You heard what your mother said," St. Peregrine added. "Stay put. Stay out of danger."

"We've got four minutes," Ella reminded Brigit. Ms. Paige would do an hourly check-in soon. They were under strict surveillance. She went over the plan again: Fill their beds with pillows to make it look like they were sleeping. Meet Jason in the Stariary to get to the Arcanum dock.

"I don't think so, young ladies," St. Andrew said.

"I've blessed your mama's travel," St. Christopher threatened. "Don't let her down."

Ella draped her quilt on top of them to muffle their fussing, then arranged her headscarf on the pillow. That would have to do. Hopefully, Ms. Paige wouldn't look too hard.

Brigit cracked open the door. She peeked her head out, looking left and right. Ella inched right behind her. The sudden buzz of wings made Brigit stumble backward and crash into Ella. She swatted her hands all around. "Get out of here."

One of Siobhan's pixies bolted inside the room. Its high-pitched gibber gabber alarmed the saints again.

"Why can't she keep these things in their cage?" Brigit threw a shoe at it.

The pixie continued to fly around wildly. "Everyone's going to hear it. We'll get caught if we don't act fast." Ella pulled the marvel light from deep down inside her and shouted her first Marvellian incant: "Shan-thee." Just as Masterji taught them.

The pixie settled, relaxing. Ella listened for her bottle tree's pulsing life force and began to sing. The branch stretched out and curled around the tiny pixie's body, trapping it in place.

Brigit scowled up at it. "Serves it right. I hate those things."

Ella took another petal from Reagan's luck root and went to the door. Brigit stopped her for a second. "We'll get Feste when we come back, right?" Panic quavered in her voice.

"Yes, I promise." Ella nodded. "Let's go."

They tiptoed through the Hydra Tower. Her minder automat sat in the corner asleep. Ms. Paige's snores and telebox rumbled. Open windows let in the scent of the starfruit flowers. The Institute's spring clouds had been released, and the window boxes bloomed.

Ella peeked her head into the next hallway. Three coppers surveyed. Their brass buttons caught the night-lantern light. Ella held her breath until they passed. She looked left and then right before easing into the hallway.

"This way," she whispered to Brigit. They shot down various corridors to get to the Vision Tower.

Ella approached the side door that would take them outside and to the path that led to the Stariary. She slipped the luck root petal into the lock. It stretched, pushing against the thick bolt.

The door creaked open. Ella and Brigit eased outside, leaving the door ajar in case Jason came behind them. They ducked past spring topiaries and the Founder's fountain as they made their way to the Stariary.

The sound of a whistle made them freeze.

"Star's teeth!" Jason eased from behind a bush. "What took you so long?"

"The saints and Siobhan's pixies." Ella led the way inside the mail center.

Tiny doors opened and closed, and a storm of letters swirled over their heads, waiting for their star messengers to catch them.

Aries blocked their path, his furry hands on his hips and brass spectacles sitting on his button nose. "You're not supposed to be in here. Again. I thought you would've learned your lesson by now."

Ella stood her ground. "You owe us after putting that sleepy powder in our faces."

"Yeah," Brigit chimed in. "And kidnapping me."

"The starfolk don't *do* favors. Especially for non–starfolk. We stick together. No exceptions." Ella had read about the starfolk in *Curious Creatures of the Marvellian World*, and it was true, they weren't prone to favors.

"But it's an emergency," Ella pleaded.

"Please," Jason added, then spoke a strange language Ella's translation crystal couldn't decipher. Clearly it was one Aries understood. They went back and forth.

The worries buzzed inside her. Maybe the starfolk was stalling? Maybe one of the instructors would show up any minute? Maybe her minder automat would escort her back and she'd earn detention again and more demerits? Maybe they'd never get a chance to help Masterji Thakur? Maybe she'd never clear her name—or the reputation of the Conjurors? Maybe she'd be kicked out of the Arcanum for good?

Aries took a big sigh and tapped his furry foot. "Jason told me everything. Let me see the poster and the key."

Ella motioned to Brigit, who pulled everything out of her satchel.

"You should tell the coppers and the Headmarvellers," Aries warned.

"They won't believe us. Everyone's mad at Conjurors. They think we had something to do with Gia Trivelino's escape. I have the meeting with the discipline board, and they're going to kick me out too. I didn't even do the thing they're accusing me of. Only Masterji knows the truth. I have to show them." Ella's voice cracked. Tears rushed down her cheeks, and she couldn't stop them. She hated crying in front of anyone. She hated crying period. She felt like everything had caught up to her.

Both Jason and Brigit took her hands and squeezed them.

"It's okay. It's okay." Aries put a paw on her shoulder. "Fine. I'll help you."

"Can you take us down in the car-lift?" she said through sniffles.

Aries stepped back. "I can't drive those unauthorized, and they're locked to the platform at night."

Ella's plan burst like a popped balloon, all the air rushing out in several directions, as well as her last ounce of hope. More tears rushed down her cheeks.

"But . . ." Aries scratched his head. "I *do* have the keys, and no one really watches those late at night. They're more concerned about the sky-ferries."

Their plan was in motion again.

✦　◼　✦　◼　✦

THE ARCANUM CABLE CAR SAILED DOWN THICK CABLES HEADED for Betelmore. Its golden nose pierced through thick clouds, and light spring rain pattered against the metal.

Aries pulled levers in the driver's chamber. He turned a series of cranks. "I have to keep forcing it to move without the use of the cable system," he said. "It's going to be bumpy. Hold tight."

Ella gripped the cushions beneath her and gazed out the window. She couldn't see the city below. Thick clouds still blocked their view, as if warning them to go back to their warm beds.

This wasn't exactly how Ella had pictured her first visit to a Marvellian city. She'd spent so much time thinking about these three great moving cities full of Marvellians who'd left the Fewel world behind hundreds of years ago. She'd spent so many hours drawing maps based on her research—winding high streets full of eccentric shops, shady low streets full of illegal goods, and the networks of cable wires pulling air-trolleys overhead. At times, she wished New Orleans could lift up off the Mississippi River and take flight just like Astradam, Celestian City, and Betelmore, so the Conjure folk wouldn't have to deal with Fewels anymore. Maybe all the Conjure folk of the world could take to the sky and be safe too.

The dashboard's brass hourglass measured the time; twenty minutes until arrival. Ella tried to contain her anxiety, but it started to spill out over the edges of her, and her legs and arms and hands quivered with fear.

This was a *serious* mission.

A rescue mission.

As they descended lower, she could soon see the tops of the city crested over with spring ivy and little oval windows bursting with flower boxes. The starfruit glittered like tiny, tethered stars.

Ella put a hand to her stomach.

Jason tapped a beat along his seat.

"Can you *not?*" Brigit barked at him. "Too loud."

Ella pressed his hand flat. The noise stopped. He smiled, flashing the tiny gap between his front teeth. His locs jumped around his shoulders, his nervous energy radiating with nowhere to go. A rottie peeked her head out of his mantle hood.

"Sweet Pea, what are you doing here?" Ella gazed into her beady little eyes.

"She stays close when I'm nervous," he admitted.

"We have to keep her safe."

Jason agreed and unfolded a map of Betelmore. "Got this from my brother. We should walk and not use the air-trolleys. Coppers probably everywhere."

Ella held her breath as the station came into view. The Crimson Line. There was no going back now.

"Here!" Aries called out.

The cable car approached the platform. Aries bounded out of the driver's chamber. "Now, you three, I'm going to wait here for two hours. If you don't come back by then, I'm coming after you, and calling the Headmarvellers and the coppers too. That's as far as the favor goes. Chins up, little heroes."

They nodded at him.

Ella didn't feel the closest bit like a hero. In the stories she read, heroes saved the world; they were chosen ones sent to rescue people. But most of the time, Ella felt like a chicken. Not someone with courage who was unafraid.

Ella was *very* afraid.

She heard her Mama's favorite phrase in her head: "*Some things have to be faced. They can't be avoided.*"

Aries squeezed her shoulder. "I'm leaving a stardust imprint on each of you. It's trackable. So, I'll know where to look. All starfolk will."

Ella nodded. "We'll be back." She tried to sound confident. She tried to fill her words with all the determination she felt. She'd orchestrated all of this and roped both Brigit and Jason into joining her.

They would find Masterji Thakur. They would bring him back. He could clear her name with the Headmarvellers. He could tell her why the Arcanum blueprints were conjure maps.

Everyone would know she was innocent.

He would be safe and return to teaching his sessions.

Everything would be *fine*. Better than fine.

They stepped out of the cable car and onto the platform. She willed away the tingle of terror that shot down her spine. They folded in with the crowd headed down the stairs to the Betelmore high street.

Jason led the way. Ella stole glances at Brigit. Her cheeks were red and her jaw clenched as she gawked all around. This was Brigit's first time in a Marvellian city too.

The shops and restaurants boasted different shapes and colors, some striped, some painted in pastels, some brass and silver, all lined up like eccentric hatboxes in a rich person's closet. Stellaric cars whizzed past, their golden spheres blinding them as they passed. Beautiful limestone mansions showed off topiary gardens of starfruit trees and window boxes bursting with moonflowers. Stardust fountains stretched high, ready to catch their medicinal dust.

Jason turned left off the high street and into an alley. A dark staircase lay ahead with a small sign that blinked: LOW STREET—BEWARE.

They started their descent.

Brigit paused.

Ella looked back. "You okay?"

"It just feels . . . feels familiar."

"How?" Jason asked.

"I was here before. I think." Brigit rubbed her temples. "I just can't remember when or why. It's like I have these memories that disappeared for some reason. When I think too hard about them, they hide."

Ella, Jason, and Brigit crept along the street, taking in all of its dark delights.

Brigit stopped abruptly in front of the Commedia Close. Ella almost crashed into her. She pointed at the gate. "There!"

Ella's first sight of it filled her with dread. The tiny courtyard looked like a place people whispered about and avoided. Not a place that wanted visitors. Not a place that looked inhabited. Not a place they should be headed to.

As they got closer, the world seemed like it darkened to a deeper shade of black. A faded sign spelled out the circus's name above the spiked gate columns. A restricted message flickered.

"He's really in there?" Jason whispered.

"I think so." Ella gulped.

Brigit turned the handle. It wouldn't budge. Then she took the heavy skeleton key from her pocket and jammed it into the ancient-looking lock. It clicked, and the gate opened with a tiny hiss.

CHAPTER TWENTY-SIX

THE CANAL OF MIRRORS

Ella stepped through the gate. Jagged cobblestones lined the courtyard like sharp teeth, ready to bite them. They tried to jump from cobblestone to cobblestone, careful to avoid the broken ones, as they made their way to the entrance of the Commedia Close. Ella thought it looked like a great big mouth, the edges once red.

"You sure this is the right place?" Jason asked. "Seems like it's abandoned."

Ella pointed up at the dilapidated sign. "I guess. It's so creepy."

"Are we going to just march right in and say—'Give Masterji Thakur back or else'?" Jason asked.

"I've never done a rescue mission before," Ella admitted.

"I say we sneak in and look around first, then figure it out," Jason offered.

"I want to get in there, help him, and get out. Something doesn't feel good." Brigit gazed up, her hands twitching at her sides. She stumbled over a cobblestone and crashed.

Ella and Jason rushed to her side. "You okay?"

Brigit grumbled. Sharp pieces of gravel scraped her hands, and her pants were split at the knee, a nasty cut gushed. She pressed her hand to it and tried to wipe away the blood, but it splattered across the ground.

The cobblestones released a soft glow.

"What's happening?" Brigit gazed up, terrified as the aura grew over them like a gigantic bubble.

"I don't know." Ella watched as the once ugly Close transformed: the faded red, black, and white diamonds now saturated with bright color, the cobblestones perfectly in place, a ticket booth reassembled, and the start of a strange pier.

"Whoa," Jason said. "It was an illusion."

The courtyard turned out to be a pier overlooking a dark canal. Gondolas were lined up beside it like colorfully stripped candies. What kind of circus was this?

A crooked sign said: STEP RIGHT INTO THE NEAREST BOAT AND IT SHALL TAKE YOU TO THE GREATEST SHOW IN THE SKY.

Jason inspected one of the boats. "What if it sinks?"

"Then you better know how to swim." Brigit climbed down into the nearest one.

A harlequin carving sat at the nose of the boat, reminding Ella of a bigger version of Feste.

"I'm a good swimmer. We go to the Caribbean Union every summer." Jason followed Ella into the boat.

Ella tried to resist gazing into the dark waters or letting her imagination fill in what could be lurking down there. She didn't even look into the bayou when they'd go out with Gran to gather sacred water for conjure work. "Now what?"

Before Jason or Brigit could answer her, the boat moved forward on its own. Ella gripped the wooden bench beneath her.

"You scared?" Jason's eyes darted between Ella and Brigit.

"Are you?" Ella tried to put on her best brave face. She knew they would come face-to-face with Gia Trivelino to rescue Masterji Thakur. All the things she'd read about her raced through her mind:

The Ace of Anarchy.

A criminal who killed her own kid.

Someone who wants to see the world burn.

She was terrified.

"Yeah," he replied.

"Me too."

Brigit didn't say a word, her gaze focused on everything around them.

Tattered posters hung from the cavernous ceiling, advertising strange, masked figures: il Dottore, Pantalone, Zanni, and more. They all had the same blue eyes and sloping red grin.

"But where could Masterji Thakur be in here?" Ella felt like this place was a labyrinth. They might never find him.

Half-lit lanterns sparked as they passed. The trickle of music played, then peals of laughter. A sign fluttered overhead: THE HALL OF FACES.

Large mirrors appeared on the cavern walls, cresting overhead. Ella spotted distorted versions of herself. "What is this?"

"Maybe a funhouse?" Brigit leaned over the edge of the boat.

"Is this what you call fun?" Jason gazed at the ceiling, watching an image of himself stretch into two.

The gondola sailed ahead.

A creaking noise echoed.

They froze.

"What was that?" Brigit asked.

"Who are you?" a deep, rumbling voice called out.

The three of them scrambled to the center of the boat, standing back-to-back, staring around for the source of the voice.

"Who's there?" Jason shouted.

"Where are you?" Ella added.

The voice laughed at them. The rattle of it sent shivers over Ella's skin.

"I don't see anyone." Brigit grabbed her hand.

"Me either." Ella flashed her a panicked look.

"Because none of you are really looking," the voice taunted.

Laughter echoed, bouncing off the glass. "If you have to ask who I am, you have no business here."

A face appeared in one mirror, half-obscured by a beaked mask that looked like a twisted pelican.

"Look, there!" Jason pointed.

The face moved.

"No, here!" Ella raced to the gondola's edge, but it moved again.

"Is this real?" Brigit whispered.

"I don't know." Jason quivered with fear.

"Stay back. Get away from us!" Brigit screamed as the boat sailed forward.

"It is you who should stay away. It is you who have found a way into a place you don't belong."

"Where is Masterji Thakur?" Ella yelled.

The voice went silent.

The waters turned rough, slapping the gondola. The three of them huddled together.

The boat bottom splintered. Water pooled around their feet, and Ella screamed.

"What are we going to do?" Brigit climbed on the gondola's edge.

"Get ready to swim!" Suddenly Jason's feet fell through, his head submerging.

Ella's heart flipped as she fell headfirst into a tornado of dark water.

CHAPTER TWENTY-SEVEN

THE GRANDEST ILLUSION

E lla's mantle clung to her sides and water rushed up her nose as she plunged deeper and deeper. For a long, horrifying moment, it was like falling down a tunnel until she found the sheer will to kick herself back to the surface.

A hand grabbed her. Her vision sharpened. Brigit stared back at her, sputtering and all red.

"Where's Jason?" Ella treaded water and searched all around. The mirrors showed no reflections now, and the candles left tiny balls of light on the water's surface. A few broken gondola pieces floated about.

"I don't see him." Brigit dove back under, swimming around in circles before surrendering to come back up for air. "Nothing. I can't see anything."

Panic shot through her. Was he okay? What about Sweet Pea? Could rotties swim? Was she still in his hood? She gazed back at the entrance to the circus and thought about turning back.

Ella took a deep breath. They could never leave him behind.

She took Brigit's shaky hand, the trembles in her own adding to Brigit's quivers. "We have to find Jason and make sure he's okay, then we get to Masterji Thakur." Ella dipped her head in and out of the water, searching for him and shouting his name.

They swam a few feet.

"Ella!"

"Ella!"

She looked back at a thrashing Brigit.

"Something's down there," Brigit screamed. "I can feel it."

A deep rumble shook the water, and the darkness illuminated. A long creature swam beneath them, its sapphire scales glowing. Brigit clasped Ella's hand, and they paddled to the cavern wall.

"What is *that*?" Brigit gripped her even tighter.

The creature's head poked above the water. A huge black eye stared back.

"It's going to eat us! It's going to eat us!" Brigit panicked.

What is it? Ella thought as the creature stretched out of the water. It resembled a cross between a dragon and a snake.

"Of course it's not." Jason's grinning face emerged from right behind the creature. He clung to one of its thick fins. Sweet Pea poked out of Jason's hood and shook the water from her fur.

A wave of relief rushed through Ella.

"This is Poco. He's a baby leviathan." Jason grinned. "Come. He'll give us a ride."

"Where?" Brigit said.

Ella looked behind her. They could leave right now, return to the pier and outside, or go forward, deeper into the twisted circus. But she took a deep breath and said, "To get Masterji Thakur."

"Poco knows where he is." Jason nodded, then looked at Brigit. "You ready?"

"As I'll ever be."

Ella and Brigit climbed on Poco's back and rode through the dark canals. Ahead, a gigantic big top floated on the water with its three rings and high tightrope oscillating. The walls held cavernous sideshow rooms: ANIMAL MENAGERIE, ILLUSIONARIUM, CLOUD SWINGS, THE CAROUSEL, GARDEN OF WONDERS, and more. Thick cobwebs stretched over the elevators leading up to each platform.

Ella's eyes scanned around. Where was Gia? Where was Masterji Thakur?

They climbed off Poco, thanked him, and walked the perimeter of the big top. Glass windows stared back at them, and behind them shadowed rooms.

"What are we going to do next?" Jason squeezed the water from his clothes while Sweet Pea sniffed around.

Brigit paced in circles. "Something doesn't look right." She waved her hands in the air. Ella didn't understand what she was doing as she pulled her knitting needles from under her mantle.

Sweet Pea squeaked and started biting at the air.

"What is it?" Jason made a kissy noise to lure the tiny rottie back to him. "She's got a weird string in her mouth."

Ella realized the string resembled thread.

Brigit lifted one of her knitting needles, holding it up to the light. "Hmm . . ." She closed her eyes and began to rock like she always did when she prepared to knit. This time, her arms reached over her head, her needles stabbing at the air. Her eyes snapped open, white as snow.

Click-click-clack.

Holes appeared in the air around them. Silver lines unraveled. Suddenly, the big top dissolved, piece by piece.

Click-click-clack.

Brigit threaded and knitted and rocked.

The sound sent a ripple through Ella.

Sweet Pea hunkered down in Jason's hood. "What's happening?"

"It's an illusion. She's undoing it." Ella's heart pounded as the entire room changed from the belly of a circus to a laboratory.

A woman glared back at them.

The Ace of Anarchy.

CHAPTER TWENTY-EIGHT

MARVEL LIGHT

Well, well . . ." The woman had blond hair the same shade as Brigit's and a mouth so red you'd think it was coated with blood.

A shiver shot through Ella. The woman was terrifying. More than the news-boxes could've ever captured. As Gia stared at her, Ella felt locked in place.

Potbellied stoves boiled liquids. Mortars and pestles held spices and powders. Tables displayed empty vials and bottles awaiting elixirs. Thick books were stacked high.

In the far corner, a cage held a sleeping person. Masterji Thakur. His once striped turban now covered with dust, its tiny mirrors cracked and falling off.

"Masterji Thakur!" Jason called out.

Their teacher lifted his head, then labored to get on his feet. "Ella. Jason. Brigit."

Gia smiled, her blue eyes skating over them. "How were you able to get past . . ." Her eyes found Brigit, and she stumbled backward. "Who are you?"

"We're here to get Masterji Thakur. Give him back right now!" Ella yelled, then flinched. She felt the volatile energy of a hot plant and scanned the room for it. She gazed up. The ceiling held drying flowers. The red Quassia from the Underworld. *What was Gia doing with it?*

Gia laughed, then giggled, then cackled. "What a twist. What a great story this will make."

They all exchanged glances, puzzled by her strange behavior. She returned to her work, continuing to stopper bottles as if they hadn't even arrived. "Silly, spirited kids." Her eyes fixed on Ella. "You're that little Conjuror they let into the Arcanum. You're as famous as me."

"I will never be like you," Ella spat back.

"Oh, but you should. I would love to see it. If Conjurors really embraced all their power, they could burn the Marvellian world to dust. Send them all to the Underworld, and you'd have every right to after how you've been treated."

"Just give us our teacher back." Sweat raced down Jason's cheeks. "Right now!"

"I have no interest in giving up my good old friend Mitha, here. We still have work to do." She glanced over at him.

"I am done with your games, Gia." Masterji Thakur rattled the cage. "Now let me out."

"Why are you doing this?" Brigit asked, her voice unusually soft.

"Aren't you tired of all these rules?"

"No," Ella yelled back, trying to figure out what to do.

"But seriously, tell me. Who do they really serve?" Gia laughed. "I want to see the shadows behind people's eyes. I want to know how they will behave when there are no rules, no Paragons, no outsiders and insiders."

The red Quassia hissed, and Ella glanced up again. Fear of the plant and fear of Gia drummed through her. She needed something to distract Gia long enough to free Masterji Thakur and get them out of there. She tried to listen for the plant's heartbeat. "C'mon," she whispered to herself, trying to push her will into that of the plant's. An image of Gran and Mama flickered into her head, and she sang.

The plant exploded, its vines thickening and curling around Gia's arms and legs, pinning her in place.

"Get Masterji," Ella directed Jason and Brigit.

Ella tried to maintain her focus, keeping Gia in place as the woman fought against the vines. They burned her white arms, the poison leaving behind a constellation of blisters. But that didn't seem to stop her.

Sweat streamed down Ella's face, and her muscles quivered. *Hold it together*, she told herself. *You can do this. Just like Mama. Just like Gran.* She sang again, trying to reinforce her grip.

Jason ran to the cage, but Brigit remained stunned, stuck and still as a statue. Hers and Gia's eyes locked.

Gia stopped struggling and let the vines encircle her. She went silent. Not even a blink or a word as she stared at Brigit, inspecting her from head to toe.

"The keys are in her pocket," Masterji Thakur shouted. "But get the bottles first. You have to destroy them!"

"Brigit!" Ella hollered. "Did you hear what he said? Get the bottles."

Brigit didn't move.

"Your skinned knee. That blood." A smile broke out on Gia's face. "It's you. You're alive, just as he said."

Brigit's head cocked to the side. "Who are you?" She squinted. "I dream of you. I knit your face. Why?"

"Brigit!" Ella hollered again. "We don't have time for this! C'mon, get those bottles."

"So that's what they call you," Gia replied. "The name I gave you was Beatrice."

Brigit took a step closer.

"Don't," Ella hollered. "This is a trick. Another one of her games."

Ella's heart seized. She tried to move closer to the table with the elixir bottles, but she had to concentrate on keeping the Quassia vines wrapped around Gia. Jason flipped over a table, and hundreds of bottles tumbled to the ground, shattering into shards and spilling a fiery elixir. As the liquid rushed toward her, Ella's concentration wavered, and the vines around Gia's wrists loosened.

"Brigit, help me, please! Smash them," Ella cried out. "I can't do both!"

Jason raced to the middle of the room. He threw the rest of the bottles on the floor, smashing all of them except for one. It rolled toward Gia and Brigit.

"The biggest game has been played on me," Gia said with a laugh. "Very clever."

"I don't understand," Brigit replied. "I don't know you."

"You used to. I'm your mother."

Her words made the entire room freeze.

With a roaring shout, Gia broke out of Ella's restraints with the ease of snapping ribbons wrapped around a gift-box.

Ella crashed to the floor.

Gia stepped closer to Brigit.

"I don't have parents."

Brigit glared at Gia.

"You did once," Gia said. "Looking at you is like looking at a reflection of my younger self. Surely you can see it."

Brigit moved away, nearly tripping on the last bottle of elixir on the floor.

Ella lunged to grab it.

"Don't even think about it," Gia snapped, and the ice in her voice sent dread through Ella. She didn't move. The terror overwhelmed her. Jason pressed himself into the wall.

"I'm not like you," Brigit said back to Gia. "I'm not your daughter."

"But you are. You're a Marveller. A very talented one at that if you could get past our family's protective incants and into this space. If you could see through my threads. You are my daughter."

"I'm from New York City, and I lived at the Children's Village with my guardian."

"That dirty Fewel city." She took another step forward. "You're what I've been looking for." Her eyes cut between Brigit and the lone bottle on the ground.

Brigit snatched it.

"Be careful with that," she warned. "Your friends have made a mess of my experiment."

"Break it, Brigit," Ella hollered.

Gia turned to her. "You shut your mouth."

Ella recoiled.

Brigit held the bottle up. The red liquid writhed like an angry fire.

Ella didn't know what it was, but she figured it had to be dangerous. Gia cut her eyes at her again, and Ella took another step back.

"What is it?" Brigit fingered the glass. "Why do you want this so badly?"

Gia's gaze fixed on the bottle. "It's the only way I can make sure no one can take anything from me again."

Brigit twirled it around and around as the liquid grew angrier and angrier.

"It steals marvels," Masterji Thakur grumbled, his voice weak and gravelly. "She perverted our Arcanum Elixir of Light and found a way to strip Marvellers of their gifts."

Brigit's hand shivered as she gazed between the vial, Gia, and Ella.

"Do not listen to him. That is an oversimplification of things. A sensationalist view of it. One to encourage confusion. Many things that are misunderstood are labeled dangerous," Gia replied. "Like conjure—and Conjurors themselves." Her blue gaze found Ella again, and Ella swore the heat of it might burn her skin. "Like we once were, Mitha. Like the Aces. This is for our protection. My protection. Our protection," she repeated. "With more than one marvel, I can harness all the light. I will be the most powerful Marveller in the world. No one will be able to take anything from me again. Not you, Brigit, not anything. I'd offer this up to others who have been made targets. Others who have had things stripped from them."

Brigit uncorked the bottle and held it to her lips.

"Don't," Gia yelled.

"You don't get to tell me what to do," Brigit barked.

Gia's face and hair suddenly changed, the white blond darkening to brown and swirling up into a bun.

"Ms. Mead." Brigit almost dropped the bottle.

"It's not real!" Ella shouted.

Gia lunged for Brigit. Ella knocked her to the left, but Gia shoved back, and Ella tumbled into a nearby cabinet, clobbering her head. Black and white spots blurred her vision.

Brigit put the bottle to her mouth and guzzled it. "Now I have no marvel. Now we're nothing alike."

"Nooooo!" Gia screamed.

Brigit collapsed. Her skin flushed red. Her veins swelled. Her mouth opened and a beam of light escaped like a white ribbon.

Ella rubbed her head and struggled to her feet. Was that Brigit's marvel? Instinct took over, and she raced to a nearby table and scooped one of the empty bottles. She had to save Brigit's gift, if she could. She kneeled beside Brigit, pulling the glowing thread of light into it like how Mama made her catch tendrils of smoke above her skillets to preserve good conjure work.

Gia tried to lift Brigit, but Ella yanked her back.

"Don't touch her!" Ella screamed.

Jason got Masterji Thakur's cage open with the help of Sweet Pea's lock picking skills. They rushed forward to help.

Pounding footsteps and sirens sounded. The bark of wolves sliced through Gia's shouting. A swarm of black ravens swarmed the space, their caws deafening. Marvellian coppers flooded the space.

Gia leaped to her feet and clicked open her pocket watch.

Ella felt her head go light. The world slowed around her.

Gia grabbed one of the metal tools from her long table. Before Ella could blink, Gia had stretched the instrument into a small archway, walked through it, and disappeared.

Time snapped back to normal.

Ella cradled Brigit's head, then leaned down. She pressed her head against Brigit's chest, listening for a heartbeat. "Brigit, wake up," she said. "C'mon, open your eyes." She felt Brigit's heartbeat thumping slow but steadily. "You're going to make it. You have to."

The Astradam Tribune

BREAKING NEWS
CONJURE KID SAVES BELOVED ARCANUM DOCTOR FROM NOTORIOUS CRIMINAL

Beloved Arcanum instructor Masterji Thakur got tangled in Gia Trivelino's twisted web, reporters learned. Add kidnapping to her list of deadly charges. But recently admitted conjure trainee Ella Durand is rumored to have saved the day.

When asked about the incident, the family gave a statement: "Ella has been raised to stand up in the face of evil, and she did what she was taught. Nothing more and nothing less."

Upon further inquiry, we've discovered that there's a pending case against her at the Arcanum Institute, and while this might be a time of celebration . . . who knows how much longer she will be a trainee.

We'll keep you updated with the latest. Be sure to order a weekly news-box subscription!

CHAPTER TWENTY-NINE

TO BE A MARVELLER . . . OR NOT TO BE?

A week later, Ella hovered outside Brigit's infirmary room. Her stomach tangled and untangled, then flipped and flopped as she gathered the courage to enter. Brigit had been transferred from the Betelmore Hospital back here, and Ella didn't know what state she'd find her friend in. That terrified her. Brigit and Jason had become her first *real* friends at the Arcanum, and she didn't know what she'd do if she lost one of them.

She gripped the gift she'd brought in her hands.

"She's awake, dearie," Nurse Peaks said in passing. "That little balloon above the door's glowing, so go right on in. And be quick about it—you're missing Marvel Combat. First bout begins in fifteen minutes."

Ella took a deep breath and turned the doorknob. Would Brigit be all bandaged up? Would she still look like herself? When Marvellers lost their marvels, what happened to them?

Brigit's bright room spilled over with Get-Well blimps and Well-Wishing sparklers darting about. A table exploded with sweets: wiggly chocolate eggs ready to hatch milk dragons, rainbow corn bags, towers of chocolate Paragon coins, fireball fizzies, caramel crystals, stacks of Marveller-bars, and a tower of medialunas beside a glass of milk.

Brigit sat up in bed. "Hey."

"Hi." Ella eased into the room.

Brigit was paler than usual, her eyes droopy, and Ella hoped it was because she'd just woken up from a nap.

"They didn't kick you out yet?" she asked with a smile.

"Not yet," Ella replied. "The hearing is tomorrow."

"But you're a hero. We're heroes. I saw those news-boxes. Everyone's talking about us."

"I guess it doesn't matter. Procedure and protocols must be followed," Ella mimicked Headmarveller Rivera with a shrug. "I brought you some things from the room and this." She held up the gift-box. "Though it looks like you don't really need more presents."

"I don't even know who they're from. All the cards are anonymous," she added, showing Ella one of them and its cryptic get-better messages.

Ella took another step closer and inspected Brigit. She looked for scars or bruises or something that showed why her friend had been in here so long. Ella had been waiting for her to come back to their room, checking in with the nurses every day for a week.

"You're staring," she said. "What is it?"

"Nothing . . ."

"How's Feste?" she asked.

"Waiting for you in our room. He keeps cleaning and making your bed. He wanted everything to be perfect for when you come back." Ella and Feste hoped she would. "Oh, and I brought this." Ella ruffled through her satchel and pulled out Brigit's malyysvit. "It started to shake last night."

"Let's see if it's really a desert universe." She ran her fingers over its dusty rose exterior. "This is the only thing I've really liked up here. It's the only thing I've ever won."

An uneasy silence crackled between them. Their eyes going back and forth between the egg and each other. Ella's past jealousy felt so silly and petty in the wake of everything that had happened, especially since the egg meant so much to Brigit, who had very little, while Ella's parents would've gotten her anything she'd asked for.

The shame piled up inside her. She'd spent so much time stirred up about the egg and the attention Brigit received, and the fact that she'd discovered her timesight marvel long before the end-of-the-year Marvel Exam, that she never realized how much of a good friend Brigit was. So loyal that Brigit had given up her marvel to save her friends.

Ella hoped that given that chance she would make the same decision, but she wasn't so sure. "So . . . ," Ella started. "How are you feeling?"

"Better. I mean, like, not in as much pain anymore." She tucked her knees to her chest. "The headaches are still bad."

The memory of the light ribbon—Brigit's timesight marvel—flashed in Ella's mind. She wondered if somewhere nearby it was sitting in a jar, waiting.

"Do you feel different?" Ella always wondered how Fewel people felt. Empty? Confused? Dulled? A world without conjure felt so sad to her. Would that happen to Brigit?

"I never felt different, if you know what I mean. The people here are always like 'We're special' and 'We have all these marvels.' But I was just a kid who could knit. I didn't know anything else."

Ella hovered on the edge of the bed.

"It's not contagious, you know," she teased. "You won't lose your marvel too."

Ella's eyes bulged and she flushed with guilt. "It's just . . . I just . . ."

"Just be regular, okay?" Brigit patted the spot next to her.

Ella sat closer and handed her the gift she'd brought. Brigit ripped it open. Three balls of glowing light-thread sat on a cushion of tissue paper and a pair of the conjure crochet hooks her Gran used.

Brigit's face softened and tears welled in her eyes.

A hot flash hit Ella. What if Brigit couldn't knit anymore? What if this was the wrong thing to give her?

"What are these?" Brigit touched them.

"It's light-thread. My gran makes it. Weaves it into her quilts so you'll never be afraid of the dark." Ella suddenly regretted giving this present. "But now I'm realizing maybe it's not the best gift . . . since . . . you know . . . you haven't gotten it back."

"My marvel," Brigit replied. "You can say it."

Ella's cheeks warmed.

"I don't know if I want it back," she admitted. "If I don't, I get to go home. Well, back to New York City. I will probably forget this whole place. But the nurses said I wouldn't be able to knit again . . ." Her voice trailed off as she ran her fingers over the thread.

A prickle of sadness rushed through Ella. Who would Brigit be without her knitting needles? It made Ella think about who she would be without conjure. What would she feel like if she couldn't feel the tingle of it in her bones or the growing mark on the back of her neck?

"You love to knit," Ella whispered.

"I don't know who I am without it," she said. "But if I get my marvel back, I have to stay here and deal with the fact that my mother is the most evil person in this world. I'll be hated."

"Jason and I won't tell anyone," Ella said. "I promise." Ella couldn't imagine how it felt to be her now . . . to go from having no mother to having one like Gia Trivelino. She patted Brigit's hand. "We could be hated together. Start a band. Everyone Hates B and E. Get posters made! Hah! If you decide to stay."

Brigit laughed.

She really, really wanted Brigit to stay. She could list at least twenty reasons why she should. But she didn't share them. Brigit was like one of the cats from home; if you came up on them too quick, they'd screech, scratch, and hide.

"I just don't know if it'll hurt," Brigit said. "It's already been so painful without it."

"Did they tell you anything about how to get it back?"

"Surgery. But I told the nurses I didn't want the details." She glanced at the light-threads in the gift-box.

"Oh, I love details," Ella proclaimed.

"I know." She laughed. "How's Masterji Thakur?"

Ella fished out an appointment card. "I get to see him . . . after the disciplinary hearing. He said he's feeling better."

"That's good." Brigit sat up straighter in bed. "Are you scared?"

Ella reached for her hand. "Not anymore. I didn't do anything, and tomorrow everyone will know that."

Brigit nodded in support. "I wish I could be there."

Another curious (and, as Mama would say, nosy) question jumped around in Ella's brain. She bit her bottom lip to keep her from asking.

"What is it? Spit it out." Brigit jostled Ella's arm.

"It's nothing," she lied.

"Your face gets all weird when you have something to say and you're not saying it."

"Does not."

"Does too."

Ella avoided eye contact. "Okay, fine." She eased her question out: "Do you remember her now?"

Brigit waited a little bit before answering. "Some things. It was almost like seeing her unlocked this place in my brain where she'd been stored away. Glimpses. A smile. A strange laugh. But I don't know if I want to remember her." Tears welled in her eyes again. "I've never had anyone. I don't know how to have someone."

Ella gently rested her hand on Brigit's. "You've got me."

The egg shimmied. Brigit sat up more, and Ella shifted closer on the bed.

"It's happening." Ella clapped excitedly as lightning bolt–shaped cracks spread across the shell. Each shard fell, revealing a tiny little desert. "Wow!" It reminded Ella of a living snow globe.

They leaned forward, touching an iridescent film protecting the tiny world.

"It's nighttime! Look . . . there's a moon."

"Five camels are snoring. Listen."

"They have wings."

Ella and Brigit laughed.

A knock rattled the door.

Jason barreled into the room. "You get your marvel back?"

"Way to say hello," Ella said.

"Inquiring minds want to know." All the wombies trundled in after him, climbing into the bed, and then came the rotties. "So, did you?"

"Not yet, but I'm going to." Brigit smiled and squeezed Ella's hand.

THE ARCANUM TRAINING INSTITUTE FOR MARVELOUS AND UNCANNY ENDEAVORS

+ ——————— DISCIPLINE BOARD SUMMONS ——————— +

Dear Ella Durand,

Please arrive at Dean Nabokov's office at 9:30 a.m. sharp for the start of your hearing.

Following Institute protocols, we will have a disciplinary review to go over the statements and evidence and determine whether you will continue to be enrolled at the Institute. Despite all the latest current events, order and tradition must be maintained.

Dean Nabokov

CHAPTER THIRTY
THE DISCIPLINE BOARD

Ella walked into the disciplinary hall. Along its octagonal walls, bright banners displayed each Arcanum tenet: integrity, self-control, perseverance, goodness. A panel of Arcanum instructors gazed down at her from a high table. The Headmarvellers sat at the very center.

Ella stood before them. Her parents flanked her. Mama held one hand and Papa the other. Her legs shook as if she'd swallowed an earthquake.

It's going to be fine. Mama's words echoed in her mind, and she hoped she was right.

But a thick knot coiled in her stomach as she awaited her fate. Jefferson Lumen, his wife, and Clare sat on the opposite side of them looking like three angry red-headed dolls gleefully ready to watch her get kicked out. News-blimps skated past large floor-to-ceiling windows. Reporters dangled out of them, trying to grab the perfect shot for their news-boxes. Camera clicks echoed.

Dean Nabokov walked to a lectern. "Good morning and

good marvelling to you all. We are here to investigate the disciplinary charges against Level One trainee Ella Durand. She has been accused of two charges—stealing from a fellow student and attacking another student. What does the accused have to say?"

Ella gulped, stood straight up, and steeled herself. "I didn't do either of those things, Dean Nabokov."

"Very well. We shall begin." She motioned for Clare to come forward. "Please tell the board what happened to you on December eighteenth."

Clare's parents glared at Ella and her parents.

Clare thumbed her necklace, the flicker of it making her pale skin almost glow. "I was on my way to see Dr. Bearden for an extra lesson working with the stellacity sphere when Ella Durand came out of NOWHERE and jumped on my back. She started hitting me and said that I'd been better than her in class." She whimpered as her mother pretended to wipe away tears. "Then she sent me threatening notes, saying if I told anyone she'd put a conjure hex on me. I was too afraid to come forward until my parents found the notes."

Ella's pulse raced. She'd never fought with anyone besides Winnie, and she didn't even know if Conjurors could cast hexes. She'd never heard of that before.

"We don't even do that kind of thing." Mama sucked her teeth.

Dean Nabokov raised her hand. "It will be Ella's turn to speak momentarily. I will now play the evidence." She projected the heliograms from the photo-balloon and turned the crank of a record-box.

Ella saw a blurry version of herself and heard her own voice.

Dean Nabokov nodded at Clare. "Thank you for your testimony." Then she turned to Ella and her parents. "What do you have to say about this, Ella?"

Mama patted her back, giving her courage. "I have several witnesses . . . and letters." She held up the letter Brigit had sent from the infirmary and another curious one Ella hadn't seen before. A starfolk delivered them to Dean Nabokov.

Jason and Masterji Thakur stood and raised their hands, ready to speak.

"We shall hear them all," Dean Nabokov replied. "But first, the letters."

She began to read the first one aloud:

"Dear Arcanum People,

My name is Brigit Ebsen, and I am one of Ella's best friends. I didn't want to have any friends here. I didn't even want to be here. But if it wasn't for her, I wouldn't have survived. She never gave up on me. She was always positive even when people weren't kind to her. She is the best kind of person to have as a student and as a friend. She's the best you have here. Heck, her marks are so good. Way better than mine. If you're going to kick anyone out . . . let it be me. I would give her my spot. That's how much I love her.

Brigit Ebsen."

Ella tried not to grin too hard. A burst of gratitude warmed her.

"Our Brigit," she heard her mama whisper. Gumbo slapped

his heavy tail on the ground, and Greno did a backflip on Papa's shoulder. Even the conjure companions were proud.

Dean Nabokov cleared her throat and read from the second one:

"Dear whomever,

Ella isn't so bad. She's different, but she's nice, too. Please don't kick her out. She helped me when I needed her. We might be able to be friends.

Abina

P.S. You should spend your time finding out who messed up her room."

The ceiling sparked, the high arches of the disciplinary hall filling with light and raining down with starposts. They pummeled Dean Nabokov one after the other.

Ella tried not to chuckle.

Dean Nabokov tried to neatly organize them. "It seems you have many fans, Ms. Durand. I'll see to it that this is reflected in the records." She passed many of the envelopes to the other instructors to open. "But we will now move on to witness testimony."

Dean Nabokov motioned to the witness stand. "Jason Eugene is next."

Jason's locs jumped at the sound of his name, and he walked down the aisle and took his seat in front of everyone. "Ella would never hurt another student. She would never hurt even an animal."

"I haven't asked any questions yet," Dean Nabokov said.

"Oh, sorry." His terrified gaze found Ella. She tried to

smile at him, make him less nervous about this, but she too was afraid. They'd been called heroes only weeks ago. They'd saved the day. Yet she was here now, needing to save herself.

"State your name for the clerk," Dean Nabokov said.

"Jason Eugene," he replied.

"How do you know the accused?"

"She's one of my best friends."

"How did you meet the accused?"

"The Headmarvellers told me to show her around. I was her Arcanum guide."

Dean Nabokov nodded. "Have you ever known her to be vio—"

"This line of questioning is irrelevant." Masterji Thakur stood, walking slowly forward with the use of a cane.

"Masterji Thakur, that is out of order. You will have your time to speak in due course." Dean Nabokov's eye twitched with irritation, and she looked up at the Headmarvellers for reinforcement.

Ella held her breath.

"It *is* time for me to speak now. To put an end to all this foolishness." Masterji Thakur turned to the panel of Arcanum instructors. "You say that we must honor the Marvellian way. To honor order and tradition. But what happens when most of it is rooted in prejudice?" He glared at each and every Arcanum instructor. "We recently opened our doors to Conjurors as we should have done long, long ago, but we placed Ella Durand under a microscope. She had to be perfect, and even then, she was not accepted. Our society has always struggled as new people joined, but the way we've treated the Conjure folk of the world is abhorrent. Only some of us get second chances. Or third chances."

He paced before the rapt audience. "I know I have. All of you know that I was a misguided youth, and yes, part of the Aces. I once considered Gia Trivelino my best friend."

A series of gasps echoed through the room.

"The whispers are true. But you found space for me here and believed me when I said I'd learned and changed. You make space for some and not others. Yet you resist Conjurors and feed into anti–Conjure folk rhetoric and behavior. All of you in this room have been guilty of it. All in the name of our traditions. It is time for new ones."

Dean Nabokov crossed her arms over her chest. "Are you finished?"

"I am *not*." Masterji Thakur scowled. "On the date and time in question, Ella Durand was on a tour of the Arcanum's Founder's Room with me and nowhere near Clare Lumen."

Gasps crackled through the room. The panel of Arcanum instructors erupted.

"Why would you take her there?" Dr. Winchester shouted.

"Students aren't allowed," Dr. Zolghad replied.

"It's against our policies," Dr. Bearden remarked.

"Ella needed to know that she belonged here. Our world pretends that it's open for all when it is only open for a few. Those who walk the line that has been drawn for them. Our history is checkered. We haven't always seamlessly come together. Not in the way we like to propagate. We do a lot of talking. It's one thing to be told you belong somewhere and another to be shown it." Masterji Thakur took a deep breath and squeezed his throat before shouting, "The original architect of the Arcanum was a Conjuror."

The room exploded. Mama gasped and Papa sat in the nearest chair. Both stunned to silence and in shock. Masterji Thakur began to choke and sputter, but a nearby Arcanum instructor handed him a drink.

Shouts echoed.

"Blasphemous talk."

"Liar!"

"You ought to be thrown out for your conspiracy theories!"

Dean Nabokov slammed her gavel down. The sound reverberated ten times louder, bringing the room to silence.

Ella's heartbeat thumped so hard she put a hand to her chest.

"Then who attacked Clare? This does not explain that!" Mr. Lumen shouted. "They need to be punished."

The doors snapped open and a voice shouted, "WAIT!"

Samaira and her mother, the President of the United League of Marvellers, marched in. Her beautiful pantsuit and matching hijab sparkled under the light. A fleet of coppers trailed her. Everyone stood to greet her and pay their respects.

"What is the meaning of your auspicious visit, Madame President?" Headmarveller MacDonald rushed down from his seat.

Headmarveller Rivera trailed him, her cane sparking the faster she moved. "We are so happy to have you here."

"My daughter has something to tell the board," the President announced.

Ella's heart did a flip.

President Al-Nahwi ushered Samaira to the center of

the room. They were copies of each other: beautiful, jewel-trimmed hijabs and light brown faces.

Samaira held out her lantern. "I found it this morning, along with many other missing things, beneath the floorboards in the Ursa Minor Tower. I have the culprit trapped in my satchel." She pointed to the copper, holding up her bag.

Ella leaned forward watching Samaira's every move. What could it possibly be?

Samaira unzipped it and yanked out a pixie by the ear. One of Siobhan's pixies. Its green skin flushed red with anger. "I caught it trying to take my hair ribbons too."

"Who does this belong to?" Headmarveller Rivera plucked the culprit from Samaira's grip. She snapped her fingers and her papel picado transformed into a tiny paper prison around the little beast.

"Send for Siobhan O'Malley immediately," Dean Nabokov ordered.

Three automats whizzed out of the room.

Dean Nabokov stared into its bulging eyes. "What have you done?"

The pixie answered in gibberish.

"Anyone here speak Pixish?" Dean Nabokov asked.

"I'll send for Dr. Doyle," Headmarveller MacDonald said. "These creatures are known to cause trouble."

The doors reopened. A sullen Siobhan shuffled her way inside, surrounded by three automats. The other two pixies perched on her shoulders, hissing and baring their teeth at onlookers.

The caged pixie started to screech.

"Siobhan O'Malley, are these yours?" Dean Nabokov asked.

She nodded. "They're night pixies."

"Did you know that they continued to steal after your first warning?"

The pixies hid their faces.

Siobhan spoke to them in a strange language Ella's translation crystal could not decode.

Dr. Doyle raced in, red-faced and out of breath. He mopped his sweaty forehead with a polka-dot handkerchief. He looked left. He looked right. He looked up at the sky. He looked down at his feet. He shrugged at the sight of the pixies and spoke to them.

They cowered.

"What are you saying?" Dean Nabokov asked.

"Telling them to fess up about the mischief," Dr. Doyle replied. "They understand English perfectly. Despite what the stories say."

"We are guilty," one of the pixies admitted. "We did not want our Siobhan, our sweet Siobhan, to have so many people being mean to her, watching her. So, we made trouble."

"We make the girl Ella's voice. We make it sound like her," the other replied. "We copied her. Made ourselves look like her."

"But we were paid. Lots of gold. Lots of ribbons. Our favorite. They gave to us to make mischief," the third proclaimed.

Siobhan balked. "By whom?"

"I've had enough of this circus." Dr. Winchester slammed his hands on the table and prepared to leave.

The pixies swarmed him, and he tried to fight them off. "Him! He gives us shiny things."

"I have no idea what they're talking about." He swatted them away. "Night pixies are notorious liars!" he stammered out, his face tomato red. "How could you believe anything they say?"

Dean Nabokov's eyes narrowed. "Do I need to ask Dr. Schwab for a truth elixir?"

Dr. Winchester went purple. "YOU THREATEN ME WHEN THE STATE OF OUR SOCIETY IS AT RISK!" He threw his hands up. "Conjurors will be the end of us. I've seen it. The eye is wise! I tried to stop it. You'll thank me one day!"

Mama gasped, and Papa's fists balled. His words burned inside Ella.

President Al-Nahwi motioned to the coppers. They plucked Dr. Winchester from the center of the room like he was nothing more than a doll to be carted off.

Once the room had been cleared and quieted, Dean Nabokov and the Headmarvellers stood.

"Charges dismissed," Headmarveller MacDonald announced.

Ella fell into Mama's and Papa's arms. They kissed her a million times. All at once, she felt her cheeks warm.

"The truth always comes to light, baby girl." Mama cupped her chin, then glanced at Papa. "Let us go have a word with the Headmarvellers, shall we?"

Ella walked over to Siobhan and hugged her from behind. The pixies petted her braids and whispered, "We sorry."

"I'm sorry," Siobhan said through tears.

Mr. Lumen and his family stormed out of the room. The reporters flooded in. Ella and Siobhan were bathed in light as their cameras flashed.

This time, she smiled as wide as possible.

THE ARCANUM TRAINING INSTITUTE FOR MARVELOUS AND UNCANNY ENDEAVORS

— LOWER SCHOOL —

FIRST YEAR LEVEL ONE FINAL MARKS
Name: *Ella Durand*

CORE REQUIREMENTS:

Introduction to the History of Marvels and Marvellers 5

Introduction to Marvel Light 5

Conjure for Beginners 5

Universal Incants and Their Origins 5

PARAGON REQUIREMENTS:

Future Forecasting 1—Divining the Future Around the World 5

Global Elixirs 5

West African Oral Story Incants 5

Global Elementals—Water and Air 5

SCORING RUBRIC:

5 = Showing signs of mastery

4 = Showing signs of proficiency

3 = Satisfactory

2 = Needs Improvement

1 = Failing to Show Effort and Progress

NOTES: *Ella is more than proficient.*

MRS. VICTORIA
BAUDELAIRE'S
PERFUME ATELIER

B lue summer skies thinned to an orange dusk over the rooftops of Paris, and Gia lifted her skirts away from a puddle as she prepared to step inside the most beautiful store off the Champs-Élysées. She thought it looked more like a tiered wedding cake than an actual place where one could visit. Painted cream and pink, glass windows were piped with ribbons of gold and curlicues of crimson. A sign dropped like a spider from above its doorway, and in bright cursive announced: VICTORIA BAUDELAIRE: L'ATELIER DU PARFUM.

When she stepped inside, the tiny tinkle of a bell announced her arrival. Just how she liked it. Subtle. Elegant.

Two silver swans spewed jasmine-scented water from their beaks into a massive fountain in the center of the shop. She was greeted by the beautiful display: clear jars and magnificent flasks contained oils, balsams, and waxes.

A metal automat whizzed by her, toting baskets and placing them on nearby shelves, and then dropped off items to a woman behind a counter. Beside the woman stood what looked like a tiny version of her. The woman and girl both shined like a pair of new gold stellas beneath the window globes, their arms willowy like dolls, as the older woman taught the girl how to tie a bright gossamer ribbon around a box.

She glanced up, meeting Gia with a smile. "Welcome to the best perfumery in all of Paris. It is full of distillations, aromatics, concoctions, and one-of-a-kind perfumes," she said in French. "May I help you find something special?"

Gia smiled. "I think so."

"Looking for a gift?" Beside her stood an ornate table featuring three tiny golden bottles etched with Mrs. Baudelaire's emblem—a bouquet of flowers tied together by a serpent—and a pile of lace handkerchiefs and three glass rods. Solid and liquid perfumes wore price tags. Powder puffs, brushes, and pots of rouge sat like macaroons on a candy tray.

"Are you *the* Mrs. Baudelaire? The famous nose of all of Paris? You look too young."

She chuckled. "Indeed, I am. And this is my daughter, Amélie."

The little girl flashed bright hazel eyes at Gia.

"My perfumes . . . have, how do you say . . . have restorative properties. Scent can keep you young and remind you of younger days."

"Is that so?"

"You may say, Who needs perfume? Who needs bath salts? Or lotions and pomades? You might say that it's unnecessary. But I urge you to think again. The art of perfume has been around since the ancient Egyptians. Does anyone know why it's stood the test of time?"

Gia didn't say a word, for she'd come precisely to hear this little speech—and for what would follow.

"Because scent delivers a memory to the mind that isn't impaired by time. You can go back to places you want to visit. You can recapture things that are lost. You can even open *worlds* . . . if one is clever enough." She waved her hands in the air. "Your first trip to the forest—the smell of pine and burning wood. The first flower you ever sniffed—petunias, a red rose, a lily. The scent of your grandmother's house—warm bread and sugar." She blew glittery dust into the air that seemed to float above the counter. Gia could smell oranges and lavender. "These memories go missing. Slip out of your mind over time. But the power of scent can restore them. I even have a special blend that can keep every memory you've ever had safely in place."

"You speak about perfume as if it is"—the word stuck to Gia's tongue like peanut butter—"magic."

"Oh, because it can be," she replied. "Let me make something for you."

"Make sure it's marvelous . . . since you're a Marveller."

The woman froze. "I don't know what you mean. What is that word?"

Gia smiled, then used her marvel to crush the perfume bottle on the counter. "I'm here for something else. I heard you collect and create parfum de mémoires."

She turned to Amélie. "Please go to the storeroom. I need a moment with our guest."

Amélie scampered out of sight.

"Who are you? And what do you want?" The woman's eyes cut from Gia to the bloated purse she held up.

"What I asked you for."

The woman shrugged, then retrieved a music box from a bottom shelf.

Gia's heart fluttered a bit as she lifted the lid.

A tiny tinkle escaped it as Mrs. Baudelaire lifted a velvet interior shelf to reveal another compartment.

Thoughts of Gia's daughter, Beatrice . . . or Brigit as she was now known, reinvigorated her, made her certain that what she was doing was right.

In the hidden area within the music box were ninety-two full glass bottles and eight empty ones. The woman flashed them at Gia. Inside each, tiny golden threads appeared and disappeared within the liquid. To an untrained eye, the bottles would appear like simple vials of perfume. But each one contained a memory. Good ones. Bad ones. Those in-between. And Gia needed memories. Memories of marvels, and of powerful Marvellers of the past.

"More," Gia replied, not daring to look away.

The woman took two empty jars, removed their stoppers, and poured them into the glass cylinder. She ran her fingers over them like these tiny bottles were more precious to her than all the jewels in the world. They clinked like coins.

"You will be coming with me," Gia demanded.

"What for? I'm not part of that world anymore."

Gia removed one of Fournier's watches from her pocket, and when she opened the lid, brown night moths froze flat against the windowpane. Liquid boiled in the jars. Papers scattered all over the store, glass jars crashed onto the ground, and the cupboards and shelves shook, ready to topple.

The woman gripped the edges of the counter.

"One of my Aces so far away from home. You owe me a favor. I've come to collect." Gia allowed her true face to be seen. "I'll need Amélie too."

"Gia?" the woman whispered. "You're still alive."

"You must not be keeping up with Marvellian news," she answered. "Very much so."

CHAPTER THIRTY-ONE

THE MARVEL EXAMINATION

Ella sat across from Masterji Thakur at the table in his lab. A steaming pot of tea rested between them.

"Are you feeling better?" she asked.

"Little by little each day, and I have you to thank for even being here," he said.

Ella's cheeks warmed. "Thank you for the things you said about me today."

"I'm hoping you realize you belong at the Arcanum now. You're a hero." He struggled to stand with his cane.

She started to rise from her chair.

"No, no. Sit. I have something for you." He ambled to one of his cabinets and returned with a small ornate chest. "In case you were still questioning your place, I wanted to bring you something to study over the summer. You can send me starposts, and I'll be ready to hear about all your discoveries."

"You're coming back?" Ella's heart lifted. A rumor had

circulated that he wouldn't be returning after his ordeal. She couldn't blame him.

"I'd never let anyone chase me out . . . and neither should you." He gestured for her to open the chest.

Ella ran her fingers over the jeweled lid, and it popped open. The Arcanum blueprints fluttered out and unfurled between them.

She gasped. "Am I allowed to have these? Won't they find out?"

"They won't find out for a while." Masterji Thakur smiled. "I took care of that and left behind some decoys to buy you some time to investigate." He winked at her and she smiled.

Ella opened her notebook to the spell her mother had taught her over the winter break, one that forced conjure paper to reveal its scribe. "Can I try something?"

He nodded.

She carefully ran her fingers above the old blueprints, the way her mother always did when they prepared to travel via the Red Book maps. With a deep breath, she sang, "Reveal your secrets, tried and true; my heart is here to hear them too."

Ella's will crossed into the paper's fibers, forcing it to expose its maker.

The outlined silhouette of a Black man projected from it. An owl conjure companion sat on his left shoulder, and a charcoal pencil poked out of his long locs. Spectacles slid down his nose, and he looked out with beautiful, dark eyes—her papa's eyes.

A tiny signature in the corner of the map revealed itself.

JEAN-MICHEL DURAND.

Her heart jumped.

"Wow, Ella. This is incredible." Masterji Thakur leaned closer to the silhouette. He rubbed his now salt-and-pepper beard. "Do you know that name?"

"I've seen it on my papa's family tree." She couldn't stop looking at him. "What does this mean?"

Masterji Thakur took a deep breath and pulled down his collar. A branded *M* sat on his clavicle. He shook his head. "I cannot speak of it . . ."

The Muzzle.

"Who did that to you?"

Masterji Thakur pointed to his throat again.

"Please don't say anything." Ella couldn't bear to see him break into a fit again. "When can you have that removed?" She couldn't believe this had happened to him.

He shrugged.

Ella felt sad and worried for him, thinking about how painful it must've been.

"You are a person who likes to know things, and I have no doubt you won't stop until you've answered all the questions," he said, then took a long sip of tea.

Her questions swirled in her head: Was Jean-Michel a founder? What had happened to him? Why had the Institute hidden this truth? Ella's papa used to tell her that life was a massive and intricate clockwork gear—a mechanism of cogs and springs and cams charged with a purpose, each element having to do its part. And in this moment, she felt like hers had just exploded. Everything she'd learned in her sessions this year had been missing a piece.

Masterji Thakur drummed his fingers on the table. "I can almost hear the questions in your head."

"What's going to happen? What should I do?"

His eyes filled with compassion. "Whenever you feel like you don't belong or you question it . . . think of these blueprints. And never stop asking the hard questions."

Ella asked the blueprints to hide their secrets once more, and she placed them back in the chest. "Were you really friends with that woman?"

His eyes filled with shame. "You can say her name."

"Gia," she whispered.

"I was. I knew her long ago before she was *that* person. Before she was evil."

"How did she kidnap you?"

"She can make doors and enter any space she wants. As long as she has the right tools to connect her. She must've gotten something from my office. I haven't figured out how yet, but I will." He patted her hand. "But don't worry. She is gone now, and we are safe. It's time to focus on the future. Today is a big day. Your exam."

Ella filled with a nervous excitement. "What do you think the Marvel Examination will see in me? What will the Elixir of Light show?"

"Whatever Paragon you end up in will be lucky to have you. Are you ready?"

"Yes." Those words gave her a tiny flutter of hope.

✦ ❋ ✦ ❋ ✦

ELLA SANDWICHED BETWEEN JASON AND BRIGIT IN THE BELLY OF the assembly hall, waiting for the Marvel Examination to start. Striped balloons sporting the initials A.T.I. were fat summer clouds leaving a storm of confetti instead of raindrops. A table with seven instructors floated high above, looking down at them like they were the gods of the Arcanum Institute.

Older trainees sat in risers and held banners representing each Paragon. They whistled and stomped at the Level Ones.

Ella felt she was at the very bottom of a fishbowl, everyone gazing down at her, waiting for her to do a trick. This was the day she'd waited for all year.

The room cheered as a microphone hovered before Headmarveller MacDonald. "Welcome, my glorious pupils, my brilliant trainees, to the last day of sessions."

The room burst into applause again.

Headmarveller MacDonald waved his hands in the air to silence the excitement. "So, you know what that means? Time for the Marvel Examination and placing our Level Ones into their Paragons." His eyes grazed over them. "I know they are ready to find their true homes at the Arcanum. The lower school is where you start your Marvellian path."

Ella's heart fluttered.

Headmarveller Rivera whistled, silencing the noisy room. "This examination has been part of our community since the first day the institute opened. Just as we group our stars above, we organize the light within, making sense of chaos, and giving everyone a place. Our founders wanted no one left behind." Her eyes found Ella and she smiled. "It provides camaraderie and connection between our very different selves. We can't wait to meet the newest stars to our Arcanum constellation."

Headmarveller MacDonald walked down a set of floating stairs. A starfolk tugged a gigantic machine to the center of the room. It glowed like a molten sun.

The whole room oohed.

"I will administer a tonic to your forefinger. Our Elixir of Light." He pulled a bottle that looked like an hourglass from inside the machine. He held it up for everyone to ooh and aah. "This will grant me a drop of the light inside you. I promise it won't hurt. It's been made by our very own Masterji Thakur, whom we welcome back."

The trainees cheered and whistled.

Headmarveller MacDonald touched the machine, causing etchings to illuminate like veins pulsing through the brass. "Let's see what it reveals." He motioned to the wall to his left.

A gigantic board flipped over, labeled with the words **ARCANUM PARAGON REGISTRY.**

"We will note your marvel and the Paragon it belongs to, then you'll go join your new family." He pointed at the Paragon symbols along the machine's belly. "You will receive your official pin. And if you're lucky enough to be not just marvelous but extraordinary, you might become a champion and represent said Paragon in our next year's Marvel Combat Tournament." A grin spread across his entire face. "We congratulate the Paragons of Sound for winning this year's tournament."

Trainees in the back corner chanted: "The ears listen well!"

"I'll pull your names at random from the machine. Please come when called," Headmarveller MacDonald directed.

Ella gazed all around the room, wondering if this is what her great-great-great-grandfather had dreamed up. The secret burned on her tongue. Before her parents had left for home, Mama had lifted her braids and held up a hand-mirror. In the reflection, Ella had spotted a change in her conjure mark.

The bean-shaped mole had split, and a line trailed down her neck like a kite's tail.

She was ready to be named a Marveller with a conjure marvel.

Ella sat up straighter. Headmarveller Rivera read names out loud. Each one hit her with a ripple of excitement.

Any minute now. Anxiety drummed through her.

"Clare Lumen."

"Macklin Feldman."

"Erin Stein."

"Luz Santos."

"Lian Wong."

"Samaira Al-Nahwi."

"Matthew Ringler."

"Tiffany Liao."

"Julie Murphy."

The kids all leaped up, almost running to the machine, hands outstretched, eager to confirm their marvel and join their Paragon. They proudly put their pins on their mantles. The pattern repeated over and over again.

"Siobhan O'Malley."

A few older kids booed as she skulked up to the machine. The pixie on her shoulder taunted onlookers. Ella felt sad for her. She'd accepted her apology, but that didn't matter to the others now that the news-boxes had reported about the incident. Everyone knew what the pixies had done. The spotlight dug up bad stories about her parents. As soon as Siobhan was placed in the Paragon of Sound with a kindred marvel, Ella stood and clapped for her. Curious eyes burned into her back, but the slight smile on Siobhan's face made it worth it.

"Jason Eugene."

All the Eugene siblings cheered, setting off a tidal wave. Ella heard Jason gulp and watched his locs jump. She flashed him a confident smile and whispered, "You got this."

Brigit shoved his arm. "Don't be a chicken."

He took a deep breath, stood, and pulled his locs away from his face and into a loose ponytail.

Ella chewed the inside of her cheek as he walked down the aisle and to the front of the room. She knew what Paragon he'd end up in, but her mind buzzed. Would they still be friends if she didn't end up a Sound?

Jason stood in front of the machine.

His pin spat out.

"Paragon of Sound. Kindred marvel," Headmarveller Mac-Donald said.

The group shouted: "The ears listen well!"

Jason turned back to Ella and Brigit and flashed a big toothy grin. He went to sit with his new Paragon family.

Headmarveller MacDonald pulled the lever. "Ella Durand is next."

Ella leaped up like a firework had gone off under her chair. The other trainees whispered.

Shush-balloons flooded the room. It became so quiet, Ella thought everyone could hear how hard her heart thumped.

She'd count her way through this.

One . . .

Sweat skated down her forehead like it was the hottest summer day in New Orleans.

Two . . .

She gulped and glanced up at the Paragon banners.

Three . . .

She reached the end of the aisle, and her eyes found Masterji Thakur. He winked. She stood up a little straighter.

I'm ready, she thought.

"Ella Durand," Headmarveller MacDonald said. "Welcome to your Marvel Examination."

The machine's warmth radiated as if the sun had been twisted into brass. Up close, the apparatus had several compartments marked with the five Paragons: an eye, an ear, a mouth, a hand, and a heart. Its smooth surface held etchings of the constellations.

"Are you ready?" he asked.

Ella found her godmother in the room before answering yes. Aunt Sera smiled at her, and she felt even more determined.

"Yes," she said a little *too* loudly, then mimicked all the others, stretching out her hand.

Headmarveller MacDonald pulled the cork from the bottle, inserted a pipette, and drew out a bit of the liquid. He placed a drop in the cradle of her hand.

Part of her couldn't believe that this was the same elixir Gia Trivelino manipulated to steal marvels and hurt people. Ella's eyes grew wide as the warm bead stretched along the grooves in her palm and traveled down the slope of her pointer finger and collected at the very tip, now a glowing pearl filled with a violet light. Headmarveller MacDonald scooped up the bead with a metal instrument and jammed it into the machine's compartment.

He pulled a lever. All the Paragon symbols illuminated.

Her pulse raced as she waited.

The lights flickered out. A slot spat out a pin.

He swiped it and held it up. "A Paragon of Vision. Carto-manic marvel."

"The eyes are wise!" The room shouted.

Ella gazed up at him confused. She'd never heard that word before.

"Cards. You will be able to determine fortunes."

Ella filled with warmth. She'd thought this moment would feel different, like a puzzle piece finally getting its place. But she realized after everything she'd been through and everything Masterji Thakur had shown her . . . she already belonged here.

He handed her pin to her. The metal heated her hand like a biscuit straight from the oven. She studied every aspect of the tiny disk as the etched eye symbol blinked at her.

Everything was better than fine.

Everything was *great*.

THE ARCANUM TRAINING INSTITUTE FOR MARVELOUS AND UNCANNY ENDEAVORS

LOWER SCHOOL

SUMMER TRAINING SESSION
LEVEL ONE TRAINEE TIMETABLE

Name: *Brigit Ebsen*

Overview of Marvellian History	Dr. Dorothy McGee
Remedial: Astrology	Dr. Isabel Acevedo
Remedial: Marvel Light Workshop	Dr. Amelia Bearden
Remedial: Forecasting	Dr. Tanisha Johnson
Remedial: Incants	Dr. Ellen Oh

NOTES: *Passed*

𝕸𝖆𝖗𝖛𝖊𝖑𝖔𝖚𝖘 𝕴𝖓𝖖𝖚𝖎𝖗𝖎𝖊𝖘

GOVERNMENT COVER-UP! NEW CRIME SCENE EVIDENCE FOUND IN THE CARDS OF DEADLY FATE!

Ronald Rumple Jr.

JUNE 22

The Marvellian government is hiding things, dear readers! They wouldn't want me to tell you this . . .

They want to cover it up!

They want to pretend that all order has been restored!

But no . . . no.

It's a lie.

My sources say that there was a piece of evidence that's gone missing from the reports about the breach of the Cards of Deadly Fate. A skeleton key etched with the initials C.B. This wasn't presented to the public. This was hidden. Who does that key belong to? Did they ask Marvellers with an iron marvel to examine it?

What are they hiding?

I know what . . .

Someone helped that clown out of prison.

WANTED!

GIA TRIVELINO

WARNING:
DANGEROUS!

ACKNOWLEDGMENTS

This book is my heart made into words. As a kid, I'd always waited for a wondrous adventure outside my window, where people who looked like me possessed immeasurable magic. I wanted all the magic, all the time, and it would've meant the world to me to see my community and family wind up in the thing I loved most—books ... and especially books about magic schools. I remember when I first read *The Worst Witch* and wanted desperately to find myself at Miss Cackle's Academy for Witches. The magic school story is a ubiquitous evergreen and staple of children's literature, and it always seemed to be missing so many kinds of kids. Kids who looked like me, kids who looked like the ones I taught for so many years. So I built the Marvellerverse for those who felt invisible but craved magic and adventure.

It took many years and an entire village to help bring it to light.

I'd like to thank my editors, my Headmarveller pair: Tiffany Liao, who pushed me to go deep with every draft and got in the trenches with me to organize and reorganize my plots no matter how many drafts it took. Brian Geffen, who is a surgeon of precision, pushed me to refine and sharpen my world. Your brilliant insights and guiding hands helped bring this book to fruition.

I'd like to thank my brilliant agent, Molly Ker Hawn, who always believed. Thank you for going into the Petty Palace with me, talking me off all the ledges, and seeing the vision. You are a fierce champion, and I'm grateful to have you.

I'd like to thank the entire Macmillan Publishing Team: my beloved friend Ann Marie Wong, who is my great champion and I hers; the fabulous Liz Dresner and Trisha Previte, who made magic with their designs; and Molly Ellis, Brittany Pearlman, Mariel Dawson, Katie Quinn, Johanna Allen, Kathryn Deaton, Kristen

Luby, Leigh Ann Higgins, Megan McDonald, and Teresa Ferraiolo, who make sure people know about my books.

I'd love to thank my copyeditors and proofreaders, Jackie Dever, Taylor Pitts, Mariam Syed, and Lindsay Wagner, who whacked my shaky grammar into place and made sure everything was in order. Thank you for your encouragement and your eagle eyes.

Big thanks to Zoraida Córdova and Jason Reynolds for taking all my incessant calls about this book and helping me figure out how to make it work and feel impactful. I treasure both of you... especially your masterful brains and your endless wells of patience with my shenanigans.

I'd like to thank all the people I pestered with questions about my global world and who gave me their wisdom and guidance: Candice Iloh, Tracey Baptiste, Olugbemisola Rhuday-Perkovich, Ashley Woodfolk, Nic Stone, Bethany C. Morrow, L. L. McKinney, Kwame Mbalia, Karen Strong, Tracy Deonn, Tiffany D. Jackson, Lamar Giles, and Ellen Oh.

I'd love to thank all my early readers: Mark Oshiro, Ebony Elizabeth Thomas, Navdeep Singh Dhillon, Margeaux Weston, Clay Morrell, and Carlyn Greenwald for their invaluable insights.

To my cover artist, Khadijah Khatib—you brought my world alive on this beautiful cover. Thank you for setting the tone and making this book look like something ten-year-old Dhonielle would lose her mind over.

To my Marvellian mapmaker, Virginia Allyn—you are a gold star. Thank you for creating maps that make readers want to forever find doorways into my worlds. You are so talented, and I am so blessed to work with you.

I'd like to thank Victoria Marini, who believed in this world from the start and found the perfect home for it all those years ago in 2017.

To Mom and Dad, thanks for filling my childhood with magic. This book is born of that.

And to my readers, welcome to the Marvellerverse. I hope you come to call it home.

THE ARCANUM TRAINING INSTITUTE FOR MARVELOUS AND UNCANNY ENDEAVORS

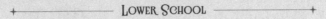

LOWER SCHOOL

Greetings, Best Regards, and Warm Welcomes!

This is your mini guide to the Marvellerverse. Grab a fresh stylus from your satchel. These secret pages contain special information you'll need to join Ella, Jason, and Brigit at the Arcanum Training Institute for Marvelous and Uncanny Endeavors for Level Two.

Be sure to memorize everything, then hide this book. Fewels are always watching and looking for magic. They aren't allowed to know about it. They'd ruin it.

All the good marvelling to you.

Best,

Laura Ruby

Executive Assistant to Headmarveller MacDonald and Headmarveller Rivera of the Lower School

P.S.: Trust me, you don't want to show this to Fewels. You'll regret it.

P.P.S.: Also, keep this away from Gia Trivelino. We don't want her to know you're headed to the Institute to help—she'll be very mad.

You've spent a year following Ella, Jason, and Brigit through their classes—and drama!—so we must figure out where you belong. Just like Ella, Brigit, Jason, and all their classmates at the Arcanum Training Institute (ATI), you too have light in you and have a Paragon waiting for you to be sorted into. Take the quiz to find out!

DISCOVER YOUR PARAGON

1. **Your friend keeps being late to Introduction to Marvel Light. How do you help them?**

   1. I give them the notes that they missed; can't slow the learning.
   2. I explain to them what the consequences of their actions are; maybe they just don't know?
   3. I wait until they tell me that they want to make a change and then help.
   4. I ask them why they're late; maybe there's a good reason.
   5. I create a distraction in class so they can sneak in.

2. **You've been given an opportunity to take any class at ATI. What do you choose?**

   1. Oh, I could never choose! There's so much to learn.
   2. Introduction to the History of Marvels and Marvellers; I want to have as much knowledge as possible to be informed on what I say.

3. Spice Elixirs! I'm great at patiently waiting for the mixtures to be just right.
4. Future Forecasting! I'd love to improve my abilities to interpret.
5. Conjure for Beginners! I love learning new and exciting things!

---

3. **If you could live in any city, Marvellian or not, where would you go?**

1. Celestian! So much history.
2. New Orleans! I'd love to taste all the amazing food.
3. Betelmore! A slow ride through the skies sounds incredible.
4. Astradam! There's so much people watching.
5. New York! It sounds like quite the adventure!

---

4. **What do you think about night pixies?**

1. They're so fascinating!
2. I don't love how they're troublemakers.
3. They're misunderstood!
4. I bet they're just bored of humans and need some way to entertain themselves.
5. They're fun to hang around with! Always getting into mischief.

5. **If you were featured in the *Celestian City Chronicle*, what would it be for?**

   1. Probably a feature on everything I've learned and achieved so far at school.
   2. A tell-all piece about some major news story that's being reported incorrectly. People need to know the truth.
   3. I'm a great eyewitness.
   4. Do newspapers still have advice columns?
   5. I might've, um, been the center of a bit of a ruckus downtown . . .

6. **We know it's frowned upon, but are there any forbidden stores, like the Mischief Mart or the low street in Betelmore, you'd love to see if you could?**

   1. Stores not so much, but I know there are forbidden sections of the library in ATI . . .
   2. No, absolutely not! I'd never want to go somewhere like that.
   3. No, I'd rather wait to see if any of the shops ever clean up their acts and then maybe I'd go.
   4. The Mischief Mart has always fascinated me; how did the people end up working down there?
   5. Oh, any of them! The entire low street in Betelmore is worth exploring!

7. **What's your favorite time of year?**

1. Fall! I love going back to school.
2. Spring! It's when the world starts to open up again after winter.
3. All the seasons! I like change and don't want to choose just one. It'd be like choosing one kind of music to like.
4. Winter! People are so much more likely to be their true selves when they can't go out as much.
5. Summer! All the free time to try new things.

8. **You're taking a half-open-note, half-closed-note test and you notice your textbook has the answers to the closed-note portion of the test on it. What do you do?**

1. Turn in the textbook and get a new one; I'm here to test my knowledge and don't want anything to skew the result.
2. Turn in the textbook and get a new one; it's morally wrong to cheat.
3. Turn in the textbook; I don't have to finish the test early and can wait for the right book.
4. Turn in the textbook but wonder how I got ahold of this textbook in the first place.
5. Turn in the textbook; I don't need it to get a good grade!

9. **What's one trait your friends would use to describe you?**

   1. Wise
   2. Honest
   3. Patient
   4. Intuitive
   5. Brave

10. **Are you excited to return to school each year?**

    1. Yes! So much to learn!
    2. In all honesty, I kind of wish summer would be a few more weeks.
    3. Yeah, absolutely! I've been patiently waiting to return all summer.
    4. I'm feeling pretty good about it, but I see that not all my classmates feel the same way.
    5. No, I wish I had more time; there were so many cool things I didn't get the chance to do.

11. **Do you think it's bad if someone doesn't read books?**

    1. Yes! Why close your mind like that?
    2. Yes, but I understand that it comes from my own biases about reading.
    3. No, I think all people are different and whatever makes them enjoy stories is fine.
    4. People like and dislike books for valid reasons.
    5. I don't have time for books!

Mostly 1s: VISION

You belong in the Paragon of Vision! Many Marvellers in this Paragon have marvels like fortune-telling, time travel, and dream decoding! You're very smart and value the continued path toward learning more. You're disciplined and studious, always able to be relied upon to complete tasks. Fun facts are your friend and your favorite kinds of conversations range from talks of history to how minds think to all the different places you hope to visit and learn about. The eyes are wise!

Mostly 2s: TASTE

You belong in the Paragon of Taste! Many Marvellers in this Paragon have marvels like alchemy, confectionary arts, and spice manipulation! You're an honest person through and through. You know what you value about yourself, others, and life and do your best to stick by your convictions. You want the world to be a better place and know that sometimes all you can control is how you treat others. Because of this, people around you tend to trust you. The tongue tells truth!

Mostly 3s: SOUND

You belong in the Paragon of Sound! Many Marvellers in this Paragon have marvels like drum hypnosis, kindred animal communication, and choral illusions! You tend to be quiet and hang back, taking the time to really understand all aspects of a situation before forming your opinion. Thus, you're often a very calming and trusted presence in your friends' lives. The ears listen well!

Mostly 4s: SPIRIT

You belong in the Paragon of Spirit! Many Marvellers in this Paragon have marvels like weathermancy, vanquishing arts, and ghost and spirit negotiations! You're very in tune with emotions and surroundings, whether those of your friends, strangers, or yourself. You're very articulate and able to be a discerning third party when fights emerge. You're very good at sussing out the truth of any given situation and offering worthwhile advice to anyone who needs it. The heart beats true!

Mostly 5s: TOUCH

You belong in the Paragon of Touch! Many Marvellers in this Paragon have marvels like paper arts, metamorphosis, and golem-making! You're someone who isn't afraid to take life by the horns and do what you think needs to be done. People, places, and situations don't tend to scare you. Challenges are something you face with relative ease. You are good at psyching yourself up to try new things. You're also protective of those around you and know best how to look after people when they're afraid. The hand has no fear!

PARAGON

MARVEL

We need to make sure you get the right supplies for your Arcanum sessions as well as pick the right dormitory for you. Be sure to pack your favorite pillow.

THE ARCANUM TRAINING INSTITUTE FOR MARVELOUS AND UNCANNY ENDEAVORS

LEVEL TWO SCHOOL SUPPLY LIST

Note: All items can be purchased at the Arcanum Institute store or at several approved retailers on Betelmore's high street, such as Woodfolk's Wonderous Wares, Cárdenas' Coliseo de Libros, and more. Also, please see your Arcanum attendance letter for coupons.

UNIFORMS:

All students must wear a Marvellian mantle over their clothing.

- Level One: white
- Level Two: orange
- Level Three: blue
- Level Four: purple

REQUIRED SUPPLIES FOR ALL STUDENTS:

- Incant log
- Stapier—SabreWhizz 1.5 edition only
- News-box
- Fire jar
- Vivarium

PARAGON-SPECIFIC SUPPLIES:

Vision: fortune journal, fortune stylus

Sound: tuning fork, kindred-gloves

Taste: mortar and pestle, tasting spoon kit, apron

Spirit: weather vessel, veil rods

Touch: living clay, tinker tool kit

REQUIRED BOOKS:

The Way of the East: History of Marvels & Marvellers in East and Southeast Asia by Kanlaya Chaichua

Global Sight: Telling the Future Around the World by Irina Drujko

Nearly Marvellian: The Role of Magically Adjacent Beings by Gus Galifianakis

The Great Marvellian Way: History and Theory by Pippa Wentworth

The Incant: Form and Function, the Science of Allurements and Figments by Amir Khan

DORMITORY CHOICES:

- Azure Dragon
- Black Tortoise
- White Tiger
- Vermilion Bird
- Gold Qilin

Dear new Arcanum student,

Before you get too excited about attending that so-called "prestigious" school in the sky, let me warn you . . . it's full of my enemies . . . and full of liars. They have more secrets hidden there than stars in the night sky.

I hope you have a truth marvel because as soon as you cross through those big doors, they will start filling your head with bad things about me. But not to worry—the whole world will learn my story soon.

Gia Trivelino